Prologue

6 April 1912
Berlin

A shadow moved on the opposite side of the street, a darker shape in the gloom of the alleyway. A match flared, briefly illuminating the man's face as he bent forward to light a cigarette.

David Curtis glanced through the discoloured glass towards the figure, but even in that brief split second, he knew he'd never seen the man before. That wasn't surprising. The Prussian secret police, the *Preußische Geheimpolizei*, appeared to have enough agents working the streets of Berlin to ensure he would have no chance of seeing the same man twice. But that didn't alter Curtis's certainty about the man's employer, or what he was doing. Why else would he be loitering at the entrance of an alleyway on Mittelstraße, at midnight, watching the café opposite?

Curtis knew he was under surveillance. He'd been under surveillance ever since he'd arrived in Germany, most probably, and certainly since he'd checked into his hotel in Berlin. Almost subconsciously, he pressed his left arm downwards, feeling the reassuring weight of the Webley Mark II revolver in his leather shoulder holster, a firm and reliable friend in the event of any trouble.

He wondered how much time he had left before they made their move. It would be tonight, he guessed, or tomorrow at the latest. It all depended on how accurate their information was. For the moment, he dismissed the silent watcher from his mind and concentrated on his companion.

The man sitting opposite him was a minor government official, in reality little more than a clerk, but Curtis knew that it wasn't the man's job which was important, but where he worked, and what he had seen as a result. And the previous week he had seen something startling, something which Curtis had scarcely been able to comprehend when the German clerk had explained it to him. And now he needed more details – one detail in particular.

'I need the name, Klaus,' Curtis said again, his German fluent and colloquial. 'You have to give me that, or the information's useless.'

The German picked up his glass of schnapps and held it up to the light which faintly illuminated the corner of the bar where the two men were sitting. Outside, the yellow glow from the gas lamps which lined Mittelstraße picked out the first few flurries of falling snow, adding to the layers already covering the roads and pavements. It was going to be another hard, cold night.

Klaus Trommler nodded in satisfaction as he looked at his glass, then drained the liquid in a single gulp and slammed the base of the tumbler down onto the scarred wooden table. He stared at Curtis and nodded again.

'I have a name for you, my friend,' he said, 'but I'm beginning to wonder if you can afford it. This is important information I have. You know that I'm risking my job just by talking to you.'

Curtis glanced surreptitiously out of the window towards the alleyway where a red pinprick of light marked the position

The
Titanic
Secret

Jack Steel worked in a garage, a factory, a mortuary and an operating theatre before joining the Royal Navy's Fleet Air Arm as a pilot. He served for over twenty years, including active service during the Falklands War. As a senior officer, he became involved in intelligence gathering and dissemination, in covert operations in places like Yemen, and on projects classified above Top Secret. After leaving the service, he ran his own company in his adopted home of Andorra for several years before becoming a professional author. He now divides his time between writing and lecturing, principally on ships of the major cruise firms, including Cunard. Jack Steel is a pseudonym.

The Titanic Secret

Jack Steel

**SIMON &
SCHUSTER**

London · New York · Sydney · Toronto · New Delhi

A CBS COMPANY

First published in Great Britain by Simon & Schuster UK Ltd, 2012
A CBS COMPANY

1 3 5 7 9 10 8 6 4 2

Simon & Schuster UK Ltd
1st Floor
222 Gray's Inn Road
London WC1X 8HB

www.simonandschuster.co.uk

Simon & Schuster Australia, Sydney
Simon & Schuster India, New Dehli

A CIP catalogue record for this book
is available from the British Library

Paperback ISBN: 978-0-85720-862-0
Trade Paperback ISBN: 978-0-85720-863-7

Typeset by M Rules
Printed and bound by CPI Group (UK) Ltd, Croydon, CR0 4YY

To Sally, for now and for always

of the watcher and his cigarette. Trommler, he knew, was actually risking far more than just his job. But that wasn't his problem.

'We agreed a price, Klaus.'

'For the information, yes. But the name is different, separate. The name, that will cost you more, a lot more.'

'How much?'

The German clerk glanced round the corner of the bar, but there was nobody within earshot. He leant forward and unclenched his left fist. A grubby, crumpled piece of paper dropped onto the wooden table between the two men.

Curtis reached forward, smoothed it out and read the figure that was written on it. As he did so, he tried not to show his relief. Before he'd headed out for the rendezvous, his third meeting with his new source in the German government, he had discussed this very matter with his superior at the embassy. They already knew Trommler was greedy – he was a mercenary spy, no more, no less – and Curtis had guessed that the German would make a further demand for money before he revealed the last, vital piece of the puzzle. Luckily, they had overestimated the man's avarice, and Curtis carried enough cash in his pocket to pay the sum he was demanding twice over.

'That's an awful lot of money,' he said now.

'It's a fair price for what you're getting,' Trommler insisted. 'And it is not negotiable.'

Curtis nodded, reached into one of his pockets and extracted an envelope, one of two, each containing an identical sum. He knew exactly how much money was inside it, but he lowered it beneath the table, and made a show of checking the contents. Then he placed it in the centre of the table in front of him.

Trommler grabbed for it, but Curtis immediately placed his

left hand over it. 'Not so fast, Klaus. This is a trade. You give me the name, and then you can take the envelope.'

'How do I know that it isn't just full of cut-up pieces of newspaper?'

'I've paid you what you asked each time we've met. Why should this time be any different?'

But Trommler shook his head. 'This time *is* different because this will be our last meeting. I have the information that you need, and this is the end of it. It's getting too risky, far too risky, for me to carry on. So unless I'm sure that you're being straight with me, I'm just going to get up and walk out of here, right now.'

Curtis stared at the German for a few moments, then almost imperceptibly inclined his head. 'Very well,' he said, rotated the envelope so that the open side faced his companion, and riffled the edges of the banknotes inside it, so that Trommler could clearly see what they were.

'Good.' Trommler leant forward and, in a voice that was so quiet Curtis had to mirror his actions, uttered just two words.

'You're sure of that?' Curtis asked.

'I saw it. That's the name on the document. There are two others as well, but I don't know their names, they weren't typed on the pages that I saw. But he's the important one, the leader. Everything, the whole plan, it's all his idea.'

Curtis slid the envelope across the table and nodded his head. 'Thank you,' he said simply. 'You've done us a fine service. Good luck.'

Right at the back of the bar, in gloomy shadows that the dim electric lighting didn't seem able to penetrate, two men sat at a table, half-drunk glasses of beer in front of them. But their attention was not directed at their drinks, or even at each other.

Instead, both men were looking directly at the table where Curtis and Trommler were sitting.

A whispered secret in exchange for an envelope of hard cash. That's what it had looked like, and the evidence – the envelope that was now in the clerk's pocket – would be all they'd need to prove their case.

One of the men murmured something to his companion, and then they both stood up, their beers forgotten, and walked swiftly through the bar, weaving around the other drinkers.

As he prepared to leave, Curtis knew that Klaus Trommler was going to need all the luck he could find, because if the *Preußische Geheimpolizei* were following him, they almost certainly had people mounting surveillance on everyone he met. He guessed that Trommler would probably be studying the four walls of a prison cell before the week was out. But, as he'd thought before, that wasn't his problem.

Curtis saw movement in his peripheral vision and glanced to his left. Two hard-faced men wearing long black leather coats were heading purposefully towards him, and he didn't think they wanted to join him for a drink.

Curtis stood up, grabbed the back of his chair and swung it as hard and accurately as he could directly towards the two men. Then he ran for the door, ignoring the shouts from behind.

The flying chair cartwheeled through the air. Both the approaching men ducked sideways, in opposite directions, but one of them wasn't quite quick enough and a wooden chair leg caught him squarely on the cheek. The blow knocked him backwards, and he tumbled to the ground, shouting in pain.

His colleague pulled open his coat, drew out a semi-automatic pistol and aimed it at Curtis, at the same time shouting out an order in German for him to stop.

Curtis reached the door, grabbed the handle and yanked it open. As he did so, the man behind him fired. The bullet smashed through the glass in the door, just inches in front of Curtis's face, showering him with needle-sharp splinters that stung his cheek and forehead, opening up tiny cuts that immediately started to bleed.

He didn't wait for the second shot, just bolted through the open doorway and out into the street.

He glanced quickly in both directions as he did so. Mittelstraße appeared deserted, apart from the lone watcher opposite, but he knew that appearances could be deceptive. He also knew that the shot the policeman – he presumed that was who he was – had fired would have been heard, at the very least by the watcher on the opposite side of the street.

As he started to run, he looked in that direction, and saw the red firefly of the cigarette fall suddenly to the ground. The watcher stepped into view and then began to run after him.

Curtis reached for his own weapon, the heavy Webley revolver that he'd collected from the British Embassy the day he'd arrived in Berlin, turned his body slightly as he ran down the street, and pulled the trigger. The bullet probably passed no closer than within twenty feet of the watcher, but immediately the man stopped running and began unbuttoning his own coat, clearly intending to draw a weapon.

There was another shot from behind Curtis, the bullet ricocheting off the pavement several yards in front of him. He risked a quick glance over his shoulder. The man who'd fired at him in the bar was now out on the street as well, but about fifty yards behind him, well outside the accurate range of any pistol, no matter how expert the shooter.

Curtis kept running, holstering the pistol as he did so. The conditions were so treacherous he needed both hands free to help him keep his balance.

Two more shots rang out. One missed him completely, but the other smashed into the stone wall of the building beside him, sending stone chips flying. A third ripped across the right-hand side of his forehead, opening up a jagged cut that felt as if it had gone right down to the bone. Blood poured out of the wound and ran down his cheek.

He pulled a handkerchief out of his pocket and pressed it against the cut, trying to staunch the flow of blood. The wound was more numb than painful, though Curtis knew it would sting later. He kept running.

He headed west towards the T-junction at the end of the road. If he could just get round the corner, and out of sight of the two men now running after him, he could turn left into Schadowstraße and then get to Unter den Linden. And then he'd be about four hundred yards from his destination. And safety.

He was still about a dozen yards short of the junction when he heard louder shouting from behind him. He risked another quick glance back. A group of men, some wearing police uniforms, others in civilian clothes, were coming out of the bar he had just left, Klaus Trommler a struggling figure in their midst. Even as he registered that, one of the uniformed men brought his truncheon down in a vicious arc onto the back of Trommler's head, and the clerk slumped to the ground.

Curtis looked ahead again, trying to move faster over the ice-covered pavement, the surface slippery and treacherous. He took another glance back, and saw that a third man was now running down the centre of Mittelstraße towards him, carrying what looked like a club in his right hand.

Curtis reached the corner with Schadowstraße and stopped for a few brief seconds, again pulled the Webley from his holster and fired a single shot in the general direction of his pursuers. That might, just might, slow them down a bit.

Then he holstered his pistol again and ran on. The lime trees of the Unter den Linden – the rows of trees which had given the wide street its name – were only about a hundred yards in front of him. Perhaps because Schadowstraße ran north to south and received more direct sunlight than Mittelstraße, more of the snow seemed to have melted from the pavements, and Curtis was able to run faster.

He'd just reached the end of the street when another shot came, the bullet exploding into the wall of the building a few feet to his right. The crack of the rifle was very different to the noise of the pistol shots, and that changed the odds. The third man, the one he'd seen running down the middle of the street, had obviously been carrying a rifle, not a truncheon. Curtis knew that if that man got a clear shot at him he'd be dead.

He dodged to the right as soon as he reached the end of the street, then ran over the central reservation with its parallel lines of lime trees, across to the south side of Unter den Linden. He knew that the tree trunks would offer him some protection from the bullets of the pursuing men. As he ran past a few late-night drunks, they stared at him, open-mouthed, transfixed by the blood covering his face, and a couple reached out to try to grab him. But Curtis ignored them all. Getting to his destination was all he cared about.

He stuck close to the line of trees on the south side of the wide boulevard, to make himself a more difficult target.

His breath was coming in short gasps as he reached the cross-roads with Wilhelmstraße, and he glanced behind him again.

There now seemed to be only two men chasing after him and they were about a hundred yards back.

Even as he looked, one of the men stopped abruptly and raised a rifle to his shoulder.

Curtis dodged and weaved, and then sprinted left into Wilhelmstraße just as the man fired. He heard the flat crack as the bullet passed close to him, and then the thud as it impacted on the wall of one of the buildings on the opposite side of the road.

And as he turned the corner, Curtis could see his objective right in front of him. On the right-hand side of Wilhelmstraße, about a hundred yards ahead, and dominated by four massive stone columns in its centre, stood the imposing stone facade of the former Palais Strousberg, the building which now housed the British Embassy.

Lights blazed from windows on two of the floors, and Curtis knew that tonight there would be at least two armed sentries guarding the main door.

He tried to run faster, but these pavements were more treacherous, and several times he slid, once almost losing his footing. He was drawing ever closer, but now he could hear the sound of the running men behind him, and then, quite clearly, he heard them stop. That was bad news; the only reason they would have for halting the pursuit was to end it, by shooting him down.

Curtis had nowhere to hide. All he could do was dodge and weave. And maybe distract them a little. He pulled out his Webley again. With an effective range of about fifty yards, even firing the heavy .455 cartridge, he knew he had no chance of hitting his pursuers.

Without bothering to aim, Curtis pointed the pistol up Wilhelmstraße, back the way he'd run, and squeezed the trigger.

The heavy revolver kicked in his hand, the loud bang of the pistol firing a sudden assault on the silence of the night. Without looking behind, he pulled the trigger again.

At that instant, he felt a massive blow on the left-hand side of his back, and a split second later the sound of the shot. The pistol tumbled from his hand to land with a clatter on the pavement as he fell forward, a terrible numbing pain paralysing the left side of his body.

Desperately, he staggered to his feet, his left arm hanging uselessly by his side, and tried to run forward. The best he could manage was a clumsy, drunken gait, barely faster than a walk.

In front of him, the figures of two armed men – the sentries he had been told would be on duty – emerged from the doorway of the embassy and stared down the street towards him, obviously alerted by the sounds of the shots. Both had rifles slung over their shoulders, but Curtis knew they had probably been ordered not to shoot, because of the diplomatic implications if they did.

Behind him, he heard an ominous metallic clicking as the man with the rifle reloaded his weapon, the empty cartridge case tumbling out of the breech to land with a clatter on the cobbled street.

Twenty yards to go. Blood was pouring from a gaping wound on his left shoulder, leaving a crimson trail in the fresh snow.

'Help me,' he gasped, reaching out with his right hand as if he could grab one of the men a few yards in front of him.

One sentry was just standing there in the street, his mouth open and eyes wide as he stared at the drama unfolding in front of him. The other man had stepped off the pavement and into the road, moving away from the entrance to the embassy, and was unslinging his rifle.

Ten yards, maybe less.

Then Curtis felt another solid, crashing blow. A shaft of agony speared up his left leg and he collapsed onto the unyielding surface of the pavement, his scream of pain a counterpoint to the flat crack of the rifle shot. And this time he knew he wouldn't be getting up again. The bullet had ripped through his left thigh, smashing the femur and tearing apart his flesh. Thick, dark arterial blood erupted from the wound.

He heard another shot, but much, much closer. Through his tears of agony, he saw that one sentry had raised his rifle to fire a warning shot over the heads of the pursuing men.

The other sentry ran over and knelt down beside him. Curtis grabbed the lapel of the man's jacket, his bloodied right hand leaving dark smears on his uniform. He had to pass on what he knew.

'Three men. Voss. You—'

And then a third bullet smashed into Curtis's ravaged body, ploughing through his skull and killing him instantly.

Chapter 1

6 April 1912
East Anglia

Alex Tremayne shifted position slightly to relieve the strain on his elbows and lowered the binoculars to the ground. He'd been lying prone in the hedgerow watching the farmhouse at the edge of the fens for over three hours, and he still hadn't seen what he was looking for. Not for the first time he wondered if he was right, if the trail he'd followed was the correct one.

He glanced down at his watch. It was late afternoon, the pale light of the early spring day already shading into the grey of evening. Quite soon, he hoped, the lamps in the farmhouse would be lit and then, perhaps, he might be able to see what was happening inside the building.

Tremayne lifted the binoculars again and resumed his scrutiny of the windows, and particularly those on the upper floor. And while he studied the dark oblong shapes, he mentally reviewed the steps he'd taken, the clues which had led him to this isolated and desolate spot. The trail had started, of all places, outside a jewellery shop in London's West End, but the men involved had then seemingly vanished from sight, and it wasn't until the letter had arrived at the Whitehall address that Tremayne had had any hard information to work with.

The single clue had been the name of the post office from which the letter had been sent. A tiny piece of evidence that was indicative, no more, of where his quarry might be found. Even then, Tremayne hadn't been particularly hopeful, reasoning that the letter would have been dispatched from a village some distance away from where the men were staying. But at the very least, the postmark had given him a starting point, and for almost a week he had been haunting the public houses and shops in the area, listening to local gossip and asking the occasional discreet question.

The previous afternoon, a chance remark overheard in the street had led him to a tiny hamlet, far too small to be dignified by the term 'village', and from there to the long and unmade track which ended at the small, grey stone farmhouse. But still he wasn't sure. Since he'd started watching the building, he had seen nobody in it or near it, and had heard nothing. The place appeared to be deserted, but it was clearly not derelict. Both the front and rear doors were in place, closed and probably locked, and there was glass in all the windows. And somehow the house conveyed a sense of occupancy, of cautious watchfulness, as if whoever was inside the building was paying just as much attention to Tremayne as he was to the farmhouse.

That was ridiculous, he knew, because his approach to the property had been so circuitous and had taken him so long that he was absolutely certain he'd been unobserved at all times, just as he was sure that he was effectively invisible in his present position. His clothing was brown and green, the colours of the hedgerow and the soil around him, and he was still almost 100 yards away from the house.

Then the faintest of movements caught his eye. A darker grey shape had just moved past one of the upstairs windows. At least, that's what Tremayne thought he'd seen, and he concentrated hard, straining to make out any detail. That window remained dark, but at that moment the other window on the top floor of the farmhouse flared with light.

A man appeared on the left-hand side of the illuminated window, and beside him Tremayne saw the figure he'd been hoping to spot ever since he began his vigil. The girl – she looked about twelve years of age – had blonde hair cut in a distinctive style, and was wearing a dark-blue dress that Tremayne had seen before. She was struggling in the man's grip as the two figures moved from one side of the window to the other, and just after they moved out of sight, he heard a shrill scream from the house, the sound abruptly cut short.

Tremayne's grip tightened involuntarily on the binoculars. Seconds later, the man appeared at the window again and roughly pulled the curtains closed. Moments later, one of the downstairs windows was also illuminated, but all Tremayne could see was a thin vertical sliver of light between closed curtains.

For perhaps a minute he remained immobile, studying the house. Then he eased slowly backwards out of the hedgerow until he was able to stand upright and still not be seen from the farmhouse. He had already planned the route he was going to take to the property, and now he had seen all he needed to confirm his suspicions. He knew the girl was in the house, and in which room he was likely to find her.

He tucked the binoculars into one of the capacious pockets of his shooting jacket, and then began walking away from the property, following the line of the hedgerow to the point where it terminated in a small copse. He stopped at that point and stared back towards the house. It looked exactly the same as it had minutes before, with two lighted windows and no sign of movement.

Tremayne picked a path carefully through the copse, trying to avoid treading on any broken branches or anything else that could make a noise and give away his position, although he was still far enough away from the farmhouse for that not to be a problem.

At the other side of the copse, another hedgerow ran at right angles to the first, and passed within about fifty yards of the house. More importantly, the side of the farmhouse which faced the hedgerow had neither windows nor doors, so that when he approached the building, Tremayne knew that unless one of the occupants was outside the property and looking in the right direction, he would not be seen.

The nearer he got to the house, the slower and more carefully Tremayne moved, and it took him almost five minutes to cover the last fifty yards. When he reached the closest point to the house, he stopped moving and for several seconds just stared across at the property. There was still no sign of movement, and none of the occupants was outside. The hedgerow was thick, but not impenetrable, and Tremayne was able to pick a spot where the undergrowth was reasonably sparse and where he was able to slide through with the minimum amount of noise and effort.

When he'd done so, he remained in a crouch for a few moments before he moved off. He checked all around him, then strode swiftly across to the side wall of the property. Again he waited, using his ears as much as his eyes to ensure that nobody was anywhere near him. Then he walked around to the front of the farmhouse, stepped across to the door and rapped on it sharply three times with his left hand.

For several seconds, nothing happened. Then Tremayne heard the sound of cautious movement inside the house, foot-steps moving slowly along a corridor towards the door. Then silence for another brief period, before the man inside the house spoke.

'Who is it?' His voice was harsh and guttural.

'I'm from the post office,' Tremayne said, sounding bright and cheerful. 'I have a package for you and I need you to sign for it.'

There was a grunt from the other side of the door, then the sound of heavy bolts being withdrawn.

The door opened a cautious six inches, and Tremayne found himself staring at an unshaven face. But that wasn't what seized his attention. It was the object the man was holding across his chest. The blue steel barrels of the twelve-bore shotgun gleamed in the light from the hall, and he could see that the man's right hand was wrapped around the stock, his finger resting on the trigger.

Tremayne took a deliberate half-step backwards, and allowed an expression of apprehension to cross his face.

The man opened the door slightly wider so that the whole of his weapon was visible. He'd obviously noted his visitor's look of fear, and smiled slightly as he moved the twin barrels of the shotgun downwards, making the silent threat more obvious.

'Where's the package?' he demanded.

'Here.'

Tremayne had been standing in a casual pose, his right arm tucked behind his back. As he spoke, he swung his arm around his body, his elbow locked as he brought the heavy calibre revolver up to the aim.

The expression on the man's face changed the instant he saw the pistol, and he reacted immediately, swinging the shotgun around to point it at Tremayne. But he was too late. For him, he was a whole lifetime too late.

Tremayne's finger was already resting on the trigger of his weapon, and the moment the sights settled on the centre of the man's chest, he squeezed the trigger. The Webley Model WG – a popular personal defence weapon among army officers – kicked in his hand, and the .455 bullet smashed straight into his target.

The man's grubby shirt blossomed crimson and he staggered backwards a couple of steps before crashing heavily onto the wooden floorboards of the hall, the shotgun tumbling from his lifeless hands, his face still wearing an expression of shocked surprise.

Tremayne reached down and seized the weapon by the end of the barrel, and tossed it behind him outside the door. He guessed the other man was probably still upstairs with the girl, but just in case he was somewhere on the ground floor, Tremayne didn't want to leave a loaded weapon lying around where he could grab it.

His ears were ringing from the noise of the shot, but the sound of movement somewhere upstairs was quite unmistakable. Above him, heavy boots moved quickly across wooden floorboards.

Then the creaking of a hinge told Tremayne that a door had opened on the first floor. He had to assume that the other man would be armed as well, and the landing above him was so wide that he couldn't cover all of it properly. He'd have to wait until the second man showed himself.

Tremayne pushed open the door on his right and stepped inside, his pistol held out in front of him, just in case. The room was a parlour, worn wooden chairs, a rough table and a battered old dresser the only furniture. He flattened himself against the inside wall and looked up, waiting for the second man to appear.

He almost missed it. He was looking at the wrong end of the landing when the barrel of the shotgun appeared. Tremayne glanced to his left as his peripheral vision detected the slight movement. Then he flung himself backwards into the old parlour. There was a thunderous roar, and the expanding blast of shot from the twelve-bore blew a ragged hole through the bottom section of the parlour door and part of the wall. If Tremayne had still been standing by the door, he would at best have lost a leg.

He stepped forward cautiously, and risked a quick glance upwards. He couldn't see the other man, but he could hear him stepping across the landing.

Tremayne could also hear the unmistakable metallic snicking sound as he closed the breech of the shotgun, which meant he knew what he was doing. Instead of firing both barrels one after the other, after which he would have disarmed himself, the man had clearly ejected the spent cartridge case and loaded another shell, so now he again had two rounds in the weapon. And Tremayne knew that at close quarters, a shotgun was just as lethal – in fact, arguably even more lethal because of the way the shot spread – than a pistol. The only advantage he had was that the shotgun was a full-length weapon, and so it would be more difficult to handle within the confines of the house.

His problem was that the man upstairs would have a clear

shot at him from the landing as soon as Tremayne stepped out of the parlour. What he had to do was get on the other side of the hallway, underneath the landing. And he knew he'd have to do that quickly, before it dawned on the man upstairs that he could use the girl as a shield.

Tremayne pulled the parlour door open all the way, took another look up the stairs and then immediately stepped back from the doorway. In that split second, he'd seen a bulky figure at the far end of the landing, peering over the banister rail, the shotgun pointing down the stairs.

To step outside the parlour would be suicidal, but Tremayne had no option but to try. He'd just have to hope his reactions were faster than the other man's. He took a deep breath, checked that the Webley was ready to fire, then moved forward, stopping just inside the room.

Then he thrust his right arm outside the parlour, aimed the pistol up the staircase, and pulled the trigger. The instant the weapon fired, he ran forward, taking giant strides across the hall. And at the same moment, the man above him pulled the trigger of the shotgun, the bellow of the twelve-bore much louder than the pistol shot.

Tremayne felt a sudden stabbing pain in the back of his right leg as he leapt forward, but he ignored it. He slammed into the opposite wall of the hallway, already raising the Webley revolver and looking for a target. But the man had ducked back out of sight.

Then Tremayne heard the shotgun being reloaded and knew he had only seconds before the man would probably start firing blind down the staircase. He needed to get out of range, fast.

Opposite the parlour door was a second door leading off

from the hall. Tremayne took two steps over to it and kicked it open. The man would have no doubt about what he'd just done, and hopefully would assume he now knew where the intruder was.

Tremayne stopped and moved silently back to the centre of the hall. He knew that now he held a very slight advantage. He still couldn't see the other man, but he could hear him.

Seconds later, the shotgun barrels reappeared, aiming towards the second doorway, and almost immediately the man fired the weapon.

The blast of pellets slammed into the floor just a few feet from where Tremayne was standing, and immediately he returned fire, pointing the Webley at the underside of the wooden floorboards of the landing.

The pistol roared and bucked in his hand, the heavy bullet smashing straight through the wood. He heard a curse from above him, an expression of fear, and knew that his shot had missed the target. Then the man moved quickly. And just as suddenly he stopped.

Tremayne stilled his breathing, concentrating as hard as he could on just listening, waiting for the first creak on the wooden floorboards of the landing that would indicate precisely where the man above him was.

For a few seconds, he heard nothing at all – the man must have been standing as still as Tremayne – but then he started to move. And he shouted down at Tremayne, yelled his defiance and made the threat that Tremayne had been fearing ever since he'd stepped inside the building.

'You're dead, you interfering bastard. And I've got the girl. She's my ticket out of here.'

Tremayne heard the man's footsteps quickly crossing the

landing, heading for one of the bedrooms, presumably where he'd locked the girl, and knew he had just seconds to act.

He estimated where the man had to be, aimed his pistol at the floorboards again and fired. Once, twice.

This time he was rewarded by a scream of agony. Maybe one of the bullets had found its mark. There was a clattering sound from above him – perhaps the shotgun falling – then a heavy thud and a bubbling wail of pain.

Tremayne knew he had just one round left in the pistol, and it was possible that the man above him was trying to trick him, pretending to be hit so that Tremayne would walk boldly up the stairs, thinking the danger was passed.

It was worth taking a few seconds to reload. He pressed the catch beside the hammer on the pistol to open the weapon and reveal the rear of the cylinder, shook out all six cartridges – five of them fired, one not – into the palm of his left hand and dropped them into his jacket pocket. Then he quickly slid six more bullets into the cylinder and closed the weapon again.

Only then did he step forward, the pistol pointing upwards, and begin a slow and cautious ascent of the staircase.

The man was still moaning, and as Tremayne climbed upwards he discovered that his quarry was certainly injured. The sudden dripping of blood through a gap in the floorboards, the drops splashing fatly onto the floor of the hall below, told its own story.

But still he was cautious. And as he climbed high enough to see onto the landing, his caution was justified. The shotgun barrel moved slightly towards him.

Tremayne instantly ducked down, and the blast roared over his head, blowing open a six-inch wide hole in the opposite wall.

He hadn't heard the man reload the weapon, but he took no chances. He jumped down a couple of steps, pointed the pistol at the floorboards where he now knew the man was lying, and pulled the trigger twice.

Only then did he turn round and resume his ascent of the staircase.

This time, when he reached the landing, the man's hands were nowhere near the shotgun. Instead, he was still moaning and clutching his stomach and left leg. The dark upwelling of arterial blood from between his fingers was proof enough of his injuries.

'Doctor,' he said hoarsely, his voice racked with pain. 'You've gotta get me a doctor. I'm hurt bad.'

Tremayne nodded at him. 'I hope you are,' he said. 'But you forfeited your right to civilized treatment the moment you and your partner snatched that girl off the street. She's only twelve years old.'

'We ain't laid a finger on her.'

'That doesn't matter. You kidnapped her, and then you demanded a ransom. But you made a mistake. In fact, you made two mistakes. You obviously knew the identity of the girl's aunt – Leslie Marian Valiant, better known as "May" – and you knew she would pay almost anything to get Claire released from your clutches. But what you failed to realize was that your ransom demand wouldn't be opened by the aunt, but by her husband, because he lives in Whitehall and she doesn't. Your second mistake was not knowing who her husband is, and what he would be likely to do.'

Despite the agony of the gunshot wounds, and his steadily weakening condition, the man lying on the floor looked puzzled.

'So who is he?' he demanded.

'Leslie Valiant's husband is a man named George Mansfield Cumming. You've probably never heard of him, because he likes it that way. He keeps a low profile, but he's one of the most powerful men in Britain. And he employs people like me, and I'm your worst nightmare.'

'Who are you?'

Tremayne smiled slightly. 'I'm the man who's been following your trail for the last week. I'm the man who's here to take Claire back to her family. And I'm the man who's going to kill you.'

'No, please, no. I can—'

But whatever offer or plea the man was going to make was lost in the crash of another shot from Tremayne's Webley. The man quivered once, and then lay still.

'You can't, actually,' Tremayne murmured, tucked the pistol into his jacket pocket and turned away without a second glance.

There were three doors leading off the landing, and he walked straight across to the one which had a key sticking out of the lock. He turned it, and pushed the door wide open. At first, he didn't see her, and wondered for a moment if he'd got the right room. Then he heard a faint whimpering sound from the opposite corner, and stepped further into the room.

The girl was crouched down on the floor beside a small single bed, her eyes squeezed tightly shut and her hands clamped over her ears. She was rocking slightly backwards and forward, clearly traumatized by her experience.

Tremayne walked across to her and bent down. He rested his hand lightly on her shoulder and she shuddered.

'It's all right, Claire,' he said soothingly. 'It's all over now. I've come to take you home.'

He didn't know if it was the tone of his voice, or what he was telling her, but her eyes suddenly opened and she stared at him. And then, with the kind of strength that spoke of her terror and desperation, she grabbed hold of him around the shoulders as if she would never let go, sobbing her heart out.

'It's all right,' Tremayne said again. 'We can go now.'

'They were all so horrible to me,' she said, when she was capable of speaking. 'They left me in the dark, and they didn't feed me very often. The food was horrible too. And all I had to drink was water.'

Tremayne lifted her up with both hands – she felt fragile, as if her limbs would snap if he squeezed her too tightly – and she was still trembling. He settled her body so that she was sitting on his left forearm and walked across to the door of the small bedroom. He shielded her face as he walked across the landing and past the dead body lying there, and on down the stairs.

He'd almost reached the bottom when a sudden realization struck him. In the bedroom, Claire had said that they were 'all' horrible to her. Why hadn't she said that they were 'both' horrible. She was educated, and that hadn't sounded to him like a slip of the tongue.

And as he looked out through the open front door, he saw that the shotgun he'd tossed there was nowhere in sight. He pulled the revolver out of his pocket even as he turned his head slightly to bring his mouth close to the girl's ear.

'How many men were there?' he asked her urgently.

'Two for most of the time,' Claire replied, 'but sometimes there were three of them here. And then I—'

She broke off with a sudden squeal of terror as she saw something behind them.

Tremayne whirled round as a third man stepped into the hall

from the door at the end. Like the other two, he was holding a double-barrel shotgun, and bringing it up to point it at Tremayne and the girl.

Alex Tremayne reacted instantly. He half turned his body to try to shield the girl from the shotgun blast, and at the same time raised the revolver and squeezed the trigger. The double report of the two weapons was almost simultaneous and utterly deafening in the narrow hallway. Tremayne's bullet hit the man in the left shoulder, the impact spinning him just enough for the round fired from the shotgun to miss both Tremayne and the girl.

Before the man could correct his aim and fire the second barrel, Tremayne pulled the trigger again, and then again. The man tumbled backwards, the first bullet smashing into his cheek and blowing off the back of his head, the second thudding into his chest.

Claire was still screaming, the noise piercing through Tremayne's head.

'Hush, now,' he said. 'You are sure that there were only three of them?'

He had to repeat the question twice before she finally stopped screaming and answered him.

'Three, yes, there were three of them.'

Tremayne stepped over the body of the first man he'd shot and entered the parlour.

'I'm putting you down for just a few moments,' he said. 'There's something I have to do before we go outside.'

Claire nodded but didn't reply as Tremayne lowered her gently to the wooden floor of the room. Then he opened his revolver again, removed the spent cartridge cases and reloaded it. It wasn't that he disbelieved what the girl had told him. It was just that he always believed in being prepared. And with six bullets in the chamber of the Webley, he felt able to face whoever – or whatever – was waiting outside.

'Now we're leaving,' he said, took Claire's hand and led her out of the parlour and across to the main door of the farmhouse, extinguishing the hall light as he did so. He opened the door a few inches, and for a couple of minutes he just looked outside the building into the deepening gloom of the dusk. He heard a rustle in the undergrowth a few yards away, and then saw a fox step cautiously out onto a patch of grass before moving away on its nightly quest for food.

That was enough for Tremayne. Foxes were highly sensitive to the presence of human beings, and now he was certain that no danger lurked outside the farmhouse.

Just over four hours later, a few minutes before midnight, Tremayne knocked on the door of a flat in central London. It was opened almost immediately by a tall, solidly built man with grey hair and piercing eyes. He exuded an unmistakable air of command, which was entirely unsurprising given that he was a captain in the Royal Navy, though his current command was about as divorced from the sea and ships as it was possible to be. George Mansfield Cumming was the head of the Foreign Section of the recently formed Secret Service Bureau, a spymaster rather than a sailor.

'Good evening, Mansfield,' Tremayne said, and gave Claire a gentle push in the back.

She needed no second bidding. She rushed over to Cumming and grasped him round the waist.

'Uncle George,' she murmured, holding him tight. 'I'm so glad I'm here.'

Cumming smiled down at her and ruffled her hair, then bent down and gave her a hug.

'You're not hurt?' he asked, directing his question at the girl, but actually looking up at Tremayne for the answer.

'I don't think they touched her,' he said, 'apart from just manhandling her when they needed to. But no funny business, if you know what I mean.'

'Where are they?'

'At the farmhouse, stiffening up and attracting flies,' Tremayne replied shortly. 'And there were three of them, by the way, not two as we'd thought.'

Cumming nodded. 'I'll have a quiet word with the people who need to know,' he said, 'and I think we'll probably write the whole thing off as a burglary that went wrong.'

'Thanks,' Tremayne said. 'Do you want me to hang on to the pistol or give it back?'

'I'll take it,' Cumming replied. 'It can go back in the armoury.'

Tremayne removed the revolver from his pocket, broke it to remove the shells and then placed it on the occasional table on one side of the hall. He took out the cardboard box which contained the ammunition, added the six rounds to it and then felt around in his pocket for the unfired round he'd removed from the weapon earlier. The empty cases followed.

'That's fifty rounds altogether,' he said, 'fired and fired, just so you can keep your books straight.'

'Thanks, Alex,' Cumming replied, gently disengaging Claire's arms from around his waist. He extended his right arm and shook Tremayne's hand firmly.

'Anything else I can do?'

'Not right now,' Cumming said, 'but I'm waiting for news

from Germany. There's a situation developing over there that might require the use of your unique talents. In the meantime, take a couple of days off. I'll have somebody contact you as soon as there's any news.'

Chapter 2

7 April 1912
Berlin

'But you are sure that he's dead?'

The heavyset man standing beside the window turned and walked back to his desk. Although he was the head of the *Preußische Geheimpolizei* in Berlin, he was wearing the dark-blue uniform with silver buttons of a regular German police officer. Eberhard Neumann had found that he could move about his city far more easily, and almost invariably be unchallenged, when dressed in this manner. And there were certain other advantages too.

Neumann sat down in his comfortable leather chair before he replied. 'We can't be certain, no,' he replied in English. 'My man fired five shots and, according to his companion, hit the English spy three times. In the circumstances – just after midnight, the only illumination the street lights, with snow falling and the target running away – that was very good shooting. Unfortunately, I can't ask my rifleman for any further information because he's dead. One of the military sentries outside the British Embassy shot him just after he fired the last round.'

'Have you registered a protest? Surely the shooting of a

German citizen in the heart of Berlin by an English soldier stationed at their embassy is a flagrant breach of diplomatic protocols?'

'It is, and normally we would, but this situation is far from normal. If we protest, every aspect of the matter will be placed under scrutiny, by my masters as well as by the British, and we both know that that is not a good idea.'

Neumann paused for a few moments and inspected his fingernails. 'I decided that the best – in fact probably the *only* – viable course of action was to cover up the incident as quickly as possible. I had the body of my man removed from the street, together with his rifle and all the spent cartridge cases. While my people were doing this, they noticed that the British Embassy staff were doing exactly the same thing with their spy. And there's something else that makes me think he's dead.'

Gunther Voss leaned forward in his seat. 'Yes? What was it?'

'Immediately the incident was over, and the two bodies had been removed, I ordered two of my men to walk down Wilhelmstraße. They easily found the two sites where the Englishman had been shot. There was evidence of heavy bleeding at the first spot, then a trail of blood as he got up and staggered forward, and a large pool of blood where the man finally fell.'

Voss nodded. 'Exactly what I would have expected from your description of the incident.'

'But at the second site, right outside the doors of the British Embassy, they also saw fragments of grey-white tissue. For obvious reasons – they were both being watched very closely by the sentries posted outside the building – they couldn't examine it closely, but both were convinced that it was brain matter. I think that last shot probably hit the Englishman's head. If it did, it would have killed him instantly.'

A slow smile of satisfaction spread across Gunther Voss's vulpine features.

'The only other concern is whether or not he said anything to either of the British sentries in his last moments.'

The smile faded from Voss's face. 'How much could the spy possibly have said in that short space of time? And by then he was so badly wounded that he might not even have been capable of coherent thought.'

Neumann nodded. 'You may well be right. But you should be aware that the traitor Klaus Trommler has admitted he told the Englishman your name at their last meeting that evening. He has also said that he read part of the report I prepared, and passed some of the other details on to the English spy.'

Voss stared at him angrily. 'I thought our arrangements were secret?' he snapped. 'Why did you have to write anything down?'

Neumann shrugged. 'We have our procedures. I am required to document meetings and record any information which I am given. That is the way the *Preußische Geheimpolizei* operates.'

'And then you let a clerk – of all people – read what you had written?'

'All of our employees are checked for reliability and honesty. Nothing like this has ever happened before.'

Voss snorted. 'But this Trommler man proves that your checking procedure is a waste of time.'

'He was an exception, I agree. It won't happen again.'

'What will you do with him?'

Neumann smiled and glanced up at the large clock on the opposite wall of his office. 'You can watch if you like,' he said. 'They should be ready now.'

He stood up and walked back to the window, beckoning Voss to join him. Neumann's office was on the second floor of the building, and the window looked down into a large courtyard surrounded by a brick wall fifteen feet high. In one corner a group of half a dozen uniformed policemen were standing talking together, each with a rifle slung over his shoulder.

As Neumann and Voss looked down, two other men appeared from the ground floor of the building, one either side of a man who had his arms lashed behind his back, and a gag over his mouth. He was writhing and struggling in their grip, but clearly his efforts to escape were futile. They walked briskly across to the corner of the courtyard and forced the prisoner to stand against the wall. One of the men did something behind the prisoner's back, and then both men moved away, leaving the man twisting against the wall.

'There's a ringbolt at waist level just there,' Neumann explained. 'It saves having to erect a wooden post to tie them to.'

'That's Klaus Trommler?' Voss mused.

Neumann shook his head. 'No, it's not, actually. That's one of my officers. He was the man who was stupid enough to let Trommler get his hands on the report.'

Down below, the two men who'd escorted the prisoner into the courtyard had just re-entered the building. After a few moments, they reappeared. This time, they were carrying a stretcher between them, on which another man lay. His body was secured to the stretcher with three leather straps tied tightly around his chest, waist and knees, and with individual straps securing his wrists to the side rails.

Voss looked puzzled. 'Why can't they make him walk to the wall?' he asked.

'Our questioning was a little – *robust* – shall we say. One of our interrogators broke both of Trommler's legs when he proved somewhat reluctant to tell us what we needed to know.'

The two men carried the stretcher across to the wall and propped it up there, just a few feet from where the other man was still struggling futilely, trying desperately to get free. Then they turned and walked away without a backward glance.

Another police officer walked out of the building and crossed to the two men. He took a piece of paper from his pocket and said a few words to each of the prisoners.

'He's reading the death sentences,' Neumann explained. 'Both men are lucky, really, that they're being shot. Execution by firing squad is generally considered to be an honourable death.'

Voss stared at him. 'So what other form of execution would you use?'

'The *Fallbeil*. The word translates as the "falling axe". It's like the French guillotine, and it's the punishment we reserve for traitors and criminals. But there wasn't time to get a machine here, and I wanted these two disposed of as soon as possible.'

In the courtyard below, the officer had moved away from the two condemned men, both of whom were shaking their heads violently. Neither Voss nor Neumann could hear the orders being given, but the firing squad quickly formed a single line about twenty feet from the wall, and then a ragged volley rang out. Both the victims slumped down to the extent of their bonds as the bullets ploughed through their bodies. Once the riflemen had slung their weapons, the officer stepped forward to verify that the two men were dead.

Neumann nodded in satisfaction and stepped back from the window. 'Coffee?' he asked, 'or perhaps some schnapps?'

'Schnapps, definitely,' Voss replied. He'd never seen anyone killed in quite that way before, and watching the casual double execution had left a strangely cold sensation in his stomach.

'Anyway,' Neumann said, pouring two glasses and then replacing the bottle in a cupboard behind his desk, 'we don't think the English spy could have passed on anything of significance to the British Embassy staff.'

Voss took a sip of the drink, then put down the glass on the corner of Neumann's desk. 'So the plan has not been compromised?'

Neumann nodded. 'That is our assessment, yes. But even if we're wrong, we still don't think that it matters. At this stage, everything is in place here in Germany, and the only remaining actions that need to be completed are your responsibility.'

'So even if the British guess what's happening, there'll be nothing they can do about it. Is that what you're saying?'

'Yes. You're a respected businessman. They wouldn't dare detain you, or impede you in any way. You are not guilty of any crime, nor are you wanted by any authority. As far as I can see, my friend, you have nothing at all to worry about.'

Voss looked at him, then drained the rest of his schnapps and nodded. 'I hope you're right, because this is the biggest gamble I have ever taken in my entire life, and I do have something of a reputation as a gambler. But this time I've staked everything I own, including my life, on this working.'

Neumann shook his head. 'Unless something happens that none of us has foreseen, I can't even see that this is much of a gamble. Within five years you will probably be the richest man in the world, and I, in my own humble way, will be one of the richest men in Germany.'

He opened the cupboard and poured two more glasses of schnapps.

'I'll drink to that,' Voss said. 'Now everything hinges on what happens over the next twelve days.'

A short while later, Gunther Voss glanced out of the window as Neumann escorted him down the corridor towards the main entrance of the building. At the end of the courtyard, he could clearly see the ringbolt mounted at waist height on the wall, and above that a dark-red discolouration upon which flies were already feasting. He smiled slightly at the recollection of what he'd witnessed, then walked on.

At the door, the two men stopped and Neumann extended his hand. 'When are you leaving Berlin?' he asked.

'The day after tomorrow. I still have another meeting to attend here before I go – a final session with one of your senior government ministers.'

'And then you're heading back to America?'

'Yes. I'm joining the ship at Cherbourg.'

Neumann inclined his head. 'Very well, my friend. As long as you can deliver on our agreement, I can see no reason why this scheme should not work. Of course, if there are any problems achieving the goal, that will be another matter altogether.'

Voss stopped and looked at his companion. 'Are you threatening me?' he demanded.

Neumann shook his head. 'Absolutely not. I'm just passing on a message from my masters. They have expended a considerable amount of time and effort in preparing for this operation, and they have told me that they would be displeased – most displeased – if it did not succeed. What form their displeasure would take, I have no idea. But,' he added with a smile, 'as you are so confident that there will be no problems, I'm sure everything will work out for the best.'

Chapter 3

7 April 1912
Berlin

Five minutes later, Gunther Voss stepped out of the *Preußische Geheimpolizei* headquarters, Eberhard Neumann by his side. The two men stood talking together on the pavement for half a minute, then they shook hands and Neumann walked back inside the building. Voss glanced up and down the street, and then, as a motor taxi approached him, he raised his hand to attract the driver's attention. Moments later, the vehicle stopped, and Voss climbed on board and then sat back in the seat as the taxi moved away from the kerb.

On the opposite side of the road, a black-haired and non-descript man wearing a dark suit, a brown overcoat and a trilby hat emerged from the open doorway of a building, dropped a cigarette butt onto the pavement and ground it out with the toe of his right shoe. He stared thoughtfully down the road towards the retreating taxi, then gestured behind him.

Another man stepped out of the same doorway, also looked in the direction of the departing taxi, then stepped out into the street to flag down a similar vehicle. Moments later, he climbed into the back of the cab and issued a simple instruction to the driver.

The black-haired man nodded to him as his taxi started moving, and then walked briskly away in the opposite direction.

A couple of hundred yards down the road was a large hotel. The man walked into the foyer and strode straight across to the reception desk. The receptionist listened to his request, and then gestured him towards a small cubicle a few feet away. Inside, attached to the wall, was a telephone apparatus, the microphone a black trumpet shape, and the earpiece separate, attached by a cable and resting on a two-pronged metal hook.

The man waited and when the telephone bell rang, he picked up the earpiece.

'It's Williams,' he said. 'I've just seen Voss and Neumann together, coming out of the headquarters. Harrington is following Voss right now.'

The man at the other end of the line asked a question, and Williams replied.

'No, they were very friendly. It's quite obvious they're working together, and that concerns me. I just wish we knew what Voss was up to over here. I'll be back at the embassy as soon as I can,' he added, 'but can you telegraph that report to London as soon as possible and request instructions?'

Williams paid the receptionist for the call, then walked back outside the hotel and looked around for a cab himself.

Twenty minutes later, the vehicle came to a stop in Wilhelmstraße and he walked into the embassy building. Inside, he crossed the reception hall, unlocked one of the doors opposite the main entrance and strode down a passageway to a small office at the rear of the building.

Inside, another man was waiting for him, sitting behind an ornate walnut desk. He nodded a greeting as Michael Williams removed his coat and hat and hung them up.

'Any reply yet?'

George Cartwright shook his head. 'Not so far,' he said. 'As soon as there's anything from Whitehall Court, the communication staff will bring it straight here.'

'Well, I hope they don't take too long making up their minds what they want us to do. When Voss and Neumann shook hands, I got the feeling that had been their last meeting. It looked like two people who were saying goodbye to each other. If I'm right, that could mean that whatever Voss has got planned is imminent.'

'Do you want to tell Cumming that?' Cartwright asked.

'Definitely not. He'd think I'd lost my senses. No, that's just my impression, and Cumming is only ever interested in the facts.'

A minute or so later there was a knock on the door and another man entered carrying a telegraph form in his hand.

'From London, sir,' he said, handing the paper to Cartwright.

'Thanks.'

Cartwright read the message, then passed the form over to Williams.

'That's your answer, then,' he said.

Williams scanned the words and nodded. 'I had hoped for a bit more in the way of direction,' he said. 'This is typical of Mansfield Cumming. "Imperative you ascertain Voss's motive and plan within twenty-four hours. All measures justified." What, exactly, does he mean by that?'

Cartwright nodded. 'You haven't seen the last line, have you?'

Williams looked back at the form, then raised his eyebrows. 'No,' he said. 'God, he's serious, isn't he? Can we take that risk?'

The final line of the message contained only two words: 'Neumann expendable.'

Chapter 4

8 April 1912
Berlin

Michael Williams sat in a small café, a copy of the *Frankfurter Zeitung* open on the table in front of him and, for about the tenth time that afternoon, wondered if he was doing the right thing. His instructions from Mansfield Cumming had been brief and the timescale short, but the intention behind them was crystal clear. The only latitude he was allowed was in the method he adopted to follow those orders.

At first, he'd been worried about the possible consequences, but since yesterday afternoon he'd had something else weighing on his mind. Now he was actually looking forward to what he was about to do.

He'd been sitting there watching and waiting for over an hour. He had no idea what time his target would emerge from the building on the opposite side of the road. And he still wasn't entirely sure what he was going to do when the man finally did appear. It depended on whether he was alone or part of a group, and if he walked away or hailed a taxi.

Williams had made his preparations, but he was well aware that he'd had no time to reconnoitre the target or ascertain his normal movements, and he also knew that off-the-cuff operations were far more likely to fail, often spectacularly so, than properly planned and executed missions.

If this worked, it would be a miracle, and he wasn't a man who set much store by providence. Or by luck.

He picked up the newspaper and started reading an article about German industrial output, then tensed suddenly as the main door of the building opposite swung open and three men walked out. He lowered the paper a couple of inches so that he could see them clearly, then relaxed. His target wasn't one of the three. But he kept watching them anyway. They stood for a few moments on the pavement, talking together, then they separated, two going in one direction, and the third man the opposite way.

Williams switched his attention back to the paper, but ensured that he still had the doorway clearly in view. A few minutes later, the door opened again, and this time he recognized the heavily built man immediately, though he'd never seen his companion before.

Like the previous three, these two stood together on the pavement for a moment, talking, then the shorter man returned to the building, leaving Williams's target standing alone outside.

Williams folded the newspaper, slid it into his pocket and stood up, dropping a few coins on the table to cover the cost of his drinks. He began walking along the pavement towards the building, on the opposite side of the road.

After a few paces, he slowed down. The man standing outside the grey stone building had just glanced down the street and then lifted his arm to attract the attention of the driver of a motorized taxi.

Williams smiled to himself. His hunch had proved right after all.

As the taxi drew to a halt, Williams crossed the road about fifty yards in front of it, and then continued walking along the pavement as the taxi started moving again, approaching him from behind. He undid the three buttons of his overcoat, and also the buttons of the jacket he was wearing underneath, and checked that he could easily reach his pistol.

Then he relied on his ears, listening for the sound of the taxi's engine as the vehicle got closer to him. Williams moved nearer to the edge of the pavement, and then risked a quick glance behind him. The taxi was now only a few yards away.

As it drew level with him, the driver suddenly braked, the vehicle came almost to a halt and Williams pulled himself up and sat down next to Eberhard Neumann.

The sequence of events had been so sudden, so unexpected, that the German hadn't even moved by the time Williams rammed the muzzle of his revolver just below his rib cage.

'Hullo, Eberhard,' Williams said, his German fluent. 'It's a pleasant evening for a ride, don't you think?' Then Williams switched his attention to the driver, and issued a crisp command in English. 'Get us out of here, Tom. Somewhere nice and quiet where we can have a little chat with our guest.'

Neumann finally found his voice. 'Who are you?' he demanded. 'Let me go! You have no idea who you're dealing with.'

'Actually, Eberhard, we know *exactly* who you are, and you're dead as of this moment. If you keep quiet and then answer a few simple questions, I'll make it quick and you won't feel a thing. Try and be clever, or tell me lies, and you'll take hours to die.'

The German stared at the expressionless face of his captor and, with a sudden sinking feeling in his stomach, realized that the English spy must have handed over far more information from Trommler than he could ever have guessed. And he'd severely underestimated the lengths to which the British were prepared to go. To snatch him off the street in broad daylight was an act of either desperation or genius. And he also knew that he had nothing to lose, because he was going to die no matter what happened.

He dropped his gaze from the face of the Englishman beside him, and took a deep breath, intending to yell at the top of his voice. There weren't that many people around, but those that were would certainly hear him and take notice.

But Williams had clearly been expecting something just like that, and even as Neumann opened his mouth, he reversed his grip on his pistol and smashed the butt into the side of the German's head. Neumann slumped sideways in the seat, instantly knocked unconscious.

Williams tucked his pistol out of sight and glanced round, but none of the pedestrians appeared to have noticed anything. He made sure Neumann couldn't topple out of the seat, then relaxed.

The driver – another of Mansfield Cumming's irregulars stationed in Germany – glanced behind him.

'He's very quiet,' he remarked.

'I know,' Williams said. 'His conversation was boring me, so I shut him up. I just hope he'll have a bit more to say later.'

'Oh, I think he will,' the driver said confidently, then looked back at the road in front of them.

Just over half an hour later, the taxi eased to a halt in one of the quieter roads that ran through the Tiergarten. Together, the two men manhandled Neumann out of the cab and dragged him a few yards into the woodland.

When the German finally regained consciousness about ten minutes later, he was already lashed to a tree, his wrists and ankles secured with leather straps, and a rough gag tied around his mouth.

'I have a few questions for you, Eberhard,' Williams began, removing the gag, 'but just remember what I said earlier. Oh, if you do want to shout, be my guest. There's nobody around who can hear you.'

That was actually untrue, but the Englishman was certain that Neumann would have no idea where he was, and would probably assume from his surroundings that he was somewhere deep in the German countryside.

'First of all,' Williams said, 'I'd like you to tell me a little bit about a man named Gunther Voss, and everything you know about what he's been doing here in Germany for the last couple of weeks.'

Neumann shook his head in refusal, and Williams sighed.

'Now don't be like that, Eberhard, or I'm going to have to hurt you. Hurt you badly, in fact.'

A couple of minutes later the driver, leaning on the side of the taxi smoking a Grathwohl cigarette – the brand was advertised as having *Unerreichte Qualitäten*, unsurpassed quality, which he, personally, didn't agree was the case – winced as he heard the first screams.

Then he shrugged, drew a powerful hit of nicotine deep into his lungs, and exhaled slowly. He decided he actually didn't care what Williams did to Neumann.

After all, they owed him for what his men had done to David Curtis.

Chapter 5

9 April 1912
London

Early that afternoon, after a short and unsatisfactory lunch at his club, Mansfield Cumming stomped heavily along the Victoria Embankment, barely even glancing at the water traffic on the Thames, deep in thought. In fact, deeply worried was probably a more accurate description. Almost without conscious thought about where he was and where he was going, he walked past a succession of elegant four- and five-storey buildings, following his familiar route up Horse Guards Avenue and into Whitehall Court. Outside this building he paused, as he always did, and looked up at the massive structure, a huge contiguous building that consisted of two separate constructions designed by two different architects who had somehow managed to mesh their work into a coherent whole. Built during the mid-1880s, it had always been occupied by a large number of private residents and several commercial and administrative organizations, a veritable rabbit warren of rooms and corridors and suites and staircases.

Three years earlier, in 1909, a small suite of irregular shaped and sized rooms, accessed by a private lift and located right at the top of number 2 Whitehall Court, had been requisitioned by the War Office, and the Foreign Section of the Secret Service Bureau, in the person of George Mansfield Smith-Cumming himself, had moved in. In fact, this organization was a lot less impressive than it sounded. The SSB was a joint initiative working under the auspices of the War Office and the Admiralty, and was primarily intended to conduct intelligence operations overseas, with a particular emphasis on the activities of the Imperial German Government. The problem was that the Bureau had almost no staff and a miniscule budget, neither of which Mansfield Cumming, the eccentric director of the organization, could do a great deal about, though he certainly tried.

Extracting funds from the British government had never been easy, right from the earliest days of the Bureau's existence. But occasionally, when Mansfield Cumming – he didn't normally bother with either the 'George' or the 'Smith' – was able to demonstrate that a particular threat existed, the Treasury's hold on the purse strings could be temporarily loosened.

Some weeks earlier, rumours which had surfaced on both sides of the Atlantic had prompted Cumming to approach his masters in government, with the result that certain funding had somewhat unexpectedly been made available to him. He was keeping most of the money in reserve, but he had invested in one piece of new and unusual technology for his office, a device which he still regarded with a certain amount of suspicion, but which was undeniably already beginning to prove extremely useful: a telephone.

Almost all of the messages that Mansfield Cumming received were written: signals sent by wireless using Morse code and then transcribed, printed telegrams and the like. Telephone communications, even from people who knew that he now had such an instrument, were far less frequent.

But only a few minutes after he got back into his office that afternoon, he did receive a telephone call. An international call in fact, which originated in the British Embassy in Berlin.

'I expected to hear from you sooner than this,' Cumming began, raising his voice. He knew he was talking to a man in Germany, and thought the extra volume would probably help. 'What happened?'

'We had to wait for him to leave the building yesterday evening,' Williams replied, his voice somewhat crackly and difficult to hear over the pops and whistles of the international line. 'I had another chap standing by with a taxi, and we picked him up in that. But he was a tougher nut to crack than I'd expected, and I had to collate and analyze what he'd told me.'

'Is he dead?'

'Bread? What do you mean?'

'No. Is. He. Dead.'

This time Williams heard him clearly. 'Very. We left his body in the Tiergarten. But I've got a piece of bad news for you. When Voss left the *Preußische Geheimpolizei* headquarters two days ago, I told Paul Harrington to follow him, just in case he was going anywhere else that afternoon.'

'So?'

'So Harrington hasn't been seen since. We've no idea what happened to him, but if I had to make a guess, I'd say that either Voss or more likely his bodyguards spotted that they were being tailed, and decided to get rid of him.'

Mansfield Cumming was silent for a few moments. First Curtis, then Harrington. The casualties were beginning to mount up. But the stakes were too high not to carry on.

'If Harrington turns up, or if his body is found, make sure that I'm the first to know about it,' Cumming instructed. 'But what about the information we needed? Did Neumann tell you what we wanted to know?'

'More or less. It took a while, and it was quite messy, especially towards the end, when there weren't many places left where I could stick a knife in—'

Mansfield Cumming shuddered slightly. During his career in the Royal Navy he'd always been able to live like a gentleman, but since his secondment to the Secret Service Bureau, he had increasingly been forced to confront – or at the very least, be aware of – the brutal tactics which were the norm in the dirty business of espionage. And, as in this case, he sometimes had to issue orders which he knew could lead to the death or torture of an agent of either Britain or a foreign power. But he didn't have to like it.

'Spare me the gory details, Williams. Just get to the point, will you?'

'He told me everything he knew, but actually that wasn't everything we wanted to know. But you were right. Voss is the architect of this scheme. The trouble is, we still don't know exactly what the scheme is, because Neumann clearly didn't know all the details. But what he did tell me was bad enough.'

Mansfield Cumming listened to the familiar voice of his agent in Berlin for the next few minutes, occasionally requesting Williams to say something again when the static made his voice inaudible. And twice he had to ask for a sentence to be repeated because he simply didn't believe what he was hearing, the suggestion was so monstrous.

When Williams had finished, Cumming muttered just two words: 'Dear God.'

For a few moments the only sound on the line was a faint humming interspersed with crackles, then Mansfield Cumming spoke again.

'What else did he tell you?' he asked.

'It's not just Voss by himself. He's got two people working with him, and they're the money men. Voss's field of expertise is mining. That's what he does, and that's what he's good at. But these other two have the financial resources to make things happen, and one thing in particular.'

Again Cumming listened as Williams unfolded details of the plot which had been hatched.

'Can he do that?' Cumming asked, when his agent had finished his explanation.

'Voss can't, no, not by himself. He's a very wealthy man, but not even his financial reserves would allow him to do that. But the two other men involved in the plot with him are bankers, and they do have the resources to achieve this. If they manage it, Mansfield, we really are in trouble. Serious trouble.'

'You don't have to tell me that,' Cumming replied. 'You have got the identities of these two men, I hope? And where they might be found?'

'Yes. You won't be surprised to learn that, like Voss, they're both American citizens, but they were born in Germany, and that's obviously where their sympathies lie. Their names are Jonas Bauer and Lenz Kortig, but where they are I have no idea. They might even be back in the United States by now. But there is one place you might start looking for them.'

'Where?'

'According to Neumann, Voss told him he was joining a ship at Cherbourg tomorrow, so maybe the other two men are with him.'

Williams spelled the names of the two men and Mansfield Cumming wrote them down on a piece of paper.

'Now we have their names,' Cumming said, 'we can try and find them, even if they are in Washington or New York or even somewhere over here in Europe, but obviously I'll try and find out if they're booked on a ship first. Did Neumann know if these two people were an integral part of the plot, or just recruited by Voss because of their positions? And what are they getting out of it if the plan goes ahead?'

'What they'll get is a lot of money,' Williams replied. 'I don't pretend to understand the mechanics of the way it works, but making money is probably their prime motivation. Neumann claimed he'd never met these two men, but according to Voss they're just as deeply involved in the plot as he is. I got the impression that even if you could somehow eliminate two of them, whichever one was left could – and probably would – continue what they've started. And make it happen.'

'So we have to find all three of them?'

'Exactly. We have to track them all down, find out the details of this plot they've constructed, and then kill them. As far as I can see, Mansfield, there's no other solution if we want Britain and her Empire to survive.'

'God help us,' Cumming said, his voice barely more than a whisper. 'God help us all.'

Chapter 6

9 April 1912
London

There was an air of ruthless and impatient competence about the tall, fair-haired young man who walked into Whitehall Court later that afternoon. The secretary who guarded the entrance to Mansfield Cumming's inner sanctum glanced from the smart tweed suit he was wearing to the expression on his face, and simply nodded to him to go up. Alex Tremayne had an appointment – perhaps a summons would have been a better description – and he was already late.

Getting inside was the easy part. Actually reaching the office was rather more complicated, because Mansfield Cumming had just installed a false staircase, entry to which was controlled from the director's office using a complicated system of levers and pulleys, which only occasionally worked properly.

It took three attempts before Tremayne was finally able to knock on the director's door and then step inside.

'Come in, Tremayne,' Mansfield Cumming boomed. 'You're late,' he added.

Tremayne sat down in front of the wide desk. 'I wouldn't have been quite so late if you didn't always have to fiddle about with that ridiculous staircase. Why can't you just have an office in a corridor, like anybody else?'

'Don't be impertinent, Tremayne,' Cumming replied, picking up a gold-rimmed monocle from the desk and screwing it firmly in his right eye. 'In case you hadn't noticed, the first letter "S" of this unit's designation stands for "Secret". That means nobody is supposed to know who we are, or where we are. And that staircase would work perfectly well if the people who built it for me had been competent. After all, I designed it myself.'

Tremayne didn't reply. The last sentence seemed to him to provide an entirely adequate explanation for any failings in the operation of the equipment in the building. Mansfield Cumming was a former naval officer who had been retired from the Royal Navy because of persistent seasickness, but who had shown a considerable talent for intelligence work. As far as Tremayne knew, he had no abilities whatsoever in carpentry or mechanical engineering.

'We have a problem,' Cumming began, and Tremayne knew better than to interrupt. The two men enjoyed an easy and familiar relationship, for a variety of reasons, but Cumming was still Tremayne's boss, and the summons he had received had made it clear that something serious was going on.

'We have a problem,' Cumming repeated, 'and it's all the bloody Kaiser's fault.'

That didn't come as a surprise to Tremayne. The military and economic development of Germany had been startling. In the forty years between 1870 and 1910, the population of the country had rocketed from 24 million to 65 million, and some 40 per cent of its total workforce was now employed in industry. Its industrial development was the fastest in the world. Germany had increased coal production by 400 per cent since 1870; steel, engineering, chemicals and armaments had grown rapidly, and its international trade had quadrupled. The country had the most efficient army in the world, with some half a million men under arms, and the second largest navy, though not as yet even beginning to approach the strength of the Royal Navy.

Any impartial observer would have come to the obvious conclusion that Germany was preparing for war. And Britain, with its vast Empire and almost limitless resources, was the major obstacle to the Kaiser's global ambitions, and clearly the country's most likely potential enemy.

'What's happened?' Tremayne asked, his piercing blue eyes narrowing as he stared at Cumming.

'You knew David Curtis?' Cumming asked.

The past tense wasn't lost on Tremayne. 'Yes, I did. What's happened to him?' he asked.

'He's dead, shot on the street three nights ago in Berlin.' Cumming never believed in sugar-coating the truth, no matter how unpalatable. 'He had a meeting with a low-level informer, but something obviously tipped off the German secret police. He was chased through the streets and then shot dead right outside the British Embassy. The events leading up to his killing were somewhat confused, as you'd expect, but we've received reports that the man he'd been talking to in a bar a few minutes earlier was arrested, so we presume they got the informer as well.'

The question seemed obvious, but Tremayne asked it anyway. 'If he was only meeting a low-level informer, why did he end up dead?'

Mansfield Cumming smiled bleakly. 'That's the point,' he said. 'In fact, the man was only a clerk. But he was looking for some easy money, and when one particular report was given to him to register and then file away, he read it, or part of it anyway. What he saw prompted him to contact one of the staff members at the British Embassy, with the result that we paid him quite a lot of money for details of a particularly nasty little scheme that the Germans are engaged in. Of course, he won't be able to spend it now. The Germans'll probably just shoot him.'

'So where did Curtis fit in?'

'That's simple. Most of the embassy staff are employed to push bits of paper around. They're not trained for any kind of covert activity, so after this German clerk – his name was Klaus Trommler – contacted them, they reported the fact to the Foreign Office, and the Foreign Secretary called me in and told me to sort it out.'

'So you sent David Curtis because he speaks – or rather he spoke – fluent German? His family came from Bavaria, if I remember correctly, and he came over here to Britain in his twenties. You were a bit reluctant to recruit him, too.'

Cumming nodded. 'You're right, I was, though he proved his worth to me several times over. Anyway, this should have been a simple enough job, but because of what happened I think the Germans were already watching Trommler. Either that or they'd been following Curtis. The mechanics don't matter. All that concerns us is the information that Trommler passed on, and which Curtis relayed to the British Embassy in Berlin and then on to us.'

'Which was?' Tremayne prompted.

Mansfield Cumming looked down at his desk and picked up a single sheet of paper, one side covered in closely spaced typewritten lines. 'It's a plot, basically,' he replied, after glancing at it for a few moments. 'Let me give you some background information. As things stand, the Royal Navy dominates the oceans. It's the biggest navy the world has ever seen, equipped with the most modern and most powerful warships we have been able to construct. In any maritime conflict, with any nation, the Royal Navy would prevail.'

'I'm not a sailor,' Tremayne remarked, 'but supposing Germany combined its own navy with the other maritime forces of this Triple Alliance they've set up. How would it work then?'

Cumming shook his head. 'We would still be more than a match for them. Even if Germany produced a combined fleet with Italy and the Austro-Hungarian Empire, we would still have something like a twenty-five per cent higher gross tonnage. I grant you, that would give us a much smaller margin of superiority, but it would still be enough.'

'So the only way that the German Navy could hope to achieve maritime superiority would be if the Kaiser managed to secure an alliance with another – a different – nation, one which already has a strong navy?'

Cumming smiled. 'As usual,' he said, 'you've gone to the crux of the matter. Without a new alliance, I don't believe Germany would dare to declare war on Britain. With such an alliance, it could happen tomorrow.'

'But an alliance with whom?'

'One nation Germany could contemplate linking up with is Russia. They have a total warship tonnage of over eight hundred thousand, and if that nation threw in its lot with the Triple Alliance, the combined force would be so powerful that it could take on the Royal Navy on the high seas and probably beat it. And if the time ever comes when the Royal Navy no longer dominates the oceans, the British Empire will cease to exist within one generation. Make no mistake, Tremayne, Britain is and always has been a maritime nation. Our most important single attribute, our strongest military arm and our most powerful instrument of diplomacy, is the Royal Navy.'

Tremayne shook his head. 'But Russia would never join forces with Germany,' he objected. 'The Tsar has signed a treaty with France and that puts Russia in opposition to Germany right from the start.'

Mansfield Cumming nodded. 'When the German clerk approached the Berlin Embassy with his story, that was their initial reaction as well. They were inclined to dismiss Trommler out of hand. But he was adamant that such an alliance was not only planned, but was about to be implemented, and he claimed he'd seen a document which proved it. Spelled it out, in fact.' Cumming leant forward to emphasize the point. 'But it isn't Russia that Germany is planning to join forces with. It's the United States of America. And the two of them together – America and Germany – have one goal in mind. They intend to declare war on Great Britain and destroy our Empire.'

Chapter 7

9 April 1912
London

Tremayne stared at Cumming for a few moments, then shook his head. 'I don't believe it,' he said. 'The Germans have got nothing in common with the Americans, and our relationship with them is very good. We speak the same language, we share the same ideals and values, and we have strong trading links. Why would the American people possibly want to form an alliance with Germany?'

'It's not quite that simple,' Mansfield Cumming sighed. 'America is a melting pot of different cultures and races. Though the English predominate, as you say, there's a very large German presence over there and, more importantly, many of the richest and most influential families in America are either German by birth, or have German ancestors and strong cultural links with that country.'

'Yes, but—'

'And there's something else,' Cumming ploughed on, ignoring Tremayne's interruption. 'You mentioned the American people. What they want, or don't want, is frankly of little concern to the government over there. Like all governments, the people running the United States are politicians first and foremost, and that means they'll do whatever it takes to stay in power. They'll say whatever they think people want to hear, but they'll make sure that any decisions they take are to their own advantage as far as possible.'

'That's a very cynical point of view.' Tremayne raised his left eyebrow.

Mansfield Cumming smiled. 'It might be cynical, Tremayne, but it's also true. All politicians are corrupt: it's virtually one of the qualifications for doing the job. If almost any politician is offered enough money, he'll take whatever decision the man who's paying him wants him to take, and if enough of them take the bribes, they'll ensure that the "right" course of action is followed.'

Tremayne looked confused. 'Are you saying that the German government is going to try and bribe America to form an alliance?'

Cumming shook his head. 'At the moment, we don't know what lever the Germans are trying to pull. I suppose it could be bribery, using some of the fortunes amassed by German emigrants to America, plus funds from Germany itself, perhaps, but I doubt it. That would involve too many people, who might ask too many questions. Personally, I think this plot involves something much simpler. And that's what we need to find out. The information that Curtis obtained from Trommler was only fragmentary, because the man only got a brief look at the relevant document. Our people stationed in America haven't heard anything about any kind of moves aimed at creating this unholy alliance. To me, that suggests that the architects of this scheme haven't yet made their move, and it also means that they must have some argument or information so compelling that the

American president or members of the government would have no option but to agree to this alliance once the plotters reach America, and that an announcement would follow almost immediately.'

Cumming held up his hand to forestall the question he expected Tremayne to ask.

'The answer's no, we don't know any more than that about the lever.'

Tremayne shook his head. 'No,' he said, 'I guessed that. I was going ask you how sure we are that whoever's orchestrating this isn't already in America. You said "once the plotters reach America". So how do you know they're not there right now, completing their scheme?'

Mansfield Cumming smiled again. 'Now that is something that we *do* know. Just before Curtis was murdered, he had enough presence of mind to pass a message on to one of the sentries. In the seconds before he died, he said four words to the soldier who was trying to help him. "Three men. Boss. You." Or at least, that was what the sentry thought.'

Cumming picked up a file off his desk, opened it and glanced at the first page, then replaced it, still open so that he could read what it contained.

Tremayne waited. He knew Cumming of old, knew that he would explain things in his own good time.

'The meaning of the first two words is quite obvious. This plot must obviously involve more than just one man. I'll come back to the third word in a minute, but the fourth and last word he spoke – "you"– had us fooled for a while. "You" could have been the start of a new sentence: "You need to find this man", or something like that. But it could also have been the first syllable of a new word, or the first letter of an acronym.'

Tremayne nodded. 'So "u" as in the letter. "U" meaning "United States" or "USA"?'

'Exactly,' Cumming nodded. 'And if we are right, then it means Curtis had received confirmation from his source that Germany was indeed planning to link up with the United States.'

'So what about the other word? "Boss"?'

'Actually, we don't think Curtis said that at all. He was badly wounded already, his left shoulder smashed, one lung punctured and his left femur shattered into a dozen pieces. He was clearly in agony, and his speech would almost certainly have been affected. The sentry he spoke to thinks Curtis said "Boss", but I think the word he was trying to get out was "Voss". And if we're right about that, it changes everything.'

Chapter 8

9 April 1912
London

There was a knock on the office door, and a few moments later a shapeless middle-aged woman backed into the room carrying a small tray.

'Tea,' she announced economically, in a pronounced Scottish brogue, placing the tray on the end of Mansfield Cumming's desk. Then she retreated as quickly as she'd appeared.

Cumming placed a cup on a saucer and then poured dark-brown, almost black, liquid from a small discoloured teapot, added a splash of milk and slid it across the desk to Tremayne, before pouring his own.

'So who is Voss?' Tremayne asked, taking a sip of tea, which tasted strong enough to be used as a disinfectant, or possibly as some kind of fuel. He decided that one sip was quite enough and, out of respect for his intestines, he replaced the cup and saucer on the tray.

'Ever since we first got wind of this plot, a couple of weeks ago, we've been watching every possible German and American citizen who we thought might be involved. Here in Britain, Vernon Kell has had his people from MI5 mounting surveillance on everyone they could find. But frankly, I doubted if they were looking in the right place. There would be no point in the people involved in this plot spending much time in Britain. They would either need to be in Germany, finalizing details of the scheme there, or over in America.

'We had to make some assumptions, of course. We presumed that the conspirators in this plot would either be Germans or, probably more likely, American citizens with German backgrounds. We guessed they would also be spending more time in Germany than anywhere else in Europe, and would be intending to return to America within the next few weeks.'

'That must have covered hundreds of people,' Tremayne suggested.

'It did,' Mansfield Cumming agreed. 'I've had people in America checking the passenger lists of their shipping lines and other people doing the same in Britain and Europe, and the total we came up with was just over six hundred, but it could be a lot more than that. The Continent seems to be full of visiting Americans at the moment. Then one of my men suggested a way that we could use to identify any conspirators. He reasoned that anyone involved in such a plot would almost certainly be having meetings with members of the German government or high-level officials, most probably in Berlin. That cut the numbers drastically, and we ended up with a list of about twenty people. One of them was a wealthy American businessman named Gunther Voss.'

'Voss is not an uncommon name in Germany,' Tremayne pointed out. 'It means "fox" in low German. Don't forget, I spent five years in Munich and Berlin after university.'

Cumming nodded. 'I remember. Your German isn't bad either. And you're quite right, but on our new shortlist, there was only one Voss. So if our assumptions were right, and if the German clerk gave Curtis the correct name, we might have identified one of the people involved in this plot.'

Tremayne didn't look convinced. 'I know your intuition is usually right, Mansfield, but it sounds to me as if you're basing the identification of this man, this Voss, on a series of assumptions, many of which might be wrong, and on a single name uttered by a dying man, a name that could easily have been misheard in the circumstances. At best, what you've got is very shaky circumstantial evidence, and certainly not enough to arrest this man, or even bring him in for questioning.'

'Two things. First, I have no intention of arresting or questioning this man. All we're doing is watching him. Second, Curtis was killed three nights ago, so we've known about Voss since then. Why do you think I'm only telling you about him now?'

'Because you spent the last two days investigating him?'

'Precisely. And what we've found out so far suggests that our identification might be correct. Our people in America have established that Voss is anti-British – but that's hardly a crime, of course – and he has something of a history of agitating for closer trade links with Germany. We also know that he has powerful connections within the Kaiser's government through his mining interests.'

'There must be more than that, surely?'

'Patience! Voss made most of his money in the mining industry in America, and we know from looking at various correspondence we've been able to – ahem – acquire, shall we say, that he's very keen to establish a foothold for his businesses in Africa. The problem for him is that Britain already controls many of the most important and productive areas.'

'So what are you saying? That Voss is prepared to commit America to joining forces with Germany, to fight a war against the British that Germany will inevitably start just so that he can get his hands on some South African mining concessions?'

Mansfield Cumming wrinkled his brow and frowned. 'I suppose when you put it like that, it does all sound a bit far-fetched, but that's what our information tells us is going to happen. Of course, we'll need confirmation before we take any action, and that's where you come in.'

Tremayne nodded. 'I'd already worked that out for myself. So what do you want me to do? Go over to Germany and follow Voss, hoping he'll say or do something that will incriminate him?'

'Not exactly. As soon as it was obvious that he was a person of interest, I ordered surveillance to be started on him in Germany. He was in Berlin, of course.'

'Was he in the city when Curtis was killed?'

Cumming nodded. 'Yes, but we don't think he had anything to do with his death, or not directly anyway.'

There was another knock at the door, and the same woman entered the office. She glanced down at the tray on the desk, and looked with displeasure at Tremayne, on seeing that his drink had been virtually untouched. Then she glanced across at Mansfield Cumming and from somewhere in her voluminous garments produced a buff envelope which she passed over to him.

Cumming took it with a nod. 'Thank you, Mrs McTavish,' he said to her retreating back as she left the room carrying the tray.

'Who is that woman?' Tremayne asked.

Cumming fixed him with a steely glint through his monocle. 'Mrs McTavish,' he intoned, 'is one of my wife's family's retainers. The McTavishes have been employed by her family up in Morayshire as far back as anyone can remember. May – my wife – decided that I needed somebody here in London who was completely trustworthy to act as my assistant, and Mrs McTavish fitted the bill admirably. She is very competent, superbly loyal, completely immune to bribery and flattery, and utterly devoted to me. I don't know what I'd do without her.'

Tremayne sat back in his chair. 'Right,' he said, and waited while Cumming sliced open the envelope with a paper knife in the shape of a miniature Scottish broadsword. He extracted a single sheet of paper, unfolded it and read the contents.

'This is from Berlin,' he said finally, 'sent from the embassy, and it's a complete list of everywhere Herr Voss has visited over the last two days. I've had a couple of my people working out of the embassy for the last month, and as soon as we had a possible identification of Voss from Curtis, I sent them out to keep tabs on him. Their instructions were to record where he went and who he spoke to. And it looks as if Voss has some rather unusual friends in Germany, if he really is just an American businessman.

'The first unusual point is that Voss is staying in a very good hotel in Berlin, in a large room on one of the upper floors. He's occupying the room alone, but he has also booked, and is paying for, the rooms on either side, and each of those is occupied by two men. They don't look like business associates, they look like bodyguards, and he never leaves the hotel without them by his side. Sometimes they accompany him inside buildings, where he is presumably holding meetings, but on other occasions they don't.'

Cumming looked at the large gold pocket watch which he

always placed on the desk in front of him, then back at the sheet of paper. 'Perhaps Gunther Voss's most unusual visit was two days ago, when he walked into the Berlin headquarters of the *Preußische Geheimpolizei* and spent over two hours in the building.'

'What would an American businessman want with the Prussian secret police? Unless he'd been arrested for something?'

'No. He went there with two of his men in a horse-drawn cab. And that's not all. The building is surrounded by a high wall and, once Voss went inside, obviously the only thing my men could do was stay out in the street, keeping out of sight of the bodyguards, who remained near the main door of the building. After about three-quarters of an hour, they heard a volley of rifle fire from the courtyard inside the headquarters. That could have been Klaus Trommler – the informer Curtis met – meeting his maker.'

'Would the secret police have the authority to execute him without a trial?'

'Probably, yes. From what little we know about it, the *Preußische Geheimpolizei* is very much a law unto itself. I doubt if they'd bother with anything as fair or democratic as a trial. They probably beat what they wanted to know out of him, then stuck him against a wall and shot him. Of course, we might be mistaken. It's always possible Trommler was arrested by the regular police, and the other lot were just making sure their rifles worked. But somehow I doubt it.'

'So if you don't want me to go to Berlin and follow Voss around, what *do* you want me to do?'

Cumming paused, glanced down at the file again and then looked up at Tremayne. 'I need to tell you something in the strictest of confidence,' he said.

Tremayne shrugged. 'I thought everything you told me was in the strictest of confidence.'

'This is particularly sensitive,' Cumming replied. 'What I'm about to tell you must never be repeated to anyone.'

Chapter 9

9 April 1912
London

For a few moments, Cumming didn't continue, just looked across his desk at Tremayne.

'What?'

'I was just trying to remember how long we've known each other.'

Tremayne shook his head. 'Too long, probably. You were still in Naval Intelligence, and we met in Germany. I can't remember which year, but I do know what you were doing out there.'

Cumming allowed himself a rare smile. 'Yes, and so do I. It wasn't the best idea I've ever had.'

'No. Driving around the country pretending to be a successful German businessman when you hardly spoke a word of the language wasn't what I would call a well-conceived plan.'

'It worked, though. I got some valuable intelligence information on that trip. And once you and I met at that hotel in Königsberg and teamed up, it was a lot easier.'

Tremayne nodded. 'Yes, because I could act as your driver and assistant, and then you pretended you couldn't speak because of laryngitis. At least that way one of us spoke German and it wasn't quite so obvious you were an English spy. Still a bloody risky endeavour, though. If the authorities had twigged what we were doing they'd have locked both of us up straight away.'

'But it worked,' Cumming repeated.

'True, but what's that got to do with this situation?'

'Nothing, really. I was just remembering that Germany was a thorn in our side then, and it's just the same now. Whether this scheme Voss has cooked up works or not, I still think that, one way or another, we'll have to face the Kaiser's forces soon.

Cumming dropped his gaze to the papers on the desk in front of him, then looked back at Tremayne.

'Now, we don't know for sure who ordered Curtis to be shot,' he continued, 'but the balance of probability is that the man pulling the strings was Eberhard Neumann, the head of the *Preußische Geheimpolizei* in Berlin. That's the first thing. Then, from the surveillance report I've already told you about, we knew that Neumann had spent time with Voss, and it seemed probable that Neumann was deeply involved in the conspiracy.'

Tremayne held up his hand. 'I think I can see where you're going with this one, Mansfield, but you're wasting your time. I know of Eberhard Neumann by reputation, and if you're thinking of trying to get him to betray Voss, he'll never do it. He's ruthless and he's vicious, but he only ever serves one master.'

Cumming shook his head again. 'You're wrong, Tremayne. That wasn't what I had in mind. In fact, I ordered my men in Berlin to detain Neumann and make him reveal everything he knew.'

Tremayne stared at him in disbelief. 'But when you release

him,' he said, 'he'll know it was the British behind it. You'll be lucky if the German government doesn't shut down the British Embassy completely.'

Mansfield Cumming's silence told its own story. After a few seconds Tremayne nodded.

'I see. You're not going to release him, are you? Is he already dead?'

'Eberhard Neumann,' Cumming said, 'unfortunately did not survive his interrogation.'

'You took a hell of a risk, you know.'

'I do know, but desperate times call for desperate measures, and Neumann was the most obvious source of information about this plot. We couldn't touch Voss without showing our hand, and even if we took him off the streets, there would still be the other two men involved who we'd have to find. So snatching Neumann looked like the best idea. And, on a purely personal note, I liked David Curtis. We owed something to his memory, and somebody ought to be made to pay for his death.'

'Then I just hope it was worth it,' Tremayne said.

'It was,' Cumming nodded. 'There are still a few holes in the story, but it's clear that somehow Voss has found a way to make this alliance happen, but we still don't know how. He seems to be working very closely with two wealthy bankers and, reading between the lines, it looks as if he's discovered some dirty little secret, maybe something implicating the American president, some lever that will allow him to achieve his ends. I can't stress this enough, Alex. We *have* to find out what Voss knows, and what he has planned, because quite literally the future of the British Empire is at stake here.'

'And how am I supposed to do that? What, exactly, are you asking me to do?'

'The most important thing is to stop Voss from getting to America. And that's your first and most important job. He's sailing from Cherbourg tomorrow, and I've already booked a passage on the ship for you and your wife.'

A long silence followed as Tremayne stared at Mansfield Cumming.

'Unless you know something I don't, Mansfield, I was under the impression that I was still a bachelor.'

'For the purposes of this operation I decided that you needed a partner, and a married couple will always attract less attention than a single man, and especially than two men travelling together.'

'Don't I have a choice about this?' Tremayne demanded. 'You know I always prefer to work alone.'

'No, you don't have a choice,' Mansfield Cumming replied. He reached forward, picked up a small brass bell and rang it sharply. 'Just remember, by the way,' he added, 'that this woman is your wife in name alone. She's a fellow agent and her job is to support you, to help you in situations where two pairs of eyes or hands will be better than one. I am not sending her with you for your entertainment or pleasure.'

Before Tremayne could reply there was a brisk double knock at the door. Then it opened and a woman walked into the office.

'This,' said Mansfield Cumming, with the air of a conjurer producing a rabbit from a top hat, 'is Maria Weston. Maria, meet Alex Tremayne.'

Tremayne had stood up as the woman entered the office, and now he stared at the new arrival. She was tall for a woman, probably five feet seven or eight, and wearing a tailored blue suit, the skirt ending a little above her ankles. Her dark hair was parted in the middle and, in defiance of the prevailing styles, worn long and neither curled nor waved. Intelligent grey eyes framed a short, pert nose, and her wide and generous mouth had a hint of a smile playing over it as she stepped forward to greet him.

'Mister Tremayne,' she said, her voice low and husky, the New England accent unmistakable. 'I'm pleased to meet you. Captain Cumming has told me a lot about you.'

'Miss Weston,' Tremayne replied, having noted the absence of a ring on her left hand. 'You shouldn't believe everything you're told, and especially not by former officers in the Royal Navy. They're notorious liars.'

The smile blossomed. 'That's a shame. He was really quite complimentary.'

'You're American,' Tremayne said, stating the obvious.

Maria nodded. 'Mansfield said you were observant, and I can see that he was absolutely right.'

The sarcasm was apparent. Tremayne looked over at Cumming. 'A word, Mansfield, if I may.'

Cumming shook his head. 'No, Alex. Let me explain, because this is really quite simple. This plot that Gunther Voss has conceived is designed to force America into an alliance that it doesn't want, an alliance with Germany. If that alliance came to fruition, then the probability is that Britain and America would be at war with each other within months. I've discussed this with my opposite number in America, with the head of the new Bureau of Investigation, and he has assigned Maria here to work with us. It's in the interests of both our countries.'

For a few moments, both Tremayne and Maria Weston remained looking at each other. Maria appeared amused while the expression on Tremayne's face remained unreadable.

'Sit down, both of you,' Mansfield Cumming ordered. 'Now,

I've already explained to Tremayne what the situation is, and you, Maria, have been working with me for the last week, so you know as much about this as I do.'

'I'm still not sure that it's necessary to place Miss Weston in this position,' Tremayne protested. 'I'm perfectly happy to undertake this operation by myself.'

'You may be happy, Tremayne, but I'm not,' Cumming snapped, 'and that's the end of it as far as I'm concerned. This matter is far too important to be left to just one man, no matter how competent he may be.'

'Just a minute,' Tremayne said, as a thought struck him. 'Miss Weston has been here a week?'

Maria nodded. 'I've been here a lot longer than that, working at our embassy here in London. As soon as my boss heard rumours about this plot from Mansfield, he instructed me to act as his liaison officer. He thought that having one of his own people in the loop was a good idea.'

'Now,' Cumming went on, as soon as the other two had taken their seats in front of his desk, 'we already know that Voss will be crossing the Atlantic on board ship, but we don't yet know whether the other two men who are involved will be on the same vessel. Their names are Jonas Bauer and Lenz Kortig, and they're both wealthy bankers and, just like Voss, although they've American passports, they were born in Germany. In fact, calling them "Americans" rather misses the point. These three men are really old-style, hard-line Prussians, despite the language they speak.

'We've asked for copies of the passenger lists from all the Continental shipping lines, and Vernon Kell has made the same request of the British lines. So far, that's produced no results, partly because the lists are incomplete. Passengers who embark at the port of departure are obviously included on the lists, but the names of those who pick up the ship elsewhere – its second or third port of call on this side of the Atlantic, for example – aren't known for certain until they actually board the vessel.

'So although we know that Voss will be on the ship when it leaves Cherbourg, his name is not yet on any of the passenger lists the company has been able to supply to us. Nor, as you might expect, are the names Bauer or Kortig. It's possible that they'll both be joining the ship in France as well, but we also have to consider the possibility that they are already in America, in which case we'll have to make separate arrangements to track them down. But at least we know where Voss is now, and where he'll be tomorrow, and you two will already be on the ship when it arrives in Cherbourg because it's sailing from Southampton—'

'But you still haven't explained exactly what you expect me – or rather us – to do once we've identified Voss,' Tremayne interrupted.

Mansfield Cumming closed the file in front of him and for a moment just sat there, resting his head in his hands. Then he roused himself.

'At this precise moment, Tremayne, I'm not entirely sure what orders I should be giving you. As you'll appreciate, the British government, and especially the Foreign Office, is taking a very keen interest in Herr Voss. I am constrained by what the government wants me to do, by how much they will allow me to tell you and what limits they will be applying to our freedom of action.

'The one thing that is absolutely clear is that Voss must be stopped. If we are unable to somehow neutralize his plan and prevent this proposed alliance between Germany and America, then there is really only one possible option. One way or another, we will have to prevent him from reaching America.'

'You mean arrest him?' Tremayne asked.

Cumming gave a small shrug. 'That would be difficult. He's an American citizen, holding an American passport, and as far as I'm aware he's done nothing that would merit detaining him for any reason. What I had in mind was something rather more *permanent*.'

His last sentence produced a chilly silence in the office, as Tremayne absorbed the implication of what Mansfield Cumming had said. Before he replied, he glanced at Maria Weston, who looked back at him.

'You mean you want us to kill him?' she said.

'I wouldn't put it quite that crudely. I was thinking more that he might meet with an accident. A few drinks too many after dinner, a stumble on the Promenade Deck, and our problem could be solved with nobody any the wiser. And just so that you're fully in the picture with regard to Voss and his men, one of my officers in Berlin, a man named Paul Harrington, was following Voss two days ago, and now he's simply disappeared. We don't know for certain, but the probability is that Voss discovered he was under surveillance and ordered one of his bodyguards to kill him. These are not pleasant people we're dealing with here, Alex.'

'You said Voss was working with two other men on this plot,' Tremayne said. 'So are you expecting us to kill them as well?'

Again, Cumming looked slightly pained at Tremayne's choice of words. 'Voss is understood to be the ringleader,' he replied. 'If he were to meet with an accident, we're not sure whether or not the other two men would continue with the plot.'

Cumming paused for a moment, then shrugged and continued. 'But just to be on the safe side,' he said, 'three late-night stumbles on the Promenade Deck would probably be advisable.'

Chapter 10

Tremayne sat in silence for a moment. To be baldly ordered to execute three men, none of whom he knew or had ever met, was something of a first, even as an agent of the Secret Service Bureau. He had killed before, both on official business, as it were, and also when it was a personal matter. But he wasn't a paid assassin, and never had been.

What had happened a few days ago with Cumming's niece in the Essex farmhouse was one thing. Then, Tremayne had known exactly what the three men had done, and he had felt entirely justified in taking the action that he had. What Mansfield Cumming was now ordering him to do was completely different, and he wasn't sure that he liked it.

'Just to get this clear, you're ordering me to carry out three assassinations?'

Cumming nodded. 'If it comes to it, and if we can find no other way of stopping this plot, yes, that's exactly what I'm ordering you to do. Do you have a problem with that?'

'I'll need to be certain that there's no alternative, that there's nothing else we can do. As far as I can see, Mansfield, all the evidence you've got is circumstantial at best. There could be other reasons Voss was in Berlin, meeting officials there, and the other two men might just be his friends, nothing more. If they really are orchestrating this plot, I'll have no qualms about eliminating them, but I won't spill innocent blood unless it's unavoidable.'

'That's another reason I'm sending Maria with you.'

Tremayne glanced at the woman. 'You mean she's going to stiffen my resolve, and make sure I do the right thing?' he asked.

'That, and to take over from you if necessary. Don't let Maria's gentle smile fool you. She's a fully trained American agent and she's often worked in the field. Her boss was somewhat vague on the details, but he did say her knowledge of combat wasn't purely theoretical. He implied that she'd killed in the line of duty, maybe more than once. That's the other reason why she'll be on the ship with you.'

Tremayne stared at Maria, a somewhat startled expression on his face, and she smiled back at him.

'They were all people I didn't like very much,' she said defensively.

Tremayne nodded. 'I'll try and remember to keep in your good books then,' he murmured.

Cumming pulled open one of the desk drawers and took out two polished wooden boxes which he placed in front of him. He turned a small key in the lock of one of them, lifted the lid and took out a compact, black semi-automatic pistol.

'This is the new Browning 1910 model,' he said. He pulled back the slide to check that the chamber was empty, pressed the catch at the base of the butt to release the magazine, and passed the weapon over to Tremayne.

'I have two of them here, both identical and chambered for

the 7.65 Browning cartridge, with a seven-round magazine, and a suppressor. These weapons are intended for your personal defence, and I expect you to return them to me, along with any unused ammunition, when this mission is over. But I'd like to emphasize that it would be preferable if you found some other way of disposing of Herr Voss and his associates – assuming it comes to that, of course – than by shooting them. It's difficult to pass off a death as an accident if the corpse is full of bullet holes.'

Tremayne examined the pistol closely. It was a neat, slim design, which would slip easily into a pocket, or a woman's purse. On the rear of the butt was a feature that particularly impressed him – a grip safety, meaning that the weapon would not fire unless it was being held in the hand. He was familiar with Browning's earlier pistol design, the 1903, but this latest model seemed a huge improvement.

He passed the weapon over to Maria, who handled it with an easy competence that implied a long familiarity with pistols, and then she passed it back to Cumming, who replaced it in the wooden case.

'Mrs McTavish has the appropriate papers for you to sign in her office, so please ensure that you do that before you leave the building. She will also provide you with your tickets and a cash advance in sterling for your expenses on board the ship, and another in dollars for your use in New York when the ship docks there. She also has new passports for you both, issued this morning here in London in the names of Alex Maitland and Maria Maitland. They're absolutely genuine, so you should have no trouble using them. We decided to use your real Christian names because we thought it would make it more natural in conversation.'

Cumming paused, as if considering his next words with some
care. 'I know you're not happy about this mission, Tremayne,
but I cannot overemphasize how important it is. I have no doubt
at all that the information David Curtis obtained from the
German clerk was accurate, and that there is a very real threat
to the security of Great Britain and her Empire. We believe that
this plot is being orchestrated by Gunther Voss for his own self-
ish desires, and as far as I can see the only sure and certain way
of stopping it is to dispose of Voss and his cronies. That is not
a course of action that I'm comfortable with, any more than you
are, but at this moment I see no possible alternative.'

Tremayne still looked unhappy at what he was being asked
to do.

'And if Voss is an entirely innocent party?' he asked. 'If all
the evidence you think you've found is actually circumstantial,
and I kill these three men, what then? How do you think the
American government will react to a British agent popping up
and executing three prominent US citizens? The diplomats will
have a field day, on both sides of the Atlantic. And it probably
wouldn't be a lot better if Maria pulled the trigger, so to
speak.'

Cumming shook his head. 'If it comes to that, we'll do our
best to protect you, protect you both, obviously.'

'That's easy enough for you to say. You'll be safely ashore
here in London while Maria and I are dicing with death on the
high seas.'

'We'll be in regular radio telegram contact with you, and I'll
ensure you're kept abreast of all developments.'

'So it has a Marconi Office, does it, this ship? And what
vessel is it, come to that?'

Cumming smiled slightly. 'I was saving that piece of good

news until the end. You'll be travelling in a First Class suite on board the *Titanic*, on her maiden voyage.'

'So at least we'll be comfortable while we're plotting how best to kill these men.'

Cumming looked somewhat pained at Tremayne's expression. 'Well, good luck to both of you.'

The briefing was clearly complete. Mansfield Cumming stood up, handed over the two boxes containing the Browning pistols, then strode across to his office door and pulled it open.

'Good luck,' he said again as they filed past him. 'And God help us all if you fail.'

Chapter 11

10 April 1912
Southampton

For over a minute, Alex Tremayne just stood still and stared. The overwhelming first impression he had of the *Titanic* was simply its scale, as he and Maria stood on the dockside at Southampton facing a seemingly endless wall of painted steel. He marvelled that anything so big could move under its own power. It dwarfed and dominated the harbour, and all the other ships moored anywhere near it.

When it was launched on 31 May 1911, the RMS *Titanic* was the largest passenger steamship in the world, and in fact the largest man-made moving object ever created. The 'RMS' abbreviation, rather than the more usual 'SS' meaning 'Steam Ship' – stood for 'Royal Mail Ship', meaning that the vessel was contracted to transport international post, a designation issued only to ships operated by the largest and most important lines.

Tremayne knew nothing about that. He just knew the vessel was huge. It was almost 900 feet long, 175 feet in height, from the keel to the top of the four funnels, and displaced over 52,000 tons. With a full complement of over 3,500 passengers and crew, the ship was designed to cross the cold Atlantic waters at a speed of twenty-one knots, driven by three massive bronze propellers. A triumph of British engineering and an indication of the enormous power and wealth of the Empire.

Looking up, Tremayne could see wisps of smoke rising from three of the four enormous funnels and the mighty vessel was clearly already a veritable hive of activity as it prepared to sail.

And it wasn't just the ship itself. The harbour was thronged with people: passengers waiting to board, ship's officers and members of the ship's company, stevedores and porters, officials of the White Star Line, administrative and other staff from the port of Southampton itself, and even a few police officers. And, of course, crowds and crowds of spectators, drawn by the unique spectacle of seeing the biggest ship in the world set sail on her maiden voyage. Tremayne found himself looking at a sea of upturned faces, all clearly marvelling that anything so big and heavy, a man-made and steam-powered leviathan fabricated from steel and iron, could possibly even float on the surface of the ocean, far less move under its own power.

'It's massive,' Maria gasped, craning her neck to stare up at the huge vessel.

'It is that,' Tremayne replied. 'The biggest ship I've ever been on up to now is a cross-Channel steamer, and that's like a rowing boat compared to this.'

They'd caught an early train out of Waterloo down to Southampton. Passengers had been instructed to board the vessel between nine thirty and eleven thirty that morning. Their train had arrived a little before ten, allowing them plenty of time to get down to the dockside.

He looked around at the scene of organized, or possibly disorganized – it was difficult to tell – chaos. Various gangways linked the starboard side of the huge ship to the dockside, and there seemed to be a constant stream of people both embarking and disembarking, or at least streaming up and down the gangways. The massive vessel seemed almost to be alive, as if it had a beating metallic heart buried somewhere below the waterline which, Tremayne supposed, wasn't really that bad an analogy. The engines and the generators were almost certainly already running, pumping warm air through the vessel's ventilation system, and sending electricity through the tens of miles of cables to illuminate the cabins and public rooms. And those same engines would then provide the motive power to drive the mighty vessel through the worst weather the Atlantic Ocean could throw at it, all the way to New York, whilst keeping the passengers warm and safe inside. Not for the first time, Tremayne marvelled at the march of technology, and how man's ingenuity and engineering know-how were beginning to conquer even the most inhospitable environments on the planet.

'You a passenger, sir?' a voice asked from just beside him, intruding upon his thoughts.

Tremayne glanced to his side to see a uniformed porter standing there expectantly.

'Yes, yes we're both passengers,' he replied, and gestured towards their cases, each bearing a bright red and white sticker showing the name 'White Star Line' and the important word 'Wanted'. Luggage was divided into two groups: 'Not wanted on voyage', meaning it would be locked away in one of the ship's cavernous holds and be inaccessible throughout the voyage, and 'Wanted', luggage which would be delivered to the passenger's cabin or stateroom. Tremayne and Maria needed all their luggage immediately available, for several reasons.

Tremayne felt in his jacket pocket for the tickets and boarding cards which Mansfield Cumming's Secret Service Bureau had provided for them.

The porter scrutinized the tickets for a few moments and then nodded sagely before handing them back to Tremayne.

'You're first class passengers,' he said, 'so that means you have to embark through the forward entrance.'

He pointed towards the bow of the ship, and to a gangway which Tremayne had already noticed, chiefly because it seemed to have fewer people using it than the others.

Tremayne looked back to see that the porter was already loading Maria's suitcase onto the trolley which stood beside him and moments later Tremayne's own case followed it. Their two small portmanteaus went on top, and then the procession began making its way along the quayside towards the bow of the ship.

It took a while, simply because of the crowds that milled about the area, people in constant motion, back and forth as they moved towards or away from the vessel, while others stood still in groups, forcing the porter to steer his trolley around them. But eventually they reached the foot of the gangway, where a ship's officer was waiting, obviously stationed there to ensure that everyone who passed the spot where he was standing was entitled to do so.

The porter removed their luggage from the trolley, and then stood waiting expectantly close by them. Tremayne nodded his thanks and handed him a few coins. The man touched his cap in acknowledgement, then seized the handles of his trolley and started walking back towards the milling crowds of people to seek out another customer.

There were a number of people already waiting to board the ship, all elegantly dressed passengers, several of them accompanied by personal servants, chambermaids and valets. Almost all appeared to own small mountains of expensive and matching leather cases. The piles of luggage on display made him wonder what else he and Maria ought to have brought with them, and he realized how little he really knew about the world he was about to enter.

There's no such thing as an average English family, but Tremayne often thought that if there was, his background would have matched it perfectly. His parents lived on the outskirts of a small Kentish village, his father employed as an accountant at a local firm, a job he'd held ever since he left school. His mother kept house, and had never worked outside the home. Tremayne had a younger sister, Veronica, who had undergone secretarial training but realistically never expected to have to use that knowledge: the local doctor's son had been walking out with her for some time, and their future together seemed as assured as it was inevitable.

Tremayne himself was the odd one out. As soon as he was able to, he'd shaken off the shackles of village life and moved to London, supporting himself by working at whatever jobs were on offer, some legal, others less so. He'd always been handy with his fists, and had never been averse to using them to end arguments that other people had started. But he'd soon tired of that style of living, and had left the capital. He had a flair for languages, and had picked up conversational German quickly after he'd worked his passage on a steamer going to Hamburg. He'd been in Königsberg in East Prussia, near the coast of the Baltic, when he'd encountered an eccentric Englishman trying to book himself a hotel room, and from that moment on, his life had changed.

Mansfield Cumming had been working for British Naval

Intelligence since 1898, and had come up with a plan to travel Germany to try to glean information about the country's naval preparedness. That wasn't such a bad idea, but Cumming's decision to portray himself as a successful German businessman was. Tremayne had used his fluent German to smooth over Cumming's hideous mangling of the language, and within two days he'd been recruited as an unpaid British agent: at that time Cumming had virtually no access to funds.

He'd worked for the man ever since, moving with him in 1911 when Cumming had been appointed as the head of the Foreign Section of the newly formed Secret Service Bureau. Tremayne was now in receipt of a salary, but still lived the sort of modest, middle-class life he found most comfortable. High society had never interested or attracted him, most of the examples of that type of person he'd encountered seeming both vacuous and useless, the men especially. And now, at a stroke, he was going to have to pretend to be a member of that level of society himself.

Tremayne and Maria were clearly imposters in this world of first-class elegance, but that didn't bother either of them. They were on the ship to do a job, and that was the end of it. Exercising typically British reserve, their fellow travellers simply nodded at them, but refrained from speaking, which again suited both Tremayne and Maria.

The genteel queue in front of them steadily diminished as the other passengers moved forward towards the gangway. When they reached the officer, Tremayne again took their tickets out of his pocket and handed them over for inspection, together with the boarding cards.

The officer kept the cards but checked the tickets, nodded, and handed them back. 'Welcome to the *Titanic*, Mr and Mrs

Maitland. You can board immediately, and your luggage will be delivered to your stateroom within the hour.'

'Thank you.'

Tremayne stepped back to where their luggage was stacked on the dockside, picked up his own portmanteau and took a couple of steps towards the gangway.

The officer waiting there stopped him with a gesture. 'Our stewards can attend to all your luggage if you'd prefer it, sir,' he said.

But Tremayne shook his head. 'I can manage this, thank you. I have some important papers and documents inside this case. I don't want to let it out of my sight.'

'As you wish, sir.'

In fact, Tremayne did have one sealed envelope in the portmanteau which Mansfield Cumming had had delivered to them immediately before they'd boarded the train to Southampton, along with instructions to open it only when they were on board the ship and in a location where the documents inside it could not be seen by any third party.

But that wasn't the main reason why he insisted on carrying that particular case himself. Inside that portmanteau were the two Browning pistols, two suppressors and a quantity of ammunition, plus a number of other objects which had been supplied by Mansfield Cumming to assist them in the task he had set. If any of the ship's staff had seen two of the items in particular, Tremayne was quite certain that not only would they not have been allowed on board the *Titanic*, but quite probably they would have been handed over to the police.

Once they stepped on board, they found stewards waiting to conduct the embarking passengers to their suites, staterooms or cabins. Tremayne showed one of the stewards the tickets, and the man immediately smiled and nodded.

'Welcome aboard the *Titanic*, Mr and Mrs Maitland,' he said echoing the words of the officer at the foot of the gangway. 'My name is Alfred. Would you like me to carry that for you, sir?' he asked, gesturing towards the portmanteau that Tremayne was still holding.

Tremayne shook his head. 'No,' he replied. 'It's not very heavy. I've only got some papers in it.'

'Then if you'd like to follow me, please.'

Alfred turned and led them through an open doorway over to the left of the lobby they were standing in, and they found themselves in an elegant open area which Tremayne thought looked like a reception room of some sort.

Alfred confirmed this immediately. 'This is the first-class reception room,' he said, pointing in front of them, 'and through those doors over there is the main dining saloon. And to your right—'

But he was immediately interrupted by Maria, who was staring in that direction.

'Wow!' she exclaimed. 'Will you take a look at that staircase? It's gorgeous.'

It was undeniably magnificent. The vast wooden structure was essentially two staircases joined together, the outer sections leading down on either side to a half landing, from which the lower part of the staircase descended in a pair of elegant sweeping curves, separated by an ornate central banister. At the end of the banister, surmounting an intricately carved wooden pillar, stood a bronze carving of a cherub, holding aloft a light in the shape of a flaming torch.

'That really is impressive,' Tremayne remarked, thinking as he did so that the light seemed ridiculously ornate and complex for the simple task it was intended to perform.

'That is the forward first-class staircase,' Alfred explained. 'It serves five decks, all the way from the Boat Deck down to D-Deck, which is where we are now. Then, below here there's a normal staircase that leads down to E-Deck. I should explain that the decks on a ship are labelled from the top down, but usually the decks are named as well.'

'So what's D-Deck called?' Tremayne asked.

'They try to name them after the most important feature on that deck,' Alfred said, 'so on this ship we have the Boat Deck, Promenade Deck and so on. This deck is known as the Saloon Deck, because we have the main dining saloon here.'

He led the way over to the staircase, but paused just to one side of it before he led them up. 'If you look here,' he said, pointing upwards, 'all the way to the top, you can see that there's a huge glass dome covering the top of the staircase, up on the Boat Deck. So it's really light and airy all day.'

Although electric lights were burning on the landings and around the staircase itself, most of the illumination came from the very top of the staircase. Tremayne looked where the steward was pointing, and high above them he could see what looked like a part of a glowing ball, as the glass dome was illuminated by sunlight.

'At night,' Alfred said, 'you get the opposite effect. If you're out walking on the Boat Deck, there's this wonderful glow as the dome's lit from below by the staircase lighting. Now we need to go up to the deck above.'

They followed him as he began climbing the stairs. 'There's another staircase,' he added, 'a smaller and less ornate version, further aft. They're both reserved for use by first-class passengers only. The second- and third-class passengers have their own separate staircases located elsewhere on the ship.'

'So which deck is our cabin on?' Tremayne asked, as Alfred led the way up the staircase.

The clear division and segregation of the different grades of passenger didn't surprise him. In fact, he thought it slightly amusing that so much trouble had been taken to ensure that first-class travellers would never have to be offended by the sight of a third-class man or woman, in case it put them off their luncheon or dinner. In Tremayne's opinion, the reverse case was probably also true, and he knew that he, personally, would probably find life far more comfortable and agreeable in the lower-grade accommodation than where he would actually be spending his time on board.

'Second-class passengers have cabins, sir,' Alfred replied, smiling. 'You're first-class passengers, so you have a stateroom, and it's on the deck we're coming on to now. This is C-Deck, also known as the Shelter Deck. Now, before I take you to your accommodation, we have to visit the Purser's Office to have your tickets inspected – that's the last time, I promise you – so if you could just follow me just over here, please.'

Alfred walked across the landing to an office off to the starboard side, a long counter framed in polished wood, behind which two uniformed men were dealing with a small number of other first-class passengers.

'As soon as one of the officers is free, please show him your tickets,' Alfred said.

It wasn't a long wait and once the formalities were over, Alfred led them across to the port side of the ship and turned aft down the passageway, past more first-class suites and staterooms.

Other passengers were already on board, strolling around this area of the ship, many of the stateroom doors standing wide open to reveal chambermaids and valets unpacking trunks and suitcases. Tremayne spotted a distinguished-looking man walking towards them, a much younger lady, clearly several months pregnant, holding on to his arm. Maria nudged Tremayne as they passed in the corridor.

'That's Colonel John Jacob Astor,' she murmured. 'He's one of the richest men in America. He could probably afford to buy this ship, not just buy a passage to America on it.'

'And he's travelling with his daughter, by the looks of it,' Tremayne replied, glancing behind him at the couple.

Maria giggled. 'That's not his daughter,' she said. 'That's Madeleine Talmage Force, his second wife. He's forty-eight and she's nineteen, and they married last year. It was a big scandal in the States, just him getting divorced, and when he married a girl who's a year younger than his son from his first marriage, you could hear a drum roll of jaws dropping right across America. I think he came over to Europe to wait for the heat to die down.'

'If he's as rich as you say he is, I don't suppose he's too bothered about what people think of him.'

'Probably not. That kind of wealth acts as a really good insulator against the world.'

'These staterooms are some of the biggest on the ship,' Alfred said, indicating the doors on the right-hand side as he continued down the corridor.

Astor wasn't the only American Maria spotted. As they moved through the ship, she pointed out Benjamin Guggenheim, another millionaire who was accompanied, she said, by his mistress, as his wife and family were at their home in New York.

Alfred led them down the port-side passageway, showed

them the barber's shop and stopped for a few moments in the aft staircase lobby. Then he continued further down the passageway and stopped a few doors before the end.

'This is the port side of the ship, the left side if you're looking towards the bow, the front end,' he said. 'For the first day or so, finding your way around might be a bit tricky, just because of the size of this ship. One easy way you can tell which side of the vessel you're on is by looking at the numbers. Everything on the port side – all the doors and openings and so on – are marked by even numbers, but on the starboard side, the right side, the numbers are odd. And the numbers start from the bow and increase as they get closer towards the stern. So if you remember those two points, you'll always know which side of the ship you're on and which way to turn to reach your destination.'

His introductory lecture over, the steward opened the door of one of the staterooms and stepped back to allow them to enter first.

'This is very nice,' Maria murmured, looking around her at the opulent surroundings. Tremayne had to agree with her. The stateroom looked like a luxury suite in a really good hotel, not that he was particularly familiar with the more upmarket establishments. It was difficult to believe they were on a ship at all: the only giveaway was the small window opposite the door of the stateroom. In a hotel, he would have expected French doors leading onto a terrace or balcony. Whatever the outcome of their mission, they were certainly going to be comfortable , and for a brief second or two Tremayne wished that the circumstances were different, that he and Maria were just on board the ship to enjoy the voyage, nothing more. But that, he knew, was not to be.

Mansfield Cumming had clearly not stinted on the cost of their accommodation, though he was certain that this was a case of operational necessity overriding budgetary considerations. To get close to Voss, they had to be able to move at will anywhere on the ship, which they could only do as first-class passengers. As Tremayne had already noted, the *Titanic* operated a rigidly defined class system, and passengers travelling on second- or third-class tickets were forbidden from entering any of the first-class spaces.

The cabin was panelled in wood – Tremayne thought it was probably walnut, but he was far from certain – inlaid with smaller panels containing an attractive red velvet. The floor was carpeted in a light gold colour. Against one wall stood a comfortable-looking double bed, and the other furniture comprised a dining table with two chairs, plus an occasional table and an easy chair with an elongated base, something like a modified chaise longue.

The steward showed them the wardrobes and cupboards, and advised them that their luggage would be delivered to the stateroom shortly.

'This stateroom does not have a private bathroom, I'm afraid,' he said, 'but there are bathrooms and ladies' and gentlemen's toilets on the other side of the corridor. The first-class dining saloon and the reception room are all on D-Deck midships. There's information about the ship on the table over there, including things like restaurant menus and, of course, the first-class passenger list. Now, is there anything else I can help you with?'

Tremayne shook his head, followed the steward to the door and slipped a few coins into his hand.

'How much did you tip him?' Maria asked. 'I mean, what's the usual rate on board a ship like this?'

'I gave him half a crown, but I've absolutely no idea if that's the right amount,' Tremayne replied. 'As I said, the only other vessels I've ever been on as a passenger are the cross-Channel steamers. But I thought it was a good idea to pay him something, because if we need anything during this voyage, we're much more likely to get it if the steward thinks he'll get a good tip if he delivers what we want.'

Maria looked around the stateroom again, and then her eyes settled on the double bed.

Tremayne followed her glance.

'Don't worry, that's not a problem,' he said. 'We're supposed to be married, and that means we have to keep up the pretence. The last thing we want is for the stewards or chambermaids to start wondering why a young married couple aren't sleeping together. But that chaise longue thing looks perfectly comfortable to me, so I'll sleep there and you can take the bed.'

Any further discussion was halted by a discreet tap on the door. Tremayne opened it, and two other stewards stepped into the stateroom carrying their luggage.

'Would you like us to put your clothes away for you, sir?' one of them asked, lowering the cases to the floor.

'No thanks,' Tremayne replied briskly. 'My wife always insists on doing it herself. But thank you anyway.'

Tremayne was very conscious of the weapons and ammunition concealed in his portmanteau. Under no circumstances did they want anyone to discover them.

Once the stewards had left the stateroom, Tremayne walked across to the table and picked up the information sheets which Alfred had mentioned. He looked at the first-class passenger list and quickly scanned through the names. Then he nodded.

'Mansfield Cumming was right,' he said. 'The only section of a passenger list which is accurate is the first leg of a voyage, from the vessel's original departure point. After that, it gets increasingly inaccurate as some passengers disembark and others join the ship. This list was probably prepared today or yesterday. Our aliases, Mr and Mrs Maitland are on it, but although we know that Gunther Voss will be joining the ship at Cherbourg later this afternoon, his name isn't included. I was hoping we might be able to find out his stateroom number from this, but it looks like we'll have to do it the hard way.'

He looked at the front of the passenger list and then chuckled.

'What is it?' Maria asked.

'It looks as if this ship might be more than just a luxurious way of crossing the ocean. According to this note in the passenger list – the White Star Line calls it a "Special Notice" – it looks like it might be a floating gambling den as well. Listen to this: "The attention of the Managers has been called to the fact that certain persons, believed to be Professional Gamblers, are in the habit of travelling to and fro in Atlantic Steamships. In bringing this to the knowledge of Travellers, the Managers, while not wishing in the slightest degree to interfere with the freedom of action of Patrons of the White Star Line, desire to invite their assistance in discouraging Games of Chance, as being likely to afford these individuals special opportunities for taking unfair advantage of others." So if anybody invites us to sit down for a friendly hand or two of cards, it might be as well to decline.'

He looked across at Maria, who was now sitting on the side of the bed.

'Let's get our stuff packed away,' Tremayne suggested, 'then we'll go and have a drink and familiarize ourselves with the layout of this ship. Then we ought to sit down, read Mansfield's latest instructions, and work out how on earth we're going to do this. If we have to, that is. Maybe he'll have found another way of stopping Voss.'

Maria nodded, the reality of their situation hitting home powerfully. 'We can always hope, but if he had, I think the first thing he'd do would be to recall us and save the cost of the passage. I'm really afraid we might have to go through with this,' she finished, almost sadly.

Chapter 12

10 April 1912
RMS *Titanic*/Southampton

After they'd unpacked their cases, Tremayne led the way out of the stateroom, locking the door behind him. His portmanteau with its selection of weapons was in one corner of the stateroom, still locked, but the envelope sent to them by Mansfield Cumming was in his jacket pocket.

They walked along the same corridor they'd used previously, heading back to the forward first-class staircase. As they did so, Tremayne and Maria looked around them with interest. Most of the stateroom doors were closed, but a few were still open and the figures inside – some of them obviously personal servants – were opening suitcases and trunks, and packing clothes and personal belongings away in drawers, cupboards and wardrobes.

'I feel deprived,' Tremayne murmured, as they glanced into one enormous suite where two valets and a chambermaid were bustling around under the direction of a large, well-padded and imperious looking woman. 'Perhaps I should have brought along somebody to help *me* get undressed.'

Maria looked at him with a grin. 'Don't get any ideas, buster. This is a strictly professional arrangement. You take off your clothes, and I'll take off mine, but we certainly won't be doing it at the same time.'

'Heaven forbid.'

The ship was like a floating city, a seemingly vast and confusing maze of corridors and passages and staircases. There were doors everywhere: doors to cabins, crew spaces, restaurants and public rooms.

Their biggest challenge, at least in the short term, was going to be simply finding their way around. One of the very first lessons Mansfield Cumming had impressed upon Tremayne was the importance of always knowing where the back door was, of establishing the location of all possible exits from a particular building. There were of course no exits on a ship, apart from using the gangways or jumping over the side, but both of them were experienced enough to fully appreciate the importance of quickly acquiring an intimate knowledge of their surroundings. Knowing precisely what lay on each deck, and how to get from one place to another, would be absolutely vital for what they planned to do, and could easily make the difference between life and death.

They made their way to the forward staircase, and decided first to go back down to D-Deck, the Saloon Deck, to look at the area which lay forward of the first-class entrance. At the bottom of the grand staircase, they glanced round the reception room, where at that moment there were only a few people, then walked across to the doorway which gave access to the first-class entrance, and stepped through it. Tremayne led the way down a short corridor marked by cabin doors located at regular intervals down the left-hand side, and by shorter, narrow corridors on the right, each with two doors on either side, each corridor serving four cabins.

'I think this is all still first-class accommodation,' he said. 'It looks like a mixture of small inside staterooms and larger suites on the outboard side of the corridor.'

At the end was a passage which led them across to the opposite side of the ship, again with cabins or staterooms on both sides, and back to the first-class entrance. Then they walked through into the reception room, crossed it and took a look into the dining saloon, a huge room able to seat over 500 people at a time. It was, Tremayne had read somewhere, the largest room on any ship afloat. Perhaps the single most arresting feature was the ceiling, covered in intricate mouldings that were reminiscent of a London club, which was presumably the intention, supported by fluted pillars, all painted off-white. Large windows with rounded tops marked the edge of the room, the light streaming through them contributing to the ambience.

The room was under half full, but was alive with the hum of conversation and the chink of knives and forks on crockery. Waiters bustled to and fro, delivering full plates and removing empty ones. Sommeliers strode round the occupied tables, ensuring that the correct wines were being served for each course. Tremayne and Maria weren't eating there, at least, not yet, so they just looked around, then turned away and walked out.

'Right,' Tremayne said, 'let's go all the way up to the Boat Deck, but we'll take a walk around each deck as we climb.'

Almost twenty minutes later, they finally reached the top and stepped out onto the first-class promenade. They walked over to the side rail of the ship and looked down at the dockside. It was still an ant-hill of activity, the crowds of people apparently un-diminished in size, although the departure time was fast approaching and Tremayne knew that quite soon the crew and dockyard teams would have to start unshipping the gangways and preparing to leave.

Forward and aft of where they were standing, lifeboats hung from davits, and above them, the four massive funnels, by far the most dominant feature of the ship, soared towards the sky, two forward of where they were standing, and the other two aft. Tremayne already knew that only three of the huge structures actually functioned as funnels, venting smoke from the engines down below. The fourth funnel, the one closest to the stern of the ship, was actually a dummy, a part of the ventilation system, but had been specified by the White Star Line because it was felt that four funnels would make the ship look more impressive than only three.

'I need a drink,' Tremayne said. 'Let's go down and find somewhere to sit. Maybe there are still a few vacant tables in that reception room,' he added.

They retraced their steps down the staircase as far as D-Deck and the reception room itself, and found that there were in fact plenty of spare seats. They chose one on the seaward side, looking out at the harbour, and Tremayne ordered a couple of drinks – a tall gin and tonic for Maria while he had a small Scotch – from one of the waiters.

When the glasses were on the table in front of them, Tremayne checked that they could neither be heard nor observed, then took the envelope out of his pocket, broke the seal and extracted the sheet of paper that it contained. There was also a black and white photograph of the face of a heavily built man, looking towards the camera. On the back of the picture was the pencilled name 'Gunther Voss'. Tremayne glanced over the typewritten paragraphs quickly, and then read it all carefully. In fact, there wasn't much in the briefing sheet that was new.

The latest news from Washington was ambiguous. There were vague rumours about changes in American foreign policy, but there were often such suggestions, and nobody could find any specific information to suggest why any such action was being contemplated. Every enquiry made by the British diplomats over there at first seemed to produce convincing evidence that some change was imminent, but upon closer examination, no solid facts could be found to back up the story. It was all simply rumours and speculation – just 'smoke and mirrors' as one senior British diplomat had apparently described it.

But the mere fact that there were rumours on the diplomatic circuit, Mansfield Cumming suggested, meant that something was going on and that, together with the information obtained from Klaus Trommler, plus Voss's unusual series of appointments in Berlin, had simply confirmed his certainty that there was a plot and that Voss was the architect of it.

'Anything new?' Maria asked as she sipped her drink and kept checking the room to ensure that nobody was moving close enough to hear what they were saying.

'Not really,' Tremayne replied. 'Apart from this picture of Voss, of course.' He passed the photograph across the table to Maria, who looked at it carefully, trying to commit the man's features to memory. 'Most of this is stuff that we already know.'

'But . . .'

'But what?' Tremayne asked.

'The way you said that, it sounded to me as if a "but" should have been tacked onto the end of that sentence.'

Tremayne smiled at her. 'You're right,' he said. 'The only new bit, really, is the last paragraph. Before, it was a strong possibility, but now Mansfield has made it an order. He's now specifically instructed us to ensure that our friend does not complete his journey.'

Although they were sitting at a secluded table, well away from those occupied by other first-class passengers, Tremayne was still aware that voices carry, and so they both needed to be circumspect in what they said, and what words they used.

'And his friends? The ones we haven't even identified yet, and who might not even be coming on board this ship. What about them?'

'The same instructions apply,' Tremayne said. 'I was hoping, really hoping, that this would all turn out to be some kind of mistake, or that there might be some other way of resolving the situation. But unless something changes, it looks as if we'll have to go through with it.'

Maria nodded. She, too, looked uncomfortable with the reality of the situation in which they now found themselves. Like Tremayne, in her brief career with the Bureau of Investigation she'd been forced to take a human life. In fact, she had been forced to take five lives, but in every case she had been involved in a covert operation and had either been defending herself or protecting a fellow agent. The idea that she would have to be involved in the cold-blooded killing of another person, and at the whim of a man she'd only recently met, made her feel very uneasy, despite the importance of the mission.

'Anything else?' she asked.

'Yes, though the last bit doesn't seem to me to make too much sense. Cumming has specified the wording of a particular telegraph message that we have to send from the ship as soon as we've completed what we have to do: that's after all three of them have been taken care of. He says that we have to send the message no later than zero nine hundred hours – nine o'clock in the morning – on the fifteenth, otherwise he will, and I quote, "have to make an alternative arrangement to resolve the situation".'

'That doesn't sound like Mansfield,' Maria remarked. 'I haven't known him that long, obviously, but usually he spells everything out in words of one syllable. What do you think he means?'

'I don't know,' Tremayne admitted. 'Unless he's trying to organize some kind of a reception committee in New York, and he needs the extra couple of days before the ship reaches port to get that in place. But that's just a guess: I really don't know. But what is obvious is that he's given us a deadline. We have to finish this assignment by that date and that time. And we can't do anything until Voss joins the ship at Cherbourg later today.' He paused and glanced at his watch. 'If the ship's on time, we've got just under one hundred and ten hours to do this, and the clock is ticking.'

Chapter 13

10 April 1912
RMS *Titanic*/Southampton

About half an hour later, as they sat talking together in the reception room, two empty glasses in front of them, the bellow of the ship's siren sounded in a long, deafening blare. Tremayne glanced at his watch: it was just before noon.

'It sounds like we're about to leave,' Maria said. 'Let's go up to the Boat Deck and watch.'

Rather than climb up the grand staircase, which was already crowded with people, they walked behind the ornate structure and entered one of the three lifts which had been installed there.

On the Boat Deck, the rails were already lined with passengers, waving handkerchiefs and scarves at the anonymous hordes of people still surging around on the dockside below. Tremayne spotted a small gap at one end of the rail, and taking Maria gently by the elbow, led her over to it. They peered down the steel side of the ship to the stone jetty below them.

The gangways which had linked the liner to the dockside had already been removed, lifted away by cranes and moved well clear of the side of the ship. Teams of dockyard workers were busy attending to the mooring lines which still held the massive ship in position, and Tremayne guessed that there would be tugs waiting to help manoeuvre the ship away from the harbour wall, probably already with lines attached on the other side of the vessel.

They watched as the last of the lines were released, the heavy lengths of rope splashing into the water as the *Titanic* began to move slowly away from the quayside. Powerful winches on board the ship recovered the ropes, and within a minute or two the last of them had vanished from sight.

Several of the passengers now strolled across to the opposite side of the Boat Deck to watch the activities as the tugs pulled the liner sideways, manoeuvring the ship out of her berth and into open water. Already, they could feel a slight vibration through the deck; the propellers were beginning to turn more quickly, assisting the efforts of the tugs.

It didn't take long for the *Titanic* to start moving forward under her own power, and Tremayne was surprised by how quickly the ship started to pick up speed, as it began to move past the other vessels which were moored nearby. To him, it seemed that the vessel was going a little too fast in the restricted waters of Southampton's harbour, but he presumed that the crew knew their business. Moments later, it looked as if his slight concern was justified.

The *Titanic* was passing alongside and fairly close to two other ships, one moored outboard of the other, so that they were side-by-side. The ship secured directly to the quayside was another White Star Line vessel, the *Oceanic*, and moored alongside her was the ocean liner the SS *New York*. The *Titanic*'s passage past these two vessels was creating a substantial bow wave and, as Tremayne looked behind, he could see a deep wake forming behind the ship.

Then things seemed to happen very quickly. The *Titanic*'s

wake was so large that it lifted the much smaller SS *New York* high up in the water and then, as the wake passed, the vessel crashed down into the trough behind it. Tremayne clearly heard the loud snap as some of the ship's mooring lines parted.

Immediately, the stern of the SS *New York* began to swing out into the seaway, directly towards the side of the *Titanic*. Shouts of alarm sounded as crew members suddenly realized what had happened, and the danger they faced if the sideways motion continued and their vessel hit the *Titanic*.

Tremayne felt a suddenly increased vibration through the deck, and presumed that the captain had ordered the propellers to go astern to try to slow the ship down and reduce the wake. But still the stern of the SS *New York* continued to move quickly out into the seaway. It looked to Tremayne as if a collision was both inevitable and imminent.

'I think it's going to hit us,' he said to Maria. 'Grab hold of something, just in case.' He suited his actions to his words, seizing the top of the rail in front of him as he continued staring down at the drama unfolding below them.

Then he heard the roar of a powerful engine, and turned to see a tug – he spied the name *Vulcan* painted on the bow – moving quickly towards the SS *New York*, obviously intending to manoeuvre the ship back into its correct position. Within seconds, a line snaked down from the stern of the American ship, followed quickly by a hawser which the tug's crew swiftly attached. The rope tightened as the tug started manoeuvring, trying to stop the swing of the ship and to drag it back alongside the *Oceanic*, the water behind the tug turning to white foam as the vessel's propeller turned at maximum revolutions.

Other tugs, possibly those which had been used to assist the

Titanic in moving from her berth, then appeared, engines roaring as they hurriedly moved into position.

The sideways movement of the stern of the SS *New York* had slowed, but it was still moving. Tremayne could clearly see members of the crew running away from that end of the vessel as it neared the side of the *Titanic*, trying to get out of danger.

The *Titanic* was quickly reducing speed, but it still looked as if it was too late, as if the two vessels were going to collide.

And then, almost as quickly as it had started, the incident came to a halt. When the stern of the smaller ship was within three or four feet of the side of the *Titanic* the actions by the tugs finally stopped the sideways movement. Within a few seconds the gap began to open, and the *New York* slowly began to be moved back to her berth, the *Vulcan* and other tugs fussing around her.

'That was really close,' Maria said. 'I do hope that's not an omen for the rest of this voyage.'

They stayed up on the Boat Deck for a few minutes longer, watching as the SS *New York* was again secured alongside the *Oceanic*. The *Titanic* had come to a complete stop, and didn't move for some time.

In the end, it was about half an hour before they again felt the propellers start to turn, and the ship started to move away, heading out of Southampton towards the open sea and the ship's first port of call: Cherbourg.

Once out of the harbour, the ship began to increase speed as it made its way south-east down the Solent. The heading altered slightly to the east once it cleared the mouth of the estuary to pass between Portsmouth and the Isle of Wight, and then as the *Titanic* reached a point east of Bembridge on the island, the helm was clearly altered again and the vessel turned well over to starboard on a direct track for the French port.

They remained on deck for a little while longer, watching as the Isle of Wight and the south coast of England steadily slipped away behind them, beyond the arrow-straight wake that the *Titanic* was carving through the choppy waters of the English Channel.

For most of the time they stood in silence, alone with their thoughts and oblivious to the chatter of other first-class passengers wandering the deck and taking the air. When they could no longer discern the individual towns lying along the south coast, and the coastline itself had started to fade into a faint grey-brown line, Tremayne turned at looked at Maria.

'Are you superstitious?' he asked, with a slight smile.

She shook her head. 'Not especially. Why?'

'What you said about us nearly hitting that other ship being an omen. Sailors are about the most superstitious bunch of people on the planet, and I'll bet they're down in their messes right now, muttering about the *Titanic* being doomed because of what happened.'

'It was a close thing,' Maria replied. 'And if it *had* hit us, that would probably have ended this ship's maiden voyage right then, and that might have got us off the hook. Voss would have found some other ship to take him to America, and there probably wouldn't have been time to get us on board the same vessel.'

'I hadn't thought of that,' Tremayne admitted, 'and you're right. Maybe we were unlucky the collision never happened. I don't think I'm particularly superstitious, but I can't shake off a sense of foreboding about this voyage, and not just about what we have to do.'

'It's probably just a touch of seasickness,' Maria said briskly. 'Another Scotch should sort you out.'

Chapter 14

10 April 1912
London

Mansfield Cumming had spent quite some time preparing the briefing sheet which he had given to Tremayne before he left for the railway station. That had been his highest priority, but once he completed that, he turned his attention to an Admiralty chart of the north Atlantic, and carefully plotted the route he had been told, through a contact at the White Star Line, that the *Titanic* would be taking after its last European port of call at Queenstown in Ireland. As well as the route itself, he also plotted the estimated position of the liner at noon and midnight on each day of the voyage.

The track he'd ended up with was, he realized, far from accurate. The actual course the ship would follow would be determined by a number of different factors, including the weather, and particularly the sea state, which could affect the cruising speed, and the vessel's time of departure from Queenstown. All of these were imponderables, estimates at best, and the *Titanic*'s departure from Southampton, the only fixed time for the entire voyage, had already showed him how quickly the situation could change. After the near-collision the ship had had with the SS *New York*, the *Titanic* had been delayed there for almost thirty minutes. Cumming's contact at the White Star Line had informed him of what had happened just a few minutes earlier.

He had stared at the chart for some time before coming to a decision. He drew a circle in pencil around one specific point on the route across the Atlantic, noted the date and time and the geographical coordinates, the latitude and longitude, of the location on a piece of paper, and then picked up the telephone earpiece and microphone, turned the handle to alert Mrs McTavish that he wanted to make a call, and instructed her to get him a particular number at the Admiralty.

When the senior officer answered, Cumming passed the information to him, waited while the details were read back, then ended the call. He had already put the arrangements in place earlier in the day, and the date, time and position he had calculated were the last pieces of information he had needed to convey.

He had only arrived at the decision to implement this phase of the operation after exhaustive discussions both with senior naval officers at the Admiralty, and with ministers and ministerial aides, the people who were his military and political masters.

It was, all parties admitted freely, a desperate last-ditch gamble, forced upon them by the bizarre circumstances of the so-called 'Voss Plot', and everyone who had knowledge of what was planned fervently hoped that the signal to execute the final phase would never have to be sent. But it was also abundantly clear to all of them that, in the end, this might be the only course of action open to them, the only way that a bloody war might be averted. They all agreed that a tragic accident, of the sort Mansfield Cumming was proposing, was infinitely preferable to the alternative.

Chapter 15

10 April 1912
RMS *Titanic*/Cherbourg

The crossing of the English Channel had been smooth. In fact, at times, it was difficult to believe that they were actually on board a ship at all. Tremayne supposed that it would take a fairly rough sea before travelling on a vessel the size of the *Titanic* would become uncomfortable. He'd spent some time working as a deck hand on merchant ships before being recruited by Mansfield Cumming, and had only very rarely suffered from *mal de mer* even when those vessels were bouncing around quite a lot. He didn't expect to have any problems on the *Titanic*.

Although they talked about how they would ensure that Gunther Voss would end up leaving the ship somewhere en route to New York, the reality was that they could make no definite plans until they knew where their target's stateroom was located and, perhaps even more importantly, whether or not his two associates – Jonas Bauer and Lenz Kortig – would also be undertaking the voyage. At that moment, all they could do was make sure that they knew their way around the ship, and then, when the *Titanic* arrived at Cherbourg, try to spot Voss as he boarded.

A few minutes after six p.m., the ship began to slow down noticeably, and Tremayne and Maria headed back up on deck again, this time to watch their arrival at Cherbourg.

When they stepped out on the Boat Deck, the small French port was already clearly visible in front of the ship. Tremayne had a small pair of binoculars slung around his neck, and for a few minutes he studied the harbour through them as the *Titanic* drew closer.

'This ship will never get in there,' he said, 'the harbour's much too small. We must be going to anchor outside the entrance.'

He was right. Just before six thirty, with a rumble and a vibration which could be felt all over the ship, one of the vessel's anchors was lowered to the seabed, and a few minutes later they realized that the propellers had stopped turning and that the ship was now stationary.

Tremayne and Maria shared the binoculars, studying the harbour and the activity there, both of them keeping their eyes open for any sign of Gunther Voss. It was evident that the arrival of the *Titanic* was quite an occasion. Enormous crowds of sightseers lined not only the harbour itself, but also the streets on both sides. Estimating numbers at that distance was difficult, but Tremayne was certain that the mass of people staring at the ship must have amounted to thousands rather than hundreds.

Then they spotted two vessels with steam up inside the harbour, and Maria guessed that they were the tenders which would be used to ferry passengers out to the ship.

When Tremayne saw one of the ship's officers at the other end of the Boat Deck, he walked quickly across to him and held a short conversation before returning to where Maria had remained at the side rail.

'You're quite right,' he said. 'Those two vessels are specially constructed White Star Line tenders, based here at Cherbourg to service the transatlantic liners. They're called the *Nomadic* – that's the big one, over a thousand tons, according to that officer, and it's reserved for first- and second-class passengers – and the *Traffic*, which will be carrying the mailbags and the third-class passengers. He said we're embarking about three hundred passengers here, in all classes.'

Maria nodded and took the photograph of Gunther Voss out of her handbag to stare at it once again. Then she replaced it and again focused the binoculars on the crowds of people waiting near the two tenders.

'I think we can safely assume that Voss will be travelling first class,' she said, 'so that will give us a smaller group of people to study. We're too far away at the moment to tell for certain, but it looks to me as if there are about twice as many people getting on board the *Nomadic* than there are on the *Traffic*, but hopefully most of them will be second class, not first. Let's make sure that when the *Nomadic* gets a bit closer, we take turns in looking at the passengers, and try to spot him.'

'We'll probably find it easier once he gets on board,' Tremayne suggested.

'I know. What I was rather hoping was that we'd see if he was travelling with anybody else.'

A few minutes later, the *Traffic* moved away from its mooring in the harbour and headed out towards the *Titanic*.

Tremayne leaned over the side of the ship and looked down. 'There are two short gangways already rigged down there, so I presume one of the tenders will go to each of them.'

Maria looked where he was pointing. 'The third-class passengers will probably disembark at the forward gangway, because most of their accommodation is in the bow and stern sections, and those are the noisiest and least desirable parts of any ship. And from here we've got a good view of the other gangway, so we might as well stay where we are.'

They watched as the *Traffic* came alongside the ship and, exactly as Maria had predicted, pulled up alongside the forward gangway. As passengers began to stream off, and crewmen began carrying the mailbags on board, they switched their attention to the *Nomadic*, which was now steaming out of Cherbourg harbour directly towards the *Titanic*.

Maria studied the approaching vessel through the binoculars, then shook her head in frustration.

'There are too many people,' she said. 'Trying to spot Voss in that kind of crowd, and especially from right up here on the top deck of the ship, is pretty much impossible. I think the best thing we can do is go down again. We know he'll have to go to the Purser's Office once he gets on board. There'll probably be quite a crowd of people there, so maybe we can lose ourselves in amongst them, but keep our eyes peeled for him at the same time.'

Tremayne nodded. Frankly he hadn't got any better ideas, so as soon as the *Nomadic* had slowed down to draw alongside the *Titanic*, they turned round, left the Boat Deck and walked down the forward first-class staircase as far as C-Deck.

But by the time they reached that deck, there was already such a large crowd of people waiting outside the Purser's Office that they realized their task was fruitless. Not only was there very little space in the lobby, but there was nowhere they could sit down, and if they just stood there, they ran the risk of being noticed by Voss. That was the last thing they wanted.

'This isn't going to work,' Tremayne murmured to Maria. 'I

think our best bet is to go and sit in the reception room or somewhere, and try and spot him if he comes in. If we don't see him now it doesn't matter. There's still a long way to go, and if we don't find him today, then we will find him tomorrow.'

There were more people in the reception room this time, but they still found a table without any difficulty. They sat there, nursing drinks – Maria had again opted for a gin and tonic, and this time Tremayne had ordered the same – and covertly watching the entrance doors, novels behind which they could hide lying on the table in front of them, but nobody who resembled Gunther Voss entered the room.

At seven thirty, they guessed they'd missed him, and that he'd already been shown to his suite, so they got up from the table, ascended one deck, and walked down the passageway to their own stateroom to dress ready for dinner.

Tremayne had brought a plain black dinner suit with him, together with three shirts and two bow ties. Maria's wardrobe was rather more extensive – and almost certainly more expensive, he noted – and she eventually settled on a full-length dress in some kind of purple material which shimmered in the light. They got dressed, on opposite sides of the stateroom, both being careful to keep their eyes averted from each other, but both obviously very conscious of each other's physical presence in the room.

'How do I look?' Tremayne asked as he put on his jacket.

Maria turned round and glanced across at him. 'You look like most men do when they're wearing that kind of outfit. Like a waiter in an upmarket restaurant somewhere downtown.'

Tremayne smiled at her. 'Well,' he said, 'I suppose that's better than a downmarket restaurant.'

'Not necessarily.'

'No matter what I look like, you look simply beautiful,' he said.

Tremayne let his eyes rest on Maria for perhaps a little longer than necessary, and again he wondered briefly about her private life. She wasn't married, he presumed, but perhaps she had a man in her life back in America. And he hadn't been exaggerating – she was beautiful, the more so in her evening dress, the colour of which seemed almost to give a glow to her complexion – and he guessed she had plenty of admirers. Maybe the reason she hadn't married was much the same as for him: with the kind of work they both did, neither could ever have a normal home life. And when you lived your life on the edge, it was probably unfair to even expect another person to get deeply involved with you.

'Enough of the flattery, Alex. You know it's not going to get you anywhere. If you're ready, let's go.'

Chapter 16

10 April 1912
RMS *Titanic*

'Where to?' Maria asked.

'I'd still like to get a look at Voss today if possible,' Tremayne replied, 'so why don't we go down and sit in the reception room and see if we can spot him as he goes into the dining saloon?'

'That works for me,' Maria said.

They walked down the forward grand staircase and into the reception room. They spotted a vacant table over on the starboard side of the room, and sat down. Outside, the evening light was starting to fade. Just then, they both felt a faint vibration run through the ship, and Tremayne stood up and walked over to the window to peer out. He glanced at his watch.

'It's ten past eight,' he said, 'and she's just started moving. I suppose that's not bad going. The ship was only at anchor for a little over an hour and a half, by my reckoning. So now we've got just one more stop in Ireland, and then we start the crossing in earnest. And no matter what happens this evening,' he added, lowering his voice slightly, 'obviously we don't do anything except identify him until we're well on the way across the Atlantic.'

A waiter walked over to them and took their order for drinks, and then returned a few minutes later carrying two glasses of champagne on a silver tray. After all, Tremayne had rationalized, you only get to enjoy any ship's maiden voyage once, so why not make the most of it, at least until they confronted the reality of their task.

'It's a beautiful ship,' Maria remarked, as he set the drinks in front of them.

'It is, madam. It's a privilege to be on board.'

'My wife and I were wondering if the ship was full,' Tremayne enquired.

'No, sir, it's not. We would normally have a crew of about eight hundred and fifty but, because this is the ship's first voyage, we have almost nine hundred. And altogether, in all classes, the *Titanic* can carry almost two thousand seven hundred passengers, but at the moment we have about thirteen hundred, so it's not even half full.'

Tremayne nodded and pointed towards a closed door at the aft end of the room. 'And I understand that the dining saloon is through there?'

'Yes, sir, but I'm afraid you're too late for dinner tonight. First-class passengers dine in there at seven sharp every evening. But the à la carte restaurant – that's located aft on the Bridge Deck, two decks above this one – is open all evening as usual.'

When the waiter had walked away, Tremayne and Maria lifted their glasses to each other in a silent toast. Then Tremayne leant forward, and Maria did likewise, cradling her drink.

'The fact that the ship's only about half full might help us,' Tremayne commented. 'The fewer passengers there are about when we have to make our move the better. Fewer potential witnesses mean there's less chance of us being seen.'

'But surely Mansfield Cumming will make sure we'd be protected if the plan came to light? We are carrying out his orders, after all.'

Tremayne shook his head. 'I'm sure he'd do his best, but we're in an unusual situation. If we were unfortunate enough to be seen giving Herr Voss a helping hand over the side of the ship, the chances are the captain would order us to be locked away in some secure space. Then, when we reach New York, he'd hand us over to the American police, and I don't think they would feel particularly benevolent towards us if we'd just been seen murdering a prominent businessman who held an American passport. I don't know how much sway Cumming and his Secret Service Bureau would have if we found ourselves in that position, but my guess is not very much.'

'I hadn't thought of that,' Maria admitted. 'We're going to have to be really careful.'

Tremayne took another sip of his champagne. 'And there's another potential problem as well. If Cumming is right and the three men involved in this plot are all here, on board the *Titanic*, the first thing we have to do is identify the other two of them. And that won't be easy, in amongst thirteen hundred other passengers, especially as Cumming didn't manage to get photographs of them. I suppose the only thing in our favour is that they're most likely travelling first class, like Voss, and there are probably only about three hundred or so passengers in this section of the ship.'

'Do you have a plan?' Maria asked.

Tremayne grinned wryly. 'Not really, no,' he said. 'For the moment, all we can do is watch and wait. First, we find out where Voss spends his time, and we make sure that we do the same, either together or individually. With a bit of luck, his fellow conspirators will at some point appear in plain sight and talk to him. Or maybe they are actually travelling as a group. At the moment, there's no way of telling. But if we can't identify the other two men, then we obviously can't follow all of Cumming's instructions. And if he's right, just eliminating Voss might not be enough to stop the plot going ahead.'

'And there's another factor here, isn't there?' Maria asked, looking closely at Tremayne, her grey eyes flashing. 'Mansfield Cumming told you that I had "killed in the line of duty, maybe more than once", I think that was the phrase he used. Some day, I might want to tell you what happened and what the circumstances were, but not now. All I will say is that I knew absolutely what all of those men had done, and because of the situation I found myself in, I could see no good reason why they should be allowed to remain alive. If I found myself in the same position next week, I would do exactly the same again. I have no regrets.'

She paused, but Tremayne didn't respond, just continued looking at her over the rim of his glass.

'I know you have your reservations about this, Alex, because we've already talked about it, and I'm the same. Before I take another person's life I need to be convinced beyond all reasonable doubt that they deserved to die. All we have in this case is what Mansfield Cumming has told us, and that was based upon a single written report which a German traitor claimed to have seen. It's not exactly what I would describe as concrete evidence. Apart from this German, nobody has seen any written details of this plot. I don't know about you, but I still have a nagging doubt at the back of my mind which is telling me that this could all be a big mistake.'

Tremayne nodded slowly. 'I know exactly what you mean.

Obviously Voss isn't going to sit down at a table in the dining saloon and explain to his co-conspirators in a loud voice exactly how well the plot to destroy Britain is going. But what he might have is some written information hidden in his cabin which confirms his involvement. So as soon as we find out which stateroom he's occupying, I say we get inside and have a look through his belongings.'

'Are you any good with locks?' Maria smiled.

'Actually, I'm not bad. One thing about working for Mansfield Cumming is that he makes sure his agents are taught any skill which he thinks they might find useful. I spent a month or so with a London locksmith a couple of years ago. Assuming that the lock on his stateroom door is the same type as ours, I don't think it'll give me too much trouble. And if you can keep watch outside, I should be able to get in and out, and do a pretty thorough search of the room, in about fifteen or twenty minutes.'

Maria nodded, then glanced behind Tremayne towards the grand staircase. 'Well,' she murmured, 'at least we know that Voss won't be having dinner in the dining saloon this evening. He's just walked down the staircase. I'm sure that's him.'

Tremayne forced himself not to turn round. 'Who's he with?' he asked.

'He's by himself. No sign of anybody else hanging around near him, no bodyguards or anyone like that. I guess he feels that in a closed community like a ship he doesn't need close protection.'

'What's he doing now?'

'He's talking to one of the stewards.' She narrowed her eyes. 'The steward is pointing up the staircase, where the other restaurant is located, and now Voss is heading back that way.'

'Good,' Tremayne said. 'We'll give him a few minutes to get seated, and then we'll follow and try to get a table where we can see him. Leave your drink,' he added, putting down his own glass. 'We'll get another one upstairs, and keep it to just a couple this evening.'

'I thought you British could hold your liquor?'

'We can,' Tremayne replied, 'but from now on we need our wits about us, and that means watching how much we drink.'

A few minutes later, they sat down at a table on one side of the à la carte restaurant on the Bridge Deck. As soon as they were settled, Maria leaned over to Tremayne and whispered in his ear.

'Smile,' she said, 'as if I'm telling you a joke or telling you that I love you or something. Voss is right in front of us. He's sitting by himself at a table for four about twenty feet away.'

Tremayne smiled as he been instructed, nodded and then whispered back to Maria.

'I know,' he said, breathing deeply and inhaling the delicious fragrance of her perfume. 'I'd already recognized him.'

'Good.'

Maria and Tremayne studied the menu for a few minutes and then placed their order, both of them keeping one eye on Voss the whole time. When the waiter had left their table, Maria reached out and squeezed Tremayne's hand.

'Is it something I said?' he asked with a smile. 'Or have you decided that you really *do* love me?'

'Definitely not,' she said firmly. 'Our mutual friend has just waved to somebody who's walked into the restaurant. Unless he has a talent for making new friends very quickly, this is someone that he's known for some time.'

She fell silent as one of the waiters led a tall, corpulent but elegantly dressed man past their table, and ushered him over to where Voss was waiting, now standing up with his hand outstretched. The two men exchanged greetings, and then sat down.

Less than five minutes later, another man approached the same table. He was the polar opposite to the first arrival, short and slim with light hair and a fair complexion, and was greeted by both Voss and the other man in a friendly fashion.

For a few moments, Maria and Tremayne stared across the elegant restaurant, surrounded by the ebb and flow of conversation, by voices raised in laughter, by the wonderful aromas of the food being served and the chink and clatter of people enjoying the finest dining experience afloat, silently memorizing the faces of the two new arrivals, and both wondering if they were looking at the other two men they were going to have to kill.

Then they both picked up their soup spoons and began their dinner.

Chapter 17

10 April 1912
HMS *D4*

HMS *D4* was a D-Class submarine, the fourth of her class, which had been built by Vickers at Barrow-in-Furness in Cumbria. The D-Class boats had evolved from the earlier C-Class submarines, but offered a number of significant improvements, including diesel propulsion while surfaced instead of the far more dangerous petrol engines, and wireless transmitting and receiving equipment. They were also larger vessels with much better buoyancy. *D4* herself was the first boat in her class – and in fact the first submarine ever – to be fitted with a quick-firing deck gun forward of the conning tower for surface attacks. As a refinement, the weapon was constructed so that it could be retracted into the deck when not in use.

Also unlike the earlier types, this class of submarine was designed from the start to be capable of operating far beyond coastal waters, with a range on the surface of some 2,500 nautical miles at a speed of ten knots, about two-thirds of the boat's maximum speed.

It was this fact, together with the wireless equipment installed in the vessel, which had allowed Mansfield Cumming to formulate his backup strategy. The fact that it would require the submarine crew to do two things they had never attempted before simply piqued his enthusiasm. Cumming was still a Royal Navy captain at heart, despite his enforced change of career.

It has to be said that Cumming's enthusiasm for the task at hand was not entirely shared by the commanding officer of *D4*, Lieutenant Bernard Hutchinson, but his orders had allowed him no leeway.

Two days earlier, he had received an order to fuel his boat and then put to sea 'with all possible dispatch', to head west out of Dover, his vessel's home port, and then to make the best speed he could down the English Channel and continue further out into the Atlantic. Additional instructions, the order had stated, would be provided by wireless.

Hutchinson had been somewhat perturbed by his sailing orders, not least because, at the boat's maximum speed on the surface of fourteen knots, its fuel consumption would be significantly higher, and the vessel's range markedly less, than if it was travelling at its normal cruising speed. He was also aware that unless he was ordered to turn back, he would fairly quickly reach the point of no return, when he would have insufficient fuel to make it back to any British port.

The first signal he received over the wireless clarified that point, but raised a number of further questions. When he'd decoded his new orders, he summoned the off-watch officer and the handful of NCOs under his command – the D-Class submarines had a total crew complement of only twenty-five, three officers and twenty-two men – to his tiny cabin, little more than a cubicle immediately adjacent to the control room, the nerve centre of the submarine. There he explained not what he had been told, but what he had been told to tell them, which was not anything like the full story.

'We have been chosen by the Admiralty,' he began, 'to undertake a long-distance trial to assess the feasibility of supported deep-water offensive operations. Our first task will be to rendezvous with an oiler approximately seven hundred and fifty miles off the west coast of Ireland to refuel.'

He glanced around at the surprised expressions on their faces. 'I know,' he went on, 'that this will be a new experience for all of us. Normally, this boat is refuelled when it's secured to a nice solid concrete jetty in Dover Harbour. Exactly how we'll fare, being tossed around in the Atlantic next to an oiler that will be doing exactly the same thing, I have no idea. But the technique will obviously be just the same. They will lower a fuel line, we will connect it to the refuelling point, and then they will pump diesel fuel into our tanks.'

Hutchinson looked down at the decoded signal once again. 'Once we have completed that evolution, we will head deeper still into the Atlantic and eventually rendezvous with a second oiler, when we'll repeat the process. After that, unless I receive any instructions to the contrary, we will turn and head eastwards, rendezvous for a second time with the first oiler, and then return to Dover.'

He folded the order and slipped it into the inside pocket of his uniform jacket. 'Reading between the lines, gentlemen, I think their Lordships believe that a conflict is coming with either the French or the Kaiser, and if we do go to war, our submarine force will play a vital role in striking at enemy shipping. What we're doing looks to me like a trial run for a long-distance interception. So we'd better make sure that we do it right. Dismissed.'

Chapter 18

11 April 1912
London

Mansfield Cumming frequently slept in his office, to the very vocal despair of Mrs McTavish, on an old folding bed that creaked and groaned every time he moved. She was forever trying to persuade him to retire to his apartment – it was, after all, in the same part of the building – so that he could get a decent night's sleep.

But throughout his naval career, Cumming had always preferred to be immediately available during operations, just in case, and at that stage the Secret Service Bureau was essentially a one-man band, or perhaps one and a half if Mrs McTavish was included. There were no other officers or staff he could call on to man the section, and he knew that urgent decisions might need to be taken at any moment. So he'd collected what he considered to be the essentials – two bottles of single malt – picked up a couple of changes of clothes and his washing kit, and basically moved in.

This operation, which had started out as a simple exercise to investigate some disturbing rumours on both sides of the Atlantic had now split into three separate but related strands.

Most importantly, he had managed to get Alex Tremayne and Maria Weston on board the *Titanic*, the ship Voss had chosen to make the transatlantic voyage back to New York. What he wasn't sure about was whether or not either of these two agents – one of whom was employed by an entirely different agency – would feel morally obliged to carry out his orders. When he'd briefed the two of them, he'd been very aware that he'd made a far from compelling case, and the taking of a human life – in this case possibly three lives – was not something anyone, not even Tremayne and Maria, would undertake lightly.

That was one worry, and one of the main reasons for implementing his backup plan, which involved the submarine HMS *D4*. He would have preferred to use a warship, but that was not an option, for at least two reasons.

His concerns about the submarine were primarily logistical: when the boat reached the first rendezvous position with the oiler, would the crew be able to successfully refuel it? Cumming was keenly aware, both from his previous career and from discussions he'd had with serving senior officers, that such an evolution had never been attempted before, and for the submarine's mission to succeed, it had to be refuelled not once but at least twice, and possibly three times.

And it wasn't just the refuelling, though if that didn't work he had no possible alternative strategy to achieve what he needed to do. Even if all of the refuelling attempts at sea were successfully completed, the submarine still had to cover a tremendous distance in a short time if it was to be in a position to carry out the interception. The speed the boat could achieve would depend entirely on the weather and the sea state in the north Atlantic.

A submarine was entirely different to a surface ship; it was intended to operate beneath the waves as well as on the surface of the ocean. The hull of a warship was designed to cut through the waves, to give the vessel good sea-keeping qualities in all conditions, and that was the principal consideration. But a submarine's hull had to be a compromise. It was recognized that, because of a submarine's greatly reduced endurance when submerged, most boats had hulls which mimicked those of surface vessels to keep them stable on the surface, but which still had to be suitable for sub-surface operations. The result was that, though perfectly capable of covering long distances on the surface, no submarine could match a surface ship in rough weather.

If a storm broke out, the captain would almost certainly have to reduce speed. If it met a heavy swell, that could be almost as bad, because the submarine might have to turn to meet the waves bow on, as well as reducing speed, which would add to the distance it had to cover, and all of that would cause more delays.

And most important of all, the interception itself would be a one-shot attempt. If the boat didn't get to the rendezvous position on time, there would be no second chance.

This was one of the reasons why Mansfield Cumming had insisted on manning his office himself. Through his contacts at the Admiralty and elsewhere, he was receiving regular position reports for both the *Titanic* and the submarine. Every time a new report arrived, he would update his chart so that he could refine his estimates for the liner's progress across the Atlantic, and the corresponding track for HMS *D4*.

That morning, just before eleven, Mrs McTavish had placed a slip of paper on the desk in front of him. The message written on it was brief and to the point. It simply said: 'Queenstown. 1130. 90-120 mins', which told him everything he needed to know. The *Titanic* was expected to arrive at Queenstown, its last port of call on the east side of the Atlantic, at half past eleven, and should take between about ninety minutes and two hours to complete the embarkation of the passengers and mail there.

He walked across the office to the chart and pencilled in the new figure. The good news, from his point of view, was that the various delays the ship had experienced meant that it was already slightly behind schedule and that, in turn, should give HMS *D4* a few more precious hours to make it to the rendezvous.

For a minute or so, Mansfield Cumming stared down at the chart, mentally recalculating times and distances. Then he nodded and walked back to his desk. The moment that the *Titanic* raised her anchor at Queenstown, the clock would start ticking. He would be able to calculate the speed – and therefore his best estimate of the ship's arrival time at the spot he had selected for the rendezvous – much better once he knew the exact time of departure, and her midnight position.

He'd barely sat down again at his desk before Mrs McTavish knocked on the door and then bustled in carrying a typewritten sheet of paper.

'This is just in from Berlin, sir,' she said, then turned and left the office.

Mansfield Cumming didn't even see her go. He was already eagerly scanning the closely typed paragraphs. When he'd finished, he sat back with a satisfied look on his face. It wasn't good news. In fact it was very bad news, but it was, he hoped, just one more nail in Voss's coffin.

Chapter 19

11 April 1912
RMS *Titanic*

Just before eleven thirty the next morning, a dull rumble echoed through the ship, a tremor that could be felt underfoot as the passengers strolled along the decks. The ship had now come to anchor some distance offshore, and was awaiting the arrival of the tenders from Queenstown which would be transferring the last of the transatlantic passengers to the *Titanic*, and both delivering and collecting mail sacks.

Maria and Tremayne spent a few minutes considering the view, and then resumed their perambulations. They had spent their time since eating breakfast strolling, apparently casually, around all the first-class public spaces. This allowed them to keep their eyes open, and to find out where Voss, and the two unidentified men he had eaten dinner with the previous evening, were spending the morning. It was essential that they worked out the pattern of their targets' movements before they needed to take action.

In fact, locating Voss turned out to be quite easy. On the Promenade Deck, just behind the aft first-class staircase, was a large and elegant smoking room, accessed by doors on both sides of the ship. The only problem for Maria was that it was a male-only preserve.

'I don't smoke anyway,' Maria said, as Tremayne pushed open the port-side door and looked inside. 'It's a filthy habit.'

'Neither do I,' he replied, 'but I don't think it's compulsory. It's probably best if you go forward and wait for me in the first-class lounge.' He gestured towards the next section of the ship's superstructure. 'I'll have a quick look in here. If Voss and his cronies are inside, I'll stay for a few minutes. If not, then I'll come straight out and join you.'

Maria nodded in agreement, turned and walked away as Tremayne stepped into the room.

The smoking room was, like all of the *Titanic*'s first-class public rooms, elegance personified. Plaster mouldings decorated the ceiling, from which chandeliers descended, giving the open space a bright and airy feel. Polished beams, resting on carved wooden columns, appeared to support the roof. The walls were panelled with carved and polished mahogany in Georgian style, and inlaid with mother of pearl. The centre-piece of the room was an impressive fireplace, above which was a large painting called 'Plymouth Harbour 1910' by Norman Wilkinson. The furniture – mainly occasional tables surrounded by comfortable leather armchairs – provided convenient seating for a group of friends or acquaintances to gather to smoke, drink and talk. And, of course, there was an ample supply of alcohol.

Almost as soon as he walked inside the room, Tremayne spotted Voss sitting at a table on the opposite side. The two other men, the ones he and Maria had seen in the restaurant the previous evening, were sitting with him. All three were smoking cigars and with heavy crystal glasses in front of them which Tremayne guessed contained port. They were deep in conversation.

He ambled slowly across the room to stand in front of the fireplace for a minute or two, looking up at the painting which hung above it. It was a bright and cheerful work, showing the harbour entrance under a blue sky dotted with white clouds. A Royal Navy battleship – a dreadnought – was steaming out of the harbour through the calm water, smoke pouring from its four funnels, while behind it a flotilla of yachts, their sails bright orange against the white stone of the lighthouse, appeared to be engaged in a race. And behind them, the shape of another dreadnought could be seen in the harbour, steam up and preparing to sail.

It was an evocative scene, contrasting the harmless enjoyment of people messing about in boats with the understated but still impressive power of the Royal Navy's capital ships. In the circumstances, and knowing what he did, Tremayne thought the image somewhat ironic, especially as the people he believed intended to destroy Britain's maritime supremacy were sitting in the same room.

Below the painting, in the fireplace itself, coals burned brightly, the flames dancing and flickering, and he could feel the heat it generated.

Tremayne glanced around him, marvelling at what he saw. He was in the middle of the ocean, or at least at anchor a couple of miles off the southern coast of Ireland, but he could easily think he was in some elegant country house a hundred miles from the sea. A ship like the *Titanic* really was the only way to travel, he decided.

He turned away from the fireplace and walked across the

smoking room, passing close by the table where the three men were sitting.

As he got near, Tremayne offered them a cheerful 'Good morning', but received only nods in return. He continued strolling past them and chose another table some distance away, from which he could see the three men, but not hear what they were saying. Then he sat down and ordered a drink – a small Scotch with lots of water – from one of the waiters.

When it arrived, he sipped it slowly while he surreptitiously watched Voss and his two companions. Now that Tremayne was some distance away and unable to hear what they were saying, they'd started their conversation again. Obviously it could just be a normal business meeting, but somehow he doubted it. To him, they had the look of three men who were anticipating good news very soon. There was an air of smug expectation about them.

A smartly dressed pageboy walked into the smoking room, an envelope in his hand, and started making his way around the occupied tables, stopping at three of them and asking questions of the people sitting there. Tremayne was at the far end of the room and the last person that he tried.

'Sir, I apologise for disturbing you, but are you Mr Alex Maitland?' he asked.

Tremayne nodded his head. 'Yes,' he replied.

'Thank you, sir. I've been asked to give you this,' the pageboy said, handing over the envelope. 'I've been told it's an urgent message from your London office. If you need to send a reply, you can obtain a form from the Purser's Office and send them a Marconigram.'

'Thanks.'

As soon as the pageboy had walked away, Tremayne opened

the envelope and pulled out a single sheet of folded paper. He glanced at it, then replaced it in the envelope, slipped it into his pocket and finished his drink. Then he stood up and walked out of the smoking room.

Chapter 20

11 April 1912
RMS *Titanic*

On the other side of the smoking room, Gunther Voss glanced round him incuriously, his gaze resting for a few moments on each of the people in the room. The good-looking young man – he had obviously been English – who had spoken to him a few minutes earlier had just stood up and left.

He had looked like precisely the kind of person that Voss despised most: certainly rich – he had to be if he was travelling first class – probably upper-class, and most likely he had never held down a proper job in his entire life. Just a wastrel, a drain on the system, that was all.

He switched his gaze, and his attention, back to what Jonas Bauer was saying.

The banker was a heavy, fleshy man with a large stomach on which he was prone to lace his pudgy and beringed fingers when sitting down. He had narrow shoulders and a head that seemed a little too small for his body, giving him almost the appearance of coming to a point, rather like a pyramid. Oiled black hair, dark-brown eyes and a thick moustache completed the picture. He was a man who enjoyed the sound of his own voice, as Voss had discovered some considerable time ago.

'The timing is not critical,' Bauer was saying now, continuing to dominate the conversation. 'In fact, I've already asked some of my associates in New York to begin circulating stories about the British economy. Falling industrial output, high unemployment, inflation beginning to rise, all that kind of thing. Nothing concrete, you understand, nothing that can be attributed to any particular source, and of course nothing that can be proven – or disproven. I expect that within two to three weeks there will be a climate of uncertainty in the financial community in New York, and then a fall in the value of sterling will be widely anticipated, if indeed it has not already begun.'

'And then you'll start dumping the pound?' Voss asked.

'Precisely. Between us, Lenz and I control something like forty per cent of the banking system in New York. What we do, the rest of the financial institutions do as well, usually within a matter of days, sometimes within hours. As soon as we're back, we'll see what the market is doing, and we might start straightaway, if we think the sentiment is right. Otherwise, we'll start spreading the word ourselves. But whatever happens, I believe we can guarantee a major run on the pound will start within no more than two weeks. And you are sure that the other matter has been taken care of?'

Voss nodded. 'Yes,' he said. 'I checked the cases myself to ensure that they were correctly labelled and I watched them being loaded into the forward hold of this ship. And the other items are locked away in one of my trunks which is also stored in the hold.'

'I would have expected you to keep them in your stateroom,' Bauer said. 'Surely they'd be safer there?'

'Probably not. The holds are out of bounds to everyone while the ship's at sea, but your stateroom is at the mercy of any sneak thief who can undo the lock on the door. If we lost those two pieces of metal, the whole scheme could fall apart. That's why I put them in my trunk.'

'That makes sense,' Lenz Kortig said. 'And then we can start the second phase of the operation as soon as the cases have been delivered to the warehouse in New York.'

He, too, was a banker, but that was where all resemblance between him and Jonas Bauer ended. Where Bauer was fat, Kortig was thin, his hair and complexion fair, as opposed to his companion's dark, almost swarthy, appearance. He didn't talk very much, preferring to listen, to absorb what other people were saying. Kortig firmly believed that his ability to listen was one of the main reasons for his success in the world of finance.

All too often in conversation, people would say things which they shouldn't have divulged, information which could give an astute listener a slight but definite advantage in any future negotiations. On two occasions, information which he had gleaned in this way and then investigated in depth had allowed him to do rather more than just seize a negotiating advantage: it had allowed him to obtain substantial payments from two wealthy citizens of New York in return for non-disclosure. They had called it blackmail. Kortig had said it was just business.

And it was another conversation which the banker had over-heard that had provided both the impetus and the key which had allowed the present scheme to go ahead. A chance remark, which at first Kortig had thought he'd misheard or misunder-stood, had led him to a certain individual, a middle-aged man, living in an apartment building in Washington D.C. And that, in turn, had produced an envelope containing half a dozen documents which had first amazed, and then electrified, the banker. He hadn't hesitated, just handed over the huge sum of money that the man had demanded. Then he'd picked up the envelope and walked out of the apartment.

Kortig had arranged for the documents to be copied, as a safeguard. Two days later, he'd met with Voss and Bauer. And a week after that, they'd known exactly how the plan was going to work.

And now, depending on how long it took the *Titanic* to reach New York, they were no more than a couple of weeks away from implementing a political scheme which would change the western world for ever.

Chapter 21

11 April 1912
RMS *Titanic*

Tremayne found Maria sitting by herself at a corner table in the lounge.

'I've just been given this by a pageboy,' he said, taking out the envelope and opening it again. 'He told me that it's a message from my London office.'

'And I suppose you don't need to tell me where your "London office" is located?' Maria remarked. 'I presume that's some more information or instructions from Mansfield Cumming?'

'Probably,' Tremayne said, and showed her the sheet of paper, which was covered in what looked like groups of five entirely random letters. 'I'll let you know as soon as I've decoded it.'

He took a small notebook and pencil out of his pocket, turned to a fresh page in the book and wrote the word 'OPER-ATIONAL' across the top of the page, spacing the letters well apart.

'Mansfield always likes his keywords to have a proper military ring to them,' he remarked. 'What he's using here is a basic single transposition cipher, a very simple and effective encoding system. He made me memorize this keyword – and a few others – before we left London.'

'How does it work?' Maria asked, curious. 'I've never been involved with codes or anything like that.'

'It's one of the simplest possible ways of encoding a message, and it's virtually impossible to crack it without the keyword, because frequency analysis – that's just a very simple way of guessing which letter in the alphabet is represented by which of the coded letters, based on how often they appear in a message – and most other tools simply don't work on it.'

'I don't know what you mean by "frequency analysis". How does that work?' Maria asked.

'It's quite straightforward. If you analyse a piece of text in any language, you'll find that some letters will appear much more frequently than others. In English, for example, the commonest letter of the alphabet is "E", followed in sequence by "T", "A", "O", "I", "N" and so on. So if you think a coded message is written in English, and the letter "Z" appears more often than any other letter, it would be a reasonable guess that the person who encoded it substituted "Z" for "E". Does that follow?'

Maria nodded. 'So presumably using this single transposition method avoids that?'

'Exactly. And if you're paranoid about security, you can go through the operation twice, using two completely different keywords. That's called a double transposition cipher, and is really secure.

'With the keyword written out, you then make what's called the number conversion. That means you begin at the left-hand side of the word and put the number one below the first letter in the alphabet that appears in the word. Now, in this case and using this keyword, that's the first letter "A". Then you put a number two below the next earliest letter, which is the second letter "A", a number three below the third letter – that's the "E" – and then continue from left to right, repeating the process until there's a number beneath each of the letters.'

Tremayne put a '1' below the first 'A' in the word, a '2' below the second 'A', a '3' under the letter 'E', and then continued working repeatedly from left to right until he had placed a number below each of the letters in the keyword.

O	P	E	R	A	T	I	O	N	A	L
7	9	3	10	1	11	4	8	6	2	5

Then he counted the number of groups of letters on the type-written sheet, which came to thirty-three.

'It's important to do that,' he explained, 'because that tells me how many groups or letters to write below each number. The keyword is eleven letters long, and there are thirty-three groups of five letters each, so that means I have to put three groups vertically below each number, obviously starting with number "1". Then I write the next three groups vertically below the number "2", the next three under the number "3" and so on until I've copied all of the groups onto the grid.'

Tremayne glanced round, to ensure that nobody was close enough to overhear them, or to see what he was doing.

'Does that make sense?' he asked quietly.

Maria nodded. 'Yes, I think so,' she replied. 'It'll be clearer when you've done it, I expect. And presumably once you've written out all the groups you'll be able to read the original message?'

'Exactly. You just read it from left to right and top to bottom. Right, the first three groups are "RCSGU", "MMHDE" and

"SHVNI".' Tremayne wrote those below the '1', then copied the second three groups of 'MRWSN', 'ENDET' and 'HONEG' under the '2', then swiftly added all the rest of the groups of letters to the grid. Then the two of them studied the result:

O	P	E	R	A	T	I	O	N	A	L
7	9	3	10	1	11	4	8	6	2	5

R	E	P	O	R	T	F	R	O	M	H
O	T	E	L	C	O	N	F	I	R	M
S	V	O	S	S	A	N	D	T	W	O
B	O	D	Y	G	U	A	R	D	S	L
E	F	T	B	U	I	L	D	I	N	G
A	T	S	A	M	E	T	I	M	E	A
S	S	S	B	M	A	N	V	A	N	I
S	H	E	D	H	I	S	B	O	D	Y
F	O	U	N	D	I	N	T	I	E	R
G	A	R	T	E	N	Y	E	S	T	E
R	D	A	Y	S	H	O	T	T	H	R
O	U	G	H	H	E	A	D	N	O	D
O	U	B	T	V	O	S	S	A	N	D
M	E	N	I	N	V	O	L	V	E	D
M	I	S	S	I	O	N	I	S	G	O

Tremayne spoke, keeping his voice down. 'Mansfield must have had a report sent to him from Berlin. The plain text reads: "Report from hotel confirms Voss and two bodyguards left building at the same time as SSB man vanished. His body found in Tiergarten yesterday shot through head. No doubt Voss and men involved. Mission is go". The SSB man was obviously Paul Harrington, that officer who'd been ordered to follow Voss in Berlin.'

He folded the paper carefully and put it in his pocket, then closed his notebook with a snap.

'The news about the surveillance officer isn't much of a surprise,' Maria remarked. 'If he'd just been ill or wounded, he would have made contact somehow. I think we all knew that when he didn't check in he was most probably already dead. Does that, that report from the hotel, I mean, convince you that Voss was responsible?'

Tremayne shook his head. 'In the strictly legal sense, no,' he replied. 'Three men walking out of a building at about the same time as another man disappears from the same building is hardly conclusive evidence. At best you could argue that there was a possible link, but that's a long way from proof that they had anything to do with the killing. But in my gut, yes, I think Voss did it, or at the very least ordered one of his bodyguards to pull the trigger.'

The vehemence with which Tremayne spoke the last sentence surprised Maria, and when she looked at his face, his blue eyes were hard and cold.

'Obviously Mansfield Cumming feels the same way,' she said. 'And the last sentence is unambiguous. He's telling us to go ahead and complete the mission.'

Tremayne nodded. 'Yes. And we can certainly take out Voss. Find him on the upper deck one night, or drag him out if we have to, and then push him over the side. But what about the two men with him? They were in the smoking room sitting and talking together. But we can't just assume that they're involved in this plot and kill them as well. They might be entirely innocent, just a couple of businessmen he met on board.'

He looked at Maria, then glanced around the lounge. 'We have to be sure before we do something like this. What do you think?'

'I don't think those other two are just a couple of casual acquaintances. They seem too relaxed together to have only just met. But otherwise, I agree with you. We can't just take two human lives, even on the word of somebody like Mansfield Cumming, just because he *believes* the people might be involved in a plot. We have to be certain, completely certain, of their guilt and complicity, and right now I don't see how we're going to achieve that.'

'I think we're back to Plan B,' Tremayne said, his voice on an even keel again. 'We have to identify Voss's stateroom, and then I have to get inside.'

Chapter 22

11 April 1912
HMS *D4*

There are few places quite as lonely as the open ocean. Only people who have been to sea, and who have crossed the vast distances between the continents, can truly appreciate the fact that planet Earth is essentially a world of water, the deep-blue oceans scarred here and there by patches of land that rise above its surface. And the old expression 'ships that pass in the night' becomes particularly apposite when it is describing the reality – two tiny self-contained communities braving the waves in their fragile steel shells – rather than simply a metaphor.

Lieutenant Bernard Hutchinson had spent more months at sea than he could comfortably count, but most of the time he had either been within sight of land, or at the very least he had known that there were harbours within a day or two's sail from his location. Ever since the west coast of Ireland had receded from view behind them, that comforting thought had vanished. He wasn't venturing into uncharted territory – his boat had charts covering his entire route, of course, and his navigation instruments told him exactly where he was – but he was certainly breaking new ground in taking a submarine so far out into the ocean.

He was also uncomfortably aware that they had now travelled beyond the point where turning back was an option. Travelling on the surface at the boat's best speed had consumed prodigious quantities of diesel fuel and, quite literally, if the oiler which had been tasked to rendezvous with them failed to appear, he had no hope of returning safely to any port. When the diesel fuel ran out, he could continue for perhaps fifty miles using battery power alone, but once that was exhausted as well, the boat would be dead in the water, and at the mercy of the waves.

Which was why Hutchinson had climbed up to the top of the conning tower at first light that morning, and had stayed there almost ever since, scanning the horizon for any sign of the vessel they were supposed to meet.

He'd reduced speed marginally, just by a knot or two, to conserve a little of the remaining fuel, and had altered course slightly to port to cope with a gentle swell that was running towards him from the south-west, and which had caused the boat to start corkscrewing. But neither the speed reduction nor the heading change had any significant effect on his route. Hutchinson knew exactly where his boat was, and precisely where the oiler was supposed to be.

But as far as he could see, it wasn't.

The horizon seemed to be completely empty. No ships of any sort were visible in any direction, as indeed none had been the previous day either. They were completely alone in the vastness of the north Atlantic.

He swung his binoculars from the bow of the submarine around to the starboard beam, and then back again all the way to the port beam, covering an arc of one hundred and eighty degrees. Still nothing.

He rubbed his tired eyes with his hand, blinked a few times and then repeated the scan, with the same result. Or was it? A faint smudge, the slightest possible discolouration, above the horizon, fine on the starboard bow. There were a few clouds in the sky, quite low down, and for an instant he wondered if that's what he was looking at: just a slightly darker cloud formation, maybe the harbinger of a storm.

Hutchinson altered the focus of his binoculars as he strained to make out exactly what he was seeing. It didn't look like a cloud. It looked more like a faint almost vertical line, and for a few seconds he hardly dared to take a breath, his concentration was so absolute.

And then he did breathe again, because now there was no doubt. He knew exactly what he was looking at. It was a plume of dark smoke being emitted from the funnel of a steamship. And he knew that because now he could see the top of the funnel as well as it appeared over the horizon. Whatever the vessel was, it seemed to be heading directly towards his position.

Hutchinson bent to the voice pipe and ordered a slight change of heading, just enough to put the approaching ship directly in front of his bow, and continued to watch as the two vessels closed with each other.

Within twenty minutes, he was able to identify the ship, and knew that his silent prayers had been answered. The shape of the oiler was quite unmistakable, and as soon as it closed to a distance of a mile or so he confirmed the vessel's identity using Morse code, the messages exchanged by signalling lamps.

Now they had to undertake the difficult task of manoeuvring alongside the much larger vessel. Again the signalling lamps proved invaluable, as the crew of the oiler explained precisely what their vessel was going to do, and how the submarine should react. The oiler commenced a gentle turn to take her bow around to the south-west, so that the ship was facing the oncoming swell. Once the vessel was established in that position, her screw turning slowly to give her steerage way, Hutchinson ordered the submarine to manoeuvre slowly around to the starboard side of her hull, where fenders had already been lowered to the waterline to prevent any collisions.

For a few seconds the two dissimilar vessels matched speed, side by side, then orders were shouted on the oiler, and two crew members threw lines down from their deck onto the much lower fore and aft decks of the submarine.

These ropes, of course, were only heaving lines, far too weak to secure the two vessels together, but they were attached to mooring lines, fat brown ropes of hemp with enormous tensile strength.

'Get those lines secure, men, as quickly as you can,' Hutchinson yelled from the conning tower, watching as members of his crew pulled on the heaving lines and dragged the heavier ropes down to the deck. The aft mooring rope was attached quickly, looped round the steel bollard on the rear deck of the submarine, but for some reason the forward rope seemed to be giving trouble. Two crewmen were struggling with it, trying to get it properly fastened. At last they seemed satisfied, and both men stepped back, moving out of the danger zone as the capstans on the oiler began taking up the slack in the mooring ropes.

And one of the men stepped back just a little too far. He lost his footing, and in an instant tumbled backwards over the safety line, slid helplessly down the black curving hull of the submarine and splashed into the cold grey waters of the Atlantic.

Chapter 23

11 April 1912
RMS *Titanic*

'That might be a lot easier to say than to do,' Maria remarked, as they left the lounge and walked out of one of the side doors which gave access to the first-class promenade. 'At the moment, we don't even know on which deck Voss's stateroom is located, far less its number. And in view of the fact that he's probably still travelling with the four bodyguards Mansfield said he had with him in Berlin, if he is stupid enough to have left any incriminating evidence out on his desk in his stateroom, he might well have ordered one of his men to either guard the door on the outside, or even wait in the room.'

'I know,' Tremayne replied quietly. 'I didn't say it was going to be easy.'

They walked across to the rail and stared out towards the coast of Ireland, the emerald green of the fertile pastures clearly visible in the land which lay to the east and west of the ship. The *Titanic* had too deep a draft to safely enter Cork Harbour, one of the largest natural harbours in the world, and the vessel had come to anchor at Roches Point, the outer anchorage of Queenstown Harbour.

From the rail, they could see Queenstown quite clearly, the buildings dominated by the lofty tower and spire, grey stones and lighter-grey slate roof of the Cathedral of Saint Colman. Crowds of people were standing in the harbour, staring out at the waiting transatlantic liner, and Tremayne thought he could now see one of the tenders heading towards them.

Within a few minutes, two small paddle-wheel-driven White Star Line tenders became clearly visible, steaming out of the harbour and heading for the *Titanic*'s deep-water anchorage. Unlike the tenders which had been used at Cherbourg, these were comparatively small craft and, as they approached the ship, Tremayne could see that both their enclosed cabins and the open decks were crowded with people.

They found a vantage point where they could look down at the embarkation, and Maria guessed that probably over a hundred new passengers were joining the ship. And it wasn't just the tenders which were buzzing around the liner. Quite a number of small craft had appeared beside the *Titanic* shortly after it dropped anchor, carrying shopkeepers and other vendors from the town who were trying to sell various local specialities, such as lace and other handicrafts, to the wealthy passengers on board.

Tremayne and Maria remained by the side rail of the ship until the embarkation process was complete. A shrill exchange of whistles between the tenders and the ship acted as a confirmation that all mailbags and the passengers had been transferred, and the tenders eased away from the *Titanic* to return to Queenstown Harbour.

Tremayne looked at his watch as the paddle wheels of the tenders turned the blue-grey water into white foam, and a distant rumble and vibration showed that the *Titanic* was weighing anchor and preparing to leave.

He glanced at his watch again. 'Look, it's just gone half past one, so why don't we sit down and have lunch, and work out what our next step should be.'

Rather than go down to the dining saloon, they decided to stay on the Promenade Deck. They walked past the smoking room, where Tremayne could still see the three seated figures inside, and then entered the Verandah Café, right next door.

Intended to serve afternoon tea and light lunches, rather than the gargantuan feasts that were standard fare in the dining saloon, this restaurant and the adjoining Palm Court had been designed to look like gazebos. They had black and white chequerboard floors, elegant wickerwork furniture, and walls featuring trelliswork, the whole decorated with a profusion of silk flowers and plants. Sliding doors gave access directly onto the Promenade Deck, and opened the room to gentle sea breezes when the weather permitted, while the huge windows provided uninterrupted views of the ocean.

'This whole situation just seems unreal,' Maria said, when they'd placed their orders. 'It's one thing to sit in Mansfield Cumming's office at Whitehall Court and listen to him outline some dastardly plot against the British Empire, but it's entirely different out here on the high seas, living in luxury and surrounded by some of the wealthiest people in the world. I told you John Jacob Astor the Fourth is one of the first-class passengers.'

'I know,' Tremayne replied. 'I meant to ask you how you knew him?'

'I just recognized him,' she said simply. 'He's one of the richest men in America, in the world. He was talking to Isador Straus. He's a partner in the Macy's department store in New York, and probably another millionaire. There seem to be millionaires everywhere you turn, and then there's the two of us, living amongst these people under false pretences: I certainly couldn't afford to buy a first-class ticket on this ship. I come from Philadelphia, and my father's just a clerk in a local factory. I was the first member of my family ever to have a passport, or to leave the States. A first-class suite on this ship probably costs close to what I earn in a year. And here we are, trying to decide how to kill three of these wealthy passengers purely on the say-so of a man sitting hundreds of miles away in an office in London. As I said, it's just unreal.'

Tremayne didn't reply for a moment, just stared out of the window at the Irish coastline, past which the ship was now slowly moving. Then he looked back at her.

'Unreal it may be,' he said, 'but I've got a great deal of respect for Mansfield Cumming. If he says there's a plot, I believe him until I can prove that he's wrong. So that means we have to check out Voss, and find out the names of those other two men. We can't simply ask for the information from a steward or one of the officers, because if they do end up going over the side, anyone on board who had any contact with them, however tenuous, is going to be an obvious suspect. So whatever we do, we have to be stealthy about it. And there is one obvious way of finding which stateroom Voss is occupying.'

'I know,' Maria replied. 'We wait until he finishes lunch or dinner, and then simply follow him. All we have to do is keep close enough to him so that we can see which stateroom he enters, but not so close that he takes any notice of us.'

'Just what I was going to suggest,' Tremayne said, 'but with one refinement. Voss looks to me like the kind of man who enjoys his food, so I suspect that he'll have dinner in the dining saloon every evening. We already know from the steward that the meal starts there at seven sharp, and of course he will have to dress for the evening, which means he'll have to return to his stateroom no later than six to get ready. So what we'll do is relax for the moment, then I'll make sure I've found him by about four o'clock, and after that I'll stick with him.'

As a plan, it had the virtue of simplicity, but a lot depended on how observant Voss turned out to be. There weren't that many people travelling first class, and if he kept on seeing the same face every time he turned round, he might well decide that his bodyguards could be usefully employed finding out a lot more about the young couple who seemed to be dogging his footsteps. Or maybe even deciding that they really weren't wanted for the remainder of the voyage.

And Maria had been right. They were travelling in the newest and most advanced transatlantic liner in the world, living in sumptuous luxury, with stewards, bar staff and waiters at their beck and call, a kind of floating paradise, a foretaste of heaven.

But if Mansfield Cumming was correct and Voss already had blood on his hands, Tremayne and Maria both knew that he and his four hired thugs could very quickly turn their personal heaven into a most unpleasant kind of hell.

Chapter 24

11 April 1912
HMS D4

Hutchinson reacted instantly.

From his elevated position at the top of the conning tower, he had an unobstructed view of both decks of the submarine, and he could see things that the seamen working under his command were unaware of.

The submarine and the oiler were linked together by the mooring lines, and were moving slowly forward at about two knots, in a mercifully calm sea that was disturbed only by the slight swell. He could see the sailor, the member of his crew who'd fallen overboard, desperately trying to grab hold of something, anything, as he was swept down the side of the submarine. But there were no handholds he could grasp, and no lifebelts which could be thrown to him.

There was just one chance to save him.

'The heaving line,' Hutchinson bellowed at the men standing on the after deck of his boat. 'Throw him the heaving line.'

The line was of course still attached to the mooring rope, but that was actually an advantage because it meant that one end of the line was already secured.

One of the men looked up at him, then into the water beside the submarine, and immediately realized what he had to do. There wasn't time to coil the line and throw it, and it lay in an untidy heap beside the bollard on the deck of the boat. The seaman simply grabbed the pile of rope and lobbed it straight over the side, right into the path of the man in the water.

'All stop!' Hutchinson instructed down the voice pipe. The last thing he needed was the rope – or, much worse, the man – getting minced by the submarine's propellers, both of which were still turning slowly.

Now it all depended on whether or not the man in the water would be able to grasp the heaving line as he drifted past it.

Hutchinson watched and hoped, because that was all he could do.

The water was cold, only a few degrees above freezing, and the man would be both shocked and chilled, and weighed down by his sodden clothing.

As he neared the rope, Hutchinson saw him slip beneath the waves, and for one sickening instant he thought they'd lost him. Then the man's head and hands appeared. He grabbed for the rope, and suddenly Hutchinson saw that he'd gripped it, was holding onto it with both hands.

'Haul him in,' he yelled. 'Gently.'

The two men on the after deck began pulling on the heaving line, dragging their comrade towards the safety of the submarine. It seemed like minutes, but in fact it could only have been thirty or forty seconds before they were able to grab his arms and drag him onto the deck of the boat, where the man just lay for a few moments, panting and spitting out water.

'Get him below, right now,' Hutchinson ordered. 'Then get

those clothes off him, as quickly as you can. Get him dry and get him warm. And give him a hot drink.'

Only then, once he was sure that his crewman was being taken care of, did he turn his attention back to the oiler alongside.

'Right, gentlemen,' he shouted across the gap. 'Now we've watched the afternoon's entertainment, perhaps we can get on with what we were *supposed* to be doing.'

He checked the deck, where two crewmen were standing beside the fuelling point, waiting for the hose.

'Are you ready?' Hutchinson asked, and one of the crewmen gave him a thumbs-up gesture. He made a final check of both decks of the boat, then called out again to the crew of the oiler, telling them everything was prepared.

Another heaving line was thrown from the oiler, snaking across the black deck of the submarine. One of the crewmen seized it, then they both started hauling on it, dragging a thick black hose across the narrow gap between the two vessels. As soon as they were able, they grasped the nozzle at the end of the hose and wrestled it down onto the fuelling point.

Hutchinson waited for a few moments while they checked that it was locked securely in place. 'We're ready,' he called out to the oiler crew. 'You can start pumping.'

The hose twitched and throbbed as the diesel fuel poured down it, and Hutchinson turned his attention to the security of his boat, checking that the mooring lines were still tight, and that both vessels still had their bows turned to face the slight swell. Then all he could do was wait until the tanks were completely full.

The entire operation took almost an hour from start to finish, but he was surprised by how straightforward the actual mechanics of the refuelling had turned out to be. Of course, the conditions were almost ideal, with only a flat calm sea and virtually no wind. How easy it would be to perform the same manoeuvres in poor weather or a rough sea was another matter entirely.

As Hutchinson waved his goodbyes – and grateful thanks – to the crew of the oiler, which would now have to loiter in the same general area until he returned, he hoped that the second refuelling, much further out into the ocean, would prove to be just as easy to complete.

But, knowing what the weather conditions were normally like in the north Atlantic in April, he had his doubts.

Chapter 25

Tremayne and Maria spent most of the afternoon relaxing, making use of the ship's ample facilities. Acting, in short, just like a wealthy, upper-class couple enjoying a luxurious voyage across the Atlantic. They talked to a handful of the other passengers, exchanging the kind of aimless and polite conversation of people with little interest in each other, and who knew that once the voyage ended they would be unlikely to ever meet again.

The only unusual event which occurred was another one of the pageboys bringing them a message in a white envelope, but this one wasn't addressed to Tremayne.

'It's from my boss in Washington,' Maria told him, when she'd opened it. 'I guess Mansfield must have contacted him to ask about Bauer and Kortig, and he's supplied me with an accurate description of the two men.'

'Without encrypting the message?' Tremayne asked. 'That's a bit sloppy, isn't it?'

'No, there's no need. He's just referred to them by their initials – JB and LK – and I don't think there's much doubt that they *are* the two men we saw with Voss last night. Bauer is the fat guy, Kortig the skinny runt. Here, see what you think.'

She passed the message form over and Tremayne studied it, then nodded. Whoever had composed the message had a good descriptive eye, and the two brief word-pictures suited Voss's companions exactly.

'No argument there. So now at least we know who they are.'

Just before four o'clock, they climbed the staircase up to the Promenade Deck and, as before, they separated, Maria going forward to the first-class lounge while Tremayne walked into the all-male preserve of the smoking room. They'd walked by the windows a couple of times during the afternoon, and each time they had seen that Voss and his two companions were still in there. On the third and last occasion, the three men had been absent, but when Tremayne and Maria walked a few yards further aft, they saw that their quarry had simply moved into the Verandah Café to take afternoon tea.

They were clearly creatures of habit. In their perambulations around the ship, Tremayne and Maria had seen many of the other passengers making use of the *Titanic*'s excellent leisure facilities: the first-class section of the ship boasted a swimming pool, a Turkish bath, plus a fully equipped gymnasium and a squash court for the more energetic. Maria had even spotted John Jacob Astor in the gymnasium enthusiastically pounding away on one of the rowing machines. In contrast, the three people they were interested in seemed merely to move from one restaurant, café or lounge to another. But as Tremayne had remarked to Maria earlier, from the size of the man, he doubted if Jonas Bauer had moved at faster than a slow amble for the last ten years. And it did make Tremayne's job slightly easier, knowing that the three men would usually be together, and in one of a limited number of locations.

Now, as Tremayne walked through the door, he saw the three men again on the far side of the room. As usual they were deep in conversation.

Tremayne chose a seat in the opposite corner, and then settled down to watch and wait. He'd brought a novel with him – *Psmith in the City* by P.G. Wodehouse, an author he'd always enjoyed – and placed the book with its distinctive blue cover, showing two seated figures either side of a cluttered office desk, on the table in front of him, but realistically he didn't expect to read much more than a few words.

After about forty minutes, Voss and his two companions stood up and started walking towards the main doors of the smoking room.

Tremayne decided to give them a few seconds' start, and watched as the three men left the room.

Then, as he saw them begin descending the aft first-class staircase, he stood up and began following, keeping a few yards back. The three men were making their way down slowly, still talking, snatches of their conversation just audible.

But they didn't go far, stopping on B-Deck for a few moments to exchange some final words. Tremayne stayed on the deck above, waiting and listening. Then there was silence, and he moved quickly down the staircase. One figure – Voss – was descending to the deck below, but Tremayne moved across to the port-side corridor and glanced through the open door. Two figures were retreating down the passageway in front of him.

Then he moved back to the staircase and walked down it. Ahead of him, Voss stepped off the staircase and turned right.

It looked as if Voss's stateroom was on the same deck as Maria and Tremayne's. Tremayne smiled. Most convenient.

He watched as Voss turned right again, to walk down the port-side passageway, and made an immediate decision. He knew there were lavatories on one of the cross passages which led off the corridor Voss was walking down, and that would give him an excuse to be in the passageway.

He strode forward, a few yards behind Voss, who eventually stopped outside a door on the left-hand side of the corridor. He took a key from his pocket and inserted it in the lock just as Tremayne reached him.

Almost opposite that door was one of the cross passages, and Tremayne immediately turned right, walked a few paces, and stepped into the male facilities. A couple of minutes later, he opened the door and peered out, but the corridor was deserted. He now knew which suite Voss was occupying.

Tremayne walked across to the starboard passage, and then turned right to head back to the staircase. He climbed swiftly back up to the Promenade Deck and strolled into the lounge to rejoin Maria, who was sitting at a table beside one of the large windows.

'They've gone down to get ready for the evening?' she asked, as he sat down beside her.

Tremayne nodded. 'The other two must have staterooms on B-Deck, but Voss is on C-Deck, the same as us.'

'And you saw which door he went in?'

'Yes. It's on the same passageway as us, but quite a way further forward, almost opposite one of the cross passages. Fortunately, because of where it is, it should be easy enough to spot Voss when he comes out.'

A few minutes later they left the lounge and walked down to

their deck. Tremayne unlocked the door of the stateroom and then closed it behind them.

'When do you want to do it?' Maria asked.

'No time like the present. Let's get ready for dinner now, and as soon as we're dressed we can keep an eye on Voss's suite. Once we're sure he's gone for the evening, I'll get inside and start searching.'

'You're sure you can unlock it, then?'

'No problem.' Tremayne unzipped a compartment in his portmanteau and produced a small leather case. He opened it and showed Maria a collection of unusual-looking tools, some L-shaped, others flat, and some pointed.

'Lock picks,' she stated.

'I never travel without them.'

'Some day,' she said, 'you must tell me where you learned some of your more unusual skills.'

'As I said before, Mansfield Cumming likes his people to be competent in whatever they do. It wasn't just lock-smithing I was taught. I also spent quite some time with two circus perfomers.' Tremayne paused and looked over at Maria.

She took the bait. 'Who? Trapeze artists maybe?'

Tremayne shook his head. 'Nothing so exotic. An escapologist and a knife-thrower. Both more useful skills than being able to hang upside down from a trapeze.'

While Tremayne kept watch down the corridor, Maria quickly donned her evening clothes. This time she wore a creation of shimmering silk chiffon in a wonderful shade of lavender with a darker blue top, trimmed with white lace. In her dark hair she placed a velvet band with a cluster of jewels on one side. Again Tremayne found himself staring at her with more than a casual appreciation of a beautiful woman. Then they changed places while Tremayne got dressed. But it was another thirty minutes or so before the door of the suite finally opened, and Gunther Voss emerged, resplendent in black tie and dinner jacket. He locked the door behind him, and then strolled off down the corridor in the opposite direction.

Tremayne looked at his watch. It was twenty-five minutes past six.

'Dinner doesn't start for over another half hour, so he's probably going somewhere to have an aperitif. Just to make sure that I get a clear run, let's go down to the reception room on D-Deck. With any luck we'll see Voss going into the dining saloon.'

Voss wasn't in the reception room when they got down there, but he appeared with his two companions a few minutes later. As Tremayne had expected, the three men sat down at a table and ordered drinks and then, on the stroke of seven, the three of them walked through into the dining saloon.

'That should keep him out of our way for at least a couple of hours,' Tremayne said, as he finished his own drink. 'Let's get started.'

Chapter 26

11 April 1912
RMS *Titanic*

Tremayne and Maria walked back to their stateroom on C-Deck. At this time in the evening, the corridors, passages and staircases were largely deserted. If there was ever a good time for a burglary, this was probably it.

In their room, Tremayne unlocked his portmanteau and took out the Browning pistol that Mansfield Cumming had given him back in London. He released the magazine, opened the box of ammunition, and expertly loaded it. But he didn't pull back the slide to chamber a round and cock the weapon. He was carrying it purely for self-defence purposes, and he knew that if he had to draw it, he would have time enough then to ready it for firing: the process only took about a third of a second.

'Here's hoping you don't need to use that,' Maria said, as Tremayne slid the compact pistol into the right-hand pocket of his trousers.

'So do I. But now we're taking the fight to the enemy, as it were. We carry our weapons at all times, loaded, of course. Your pistol can easily fit inside your handbag.'

Maria smiled at him and opened the top of the bag a few

inches to reveal the black chequered butt of her Browning. 'My pistol has been with me ever since we stepped on board the ship.'

'I'm not entirely surprised,' Tremayne said, 'and I'm really glad I've got you watching my back.' He paused for a moment, then added: 'I know we only met a few days ago, and then got thrust into this situation together, but I absolutely know I can trust you with my life. And I hope you feel the same way about me.'

Maria nodded. 'You're okay, Alex. When I first saw you, I thought you were a typical English upper-class idiot, despite what Mansfield had told me about you, but now I know he was right and I was wrong. First impressions so often are. We're working well together, and you're right: I would trust you with my life.'

'Nobody's ever called me "upper-class" before. I don't know whether to be flattered or insulted.'

'Take it whichever way you like. Now we need to get to work. I'll be watching your back, as you said. So where do you want me to be, and what signals do you want me to make?'

Tremayne nodded. 'Once I'm inside, station yourself at the end of the cross passageway, where you'll be able to see up and down the corridor. Just pretend to be an irritated woman waiting for her husband to come out of the lavatory. That should come easy. I'm not bothered about other passengers or stewards, but if you see Voss, either of the other two men, or anybody who might be one of Voss's bodyguards, walk over to the door and knock three times. That'll give me time to get out of sight.'

Tremayne checked that he had his lock-picking tools, then stepped out into the corridor, which was still deserted. He walked quickly down it, Maria beside him, past the staircase lobby and the barber's shop, and stopped close to the door of Voss's suite. Again he checked that he was unobserved, then rapped sharply on the door, twice.

If Gunther Voss had left one of his bodyguards in his stateroom, then the man would now appear at the door. But there was no sound of movement that Tremayne could detect.

After another glance up and down the corridor, he took two steel tools from his leather pouch, bent down and started working on the lock. He inserted a tiny wrench into the keyhole to apply a turning force, and then used a pick to locate and move the pins of the barrel. It was delicate, tactile work, as he tried to visualize in his mind's eye what the pick was telling his fingers about the shape of the lock itself.

Tremayne had done this many times before, and in less than thirty seconds the last of the pins clicked upwards, and the wrench turned smoothly in the lock. He slid the tools back into his pocket, opened the door and stepped inside the stateroom.

At that moment, Maria was splitting her attention between Tremayne and what he was doing with the door lock and the corridor in which they were standing. As the door closed behind him, she saw two figures approaching from her left and turned to look at them, but then dismissed them as a threat: they were a middle-aged man and woman and as she watched they entered another stateroom some way down the corridor. But because she was looking that way, she failed to notice a heavily built man wearing a dinner jacket who appeared at the far end of the passageway to her right. For a few seconds, the man looked down the corridor towards Voss's stateroom, and then he stepped backwards and retreated the way he had come.

For a fleeting second, as she turned her head to the right, Maria thought she saw movement in her peripheral vision, but when she looked down the corridor, there was nobody in sight.

The room Tremayne and Maria were occupying was opulent enough, but Voss's suite provided a whole new level of luxury. Tremayne found himself standing in a large lounge panelled in a dark wood, perhaps walnut or mahogany, and equipped with a gilt fireplace adorned with flowers in front of the grate and a painting, a still life which also depicted a bouquet, in a heavy gold frame above it. On the mantelpiece stood an ormolu clock and a pair of small jewelled vases, and either side of the fireplace twin wall lights illuminated the stateroom. A comfortable sofa covered in an elegant patterned fabric, two matching armchairs and an occasional table comprised the main furnishings. Heavy curtains were draped over the large windows, the carpets were thick underfoot, and all the decoration was simply sumptuous. Again, Tremayne found it difficult to believe he was actually on board a ship.

He moved quickly across the stateroom and looked around him, checking for cupboards and drawers, anywhere that Voss might have secreted papers or documents, but saw no obvious hiding places. In fact, he could see no sign of personal belongings anywhere in the room.

In the bedroom it was a different story. Two large leather suitcases stood against one wall, but the moment Tremayne lifted them he knew they were both empty. He turned his attention to the wardrobes, opening the doors wide to reveal suits, jackets, trousers and shoes. Drawers yielded shirts, socks, underwear and ties, all entirely innocent.

On the table beside the bed were two novels – *Under Western Eyes* by Joseph Conrad and *The Olympian: A Story of the City* by James Oppenheim – and a swift flick of the pages showed that there was nothing concealed in them.

The only place left to check was under the bed. Tremayne

lifted the edge of the counterpane and looked underneath. Right in front of him, he saw a small leather case with two catches. He pulled it out and placed it on the bed.

The catches were locked, but another of his tools released them in a matter of seconds. Tremayne snapped them both open and lifted the lid.

Inside the case were two shaped recesses, and in each one was a distinctive black semi-automatic pistol, of a type that he recognized immediately: they were both Lugers, and they looked brand new, perhaps a gift to Voss from his German associates.

Then he looked inside the lid of the case, and saw a small metal plaque there, bearing an inscription in German, which he quickly translated: 'To Gunther Voss with grateful thanks from his friends in Germany for the idea and the execution.'

It was hardly concrete proof of what Voss had been doing, and there could have been a number of alternative explanations for the wording, such as some radical new business venture, but Tremayne didn't believe that for a moment.

He picked up one of the Lugers and worked the action, pulling back the unusual jointed arm which in use would eject the spent cartridge case and then chamber a new round, the well-oiled moving parts clicking smoothly as he did so. Tremayne knew pistols, and had fired Lugers on many occasions. It was a design he had always liked.

He replaced the weapon in the recess, closed the lid and locked the catches again, sliding the case back under the bed where he had found it.

He stood up and looked around the stateroom again, but saw nothing that he thought would merit any further investigation. No documents of any sort, in fact.

Tremayne took a last look round, then left the bedroom,

crossed the lounge to the door, opened it and let himself out into the corridor. Maria was waiting for him exactly where he'd asked her to.

As before, there was nobody in sight, so Tremayne quickly bent down and relocked the door of Voss's stateroom. Then he stepped over to join Maria, and they walked down the cross passage to the starboard corridor, which took them back to the forward staircase, and then they carried on to their own stateroom.

'Well?' Maria asked as Tremayne closed the door behind them.

'Not what I was hoping to find. No documents, nothing in writing at all, in fact. The only thing I found was a pair of Luger pistols in a presentation case. They'd been given to him by somebody in Germany, but the inscription didn't say who. They were thanking him for "the idea and the execution".'

Maria didn't look impressed. 'That's circumstantial evidence, at best. You and I can place one interpretation on it and think we know what it means, but to anyone else it could seem entirely different. If it had been signed by someone important – the German Foreign Minister or the Kaiser, say – that might be fairly convincing. But as it is, it's not enough. Nowhere near enough. We need more, something definite.'

Chapter 27

11 April 1912
RMS *Titanic*

In the dining saloon, the clinking of cutlery on fine china was overlaid by the buzz of conversation, a sound which rose and fell in a discordant, irregular rhythm. Voss and his two companions were seated at a table on the port side of the large room, and had already consumed two excellent courses when they saw a familiar figure approaching, wearing a dinner jacket and weaving his way between the tables, almost all of which were occupied by diners.

Voss stood up as the man approached his table.

'Yes, Vincent?' he asked. 'What is it?'

'I just went down to check your stateroom, like you asked, and there was a guy just opening your door and stepping inside. A woman was with him, but she was keeping out of sight, standing in the cross passage. Guess she was watching his back. The man might still be in there now. You want me to take care of him, maybe her too?'

Voss shook his head, unconcerned. 'There's nothing in there for him to find, unless he's just a sneak thief. Don't do anything right now. Describe them to me.'

Vincent, the leader of the bodyguards Voss had hired in New York, painted a brief picture of the two people he'd seen. He'd only caught a fleeting glimpse of the woman, but he'd had the man in sight for several seconds.

When he'd finished, Voss nodded. 'You would recognize the two of them again, I hope?' he asked.

Vincent nodded. 'You bet I would,' he replied. 'The man, anyway. And if the woman is his partner, all I have to do is spot him, and she'll probably not be too far away.'

'Right, then. Come and see me after breakfast tomorrow morning, and I'll tell you where we'll be during the day. Then you can go and check all the first-class public rooms until you find these people. Don't approach them, just come and tell me. Then I'll decide what we'll do about them.'

'You're the boss,' Vincent said, nodded and retraced his steps across the dining saloon.

'A problem?' Jonas Bauer asked.

'At the moment, I don't know. My guess is the man's probably just a petty thief, picking the lock of one of the most expensive staterooms on the ship in the hope of finding jewellery or a good watch, something like that, which he can sell once we get to New York. In that case, I'll tell Vincent to show him the error of his ways and give him a good beating.'

'But what if he isn't? Suppose he's an American government secret agent, or even a British one?' Bauer asked. 'And was there anything incriminating in your stateroom? Anything he could find that might tell him what's going on?'

Voss shook his head. 'Nothing to show what we're doing.' He touched the left side of his jacket. 'I always carry the envelope with me, in a waterproof pouch, just as I hope you two do as well, with your copies. So there's nothing for him to find.

Everything else is locked away in the hold. I told you before that was a good idea.'

'But if he is an agent?' Bauer persisted. 'What then?'

Voss shrugged. 'If he is, then I'll have to find a more permanent solution for him.'

'And the woman as well?'

'The same rules apply. Just because she's a woman, she won't get any special treatment from me.' He paused for a moment, then smiled wolfishly. 'Well, she might get *some* special treatment, I suppose.'

Chapter 28

12 April 1912
HMS *D4*

Lieutenant Hutchinson was pleased with the progress of his submarine, in view of the circumstances. The weather since he'd sailed had been basically good, with light but very cold winds and weak sunshine. More importantly, the sea had been comparatively calm, and he'd been able to keep the boat running on the surface at about twelve knots, which seemed to him to be a reasonable compromise between his maximum speed of fourteen knots and his best speed for endurance, which was a little over ten.

As a result, he was only about four miles behind the position he should have reached by noon that day, which in terms of the overall mission was an insignificant distance. His diesel tanks were still relatively full, and the weather looked as if it would stay fair for the rest of the day.

He took a last look around from the top of the conning tower, then handed over the position to the officer of the watch and climbed down the ladder. He poured himself a mug of hot coffee and took it to his tiny cabin, but he'd barely sat down before a crewman knocked on his door.

'Sorry to disturb you, sir,' the signalman said, 'but we've received a message marked most urgent, and for the attention of the captain only. It's classified "top secret" and encrypted,' he added.

'Thanks,' Hutchinson said briefly, took the envelope and signed the signal log to show that he had received it. From a small safe bolted to one bulkhead, he removed a code book and started the painstaking process of decrypting the message he'd been sent.

His coffee turned cold while he worked. The message was quite lengthy. The first section informed him that the second oiler would reach the rendezvous position the following day, as planned, and had reported generally good weather in the area, a moderate sea state and a slight south-westerly swell. That part seemed routine.

The second and third sections of the message were both much more unusual, and had been sent on the authority of the head of the Submarine Service, the first time Hutchinson had seen any message from that individual. The message baldly instructed him that HMS *D4* was to be at the specified rendezvous position on the date and time previously ordered, and was to have the two bow torpedo tubes loaded with live weapons and ready to fire on arrival. All other considerations were secondary to achieving this objective.

He was then to remain on the surface, with his wireless equipment manned at all times, and await further orders by radio. If and when those orders arrived, he was to acknowledge them immediately, and then execute them promptly and expeditiously, and without question. Under no circumstances was he to divulge any part of those orders to any other member of the crew. If the order to engage a vessel was given, as soon as he had acknowledged the instruction, the submarine was to dive and remain submerged until after the attack had been completed. Throughout that time, only the captain himself was permitted to look through the periscope at the target ship. Having read that far, Hutchinson could almost have guessed the last line of that part of the signal: after the attack, no discussion of any sort was to be permitted about any aspect of the operation.

'Just what the hell is this all about?' he muttered to himself. 'And why is Commodore Keyes giving personal and direct orders to a mere lieutenant?'

Appointed on 14 November 1910 as the Inspecting Captain of Submarines, a unique post in Royal Navy commands, Roger John Brownlow Keyes was the head of the British Submarine Service, now holding the rank of commodore.

The third section specified precisely what information Hutchinson was allowed to pass on to his crew, the cover story he was to tell them, which was barely plausible and would no doubt cause talk and speculation on board. But there was nothing he could do about that. He had his clear – very clear–orders.

Hutchinson replaced the code book in a safe, along with both the original and the decrypted signal, and locked it. Then he picked up his mug of cold coffee and walked the few steps to the control room. He studied the navigation chart for a few minutes, and then ordered a two-knot increase in speed. It was better, he thought, to cover the distance a little quicker than he'd originally planned, to make absolutely sure that the boat did make the rendezvous on time.

Because the unspoken message that he'd just read in that signal was that if he *didn't* get his submarine into position as ordered and on time, his naval career would be over.

Chapter 29

12 April 1912
RMS *Titanic*

When Voss had returned to his stateroom the previous evening, he made a careful check of all his possessions, and had found everything intact and apparently undisturbed. If Vincent hadn't seen the unidentified man enter his stateroom, he would never have known there'd been an intruder.

And that was bad news, because it meant his guess was wrong. The man who'd so expertly unlocked his stateroom door and then searched through his belongings clearly hadn't been looking for an expensive watch to sell in New York. If he had, he would definitely have taken at least one of the three which Voss had left in one of the drawers.

Obviously the Americans – or perhaps more likely the British, bearing in mind the events which had taken place in Berlin while he'd been in the city – had found some information about what he and his companions were planning to do, and had got this unidentified man and his female companion on board the *Titanic* to tail him. Well, it was still a long way to New York. It was a big ocean and a comparatively small ship. Accidents could happen.

In fact, Voss was going to make sure that accidents *did* happen.

As had become his routine, Voss and his two compatriots took seats in the first-class smoking room as soon as they'd finished breakfast, and Vincent found them there shortly afterwards.

'The man you saw wasn't a petty thief,' Voss told him, 'but someone much more dangerous. I think I know what he was doing in my stateroom, and what he wants.'

The bodyguard knew very little of what Voss had been doing in Europe, only that his employer had been involved in important meetings with senior German government staff. Vincent wasn't particularly interested. His job was to protect his employer, and to do what he was told, and he was quite happy about that.

'So as I said last night, the first thing you have to do is find that man and the woman who was with him, and then let me know where they are. I'd like to get a look at their faces before I decide what to do about them.'

Vincent nodded. 'I'll be back as soon as I can,' he promised, then turned and walked away.

Voss stared at the bodyguard's retreating back for a few seconds, lost in thought, then he turned round to look at the two men sitting at his table.

'Your bodyguard only gave us a pretty general description of this man he saw,' Bauer said, 'and he hardly saw the woman at all. I reckon the man's description could apply to a lot of people here in the first-class section. Of course, he might be travelling on second- or third-class tickets, and just took a chance and sneaked in while almost everybody was at dinner last night.'

Voss nodded. 'You could be right,' he replied, 'but if Vincent says he can recognize him, then I'm sure he can. He's very reliable. If this man is travelling in one of the other accommodation areas, it'll just take him longer to identify him, that's all.'

He glanced up as the smoking-room door opened. Half a dozen people entered and sat down at a table on the opposite side of the room, talking animatedly together. Several other tables in the room were already occupied. It was quite a popular place to relax during the day, mainly for people who enjoyed smoking, but quite a number of others seemed to just like the atmosphere. None were within earshot of the table where the three men were sitting, and they felt free to discuss their plans without reservations.

'Anyway,' Voss said, 'just forget about that couple for the moment. When Vincent finds them, we'll decide what's necessary. Let's just go over the sequence of events one more time. That way, once we get back to New York there'll be no problems with co-ordinating our actions. Jonas, why don't you go first?'

Bauer nodded, leant forward and began to talk.

Chapter 30

12 April 1912
RMS *Titanic*

Tremayne stepped into the smoking room and took a seat at a vacant table on the opposite side of the room. The three men were already there, and appeared to be deep in conversation.

Other people came and went from the smoking room, and Tremayne simply registered their movements without taking any particular notice of who they were or what they were doing. But when a thick-set man in a dark suit walked past his table and continued striding over to where Voss was sitting, he immediately registered the fact. He wondered if he was one of the bodyguards he'd been told Voss was travelling with.

As the man approached the table, Voss stood up, and for a few moments they talked quietly together. Then the man nodded, turned and walked out of the smoking room through the other door, and Voss resumed his seat.

'I wonder what that was about?' Tremayne murmured to himself, looking down at his book again.

On the other side of the room, Voss sat silently for a few seconds. Vincent had returned to the smoking room to tell his employer the unwelcome news that he'd not seen the intruder anywhere, and to ask if he should start checking out the second- and third-class passengers as well, when he'd walked straight past the table where the man he was looking for was sitting. He must have walked up one staircase to the Promenade Deck as he, Vincent, had been walking down the other.

When Voss had stood up to greet him, Vincent had needed to explain very little.

'He's here in this room,' had been his opening words. 'At the table right behind me, on the opposite side of the fireplace. The guy's by himself, fair hair, blue eyes. He's wearing a dark-grey suit, black shoes, and reading a book.'

Voss hadn't reacted, just in case the man was watching him, except to nod once.

'Thank you, Vincent,' he'd replied briefly. 'I'll let you know what I want you to do later.'

Now, he leant forward across the table, and spoke to his two companions in low, urgent tones.

'Don't turn round or react in any way,' he said, 'but the man who broke into my stateroom is sitting in this room, about thirty feet away, wearing a grey suit and reading a book. Over the next few minutes, take a glance in his direction, and try to memorize his face.'

Bauer nodded, then leant back in his chair and stretched both his arms above his head, as if to relieve cramped shoulder muscles. As he did so, he snatched a glance across the smoking room towards the table Voss had indicated.

'I've seen him before,' he said, turning to Voss. 'I believe he's been in here every day since we sailed from Cherbourg. You think he's been watching us?'

'Unless you can think of another good reason why a nonsmoker – I've not seen him with so much as a cigarette between his lips – would want to spend his days in a room full of tobacco smoke.' Voss paused, and glanced across the room. 'I've noticed him before as well,' he added. 'I assumed he was just a rich upper-class idiot, spending some of his inherited wealth on an expensive transatlantic crossing. It looks like I was wrong.'

'So you think he's an agent? British or American, I mean?'

Voss nodded. 'No other reasonable conclusion.'

'So what do we do about him?'

'*We* don't do anything,' Voss said. 'It's important that we behave absolutely normally, and remain very visible, at least for the moment, so that when that man turns up dead, or simply vanishes over the side, nobody will have any reason to suspect that we were involved.'

Chapter 31

12 April 1912
London

The telephone rang in Mansfield Cumming's office, and he reached out his hand to the instrument somewhat hesitantly: he still didn't entirely trust the new technology.

'Yes?' he barked.

'I have a call for you from Berlin,' Mrs McTavish announced. 'It's that man Williams again.'

Moments later, Cumming was connected.

'Yes?' he said again. 'Is that you, Williams?'

'Yes, sir,' Michael Williams replied. 'I have a little more information, but I don't know how much use it's likely to be. You remember that you asked me to check all of Voss's activities in the city, not just his contacts with government officials? Well, the commercial attaché has been working with me and looking at all of his movements, and two of them look interesting.'

Cumming seized a pencil and a sheet of paper while he listened intently.

'He made two visits to a warehouse on the outskirts of Berlin, and on the second one he took delivery of two large packing cases. When he left the city by train for Cherbourg, both cases went with him, and he had one of his men stationed in the guard's van of the train with the cases.'

'So what was in them?' Cumming asked.

'That's where the commercial attaché proved his worth. He managed – and I don't know how – to work out which company in Berlin had delivered the cases. It turned out to be a specialist paper manufacturer, so presumably that was what he'd bought. I can tell you the name of the company, if you wish, so that you can run checks from London, but I doubt if you'll get much information from them if I'm right about what they were doing.'

'Paper? Why the hell would he be buying paper in Germany?'

'I think the point, sir, is that it wasn't just ordinary paper.'

'You'd better explain that.'

For about a minute Cumming listened intently as Williams expounded his theory. Then he asked another question.

'If you're right, that's only half of what he'd need.'

'I know, and that's why the other visit he made to a commercial enterprise in Berlin is significant.'

'Does that company have the capability to produce what Voss would need?'

'Definitely. They specialize in precisely this kind of work. I've still got one of my men trying to find out more, but I'm not hopeful.'

Cumming glanced over his notes once more, then thanked Williams, and ended the call. He sat in thought for a few moments, then took a fresh sheet of paper and quickly composed a telegraph message for Alex Tremayne. The new information added a vital new dimension to the problem, and to the plot, though at that moment he couldn't see what Tremayne or Maria could do about it. It looked as if this aspect of the matter would have to be attended to by other means.

Chapter 32

12 April 1912
RMS *Titanic*

As Tremayne had expected, the three men he was watching stood up about forty minutes before lunch would be served in the main dining saloon, and walked out of the smoking room together. They made their way down the first-class staircase and then separated, with Voss continuing to the deck below.

When the other two men entered the port-side passageway on B-Deck, Tremayne was only a few yards behind them, and watched as Bauer unlocked the door of the first stateroom on the left-hand side of the passageway and stood talking to Kortig for a few seconds before stepping inside. The other man strode down the cross passage to the opposite side of the ship and entered his own suite, the twin of Bauer's, but on the starboard side of the *Titanic*.

As before, as soon as he'd noted their stateroom numbers, Tremayne returned to the Promenade Deck to rejoin Maria in the lounge.

'I know their stateroom numbers,' he said briefly. 'I followed them down to B-Deck, and I watched them when they opened their stateroom doors and walked inside.'

Maria nodded slowly. 'So that's it, then,' she said. 'A positive identification of all three now, and we know precisely where to find them.'

'Exactly. Now we know who the targets are.'

A few minutes later, a pageboy appeared with an envelope addressed to 'Alex Maitland', which Tremayne signed for and then opened. He read the contents quickly, then passed the message across to Maria, who read it in her turn.

'If Mansfield's right,' Tremayne remarked, 'that does add a new dimension to the plot. What I'm not sure about is what he expects us to do about it. Those packing cases will be locked away in one of the holds, and there's no way we can get in to check them. And even if we could, what the hell could we do?'

'What about the engravings?' Maria asked. 'You didn't see anything like that in Voss's stateroom, I suppose?'

Tremayne shook his head. 'No, and I searched the place pretty thoroughly. If they'd been there, I'd have found them. My guess is that he's got those locked away in the hold as well.'

'Is it worth trying to get inside the hold and checking the cases?' Maria asked. 'You could pick the lock easily enough, I guess.'

'I doubt it. I could probably get inside the hold, but I used to work on ships, and unless you know exactly what you're looking for, and whereabouts in the hold it's located, finding the cases would be almost impossible. There are always hundreds of boxes, all stacked in neat piles, and even if by some miracle I could identify the two cases Voss had loaded on board, unless they're on the floor of the hold with nothing on top of them, which is really unlikely, I couldn't get them open anyway.'

Maria held up her hands in a gesture of surrender. 'Okay,' she said, 'you've convinced me. And really, if Mansfield's information is correct, we already know what's inside them.'

'And that adds another confirmation to the reality of the plot. I don't know about you, but it really looks to me as if Mansfield is right about what Voss is planning.' He picked up the message form again and pointed to a couple of the names listed on it. 'This is hard evidence. There's no legitimate reason that I can think of for Voss making these purchases. But set against what he's plotting, they make perfect sense, and it's quite obvious what he intends to do when he gets back to America.'

'I agree. I think the evidence is now overwhelming. If we let those three men – Voss, Bauer and Kortig – reach New York and implement their plan, the world could be plunged into a bloody war within months, possibly even within weeks.'

'And the only thing that could stop that happening is if we follow Cumming's orders and assassinate the three of them.' Tremayne nodded, then looked resignedly at Maria. 'It's time,' he said. 'We'll do the first one tonight.'

Chapter 33

12 April 1912
London

Mansfield Cumming had a number of operations running simultaneously. Because the budget of the Secret Service Bureau was so limited, he had been forced to rely upon serving and retired officers of the Armed Forces, people of similar status in the merchant marine, and even some businessmen, to act as his eyes and ears in foreign countries. He had been largely successful in appealing to the innate patriotism of such people, and these unofficial agents had generated substantial amounts of important intelligence information for Britain.

At that moment, he had three groups of volunteer spies operating in Germany, keeping an eye on the ports of Kiel, Hamburg and Bremerhaven. Another small group was based in France, in Paris, trying to make sure that all was quiet in the capital of Britain's oldest and most traditional enemy, and there were others in Italy, Austria, Poland and Hungary. In addition, he had a number of lone watchers scattered throughout Europe, operating without specific briefs, and simply observing whatever military activity there was in their vicinity.

But ever since he'd first received confirmation of the plot to align Germany with America, that had dominated his thoughts and driven his actions, and he'd spent almost no time doing anything else.

That evening, he was again studying the north Atlantic chart. He'd been given the noon position of the *Titanic*, which he'd plotted carefully. That gave him the liner's course and average speed, which worked out at a little over twenty knots. The other track marked on the chart was the much slower course being followed by the submarine HMS *D4*, and was significantly more accurate than that of the *Titanic*, simply because a senior officer at the Admiralty was passing him an updated position of the boat every four hours.

Projecting the two courses seemed to suggest that he was going to have to change the rendezvous position slightly. He'd originally planned for it to occur at noon on the fifteenth, but it now looked as if it was going to have to take place twelve hours earlier. He would, he knew, have to keep monitoring the situation very closely.

His thoughts turned then to the *Titanic*, ploughing westwards across the cold north Atlantic waters, and he began to wonder what Tremayne and Maria Weston were doing. By now they should have identified the three Prussian traitors, and come up with a plan to eliminate them.

And as that thought crossed his mind, Cumming realized that there was one specific order, one vital piece of information, which he hadn't passed to Tremayne. Surely the man would already have guessed what he wanted to happen – they had talked about it, albeit briefly – but Cumming decided he couldn't take the chance. And there was one further piece of information Williams had gleaned in Berlin. It was only a confirmation of what they already knew, but it was worth passing on to Tremayne.

Quickly, he seized a sheet of paper, composed a short but clear message, and encrypted it. He took the time to check both the original and the enciphered version to ensure there were no mistakes, then walked out of the office and gave it to Mrs McTavish to send immediately.

He just hoped he wasn't too late.

Chapter 34

12 April 1912
RMS *Titanic*

'How will you do it?' Maria asked.

They were in their stateroom, and were dressed for the evening. As before, they'd taken their meal in the à la carte restaurant, which meant they could eat a smaller meal in a much shorter time than if they'd gone to the main first-class dining saloon.

Tremayne shook his head, and then unlocked his portmanteau. 'Right now, I don't know. What is certain is that I have to find one of the three men alone. There can't be any witnesses, so I'm going to have to pick my moment carefully and use whatever weapon seems to be the most appropriate at the time.'

From a small compartment at the bottom of his leather bag he took out a garrotte, a leather-covered and lead-filled cosh, and a sheath knife with a slim, stiletto-like blade.

'Mansfield Cumming believes in both belt and braces,' he said. 'Apart from the knife, which is mine, he gave me all this lot, plus an interesting selection of lethal drugs, before we left London. Just what every aspiring assassin needs.'

'I thought the idea was that there'd be three tragic accidents?'

'That's the best possible solution, yes. Three men falling overboard, or tumbling down the stairs and breaking their necks, but if all else fails we might have to ambush them somewhere, shoot them and then toss the guns over the side. But that has to be our last resort, for obvious reasons.'

Tremayne picked up the cosh, hefted it in his hand for a few moments, then slipped it into his right-hand trouser pocket, where it would be easy to reach. The Browning pistol was already out of sight in his left pocket. Then he locked the portmanteau again.

'Right,' he said, glancing at his watch. 'They should be finishing dinner within the next half-hour, so let's go down to the reception room and wait for them to come out. After that, we'll just have to see what the evening brings.'

At that moment, there was a brisk double knock on their stateroom door. Tremayne strode across the room and pulled it open. A pageboy was standing in the corridor, a sealed envelope in his hand.

'Mr Maitland, sir, good evening. I have a message for you,' he said, proffering the envelope.

'Thank you.'

Tremayne closed the door, slit open the envelope and extracted the piece of paper it contained. Written on it was a short message in the encrypted format that was now so familiar to them both.

'There are only a few groups this time,' Tremayne said, 'so it won't take too long to decipher it.'

He sat down at the occasional table, took out his notebook and a pencil, wrote out the next keyword in the sequence he'd memorized – 'INTERVENING' – and started work. In less than five minutes, he was able to read the message aloud to Maria.

'It reads, "Essential all deaths are accidental, or bodies not found at all. Use weapons only if no other method possible and ensure bodies thrown overboard." So no surprises there. I'd hoped for a moment that he was calling it all off. And there's one other snippet. Mansfield's agent in Berlin managed to find some more evidence at the engraving company. According to this, his man discovered that Voss had sent the company two pieces of paper a couple of months ago.' Tremayne paused, then finished: 'One was a mint ten-pound note, and the other a mint twenty-pound note, and nobody thinks he was using the money to pay a bill.'

Maria nodded. 'That proves it, then. It was just as Mansfield thought. Now I think we should go and finish this. The meal in the dining saloon must be almost over.'

They walked into the first-class reception room. Several of the tables were already taken, but they found one in a corner close to the staircase which gave them a good view of one of the two entrances to the dining saloon, and when Voss and his companions left the room, they would have to pass in front of them to reach either the staircase or the elevators. Unless of course they'd decided to dine in another restaurant that evening. But the three men seemed to be creatures of habit.

They'd been sitting there for fifteen minutes when the door at the rear of the reception room opened and a group of people emerged from the dining saloon, talking noisily. At the back of the group, but clearly not a part of it, were the three men.

They didn't stop in the reception room, but continued forward to the staircase and began climbing up it.

'We'll give them a couple of minutes and then we'll follow,' Tremayne said.

Chapter 35

12 April 1912
RMS *Titanic*

Although he appeared almost oblivious to his surroundings, Voss had seen the young man sitting at a table in the corner of the reception room along with a dark-haired pretty woman, and he repressed a smile. He had expected that the man would be waiting for him and his companions.

His bodyguard was nowhere in sight, which again was what he had ordered. But he knew that the men weren't far away, and if everything went according to plan, sometime around midnight two bodies would vanish over the side of the ship and plunge into the waters of the Atlantic. And then there would be nothing to prevent their plan coming to fruition. Voss could almost savour the sweet taste of victory.

Chapter 36

12 April 1912
RMS *Titanic*

Ten minutes after their targets had started walking up the staircase, Tremayne and Maria stepped out onto the Promenade Deck. The air was cool, the breeze gentle and generated mainly by the ship's passage through the water. Above them the heavens blazed with millions of tiny points of light.

'I don't know why it is,' Maria said staring up at the display, 'but the stars always seem to look brighter and more numerous when you're at sea.'

Tremayne looked at her keenly. 'You've spent some time on board ship, then?' he asked.

'Some time, yes,' she replied, with a smile. 'You're not the only one with a faintly nautical background. I've worked on a couple of liners sailing out of America. And that's something else I might tell you about some day,' she added. 'Now let's get on with the job in hand.'

They walked down the passageway to the first-class lounge. Tremayne wanted Maria to get settled there, and for him to be seen with her, before he went to the smoking room by himself.

Card games were in progress at many of the tables, and the buzz of conversation filled the air.

'I presume this is where the card sharps hang out in the evening,' Tremayne remarked.

'Actually,' Maria replied, 'I'm not so sure. I was talking to someone in here and they told me that it was the smoking room the wealthy sheep visit to be shorn. That's where the serious gambling takes place. I imagine the professionals let their victims win the first few hands for inconsequential stakes, and then raise the bets and steadily empty their wallets or billfolds. That's the usual technique. But here, these look like friendly, low-stakes games.'

'You know about gambling, Maria? I'm finding out a lot about you tonight. Do you want to find a seat and play a few hands, before I go?'

Maria shook her head. 'No,' she said. 'It wouldn't be fair.'

'You mean you don't want to play in case one of the professional card players here at one of the tables beats you?'

'No, I mean it wouldn't be fair on *them*.'

That silenced Tremayne, and he glanced at Maria with a sudden new understanding. She was an expert.

'I don't know much about cards,' he murmured, 'so I have no idea what these people are playing.'

In the centre of most of the tables were small piles of coins and, as Tremayne watched the activity at the one closest to them, the dealer completed the round, dealing two cards in front of each man, one face down and the other face up.

'That's poker,' Maria told him. 'Probably five-card stud. Depending on the type being played, they'll each end up with either two or three cards face up, and the others face down. Before each round of cards is dealt, everybody in the game has to put more money into the pot, and how much depends upon the betting. Usually, the person showing the highest card – an ace or a picture card perhaps – will open the betting, and the other players can fold, meaning they drop out of the game and lose whatever money they've put in the plot, see the bet, or raise it. Now, just watch what's happening at this table. The man on the dealer's left has a king, so he's just opened the betting. It's a bit early in the hand for anyone to drop out, so my guess is they'll all just match whatever he's bet, and that gives them the right to be dealt another card.'

Without appearing to be paying too much attention to the men they were watching, Tremayne and Maria eased slightly closer to the table.

Each of the players in turn tossed coins onto the pile, and the dealer passed each one a third card, this one face down.

'So the next card will be face up? Is that right?' Tremayne asked quietly.

'Probably,' Maria replied, 'but there are a huge number of variations and, really, it's whatever the players decide they're happiest with. Other times, it's the dealer's choice. He just says what the hand is going to be, and they all either agree to play it or opt out for that round.'

There was another round of betting, with all the men staying in, then a fourth card was dealt face up.

'There's lot of psychology involved in poker, that's what I like about it,' Maria explained, 'and the game is much more interesting when you can see part of your opponents' hands. Now, in this game, each player has two of his four cards face up and on show, and two hidden, so all of them can get some idea of the strength of the opposition. Obviously, if one man has something like two kings showing, and the highest card in your hand is, say, a jack, then no matter what the last card is, your hand can never beat his hand.'

'So obviously you would give up – you would fold?'

Maria shook her head. 'Not necessarily,' she replied. '*You* know that your hand can never beat his, but at that stage, *he* doesn't. The best poker players are those who can sit there with nothing showing on the table, and virtually nothing in their face-down cards, and still beat the man opposite who has two kings in front of him.'

'And that works how, exactly?'

'You bluff him. You carry on betting as if you have three wonderful cards face down, and raise the betting so high that the man doubts the evidence of his own senses, and eventually folds.'

'You can do that? But if he matches your bet, then you lose, right?'

'Of course. So the trick is to make the last bet so expensive for him to match that he won't take the chance.'

'It sounds as if you know a lot about poker, young lady.' The speaker was a middle-aged man – American by his accent and dress – sitting at a table just behind them, with three companions, all of whom had stopped playing and were now looking at Maria with interest.

She turned at the sound of his voice and smiled at the group of people.

'I'm so sorry,' she said. 'I didn't mean to disturb your game. My husband has never played poker, but it was my father's favourite game, and he taught me how to play it many years ago.'

The American gestured to two vacant chairs nearby. 'Why don't you and your husband join us?' he suggested. 'It's rare to find a lady who enjoys the game.'

Maria shook her head. 'No, really, I couldn't. You were having a pleasant evening with your friends, and we would only be spoiling it.'

The American glanced at his companions. 'I don't think having this lady join us would spoil anything, fellows, do you? I think she would definitely improve the evening in fact.'

The other men nodded enthusiastically, and Maria turned to Tremayne, who bent his head so she could whisper in his ear.

'We'll sit here with this group,' she murmured, 'and then, in a few minutes, you can go off and find Voss and the other two men.'

'Good idea,' Tremayne whispered back.

Maria smiled again at the American. 'I'd be happy to play a few hands with you,' she said, 'as long as you don't make my husband join in. And as long as you don't take all my money, of course.' She batted her eyelashes.

The four men laughed dutifully, and Tremayne moved the two vacant chairs to the end of the table, positioning Maria's close to the table but his own some way back so he wouldn't interfere with the play.

The American who'd spoken to Maria first introduced his friends, and Tremayne reciprocated, then sat back in his chair, where he had a good view of the table.

It quickly became clear that the group Maria had joined was not a professional poker school. The initial stake was modest, and they'd placed a table limit on the maximum bet that could be placed, so the 'pots' were always small.

Maria was clearly right at home playing the game, winning and losing with equal grace, and never demonstrating the kind of aggressive killer instinct towards her fellow players that Tremayne guessed she could employ if she wished.

On one side of the lounge was a liquor pantry, and after a few minutes Tremayne went over to it and ordered a round of drinks for Maria and the four Americans, and then excused himself from the group.

He left the lounge, walked back down the passageway and then entered the smoking room again.

Previously, he'd only been in this room during the day, and it was immediately obvious that, like the first-class lounge, it had a very different atmosphere during the evening. Illuminated by the electric lamps, and with a flickering fire burning in the grate, the air turned blue by the smoke from myriad cigars and cigarettes, it could easily have been a room in a good London club. Almost every seat was taken and, above the hum of conversation, the dominant sounds were the distinctive slap as one card was laid upon another, and the riffling noise as a pack was shuffled.

It looked as if Maria was right. There was an almost palpable air of excitement about the room, and Tremayne was certain that the amount of money being staked on the turn of a card on these tables would be substantial.

He walked further into the smoking room, looking around him as he searched for his quarry, peering through the haze of tobacco smoke. Then, over in the far corner of the room, he saw them. The three Prussians – he refused to think of them as Americans – were sitting at a table with another two people, all smoking large cigars, and with drinks beside them. Voss had just cut a pack of cards, and four of the men were watching intently as the fifth – a man Tremayne had not seen on the ship before – dealt a hand. As he surreptitiously watched the activity at the table he slowed down, glancing around and looking for somewhere to sit.

There were very few spare seats, but eventually he found one which had been put aside by a group of men who had pushed two tables together to accommodate their game. He moved it a short distance away, angling it so that he could see the table where Voss was sitting, and sat down, ordering a drink from a passing waiter as he did so.

After about an hour, he noticed that Jonas Bauer, Voss's heavyset companion, was easing his chair back from the table. Immediately, before the man had even stood upright, Tremayne stood up and crossed swiftly to the door of the smoking room. He walked down the first-class staircase to the half-landing, and waited there for Bauer to appear. The man could have been returning to his cabin, going out on deck for a breath of fresh air, or heading for the lavatories, and at that moment Tremayne had no idea which. He could even, in fact, have been going to find a waiter to order another round of drinks, and might not be leaving the smoking room at all.

It had just seemed like a propitious moment, which Tremayne had decided to seize; it might provide the opportunity he needed to tackle Bauer alone, out on the open deck.

He heard a door swing open on the deck above him, and immediately began climbing the staircase, as if he was just arriving on that deck. When he reached the Promenade Deck, he saw that the door on the port side of the lobby, which gave access to the open deck, was just closing, and he immediately strode across to it and stepped outside.

As he did so, he almost walked into two people – a man and a woman – who were taking a late-night stroll in the open air. Tremayne apologized, stepped around them, and walked across to the rail that marked the side of the ship. If there were witnesses on deck, he knew he couldn't act.

He glanced ahead, and saw a large man walking away from him along the deck towards the nearest lavatories. He didn't know for certain that it was Jonas Bauer, but it was probable that the figure was the Prussian banker. He would have to wait until the man returned and went back towards the smoking room, and hope that then the coast would be clear.

Tremayne glanced down at the black waters of the Atlantic far below, the wake caused by the hull of the ship a constantly changing, foaming white shape against the darkness of the sea; then up towards the heavens. He wasn't a religious man, but just for an instant he was tempted to ask God for forgiveness for what he was about to do.

He felt in his pocket for the cosh, ensuring that it wouldn't snag when he pulled it out, checked that his pistol was secure in his other pocket, and then glanced around again. The couple he'd seen had now moved out of sight, and were presumably continuing their perambulations along the starboard side of the ship.

He looked back, to where the dark figure had vanished a couple of minutes earlier, but for the moment the deck was empty.

Then he saw a sudden movement in the shadows ahead of him, and a man appeared. But he was obviously not Jonas Bauer. His body was the wrong shape. This man appeared to be strong and athletic rather than corpulent. It looked as if he was wearing a dark suit. And then, as he moved into the glow cast by the deck lights, Tremayne was finally able to see his face.

He knew he had never seen him before, but even so Tremayne had no doubt about his identity. It was one of Voss's bodyguards, and the smile plastered across his lips provided a stark contrast to the gleaming steel of the knife which he held in his right hand.

Chapter 37

12 April 1912
RMS *Titanic*

For an instant, Tremayne simply wondered what had gone wrong. How had Voss realized why he was on the ship? Because this was clearly not some opportunistic attempted robbery being carried out by a thug on a lone and vulnerable passenger. He and Maria had obviously made some mistake, and had been identified for what they were. And this was Voss's idea of a permanent solution.

Now he saw that Bauer's departure from the smoking room was simply a clever ruse, something to entice him out onto the open deck, where the bodyguard would be waiting. Bauer was probably already back in the smoking room, sitting down at his table and acting as if nothing had happened.

Then he sensed movement over to his right, and saw a second figure approaching. Another powerfully built man, almost a clone of the first. Another of Voss's bodyguards, he presumed. He, too, was carrying a knife.

Tremayne knew he had the Browning pistol in his pocket, but he also knew that the suppressor for the weapon was locked away in his portmanteau in the stateroom. If he fired the weapon without the silencer, it would alert everybody on the Promenade Deck of the ship, whether they were outside walking on the open deck or in one of the first-class public rooms. And if that happened, there would be no chance of completing the assignment.

Somehow, he had to finish this without firing a shot. He knew the odds were stacked against him: two men with knives should be more than a match for one man – for any man – whose only usable weapon was a cosh.

But Tremayne wasn't just any man. He'd operated in some of the roughest and most dangerous cities in the world, and he was no stranger to street fighting. He'd learned his trade in the backstreets of London's East End and the alleyways of Hamburg, and had suffered more than his fair share of unarmed combat courses since Mansfield Cumming had recruited him. And all those forms of brutal, no holds barred, hand-to-hand combat did have some rules, basic though they were. Or, to be exact, it had one very important rule: if you were going to fight, you hit first, you hit hard, and you kept on hitting.

The trouble was, Tremayne guessed that the two men, who were even then trying to crowd him towards the guard rail at the side of the ship, had probably been educated in the same way, and had learned the same hard lessons.

He slid his hand in his pocket, slipped his wrist through the loop of the cosh and eased it out, covering the end of it with his fingers so that it would remain out of sight for as long as possible.

The man on his right was bulkier, and a fraction closer than the first man he'd seen. That was another unwritten rule of street fighting – you always picked the biggest opponent and went for him first – so that was exactly what Tremayne did. He dropped the cosh so that it extended below his hand, grasped the leather handle tightly and took two quick steps straight towards the man.

His opponent's face registered surprise. Maybe he'd been expecting Tremayne to stand there and wait until they got close enough to stick their knives in him and then throw him over the side. Then he grinned and drew back his right arm, his hand gripping the knife with the cutting edge of the blade facing upwards, the way an experienced knife fighter would hold his weapon.

He lunged forward, covering the remaining few feet between him and Tremayne in a rush, his knife stabbing towards his victim's stomach in a savage arc.

But the blow never connected. The bodyguard had telegraphed his actions, and when he reached the spot where Tremayne had been standing, all his knife cut was the empty air.

At the last possible moment, Tremayne danced sideways, to the right and away from the blade. At the same instant, he powered his right arm upwards, towards his attacker's face, and the lead-filled cosh smashed into the man's jaw, sending him reeling backwards.

That wasn't what Tremayne had been intending, and he sighed in irritation. He'd been aiming the cosh at the bodyguard's nose, because a hard uppercut delivered to the end of the nose was normally a killing blow, splintering the fairly fragile nasal bones and driving them up and backwards into the brain.

The bodyguard tumbled to the deck, the knife dropping from his hand. Tremayne knew that he was only dazed, not out of the fight. Not by a long way. But there was nothing he could do to finish him off, because the other man was already stepping forward. And after what he'd just seen, he was moving more cautiously.

The bodyguard feinted, stabbing his weapon towards Tremayne, aiming low, at the soft tissue below the rib cage. Not committed attacks, just probes to see how his intended victim would react.

Tremayne knew the steps of this particular dance very well, knew that every pace he took backwards, avoiding the stabbing blade, would be taking him closer to the guard rail and closer to a position from which he wouldn't be able to escape. He'd be pinned there, and only then would his attacker step forward and deliver a lethal blow. At all costs, he had to avoid that. And he had to finish this soon, because he could see that the other bodyguard was already getting to his feet and rubbing his jaw, clearly still dazed but already looking around for his knife.

His attacker lunged again, and again Tremayne moved. But this time he didn't step backwards, but sideways, to his right. And as he did so he lifted his cosh and swung it in a vicious horizontal arc, the head of the weapon smashing into the bodyguard's left side. Delivered accurately, a blow like that could crack ribs, but the man was wearing a heavy jacket which would help protect him. Even so, it would hurt.

The man howled in pain, a yell he quickly muffled. Like Tremayne, he also had no wish to attract witnesses to what was going on. He whirled round, lunging powerfully with his knife, but again his victim stepped sideways and the blade whistled harmlessly through the air.

The stabbing blow had unbalanced the bodyguard, and Tremayne seized the minimal advantage that offered. He swung the cosh again, this time driving the weapon down hard towards the man's left upper arm, aiming to break the bone. But even as he swung his weapon, the bodyguard twisted away, and the blow never landed.

The dynamics of the fight subtly changed at that moment. For the first time since the two men had confronted Tremayne, it was they who were retreating, not him. As the bodyguard stepped away, drawing back his arm for another strike, Tremayne swung the cosh again, and this time the blow landed precisely where he was aiming it.

As the man's right arm drove forward, the blade glinting in the deck lights, Tremayne stepped close to his attacker, bringing the cosh down with every ounce of strength that he could muster. The head of the weapon connected violently with the man's arm just above his wrist, and Tremayne clearly heard the crack as the bone shattered.

The knife fell from the bodyguard's hand and dropped to the deck, and this time the man's scream of pain was loud and penetrating. Instinctively, he clutched at his wrist with his left hand, to try to ease the pain. Tremayne stepped back and swung the cosh once more, aiming the weapon at the back of the bodyguard's head. It connected with a solid thump, and instantly the man fell senseless to the deck.

Tremayne turned quickly towards the spot where he'd last seen the other man, but he wasn't quite quick enough. The second bodyguard had recovered both his knife and his senses and, as Tremayne turned, he lunged forward, the blade of his knife aiming straight for his victim's chest.

The lethally sharp blade ripped through Tremayne's shirt and he felt a sudden agonising pain as the knife slammed into his ribs.

Chapter 38

Tremayne swayed backwards, trying desperately to move out of range as the man drew back his arm for a second, and final, stab.

But as his attacker lunged forward again, Tremayne knocked the man's knife hand to one side, and reacted faster. He stepped forward and drove his left fist into the bodyguard's stomach, knocking the breath from his body. Simultaneously he lifted the cosh high above his head and, as the bodyguard involuntarily bent forward, Tremayne brought the weapon crashing down onto the top of the man's skull. Like his partner, he too crashed down to the deck, unconscious.

Tremayne looked around, but the Promenade Deck was still mercifully empty of any passengers or crew. He didn't hesitate. He slid the cosh back into his pocket and grabbed the closest bodyguard around the shoulders. He struggled to drag the unconscious man to the rail, bent him forward over it and then simply lifted his legs. The bulky figure tumbled over the side of the ship and plummeted down into the Atlantic far below.

The second man was bigger and heavier, but Tremayne was

strong and in a matter of seconds he, too, had disappeared from sight over the rail. Tremayne hadn't heard a splash as either man entered the water, because the Atlantic Ocean was a long way below the deck he was standing on, and he doubted if anyone else on the ship would have heard anything. Both of his victims would still have been unconscious when they hit the water, and would probably drown in a matter of minutes, but frankly Tremayne didn't care whether they recovered consciousness or not. They'd try to kill him and failed and, whatever happened to them, they were no longer his concern.

He looked around the deck again, found the two knives which the men had been carrying, and tossed one of them over the side rail as well. But he slipped the other knife into his pocket, because he knew he was going to need it. Only then did he open his jacket and look down at the wound on his right side. His shirt was soaked red with blood, but his probing fingers found no sign of a penetrating wound, only the ragged gash where the blade had opened up his skin.

Holding his hand over the wound to try to staunch the bleeding and conceal it from any passengers he might meet, Tremayne walked on and entered the superstructure by the forward first-class staircase, then strode down the port-side corridor. Almost at the end, he turned right into the cross passage and then right again into the gentlemen's lavatory. He locked the door and immediately washed his hands. Then he slipped out of his jacket, taking care not to get any more blood on the material, and hung it up. Next he peeled off his shirt, wincing slightly as the movement aggravated his wound, and looked carefully at his injury. Like many superficial wounds, it had bled a great deal, and looked a lot worse than it really was. He guessed it would hurt, hurt a lot, for a few days, but would not require medical treatment. Just strapping it up would be enough, but that would have to wait until he got back to the stateroom, where Maria could help him.

In the meantime, he washed the wound with warm water, which started some fresh bleeding, then took a towel and wrapped it around his torso. He took a second towel, removed the bodyguard's knife from his jacket pocket, and cut it into strips, which he bound around the first towel to hold it in place. That should stop any further bleeding, at least for a short while.

There was nothing he could do about his shirt, which had heavy bloodstains on the right side, and was in any case ripped open by the knife, but he pulled it back on and tucked it into his trousers. Then he slipped his jacket on and did up the buttons to hide as much of the shirt from view as possible, he was going to have to return to the lounge to collect Maria, and that meant appearing in the full view of perhaps fifty people. He had to look as normal and natural as possible. Dripping blood from an open wound would obviously lead to questions being asked.

Tremayne looked around the lavatory to make sure that he'd cleaned up properly, that no drops of blood were visible on the floor or the sink, took the towel he'd used to clean his wound and rolled it up so that none of the bloodstains were showing, tucked it under his arm and then stepped back into the corridor.

He walked back out onto the Promenade Deck, checked that nobody was in sight, and dropped the towel over the side of the ship. He looked around again, then re-entered the superstructure and in a few seconds was walking back into the first-class lounge. As he threaded his way between the tables, nobody appeared to take the slightest notice of him.

Maria was still sitting at the end of the table, playing poker, but looked up as he approached and then sat down beside her.

'You've been a long time,' she said, looking at him carefully.

Tremayne nodded. 'I know,' he replied. 'In fact,' he added, feeling an increased dampness from his wound which suggested that the bleeding had started again, 'I don't feel all that well, actually. Perhaps I've eaten something that didn't agree with me. I think I'd better go back to the stateroom and lie down.'

'I'll come with you,' Maria said immediately. 'Gentlemen, I'm sorry but you must excuse us. Another time, perhaps.'

She threw her cards down onto the table, picked up the money she had been gambling with and tucked it into her purse, then stood up and took him by the arm.

In the lobby by the first-class staircase, Tremayne stopped.

'Just give me one minute,' he said. 'There's something I want to do.'

He strode forward, stepped into the smoking room and walked across to stand just a few feet away from the table where Voss and the other men were sitting. For a few moments none of them seemed to be aware of his presence, then Voss looked up and stared directly at him, the colour draining from his face as if he'd seen a ghost. Tremayne met his gaze and smiled slightly.

Then he turned away and walked out of the smoking room.

Chapter 39

12 April 1912
RMS *Titanic*

As they walked down the corridor on C-Deck, Tremayne glanced round, but again there was nobody in sight.

'What happened? Are you hurt?' Maria demanded.

'I'll tell you in a minute,' Tremayne said, as they reached the door of their stateroom, 'but for now, can you just grab a couple of towels from one of the ladies' lavatories while I go inside?'

Maria immediately headed off down the cross passage while Tremayne took out the key and unlocked the door.

When she returned, a couple of minutes later, he had already taken off his jacket and hung it up. Tremayne heard, quite clearly, her sudden intake of breath as she saw the huge blood-stain for the first time.

'Don't worry,' Tremayne said. 'It looks a lot worse than it really is. It's not very deep, but it's bled a lot.'

He started to unbutton his shirt, but Maria walked straight across to him and stopped him.

'No,' she said. 'Let me do it.'

She released the buttons down the front of the shirt, and removed his cufflinks, then eased the material away from his body. Under the shirt, there was an ominous red stain discolouring the towel he had used to cover the wound.

Maria undid the knots on the strips of towel holding the pad in place, and then gently peeled away the blood-soaked material from the untidy knife wound on his side. She used some water to dampen one end of the towel and carefully wiped away the dried blood from the edges of the cut. It was still bleeding, but the flow was obviously much reduced, thanks to Tremayne's rudimentary attempt at first aid.

'You're right,' Maria said. 'It looks a lot worse than it is, and it's probably going to hurt for a few days while the cut heals. But you don't need stitches, which is good, because I suspect that a doctor would want answers to a few awkward questions. In fact, he'd want answers to the same questions that I'm going to ask you, starting with the big and obvious one: what the hell happened?'

While Tremayne explained the events that had taken place on the Promenade Deck, Maria cut one of the towels she had taken from the lavatory to form a pad, then rummaged around in her own portmanteau and removed a basic first-aid kit, which included both pads and bandages. She placed a cotton pad over Tremayne's wound, put the piece of towelling over the top, and then wrapped bandages around his torso to hold the dressing in place.

'Not the neatest job I've ever done,' she said, taking a pace backwards and looking at her handiwork, 'but I think it'll do the trick. I'll unwrap it again in the morning, just to check that there's no sign of any infection, but the wound looks quite clean to me. Does it hurt much?'

'It's pretty numb at the moment, but I suppose it'll start to ache soon. It won't be a problem. It's not the first knife wound I've ever had.'

'I noticed that,' Maria said. 'You've got one or two old scars.'

She packed away her first-aid kit, then turned back to Tremayne. 'One question, before we go any further. You tossed the two bodies over the side, and the knife one of them was carrying, so there's nothing obvious for anyone to find up there. But was there any blood on the deck that I need to go and clean up?'

Tremayne ran over the sequence of the fight in his mind's eye before he replied. 'I don't think so, no,' he said. 'There might be the odd spot from the knife blade when I was stabbed, but that would be all, and they are hardly going to be noticed, even in daylight. Certainly there were no pools or smears of blood, nothing to show what had happened there.'

Maria nodded briskly. 'Good. Now, you'd better get your pyjamas on,' she said. 'I know you probably feel perfectly well, but there's bound to be some shock in the aftermath so what you need is a good night's sleep. And tonight you'll be sleeping in the bed, because you need to be comfortable.'

Tremayne shook his head. 'There's no need for that, Maria. I'll be perfectly all right on the couch. I can't ask you to change places with me.'

'I said you'll be sleeping in the bed. If you recall, I didn't actually say that I would be sleeping on the couch. Now stop arguing and get undressed.'

Fifteen minutes later, they were lying in bed side by side, separated from each other under the covers by a chaste six inches, the lights out and both staring up at the ceiling.

'I was really worried about you tonight,' Maria said. 'Once you left I had no idea what you were doing or where you'd be. For all I knew it could have been you who'd gone over the side of the ship. I can't tell you how relieved I was when you walked back into the lounge, even though you did look a bit the worse for wear.'

'I still don't know how it happened,' Tremayne replied, after a few seconds, 'but obviously Voss or one of the others must have discovered who we are. Or at least, they know that we have an interest in what they're planning to do. Maybe they saw me breaking into Voss's suite, or coming out of it afterwards.'

'I didn't see anybody, but maybe one of his men did see us.'

'Well, it really doesn't matter now. However they found out, Voss and his friends will certainly be on their guard from now on, which is going to make our job a lot more difficult. The only good news is that I managed to eliminate two of his body-guards. So at least I've evened the odds a little.' Tremayne paused and then chuckled softly.

'What?' Maria asked.

'I was just remembering the expression on Voss's face when I walked back into the smoking room. I swear he went white, because right then, at that very moment, he knew something had gone badly wrong and that his ambush had failed, and I was still very much alive.'

Maria rolled sideways, leant over and kissed Tremayne softly on the cheek.

'And I'm really glad that you are,' she said. 'Now shut up and get some sleep.'

Chapter 40

13 April 1912
RMS *Titanic*

'So what do we do now?' Maria asked. 'Voss obviously knows that we're onto him, so he and the others are bound to be on their guard from now on. If I was him, I'd be carrying one of those Luger pistols you said he had in his stateroom, just in case we turn up anywhere near him.'

They were sitting at a table on one side of the dining saloon, finishing their breakfast, cups of coffee in front of them. There were only about twenty passengers still in the saloon, and since they'd been sitting there, they had seen no sign of either their three targets or any men who might have been the two remaining bodyguards.

In view of what happened the previous evening, both Tremayne and Maria were now carrying their Browning pistols, cocked and ready to fire, and with the suppressors already screwed on to the ends of the barrels. The weapons were much bulkier like that – Tremayne's only just fitted in his pocket – but if they had to use them, they knew that the sound of the shots would be enormously reduced.

'I don't know that one of the Lugers would be that much use

to him,' Tremayne replied. 'As I said, the pistols were clearly a presentation pair, and I saw no ammunition in the case with them. Of course, he could have a box of shells tucked away somewhere else, and I expect that his bodyguards are armed. The two I met last night were only carrying knives but they probably had pistols in their staterooms.'

'That still doesn't answer the question: what do we do now? If they're carrying weapons and they're on their guard, how are we going to kill them? We can't just burst into their staterooms firing our own pistols, because we'd be seized and imprisoned on board, and while I don't mind shooting Voss – in fact, it would be a pleasure after what his two goons tried to do to you – I'm not prepared to gun down some innocent ship's officer.'

Tremayne nodded. 'Right now,' he said, 'I don't know what we should do. I don't really have a plan. But ultimately, if we can't devise some way of isolating these men, we may have no option but to find them and shoot them down. That has to be a last resort because if we do end up having a gun battle, it's going to cause a huge diplomatic incident. And there's still the other component of this situation which we have to sort out. Mansfield Cumming wants us to find the lever Voss is intending to use to make his foul plan work. Whatever it is, it has to be highly incriminating to somebody in the American government – maybe even the president himself – so it's probably some kind of document or photograph, something like that. I didn't find anything in Voss's stateroom, so my guess is that, whatever it is, he carries it around with him.'

He fell silent and took a thoughtful sip of his coffee.

'In fact, the only sort of plan I've come up with,' Tremayne said, after a couple of minutes, 'is for us to split up. I don't know if Voss thinks you're my partner, or just with me on the ship as some kind of camouflage, but I'm sure I'm going to be the focus of his attention. And if Voss and his men are occupied watching me, you can watch my back.'

Maria nodded. 'That makes sense. Just tell me that you're not going to wander about on the open decks at night, making yourself an obvious target.'

Tremayne shrugged and gave a rueful grin. 'Not at first I'm not,' he said, 'but you know as well as I do that it might come to that in the end.'

He finished his coffee and stood up to leave.

'Where to?' Maria asked.

'I thought I might go up to the first-class smoking room, and just see what Voss is up to. There'll be plenty of people up there, I expect, and I really don't think he'll dare to try anything in such a public place.'

'You hope. Still, it's your funeral.'

'Actually, I rather hope it isn't,' Tremayne said, leading the way out of the dining saloon.

Chapter 41

13 April 1912
London

Mansfield Cumming stood in his office at Whitehall Court and looked down at the North Atlantic chart again. Then he switched his attention back to the piece of paper in his hand, a page covered with scribbled calculations. He'd done the sums four times now, and each time the overall result had been the same, albeit differing slightly in the details, depending upon the assumptions he'd made about some of the parameters.

The problem was that in these calculations there were no absolutes, only an infinite number of variables. The speed of the *Titanic* had been relatively consistent since the ship's departure from Queenstown, and the course, too, had been more or less what he had expected. But some recent weather reports from other ships operating in the North Atlantic had stated that numerous icebergs had been sighted in the area the liner would be reaching the following day, and obviously that would force the captain to either reduce speed or alter course to avoid them, and quite possibly do both. That was one uncertainty.

The weather would also affect the speed of the submarine. The south-westerly swell was believed to be increasing, and it was possible that the captain of HMS *D4* would have to alter his heading to steer into the oncoming waves, which would inevitably force him to move to the south of the planned track.

The other variable affecting the boat was the length of time the second refuelling might take. According to the Admiralty, the first time the submarine had stopped to take on diesel from the oiler, the evolution had been extremely smooth, apart from the minor incident of the man overboard, which had happily ended with his recovery from the ocean. But that refuelling had taken place in a very calm sea, and Cumming expected that the next time the boat came alongside an oiler, the weather would have deteriorated significantly, and instead of taking perhaps two hours overall, from start to finish, it might easily take twice as long. And stopping for an additional two hours meant that the submarine would be over twenty miles behind its forecast position, assuming it was making in excess of ten knots on the surface. Of course, if the refuelling took even longer than this, then the discrepancy would be even greater.

All in all, it was simply impossible for him to predict exactly where the submarine would be when the *Titanic* reached the rendezvous position that he had calculated earlier. But it was increasingly clear that, short of a miracle, the one place the boat wouldn't be was where he wanted it.

There was only one viable option available to him: he had to move the rendezvous, in terms of both place and time.

He scanned the chart again, the tip of his pencil tracing the predicted route of the ocean liner. Then he drew a circle around one particular point on the ship's course and turned his attention to the submarine's track. He decided to be generous, and allowed a five-hour delay for the refuelling operation to take place. Then he recalculated yet again, and checked his figures twice. He nodded slowly. If he moved the rendezvous to the new position, and as long as the *D4* managed to achieve a minimum speed of ten knots, even if the *Titanic* didn't slow down or alter course, the submarine should still reach the rendezvous about two hours before the liner. And that would be ample time for all the preparations to take place.

Cumming nodded again, double-checked what he had done, and confirmed the new rendezvous position's latitude and longitude, and the new time. Then he walked back to his desk to prepare two new messages: one for the captain of the submarine which would be sent via the Admiralty's communication system, and the other for Alex Tremayne, which he would encode personally.

This change was, Mansfield Cumming realized, almost certainly the last alteration he would be able to make. In order to comply with his new instructions, as soon as the submarine had completed its second scheduled refuelling at sea, it would have to immediately alter course in order to reach the position he had specified by the revised time. Trying to get the boat anywhere else in the diminishing time period which now remained would probably not be possible, so this really was the only chance he had to successfully complete the operation.

Once he'd sent signals, all he would be able to do was wait. And hope.

Chapter 42

13 April 1912
RMS *Titanic*

As soon as Tremayne stepped inside the smoking room, he saw Voss, Bauer and Kortig sitting in their usual seats on the opposite side of the room.

He chose a table close to the door, and well away from the three Prussians, all of whom had ceased talking the moment he had entered the room, and were now staring at him in a hostile fashion across the room.

Tremayne simply ignored the three men, and apparently turned his attention to the book he was carrying. After a few minutes, Voss began talking in a quiet voice to his associates, his eyes still fixed on Tremayne.

Then he stood up and began walking across the smoking room, directly towards him.

Tremayne leant back in his chair as Voss approached, his right hand drifting down to his trouser pocket, where he'd hidden his pistol.

Voss stopped a couple of feet in front of the table and looked down at Tremayne, his features contorting themselves into a forced smile.

'I don't believe we've met,' he said, and waited expectantly.

'My name's Alex Maitland,' Tremayne supplied automatically. He didn't know what Voss was going to say or do to him, but he would observe the rules of politeness. At least at first.

'May I sit down?'

'Of course. I assume you're a first-class passenger, so you can sit anywhere you like.'

Voss drew out a chair and then sat down facing Tremayne.

'I wonder if you can help me?' Voss said. 'I can't seem to find two of my associates. I was supposed to meet them last night, outside the smoking room, but they never appeared. You were here last night, but you left in what looked like a hurry, and you might possibly have seen them somewhere outside, on the Promenade Deck.'

He paused and looked across the table expectantly.

'I'm sorry, I can't help you,' Tremayne replied smoothly. 'I was feeling a bit off colour last evening – I think it was something I ate – and I went outside to get a breath of fresh air. I did see a couple, a middle-aged man and a woman, walking around the Promenade Deck. In fact, I nearly bumped into them when I stepped outside. Could they have been your associates?'

Voss shook his head. 'Of course not. I think you know exactly who I'm talking about, Mr Maitland, if that really is your name.' He glanced around the smoking room, checking that nobody else was in earshot. 'Let me put my cards on the table.'

'Be my guest,' Tremayne replied.

'I know you broke into my stateroom a couple of days ago.'

Tremayne held up his hand. 'That's a very serious accusation to make, Mr – I don't believe you told me your name.'

'My name is Voss, Gunther Voss, as I'm sure you know perfectly well. And there's no point in denying your action, because

I have a witness who saw you unlocking the door and then step inside. Normally, I would simply report the actions of a thief to one of the ship's officers and allow him to take whatever action he felt appropriate. But you, Mr Maitland, are not a thief, are you? You are a different kind of irritation. I suppose you've been sent here to follow me by your government, by that confused group of old, disillusioned, and incompetent men who are trying to run Britain – I refuse to call it "Great Britain" – in these twilight days of your once impressive Empire.'

Tremayne stared at him. 'I'm not sure that I see what you're driving at, Mr Voss, unless your purpose in sitting down at this table is to insult the country of my birth. And if it is, I would thank you to stand up and leave right now.'

Voss shook his head. 'Let's not play games, Maitland. Your nation has had its time. The Empire that you acquired by force, deception and duplicity will soon be fragmented and lost for ever. A new world order is coming, a shift in alliances that will see the final end of the decadent British Empire and the emergence of a new and vibrant nation that will dominate the world for decades to come. One of the oldest and most noble countries in Europe will finally realize its true destiny, aided by the newest nation of them all. And there's nothing you, or anyone else, can do about it. So why don't you just walk away from this? Go back to your masters and tell them that your pathetic attempt to stop this happening has failed dismally. I'll even forget that you killed two of my men.'

Tremayne smiled. 'First you accuse me of being a thief, then some kind of government spy and now, finally, a murderer. I presume you have some kind of proof of all these wild accusations, Voss? Or do you just enjoy ranting and raving at people? Is that your hobby, perhaps?'

Voss's cold eyes bored into him. 'Just keep out of my way, Maitland, or you'll regret it. We're all armed now, in case you were thinking of trying anything physical against us. You were lucky last night. Next time, luck will not be a factor, and that's a promise.'

'That sounded more like a threat to me.'

'Promise, threat, it's all the same,' Voss replied, standing up. 'Just remember what I've said, and if you want to get off this ship alive, make sure you keep out of my way.'

Chapter 43

13 April 1912
HMS *D4*

When the lookout, jammed into the tiny space at the top of the conning tower along with the submarine's First Lieutenant, reported smoke on the horizon, Hutchinson was already wearing his foul-weather gear and was standing in the control room, ready to go topside. He called the two men down, then clattered up the steel ladder himself, binoculars slung around his neck.

The lookout had reported the smoke on the starboard bow and, almost as soon as Hutchinson raised the binoculars to his eyes, he saw it as well. A distant smudge, slightly darker than the surrounding clouds. The ship which had produced the plume was still invisible below the horizon, but Hutchinson had spent the previous ten minutes studying the navigation chart on which the rendezvous position with the second oiler had been marked, and he knew his boat was within thirty miles of that location. So, assuming that the navigation officer on the oiler knew what he was doing, he'd been expecting the ship to be sighted some time that morning, and he had little doubt of the identity of the approaching vessel, simply because of where it was. They'd only seen two other ships since they'd detached from the previous oiler two days earlier, partly because Hutchinson had been instructed to keep clear of all the main transatlantic shipping routes, but mainly because the Atlantic Ocean was an extraordinarily large body of water, and ships, all ships, were comparatively small.

As the two vessels closed with each other, Hutchinson followed the same routine as he had done on a previous occasion: as soon as he could clearly see that the approaching vessel was, in fact, an oiler, he used the signal lamp to send the predetermined challenge to it, and then waited for the appropriate response. Once he'd received it, and then the instructions from the oiler as to the sequence of events which would take place, he called down the voice pipe to the control room.

'Do you hear there. All hands, prepare for refuelling. Preplanned routine. The oiler will turn south-west to minimize ship movement and slow down to maintain steerage way. We will then manoeuvre and take up position on her starboard side. Once the mooring lines are secure, refuelling will commence. All hands, I say again, all hands, involved in this evolution are to wear life jackets and take extreme care while moving around on the decks. Manoeuvring will commence in approximately one-five minutes. All hands, standby.'

Hutchinson secured the voice pipe and looked ahead again. The oiler was now clearly visible without the binoculars, inside ten miles away, and had already altered course very slightly, in preparation for the long turn the vessel would make from its present easterly heading onto south-west.

Then he raised his binoculars again and scanned the entire horizon, searching for any other ships in the area, but saw nothing. The biggest problem they were going to have, he realized, was the sea itself, because the weather today was very different to the previous occasion. It had been raining for most of the morning, but had stopped about twenty minutes earlier, which was the only piece of good news. The swell was running at probably six to eight feet, which had necessitated frequent alterations of course, and had imparted the familiar and uncomfortable corkscrewing motion to the submarine. The wind had risen significantly over the previous twenty-four hours, and was now blowing at, Hutchinson estimated, at least fifteen knots from the south, a stiff breeze which was driving white foam off the tops of the waves. It was a cold, grey and unpleasant day, typical of winter in the North Atlantic.

This refuelling session, he was quite certain, was going to be more difficult, and take a lot longer, than the first one.

Hutchinson looked again at the oiler, which was now some distance off the submarine's starboard bow, and was just commencing its right turn. The plan, conveyed in terse sentences by the signal lamp, was for the oiler to turn in front of the submarine and then reduce speed once it had steadied on its new heading. The boat would then also turn onto south-west, crossing the oiler's wake, and come alongside the larger vessel, matching speed with it as quickly as possible.

Hutchinson watched as the ship turned ahead of him, then issued the appropriate orders.

'Ten degrees left rudder. Steer course two-three-five magnetic. Set engine revolutions for five knots.'

He listened to the responses from the control room, ensuring that his orders were being followed accurately, then looked ahead again. The oiler had slowed and was steady on the heading chosen for refuelling, but was pitching up and down in the swell. As he watched, members of the ship's company began lowering fenders of various shapes and sizes over the starboard side, to act as buffers between the two vessels.

'Engine revolutions for three knots,' Hutchinson ordered, as the submarine began to close on the oiler.

The motion of the submarine was much worse, the pitching noticeably more pronounced, at this slower speed, but there was nothing they could do about that.

When the boat was within about 200 yards of the ship, he ordered the refuelling team out on deck.

'Keep hold of the safety lines,' he shouted as the half a dozen men climbed out of the after hatch, 'and watch your footing down there.'

He watched critically as the submarine nosed closer to the oiler, and ordered slight changes to the engine revolutions to match its speed. When the boat was precisely abeam the midships section of the oiler, orders were shouted on board the ship, and two heaving lines flew out, landing across the boat's fore and after decks, where they were quickly grabbed by the waiting crewmen. Immediately, they began hauling on them, pulling the heavy mooring ropes across the gap between the two vessels, and then securing them to the deck bollards.

To Hutchinson's palpable relief, both mooring lines were attached quickly, his men working smoothly and efficiently, despite the waves that were breaking over the low decks of the submarine, and the boat's pitching. Another line followed, and that was attached to a thick black hose, which his men quickly secured to the refuelling point, and minutes later the tanks were being replenished with diesel.

They had just started pumping the fuel when a signalman appeared in the conning tower holding an envelope.

'Sir. A signal for you, classified secret and marked "most urgent",' he said.

Hutchinson barely even glanced at him, concentrating totally on the refuelling, watching the actions of his men and alert for any mistakes that could injure one of them or disrupt the operation.

'I don't care who it's from or how urgent it is,' he said. 'It can wait. Take it away. I'll be down to look at it when this is finished.'

Chapter 44

13 April 1912
RMS *Titanic*

In the first-class smoking room, Gunther Voss watched with satisfaction as the British agent – because he had no doubt in his own mind that that was what the man calling himself 'Maitland' actually was – stood up and left the room.

He'd debated with Bauer and Kortig about the confrontation, but he'd come to the conclusion that he had nothing to lose by telling the Englishman that his mission was futile. Maitland could not have found anything in Voss's stateroom, because there was nothing in it to find, just as he would have found nothing if he'd searched the suites of the other two men. Each of the three had a sealed and waterproof pouch, the contents of which were vital to the success of their plan, and each of them carried their pouch about their person at all times.

So Maitland could snoop about as much as he wanted, but he wouldn't find anything. The crates of special paper, the watermarks virtually identical to those on the current British ten- and twenty-pound notes, and the professionally produced printing plates for the same value notes, which Bauer and Kortig would use to flood the currency markets with counterfeit sterling notes almost as soon as the ship docked in New York, were locked away securely in one of the *Titanic*'s holds, well out of Maitland's reach. And now Voss had told him that all three of them were armed, he doubted very much if the Englishman would dare try anything else.

'Is that it, then?' Bauer asked, as the smoking-room door closed behind Maitland.

Voss nodded. 'Probably, yes. Now he knows that we're onto him, there's nothing much he can do. He'll probably still try following us about the ship, and he might even pick the lock and try searching one of your staterooms, but it won't do him any good. He won't attack us, because I told him that we're all carrying weapons, and if he is stupid enough to try anything, we can simply shoot him down.

'The closest police force to us now is in New York City, and if one of us did end up killing him, I can pretty much guarantee we wouldn't have any problem when the ship docks. We'd be three respected American businessman who'd been attacked by a renegade Englishman who was also an accomplished thief. Don't forget that we have an eyewitness to him breaking into my stateroom, and I have powerful friends in the New York police force. In any American court – if it ever came to that, which I doubt – the verdict would be self-defence.'

Voss smiled, an expression of smug self-satisfaction crossing his face.

'No,' he finished, 'you can forget about Maitland and that woman. And if he gets *really* annoying, I'll tell Vincent to kill him, and this time he can use a gun and do the job properly.'

Chapter 45

13 April 1912
HMS *D4*

Perhaps because of the unfavourable weather conditions, which would have concentrated their minds, and no doubt also partly because of the lessons they had already learned from the previous refuelling operation, on this occasion his men made no mistakes and everything went like clockwork. Nevertheless, the refuelling took almost three hours, mainly because of the extra time which the submarine had taken to get into position and secure the lines from the oiler in the inclement weather conditions.

Hutchinson remained in the conning tower the entire time, watching everything and everyone, until the last link between the two vessels – the forward mooring line – was finally released, and he ordered ten degrees right rudder and engine revolutions for four knots, which slowly moved the boat away from the side of the oiler. And even then he remained in the conning tower for a further ten minutes, until the two vessels were well separated and the submarine was once again established on its pre-programmed transatlantic track, before he finally climbed down the ladder to the control room.

Hutchinson removed his foul-weather clothing, which dripped water onto the steel deck of his boat, poured himself a hot coffee to try to warm up, then told the signalman to bring the envelope containing the classified and urgent message to his cabin.

He signed for the message, opened the envelope, and looked at the encrypted text. Whatever it was, he didn't expect that it would be good news. For a few minutes he didn't move, just sat at his desk drinking his coffee. Then he walked across to his safe, unlocked it and removed the code book, then sat down again and started to decrypt the message.

It wasn't that long, and really only contained one additional instruction, or rather two amendments to his original orders. The rendezvous position, and the time at which he was to be there, had both been changed. The new position was several miles to the south-east of the original rendezvous, which meant the boat had a shorter distance to cover, but instead of getting there at noon on the fifteenth, he would have to be at the new rendezvous a little over twelve hours earlier. The orders specified that he should aim to reach the position by twenty hundred hours – eight in the evening – on the fourteenth, which would allow him time to loiter in the area, and the absolute latest time he had to be there was twenty-two hundred hours, ten o'clock.

Hutchinson jotted down the coordinates, the latitude and longitude, of the new rendezvous, then walked back into the control room and bent over the North Atlantic plotting chart. He took a pencil and a parallel ruler, and drew a neat cross on the chart at the precise coordinates he had been given. The position of his submarine was of course also marked, together with the time of the last fix, just under ten minutes earlier. That meant the position was slightly out, but not enough to be significant.

Hutchinson used the ruler and drew a pencil line between the last fix and the new rendezvous, and then opened up the ruler so that the other straight edge passed through the centre of the nearest compass rose on the chart, and read off the appropriate bearing.

That gave him a theoretical course to steer, but obviously the wind and open ocean currents would have an effect on the boat's track. Hutchinson did a quick mental calculation and amended the course by a few degrees. Then he turned to the helmsman and issued his new orders.

'Twenty degrees left rudder, and steer two-three-zero degrees. Engine revolutions for twelve knots.'

'Aye, aye, sir. Course two-three-zero, speed twelve knots.'

'Right,' Hutchinson said. 'I'm going to try and get my head down for a couple of hours. Number One, you have the boat. Our new course and rendezvous position are on the chart. My standard orders apply. Wake me if we sight another vessel, or if any department reports a fault, or if for any reason you are unhappy with any aspect of the vessel, its operation, or our navigation.'

The First Lieutenant, another lieutenant and a seaman officer only a few months junior to Hutchinson named William Evans, nodded agreement.

'Aye, aye, sir. Sleep well.'

'Tricky, in this sardine can,' Hutchinson retorted, then left the control room.

Chapter 46

13 April 1912
RMS *Titanic*

Tremayne had given it fifteen minutes and then, after a final glance across the smoking room towards Voss and the other two men, he stood up and walked out.

Sitting at the table near the door were two heavily built, hard-faced men. As he passed them, both men gave him a flat, cold stare, and one mimed pulling a gun and shooting him.

Tremayne ignored them both, checked that neither of them was following behind him as he left and then, a few moments later, he strode into the lounge and sat down beside Maria.

Despite his placid appearance, she could tell that Tremayne was seething inside.

'What's happened?' she asked.

'That arrogant bastard Voss has just warned me off. He's told me he knows I'm a government agent, and said, in so many words, that it was far too late to stop the alliance happening. He virtually promised me that the British Empire would crumble in a few years, and from its ashes would emerge a new and glorious German nation.'

'Not much of a surprise there then,' Maria remarked, with a slight smile. 'Did he say anything else?'

'Only to warn me that all of them are now carrying pistols and to suggest, slightly obliquely, that it would be better for my health if I didn't wander about on the open decks after dark.'

'He's obviously trying to goad you,' she said.

'Yes,' Tremayne replied, 'and he's succeeding. But don't worry,' he added, 'things like that irritate the life out of me, but they don't affect the way I do my job. It'll just make the moment I slice his throat all the sweeter.'

He leaned back in his seat and then grimaced slightly as a sudden throbbing pain lanced through his side.

Maria noticed immediately and extended her arm to help him.

'You're hurting,' she said. 'Has the cut opened up again?'

Tremayne shook his head. 'I don't think so,' he replied. 'It's just the kind of pain you'd expect from a wound like that. I've had a couple of similar injuries in the past.'

'I know.'

Tremayne looked at her quizzically. 'Has Mansfield Cumming been telling tales out of school again?' he asked.

'No,' Maria replied. 'I saw your scars, remember?'

'So you did,' he nodded. 'Well, last night didn't go anything like I planned it. I'd hoped that by now we would have taken care of at least one of the targets, and nobody on the ship would have been any the wiser. Instead, all three men are alive, perfectly well, forearmed about our intentions – or at least about my identity – and are now carrying pistols, just in case we try anything, and the deadline's getting closer with every minute that passes. All I succeeded in doing was tossing a couple of bodyguards over the side and I managed to get myself stabbed in the process. It isn't what you might call an auspicious start.'

Maria smiled somewhat sadly at him. 'I have to confess that I've never before embarked on an operation which has begun in quite such a disastrous fashion as this one. And you also didn't mention that we have no backup and no support and, as far as I can see, no obvious way of retrieving the situation. Back home, I'd say we were screwed.'

'Thanks,' Tremayne said. 'That makes me feel a whole lot better.'

'And I have a feeling,' Maria said, 'that there may be more bad news still to come.'

'What? How do you know?'

'I don't. I'm just guessing.'

She pointed towards the door at the far end of the lounge, where a pageboy had just entered. He held a white envelope in his left hand, and he was looking hopefully around the tables and chairs, clearly searching for someone.

'After all that's happened,' Maria went on, 'I'm almost prepared to bet that that's another message from Mansfield Cumming, and it'll be news that we really don't want to hear.'

'I've seen you play poker,' Tremayne replied, 'and I wouldn't take that bet.'

At the other end of the lounge, the pageboy looked directly at him, and the puzzled frown on his face suddenly vanished. He walked smartly through the room towards them, stopped a respectful two paces away and asked the question that Tremayne had been expecting ever since he'd first seen the lad.

'Excuse me, sir, but are you Mr Maitland?'

Tremayne nodded, and held out his hand for the message that the pageboy was offering him.

'Thank you,' he said, and as soon as the pageboy had left, he opened the envelope.

'Mansfield?' Maria asked.

'Mansfield,' Tremayne confirmed, scanning the columns of letters. He glanced round to make sure that nobody could see what he was doing, reached for his notebook, wrote out the correct keyword and started to decrypt the message.

About five minutes later he sat back and read the plain text version to Maria.

'Is that all?' she asked. 'He's just changed the time we're supposed to have completed this operation?'

'That's it. That's all he said, apart from reminding us again to send that signal when everything was finished, and changing the time by which we have to transmit it, because of the revised deadline. So we now have twelve hours less than we expected to complete an operation which is probably impossible.'

'Terrific. I suppose there's no point in asking you if you've had any bright ideas?'

'Not really,' Tremayne replied. 'I've only come up with one possibility, and I don't think you'll like it.'

'Try me,' Maria suggested.

'I'll tell you downstairs, in the stateroom. You go first, and I'll follow in a couple of minutes.'

Maria gave him a quizzical glance, but didn't argue or question him. She simply nodded, picked up her book and her handbag, stood up and walked out of the lounge.

Tremayne read the decoded message sent by Mansfield Cumming once more, then put the original and his notebook back into his pocket and stood up himself. He walked across to one of the large panoramic windows which were a feature of the first-class lounge, and for a few moments just stared out at the ocean.

Then he glanced round, checking that nobody was paying him any attention, turned and strode out of the room. Before he walked down the passageway to the staircase, he made sure nobody else was in sight and took similar precautions in each of the lobby areas as he descended the staircase to C-Deck.

A few minutes later, he opened the door to the stateroom and stepped inside, closing and locking the door behind him.

Maria was sitting on the edge of the bed, waiting for him.

'That was all very mysterious,' she said. 'What's going on?'

'I'm just trying to keep both of us out of sight,' Tremayne said, 'at least as a couple. Look, it occurred to me that if we just try and tackle them one by one, there's a good chance that we'll either get shot ourselves, because Voss and his cronies will pull out their pistols and start blasting away, or at the very least we'll end up under lock and key on board the ship when the gun fight's over. Neither is what you might call a satisfactory outcome for us.'

'Agreed. So what do you suggest?'

'Voss knows what I look like, that's perfectly obvious, and I'm quite sure that he'll probably start having his men watch me whenever I'm on deck or in the public rooms, just to make sure I don't get too close to him or the other two men. In fact, I'm surprised he hasn't done that already.

'He might possibly have noticed you as well, because we've been together in some of the public rooms and the restaurants, but I think he's focused on me. I'm the danger, he thinks, especially after what happened last night, when the two men he sent out to kill me vanished without a trace. He might think you're just my lookout or something. But what I'm quite certain of is that he won't see you as a threat, simply because you're a woman. And that might be the only advantage we have right now.'

'You mean you want me to do the killings?' Maria asked.

Tremayne shook his head. 'No. What I was thinking about was using you as a decoy, or maybe as a lure, putting you in a situation where you could persuade one of the men to drop his guard. Then I can step in and take care of him in a permanent fashion.'

Maria didn't look convinced. 'I'm not entirely sure you've thought this through,' she said. 'Let's just suppose I fluttered my eyelashes at Bauer – which is not something I'd normally contemplate doing in even my worst nightmares – and managed to persuade him to follow me down some dark corridor so that you could bash him on the head and then throw him over the side. That might work once but, even if I changed my appearance with a wig or something, and I do actually have a couple with me, I can't see all of them falling for it, one after the other, and certainly not Voss. We need to eliminate all three of them, not just one or two, and they're almost always together, so how could we split one off?'

'We think the same way,' Tremayne said, 'and as I see it there are only two possibilities now. We could try and tackle them all at once, by waiting until the smoking room is empty and then simply shooting them and getting rid of our weapons immediately, but that situation might never present itself.'

'I'd be amazed if it did,' Maria commented. 'And the other option?'

'What I was about to suggest. We hit them the only time when we can be certain they'll be alone: in their staterooms. You appear at the door, maybe dressed as a stewardess, and either ask them to go with you to the Purser's Office or somewhere, or just persuade them to let you inside to check something. Either way, once they've dropped their guard, they'll be vulnerable.'

Maria nodded slowly, then sighed.

'What is it?' Tremayne asked.

'I know this is going to sound stupid, but this all feels a bit unsporting, almost. I mean, I know what these three men are trying to do, and I absolutely agree that they have to be stopped. But to trick them into letting me inside their cabins, and then for you to burst in and knife them or whatever, it's like shooting a sitting bird. It's just not fair.'

'They are armed,' Tremayne pointed out. 'It's not as if they're three defenceless victims. Even if I did burst into their cabin, there's no guarantee I wouldn't come off worse.'

'I know that, Alex, I do know that, but it still leaves a nasty taste in my mouth.'

Chapter 47

13 April 1912
London

One of the problems that Mansfield Cumming was facing was the complete lack of any information about what was happening on board the *Titanic*. Or, to be absolutely accurate, he was still getting updates from his contact at the White Star Line headquarters about the ship's position, heading, speed and so on, which he was still religiously plotting on the North Atlantic chart in his office. He was also receiving a daily summary of information relating to events on board the ship, but all of this information was essentially routine, and that was now beginning to concern him, because the lack of any reports of missing passengers or unexplained deaths suggested that Tremayne had so far failed to carry out any part of his mission. Cumming had hoped that by now his agents would have eliminated at least one of their three targets.

Or, if they had achieved it, they must have managed it in such a way that nobody on the ship had any knowledge of it, which seemed unlikely at best. The absence of three first-class passengers would surely have been remarked on by somebody, and that would eventually have filtered up the chain of command to the captain, and hence would have been transmitted to the company.

Cumming, of course, had his backup plan in case the mission on board the ship failed for any reason, but he had hoped that he would not have needed to reveal details of it to Tremayne and Maria Weston; it really was a drastic solution, an absolute plan of last resort, which he had believed all along he would never have to use, and that he would have been able to keep secret for all time. But he was also conscious that time was passing, and that if Tremayne's mission didn't succeed in the very near future, he would have absolutely no option but to implement that plan.

With the greatest possible reluctance, Cumming took a new sheet of paper and began composing another message to be sent to the *Titanic*, which he again marked 'Most Urgent', and had it sent by the fastest possible method to the ship.

Then all he could do was wait for Tremayne's response.

Chapter 48

13 April 1912
RMS *Titanic*

Tremayne and Maria were still in their stateroom when there was a knock on the door. In one swift movement, Maria opened her handbag, extracted her Browning pistol and stood up, hiding the weapon behind her back. Tremayne checked that he was clear of her line of fire, then stepped across to the door.

'Who is it?' he asked.

The reply was slightly muffled, but clear enough. 'I have a message for you, Mr Maitland, sir.'

'One of the pageboys,' Tremayne said, taking his own pistol out of his pocket and tucking it into the rear waistband of his trousers, where it would be easier to reach if he was wrong about the identity of the person standing on the other side of the door. Then he released the bolt and eased the door open a few inches.

Standing in the corridor outside was one of the pageboys, clutching another white envelope, which he handed over, and then walked away. Tremayne closed and locked the door again, then tore open the flap on the envelope and removed the message that was inside.

'More orders or changes,' he muttered, then sat down and began the decoding process.

The message was long, and Tremayne worked on it for about twenty minutes before he was able to read the plain text original. Then he read it again, the colour draining from his face as he did so.

'This is madness,' he said, 'sheer madness.'

'What?' Maria demanded.

'I think Cumming has literally gone mad.' Tremayne turned in his chair at the occasional table and looked across at Maria. 'First of all, he has specifically instructed me not to divulge the contents of this message to you.'

'So why are you telling me?' Maria asked.

'Because I don't work that way. We're a team, and that means we share the risks and the rewards, and especially we share information. I'm not prepared to keep any secrets from you, and I would hope that you would have the same attitude. We're in this together, so what I know, you know.'

Maria nodded. 'I can't work any other way,' she agreed.

'Exactly.' Tremayne glanced back at the decoded message in his notebook, then looked over at Maria again. 'You remember one of his earlier instructions, when he told us we had to send a particular message from the ship once we'd completed the operation?'

Maria nodded.

'Do you know why he wanted that message sent?'

'Yes. It seemed fairly obvious. It was so that he could cancel whatever reception committee he was organizing to meet Voss and the other two men in New York after the ship docked there, assuming that we hadn't managed to kill them on the ship.'

Tremayne nodded. 'That's exactly what I thought as well, but we were both wrong. According to this message, Mansfield Cumming has put a rather more brutal solution in place. He claims that he has the full support of the British government, and that the Prime Minister has personally agreed to the course of action he has arranged. Apparently, they all believe that the threat posed by Voss and the other two men is so great that almost any sacrifice is worth making to prevent this alliance from being achieved. They are certain that if America and Germany do join together, a devastating war will start within a matter of months, and will probably involve most of the countries of the world as the British Empire fights for its very survival. There's also the matter of the counterfeit printing plates and the special paper in the crates in the hold, which Cumming is adamant should not be allowed to reach New York to avoid a massive run on the pound starting as soon as the fake currency hits the streets.'

'But we knew all that. That's why we're here.'

Tremayne nodded. 'I know. I'm just telling you what the message says. Cumming finishes that section with a sentence which I think I'll remember for the rest of my life. He says: "In this perilous situation we must act for the greater good of the greatest number." He's trying to justify the sacrifice of a small number of people against the possible death toll that might result if war does break out.'

'I know. Those three Prussian conspirators,' Maria said.

But Tremayne shook his head. 'No, not just the three Prussians. If we don't get a message to him by twenty-two hundred hours tomorrow, stating that we've completed this operation, orders will be issued to a British submarine to sink this ship using torpedoes.'

'What? He can't do that! We're in the middle of the Atlantic Ocean. The loss of life would be catastrophic.'

Her voice died away as she realized that that was precisely why Cumming had chosen the date and time. If the *Titanic* was to sink on this voyage, it had to be in deep water, to prevent the wreckage ever being recovered and showing what had caused the catastrophe, and to ensure the maximum possible loss of life, including the three Prussians.

'Oh, dear God,' she muttered. 'He's serious, isn't he?'

'He's very serious,' Tremayne replied. 'He's prepared to sacrifice the lives of everyone on this ship – over two thousand people – against the possible casualties in a war that might never happen.'

'And that includes us,' Maria said, in a small voice.

For a few moments neither of them spoke, alone with their thoughts. Then Maria broke the silence.

'We could send the message anyway, and argue about it later,' she suggested. 'I refuse to have the deaths of two thousand people on my conscience.'

Tremayne shook his head. 'I know Mansfield Cumming. I've known him for years. He'll have some kind of a checking mechanism in place. He'll have a contact in the White Star Line management who would signal the ship and tell them to confirm the whereabouts of Voss, Bauer and Kortig, and if any of the three are still on board, Cumming will know that we failed. And then he'll authorize the submarine to attack.'

'So what do we do, then?'

'As I see it,' Tremayne replied grimly, 'the only thing we can do is exactly what he told us to do in the first place. We don't have a choice. We either kill those three men – somehow – or we'll be complicit in the deaths of every man, woman and child on board this liner. And, like you, I couldn't live with that on my conscience.'

Chapter 49

13 April 1912
HMS *D4*

The good news, as far as the crew of the submarine were concerned, was that the new course the boat was steering was almost directly into the swell which was still running from the south-west. The result was that the corkscrewing motion of the submarine had virtually stopped, and the boat was now simply pitching up and down as the vessel rode over the waves. Although it was still quite uncomfortable – the submarine displaced less than 500 tons on the surface, and was much smaller than most craft that ventured out into the major oceans of the world – the pitching was much easier to cope with.

Lieutenant Hutchinson had also been able to order a slight increase in speed, only another knot, but it would mean that over the next twenty-four hours, at the end of which the boat had been ordered to be in position, he would have covered an additional twenty-four miles, the equivalent of almost two and a half hours' steaming at normal cruising speed. That would act as a slight buffer in the event of the weather worsening or the sea state increasing, either of which could result in a reduction in speed.

But if all went well, and the weather held, it looked as if the submarine would reach the designated rendezvous position at least two hours ahead of time: a slim enough margin, but a margin nevertheless.

And now it was time for the other preparations to be made, preparations which had been specified in exhaustive detail in the sealed and classified orders Hutchinson had been given. He took a last look round at the empty horizon, now barely visible in the gathering dusk, and clattered down the metal ladder to the control room. There, he checked that all the instruments were reading correctly, then beckoned to the First Lieutenant and led him into his cabin.

'I know this has been a pretty dammed strange exercise so far, Bill, but I think up to now we've acquitted ourselves fairly well. The two refuelling sessions went quite smoothly, and I think we've probably proved the point for their Lordships in the Admiralty. We've shown that a submarine can successfully operate a long way outside coastal waters, as long as it's properly supported, as we've been. I think we might have surprised a few people, actually.'

William Evans smiled. He, too, had been pleased – and, in truth, a little surprised – at how reliable the submarine had turned out to be. The new Vickers diesel engines fitted in the D-Class boats were proving to be a whole lot more reliable, and an awful lot safer, than the petrol units fitted in the older C-Class submarines. Yes, the fuel didn't smell very good, but at least there was no chance of the boat filling with highly flammable fumes that could be ignited by the slightest spark, with devastating consequences. Diesel engines, it seemed to him, definitely represented the road ahead, and not just for submarines.

'I agree, sir. I think we've done very well, better than I

expected, certainly. But I won't be sorry when we get the order to turn back and head for home. And I know the men feel exactly the same.'

Hutchinson nodded. 'That shouldn't be too long now,' he replied, 'but it's possible that we'll still have one more evolution left to perform before we turn around. I won't know for certain until I get another signal from the Admiralty, but we might be doing a live firing on a target when we get to the rendezvous position, and we need to get the preparations underway now, just in case. Tell the weapon artificers to prepare two torpedoes and then load both the bow tubes ready for firing.'

Evans nodded. 'Dummy warheads, I presume?' he asked.

'No,' Hutchinson said. 'Live warheads. Tell them to take their time, and make sure they get everything right, but both weapons must be ready and loaded in the tubes no later than fifteen hundred hours tomorrow. Any questions or any problems, let me know immediately.'

Evans nodded again, but looked somewhat quizzically at Hutchinson as he left the cabin and walked back into the control room to issue the appropriate orders.

Hutchinson shrugged. He had no option but to deceive Evans, the same way he was deceiving the rest of the crew. His orders were absolutely specific, and came from a level in the command structure which made it impossible to disobey, or even to question them. The reality was that he still had no idea what he was supposed to be doing steaming around the Atlantic Ocean in a submarine carrying live weapons.

Perhaps the next classified and encrypted signal the boat would receive would provide him with an explanation. But somehow, he doubted it.

Chapter 50

14 April 1912
RMS *Titanic*

'It's time,' Tremayne murmured, glancing again at his watch. It was just after four thirty in the morning, and both he and Maria were still fully dressed. They'd slept for a short while, until just after three, and then spent the last hour and a half trying to decide not what they should do – they already knew that, because of the unequivocal final message Tremayne had received from Mansfield Cumming – but exactly how they should do it.

And, in the end, there seemed to be only one possible way they could achieve their goal: they would have to tackle each of the three conspirators in their staterooms, one by one, when they were alone and, hopefully, asleep, and make sure they were all dead by the morning.

It wasn't much of a plan, realistically, and it largely depended on Tremayne's ability to pick the door locks quickly – and above all silently – and on the corridors of the giant ship being deserted while they moved from one stateroom to another. And, obviously, on their intended victims not being wide awake and sitting waiting for them, armed with loaded pistols.

'Have you got everything?' Maria asked, getting up from the bed where she'd been lying down.

Tremayne nodded, and pointed at the occasional table where he'd laid out the tools he was going to need. His leather case of lock picks was next to his pistol, the suppressor still attached to the end of the barrel, and beside that lay the cosh and garrotte. The last item was a small steel tin which Maria hadn't seen before.

'What's that?' she asked.

Tremayne clicked open the lid to show her. Inside was a syringe, two needles and four small glass bottles containing a straw-coloured liquid.

'What you're looking at are four cases of instant heart attack. Just load up the syringe, stick the needle in someone's arm and press the plunger, and thirty seconds later they're dead. It's quick and allegedly painless.'

Maria looked at the steel case with interest. 'That might be the best option, if you can use it,' she said. 'Somebody dying of a heart attack on board the ship is sad, but hopefully no-one would suspect foul play, and we wouldn't have to lug the body up to the outside decks and throw it over the side. Mind you, three cases of heart attack might be a bit more difficult to explain. Does that stuff leave any traces in the body?'

Tremayne shook his head. 'I've no idea,' he replied. 'The instructions, if you could call them that, didn't mention it. But even if it does, there should be nothing to link us with the simultaneous deaths of three other first-class passengers. Obviously, once we've done the job, all the evidence that we were involved goes over the side of the ship. In fact, if you think about it, a ship is an ideal place to commit a murder; the ocean will swallow both the body and the evidence.'

'I hope you're right.'

Maria still sounded unhappy about what they were about to do, and in truth, Tremayne didn't feel comfortable with it either, but they had absolutely no choice in the matter, and both of them knew it.

He slipped the pistol into the right-hand pocket of his trousers, and distributed the remaining tools, for want of a better word, into his other pockets. He had the sheath for the stiletto strapped to his left arm, under his jacket, the knife already in it. Maria would be carrying nothing apart from her handbag which contained her Browning with the suppressor attached. She would be the eyes and the ears at the back of Tremayne's head.

She opened the door of their stateroom as quietly as she could, and peered out into the corridor, glancing in both directions. Lights were burning, but there was no sign of life, no indication that anybody on that deck of the ship was awake. And that suited them fine.

They walked down the short corridor to the lobby beside the staircase and climbed quietly up to the deck above, where they knew that Bauer and Kortig had their staterooms. As they stepped into that staircase lobby they separated, Tremayne walking to one side of the ship to check the corridors in both directions, and Maria to do the same on the other side. Just as on the deck below, all the passageways appeared to be deserted, which is what they'd hoped.

'This way,' Tremayne whispered, and led the way down the corridor towards Jonas Bauer's stateroom. As with most of the first-class accommodation, not every stateroom had en suite facilities, and there were a number of cross passages running between the main port and starboard corridors, in which bathrooms and lavatories were located. The first of these passages was almost opposite one of the two doors that gave access to Bauer's suite, which would allow Maria to keep out of sight, while still being able to check for people approaching down the corridors.

'Which door?' she mouthed.

Tremayne pointed first at one door, and then at the other one, and whispered: 'Lounge, and bedroom.'

He gestured silently to her, and she slipped into the cross passage and waited there. He glanced in both directions, but neither heard nor saw anybody. He took the leather case out of his pocket, selected two of the tools from inside it, again checked that he was unobserved, then crouched down and began working on the lock of the door leading to the bedroom of the suite.

It didn't take long. In less than a minute there was a faint click, and Tremayne was able to turn the handle and ease the door open the barest fraction of an inch. Then he stopped, replaced the case in his pocket, took out his cosh and motioned for Maria to follow him. Jonas Bauer was a big man, and subduing him might be easier with the two of them.

The one thing Tremayne had not brought with him on board the ship, was an electric torch, and as he peered through the crack between the door and the frame into the darkness of the stateroom, he regretted the omission. The other obvious problem was that the corridor lamps were burning brightly and would throw a sudden flood of light into the room as soon as he opened the door fully, and that might well be enough to wake the sleeping occupant. But that was a chance he was simply going to have to take.

Tremayne glanced behind him, to make sure that Maria was there, nodded to her, then pushed open the door and stepped inside.

The light from the corridor revealed a bedchamber that looked just as opulent as the one Voss had taken. As he glanced round, Tremayne saw the same kind of luxurious furnishings – elegant chairs, tables and decorations – with the bed positioned over to his right. He took all that in, and immediately stepped forward.

The moment he did that, he noticed that although the covers on the bed showed that it had obviously been slept in, there was nobody lying there.

And as his steps faltered with the realization that his target was not where he expected him to be, a pair of hands seized him around the neck and began to efficiently choke the life out of him.

Chapter 51

14 April 1912
RMS *Titanic*

Tremayne gasped with shock, and then reacted. He reached up, grabbed the wrists of the man standing behind him, and started to bend forward, to try to throw his attacker completely over his body and break the man's grip. But before he could complete the move, there was a dull thud from behind, and the grip on his neck was immediately released.

Tremayne whirled round, his right hand lifting up his cosh, but then relaxed again. In the light spilling into the stateroom from the corridor, he could see Maria standing about four feet away, the Browning pistol held firmly in her right hand, but reversed so that she was grasping it by the slide and suppressor, effectively turning the weapon into a very efficient club. At her feet lay the crumpled figure of Jonas Bauer, blood oozing from a wound on his right temple.

'Are you all right?' she asked Tremayne, who was massaging the sides of his neck where the banker had grabbed him.

'Yes. And thank you for your intervention.'

'You didn't need me,' Maria said with a slight smile. 'I saw what you were going to do, but I just thought it might be better to knock him out before you started throwing him all around the stateroom and breaking the beautiful furniture. I hope,' she added, looking critically at her pistol, 'that I didn't bend the barrel or anything on his thick skull.'

'The Browning's a good pistol,' Tremayne said, looking around the stateroom. 'It'll take a lot more than that to do it any serious damage.'

He walked behind Maria to the open door, peered out, checking in both directions, then stepped back inside, closed and locked the door and switched on the electric light. He looked down at the unconscious man and nodded.

'I know it's not exactly the way we planned it,' he said, fishing in his pocket and producing the metal container supplied by Mansfield Cumming, 'but now we can actually make this a believable scenario.'

He took out the syringe, attached a needle and then removed the top of one of the small bottles and drew the liquid inside it into the instrument. Bauer was wearing a pair of garish striped pyjamas, and Tremayne was able to easily roll up one sleeve to expose his upper arm. He located a vein in the crook of the man's elbow, slid the needle into it and depressed the plunger on the syringe.

Nothing happened for a few seconds, and then Bauer gave a sudden shudder, twitched and then fell still, all movement in his body ceasing.

Tremayne felt for a pulse in the man's neck, and then in his wrist, but could detect nothing.

'That's it,' he murmured, carefully removing the needle and packing it and the syringe back into the metal case.

'Whatever that stuff is,' Maria said, 'it's certainly very effective.'

A tiny drop of blood had appeared where Tremayne had inserted in the needle, and he wiped it off with a towel he found in the en suite bathroom.

'If anyone even notices that,' he said, indicating the towel, 'they'll just assume that he cut himself shaving.'

He looked around the bedroom, then back down at Bauer.

'He was severely overweight, and I don't suppose a heart attack at his age and in his condition would surprise anyone too much. It'll look as if he felt unwell, got out of bed, perhaps to try to summon help, then he fell to the floor, smashing his head as he did so. Probably on this,' he added, wiping the bloodied towel on one corner of the seat of a nearby chair.

Tremayne put the towel back in the bathroom and then walked into the bedroom to stand beside the body. He and Maria stared down at the corpse, their backs to the door. Neither of them saw the handle of the door turn slowly and silently as somebody tried to get in from the corridor outside. But Tremayne had locked it, and the door didn't budge. After a few seconds, the handle turned back the other way.

'We'll take a quick look round while we're here,' he said, 'just in case Bauer has been obliging enough to leave out anything incriminating.'

He and Maria checked in all the obvious places – the drawers and cupboards and a small and clearly expensive leather case on one of the chairs – but found nothing of any interest until Tremayne felt under the still-warm pillow on the bed. Then his fingers closed around an oblong packet. He pulled it out and examined it carefully.

'This looks like a waterproof pouch,' he said, opening it at one end and extracting a sealed envelope. 'Whatever's in this is important.'

He ripped open the envelope and looked at the contents, half a dozen copies of what looked like financial documents of some kind.

'What are they?' Maria asked.

Tremayne looked at each in turn, an unreadable expression on his face. Then he handed them all to Maria.

'Here,' he said, 'these don't make any sense to me.'

Maria stared at the pages one after the other, and then nodded. 'They do to me,' she said, after a moment. 'I did some training as an accountant – not the most exciting few months of my life. These are copies of documents, of contracts and other agreements for financial transactions, and the only common factor is the signature at the bottom. The signature of the President of the United States of America. I don't know exactly what these documents refer to, but from the looks of them they provide evidence of a colossal misuse of power, of corruption at the highest possible level. And the sums of money listed in these transactions are eye-watering.'

'Would they be enough to compel the president to do what Voss wants?'

'I don't know, but because of what's been going on, I assume they must be,' she replied, handing back the copies to Tremayne, who replaced them in the envelope.

'I think that explains the lever Voss has then, doesn't it?' he said. 'But by themselves, these copies probably aren't enough, because they could be faked. What we have to do is find the original documents, and my guess is that Voss will have those.'

'You don't suppose he might have them stored in a bank vault somewhere?'

'I doubt it. I don't think Voss would trust these to a bank. These documents are his ace in the hole and he would want them with him at all times. These copies are just confirmation of their possession of the originals. I assume that Kortig will have a set as well. We need to recover all of them, and especially we need the originals, because if these fall into the wrong hands – I mean, Voss having them is bad enough – the consequences could be catastrophic. We need to find them, and destroy them.'

Chapter 52

14 April 1912
RMS *Titanic*

Ten minutes later, Maria cautiously opened the stateroom door, checked that the passageway outside was still deserted, and then left the room, Tremayne right behind her. He pulled the door closed, took out his specialist toolkit, and within a few seconds had locked the door again. When Bauer didn't appear for breakfast, Voss or Kortig would no doubt raise the alarm, but it would take one of the ship's officers with a master key to get inside the stateroom.

Tremayne hoped that his heart-attack scenario would look convincing enough to one of the ship's doctors, and it would be accepted as a death from natural causes. Of course, if Voss were to be allowed into the stateroom, and discovered that the packet of copied documents was missing, he would guess what had happened, although he wouldn't know exactly how.

But Tremayne had no intention of allowing Voss to get involved in any way at all. Both Kortig and Voss would themselves be dead long before breakfast was served in the dining saloon.

'So where's Kortig's stateroom?' Maria asked, her voice

barely audible above the distant, ever-present hum of machinery.

Tremayne moved right beside her and pointed down the cross passage.

'It's directly opposite to Bauer's,' he replied in a whisper. 'In fact, it's a mirror image of the suite we've just left.'

'We'll do the same routine, then?'

Tremayne nodded. 'Yes, why not?'

They walked down the passage, stopped at the end and looked across at the two doors which led into Kortig's suite.

Tremayne selected the correct tools, walked forward and started working on the lock. In less than a minute the lock clicked open, and he was able to turn the handle to open the door.

But as he replaced his tools and stood up again, he heard a sudden commotion from behind him, and twisted round to see Maria struggling in the grip of one of Voss's bodyguards. And before he could do anything about it, he felt a jab in his back from the muzzle of a pistol, and realized that he had badly underestimated his opponents.

Chapter 53

14 April 1912
RMS *Titanic*

The door which led to the lounge of the suite swung open, and Gunther Voss stepped out, the smaller figure of Lenz Kortig a couple of paces behind him. The two Prussians stood in the corridor and for a few seconds just stared at Tremayne.

Voss spoke first. 'We expected you to come here first,' he said, 'but we guessed wrong. Bauer was confident he could handle you on his own, but I suppose you killed him?'

Tremayne shrugged. There was no point in denying it. 'He didn't look at all well when we left,' he smiled.

Kortig's face was suffused with anger. 'You bastard,' he muttered, pulling a pistol from his pocket. 'Move out of the way, Gunther. I'll kill him right now.'

'No.' Voss's voice was sharp and commanding. 'He's going to die, but not here. Blood on the carpet and the walls would take too much explaining.' He stepped forward and stood in front of Tremayne. 'This is the end of the line for you,' he said. 'You should have walked away when you had the chance, you and this hussy that you're with.'

'She's not involved,' Tremayne said. 'She's just my secretary.'

Voss smiled. 'Maybe she is, or maybe you're just playing the classic English gentleman, and trying to protect the little woman. Either way, it doesn't matter. At the moment, I have only one use for her.'

'What?'

'You – and she – will find out soon enough. Now, if you don't want Vincent to blow a hole in your spine, and then do the same to her, put your hands in the air and stand still while I relieve you of whatever weapons you're carrying.'

'What about the blood on the carpet?' Tremayne asked.

'I'll risk it,' Voss snapped.

It's a basic rule of combat that you never surrender your weapon, and Tremayne knew this as well as anyone. The problem was that he was outnumbered four to one, all of his opponents were clearly armed, he had a gun sticking in his own back and there was another one pointing at Maria's head. In the circumstances, he really didn't see that he had any option. Tremayne raised his hands.

Voss took another pace forward, reached out and pulled the Browning pistol and the cosh from Tremayne's trouser pockets, and then found the garrotte and the metal box containing the syringe.

'What's in these bottles?' he asked, opening it and looking at the contents.

'A tonic,' Tremayne replied. 'You should try it. It'll do you the world of good.'

'I very much doubt that,' Voss said. He held the objects in his hands and looked at Tremayne.

'I underestimated you,' he said. 'I thought you'd just been sent on this ship to spy on us. But I was wrong. You're an assassin, an executioner, pure and simple. A man who is paid to kill other men. The basest possible kind of thug.'

'I see myself more as a specialist in rodent control,' Tremayne replied. 'I find rats and then I eliminate them. And I don't need lessons in morality from you, Voss. You were planning to blackmail the President of the United States of America into forming an alliance with Germany so that you could start a war. A war in which hundreds of thousands, perhaps even millions, of innocent people would die. And why? For some higher moral purpose, perhaps? Oh, no. For you, it was nothing more than simple greed. You were going to start a war just so you could get your grubby little hands on the mineral riches presently controlled by the British Empire.'

Voss stared at him. 'You are better informed than I anticipated,' he said. 'But I wouldn't call it blackmail. It makes perfectly good sense to ally Germany with America – the two nations have a lot in common – but I thought the American president might need a little nudge, a reminder, to see things that way. And I was lucky enough to find something that might help concentrate his mind. Speaking of which, I presume you removed the envelope of copied documents from Bauer's stateroom, so where is it?'

'My inside jacket pocket,' Tremayne replied, and Voss reached over and pulled it out.

'So what now?' Tremayne asked.

'Now you go away and die, Mr Maitland. But I am prepared to offer you one concession. Or rather, a concession to your lady friend here,' he added, gesturing to Maria, who hadn't said a word since they'd been surprised by Voss and his men.

'What?'

'If you go up to the Promenade Deck with Vincent in a quiet

and gentlemanly fashion, and do exactly as he tells you, he'll make sure that you're dead before you hit the water. It'll be quick and clean. And if he comes back down afterwards and tells me that you did that, then I'll let the woman live, and she can disembark in New York with all the other passengers.'

'And if I don't?'

'Then she'll join you in the ocean, but we might have a bit of fun with her first. Your choice. Vincent, as a matter of interest, would far rather that you didn't go quietly. The two men you met up on the deck the other night were good friends of his, and he would very much like you to suffer.'

As Voss said this, Vincent ground the muzzle of his pistol even more firmly into Tremayne's back.

Tremayne glanced across at Maria, then looked back at Voss and nodded. 'I'll go quietly and behave myself,' he said, 'as long as your ape can restrain himself. Just make sure that you keep your word, Voss, and let the girl go.'

'Or what, Maitland? You won't be around to see whether I do or not.' Voss nodded to the man standing behind Tremayne. 'Do it now, Vincent, and keep it quiet. Don't get any blood on the deck.'

The bodyguard shoved Tremayne hard in the back, pushing him down the short length of corridor towards the staircase.

As he stumbled forward, he heard Maria cry out.

'Alex!' she called, and then her voice was cut off, as if a hand had just closed round her mouth.

Tremayne tensed for a moment, then walked on.

Chapter 54

14 April 1912
RMS *Titanic*

'What do you want me to do with her?' the bodyguard holding Maria asked.

Voss looked over at him for a moment, then stared at Maria's face. 'I think she'd better join Maitland and feed the fish,' he said slowly, enjoying the way her face began to turn pale as he spoke. 'But not quite yet,' he added. 'Take her down to your stateroom and keep her there for a while. Try not to damage her too much, and above all keep her quiet.'

Maria glared at him. 'You lied,' she said.

'Of course I lied.' He sounded surprised at her comment. 'If I'm prepared to have people killed just because they get in my way, why would you suppose I'd tell *you* the truth? What I said was just a convenient way of getting Maitland out of here and onto the open deck where Vincent can kill him without any mess or fuss, nothing more.'

Voss paused for a moment and looked at her appraisingly. 'I still don't know who you are, though your accent is obviously American,' he said. 'Not that it really matters. I suppose Maitland might have been telling the truth, and you could be just some assistant for him. Or maybe you're an agent sent by the United States government to spy on us, or even to try to kill us. Either way, you won't be seeing New York again.'

He bent down and picked up Maria's handbag, which she had been forced to drop to the floor. Voss weighed it in his hand for a moment, apparently surprised at how heavy it was, then opened it and pulled out the Browning with the attached suppressor.

'Just a secretary are you?' he snapped, waving the weapon at her. 'Just carrying a pistol around in case his jammed, something like that?' He shook his head. 'No, I don't think so. I think you're a team, two equal partners, and equally dangerous.'

Voss switched his glance to the bodyguard. 'Leonard, make sure you watch her,' he said, 'just in case she's got any other surprises for you. Now take her away.'

The bodyguard twisted Maria's arm around her back, put away his pistol and picked up her handbag. Then he turned away and started forcing her down the corridor, towards the staircase and his own stateroom, somewhere on the decks below.

Chapter 55

14 April 1912
RMS *Titanic*

As he walked down the corridor, helped along by frequent shoves in the back from Vincent, Tremayne's mind was working overtime. Obviously he didn't believe a word that Voss had said, and he had no doubt that the Prussian intended Maria to die as well, but probably not that night: he guessed that she might end up in one of the staterooms occupied by the bodyguards for a while, as a kind of sick reward for the two men. All the stuff Voss had said about letting her disembark from the ship in New York was just talk, a transparent attempt to persuade Tremayne to go quietly to his death.

But Tremayne was actually pleased to go off with Vincent, because it changed the odds in his favour. Down there in the corridor on B-Deck he'd been faced by four armed men, one holding a gun to Maria's head, in a confined space. Up on the Promenade Deck, it would be just him and the bodyguard, odds of one to one, and the only weapon Voss hadn't found on Tremayne, precisely because he'd had his hands sticking up in the air, was the stiletto, nestling in its sheath and strapped to his left forearm. And Tremayne was good with a knife.

They emerged from the doorway at the end of the passageway, and Vincent gave him another heavy shove towards the foot of the staircase. Tremayne grasped the banister rail and began climbing slowly, but too slowly for the bodyguard, who grunted at him to get a move on.

He reached the half-landing and glanced behind him. Vincent was a couple of steps below, and out of reach, which was what Tremayne had expected.

'Which side?' he asked, gesturing at the stairs which ascended on both sides of the landing.

'You can choose,' the bodyguard replied, with a malicious grin. 'It'll be the last choice you ever make, so be my guest.'

Tremayne nodded, walked across the landing and began climbing the stairs towards the port side of the ship. He wasn't sure how much noise could be transmitted through the decks, but tackling Vincent directly above the spot where he knew Voss and the others were standing didn't seem to be a very good idea.

On the Promenade Deck, he walked across to the door, opened it and stepped outside, the bodyguard now following close behind him, the gun still held in his right hand.

On the open deck, the eastern sky was already displaying the first probing fingers of dawn, with streaks of red and yellow and gold. There was a stiff, cold breeze blowing, and Tremayne involuntarily shivered as he walked slowly towards the side rail of the ship, his right hand slipping up the left sleeve of his jacket and closing around the hilt of the stiletto.

'Frightened?' Vincent asked, with a sneer, 'because you should be. Voss told you that you'd be dead before you hit the water and you will be, I promise you that. But that'll be my last shot. The first few will just hurt you, really badly. In fact, by the end, you'll be begging me to kill you.'

Tremayne came to a stop, staring out across the dark and foam-flecked water of the North Atlantic, the point of the stiletto now grasped firmly between his right thumb and fingers, waiting for the moment. He had met people like Vincent before, and he knew the way their minds worked. Before he pulled the trigger, Vincent would want Tremayne to turn round, to face him, so that he'd be able to see the expression on his victim's face when the first bullet hit. Shooting him in the back wouldn't be anything like as enjoyable for the bodyguard.

'That's far enough, Maitland,' Vincent snapped. 'Now it's time to start dying, so turn around.'

Tremayne turned slowly to his left, lifting his right hand, shielded by his body, as he did so.

Vincent was standing about eight feet away, a smirk on his face, the pistol held casually in his right hand, obviously intending to take his time, to enjoy the punishment he was going to inflict.

But as Tremayne turned fully to face him, a flicker of alarm swept over the bodyguard's face as the blade of the stiletto glinted in the light from the deck lamps, and he immediately started bringing his pistol up to the aim.

Even as he did so, Tremayne was already swinging his right arm down and forward with all the strength he possessed. At precisely the right moment, he released his grip on the blade of the stiletto and the knife hissed through the air, a spinning sliver of death.

The tip of the blade slammed into the bodyguard's chest, the lethally sharp point burying itself three or four inches deep, and the force of the impact knocking the man backwards off his feet. He tumbled to the ground, the pistol falling from his grasp as he clutched desperately at the knife.

Tremayne had started moving the instant the stiletto left his hand, and almost before the bodyguard had hit the deck, he was on him. He wrenched the knife out of the wound, and stared down at the man's face.

'You know your trouble, Vincent?' he said. 'You talk too much.'

And with a single powerful blow, he drove the stiletto into the underside of the bodyguard's jaw, the blade slamming through the bone and tissue to lodge deep in the man's brain. It was a killing blow, and in moments the light went out from his eyes and he stopped breathing.

Tremayne pulled out the stiletto, wiped off the blood and tissue from the blade on the bodyguard's jacket, and slid the weapon back into the sheath. Then he stepped back, picked up the pistol Vincent had dropped, and checked to ensure that there was nobody in sight on the deck. It appeared to be deserted, so Tremayne swiftly searched the pockets of the bodyguard's suit and removed a suppressor and two spare magazines for the weapon, both fully charged. He slid them into his own jacket pocket, then dragged the dead man across to the guard rail. Very conscious of the knife wound he had sustained in his previous encounter, Tremayne carefully propped the body against the rail, then dragged it up until the man's waist was level with the top. Then he reached down, grabbed his ankles and simply lifted. In an instant the body tumbled out of sight, lost for ever in the darkness.

Tremayne took a moment to examine the pistol he'd taken from the bodyguard. It looked like a Browning 1903, the fore-runner of the Model 1910 which he'd been issued with, but when he looked more closely he realized it was the American version of the same pistol, manufactured in the United States by Colt.

He released the magazine, checked that it was fully loaded, and replaced it in the butt of the weapon. Then he screwed on the suppressor, chambered a round, and headed back towards the staircase.

Voss would be expecting somebody to come back from the Promenade Deck, and Tremayne didn't want to disappoint him.

Chapter 56

The Titanic Secret

14 April 1912
RMS *Titanic*

Tremayne stepped inside the superstructure, walked over to the top of the first-class staircase, and for a few seconds just stood there, listening.

He heard nothing, no voices, no footsteps. He guessed that meant they were all still in the corridor beside Kortig's stateroom, on the other side of the internal door in the staircase lobby that marked the end of the passage. Tremayne again checked that the Colt pistol was ready to fire, and began descending the staircase, one step at a time, listening out for any sounds from the deck below.

He reached the lobby without incident. Turning left at the bottom of the staircase would take him back the way he had come, but obviously he wasn't going to retrace the route he had followed with Vincent, because the moment he stepped through the doorway, he guessed that Voss would simply shoot him down. Instead, he turned right, towards Bauer's stateroom. That way, he could approach the men using one of the cross passages, which would give him the element of surprise. Tremayne knew that he was still outnumbered and outgunned, and any slight advantage he could find was hugely valuable.

He opened the door at the end of the passageway as quietly as he could, and looked down it. It appeared to be empty, and what puzzled him was that he couldn't hear even the slightest sound of voices, when he was only a matter of feet from where he had last seen Voss and Kortig.

Tremayne stepped into the corridor and eased the door closed behind him. Then he walked forward until he reached the end of the first cross passage. He looked in both directions, checking that nobody was approaching him from behind or in front, then took a quick glance down the cross passage itself. It was empty, and that was where he had last seen Maria and the bodyguard who had grabbed her. That meant they must have moved, but possibly only as far as the longitudinal passage that ran down the starboard side of the ship, the one opposite to the corridor Tremayne was standing in.

He knew there was another cross passage a few yards further down. He took another look all round him, then moved quickly down the corridor, checked the cross passage, and walked down it. At the end, where it linked with the starboard longitudinal passage, he stopped before looking in both directions.

But the passage was empty. Voss and Kortig – and, more importantly, Maria and the remaining bodyguard – had vanished, and at that moment Tremayne had absolutely no idea where they had gone.

Chapter 57

14 April 1912
RMS *Titanic*

For a few moments, Tremayne didn't move as he worked out what he should do next.

He didn't think that Voss could possibly know what had happened up on the Promenade Deck, so it was unlikely an ambush had been laid for him. As far as Voss and Kortig were concerned, he was already dead.

Maybe they'd just decided that standing in the passageway in the early hours of the morning wasn't a good idea, and had moved into Kortig's stateroom. On balance, that seemed to Tremayne to be the likeliest explanation.

He stepped out of the cross passage and walked slowly down towards the two doors that gave access to the Prussian's suite, checking the length of the corridor constantly. Still he neither saw nor heard anyone: it was as if he was alone on the ship.

Tremayne pressed his ear against the wood of the door which led into the stateroom's lounge, and listened intently. But he heard nothing apart from the usual sounds of the ship, an amalgam of machinery noises and the distant roaring as the hull cut through the water. That, of course, didn't mean anything. All the doors on the *Titanic* were thick, and it was quite possible that a group of people talking inside the stateroom would be entirely inaudible outside in the corridor.

He moved the short distance to the bedroom door and repeated the process, with precisely the same result: he heard nothing that resembled people talking.

His lock-picking tools had been taken from him by Voss when the Prussian had disarmed him, so Tremayne had no way of undoing the lock on the door quietly, so that left just two alternatives. He could try kicking it, smashing the heel of his foot against the lock and trying to burst the door open. There were two problems with that approach. First, Tremayne already knew that the doors on the *Titanic* were solid and the locks were of good quality, so it might not even be possible to break one down, even with repeated kicks. The second reason was in some ways even more compelling: if he tried that, the racket he would cause would be bound to wake up the passengers in the nearest staterooms, and the most likely result would be his detention by the ship's officers.

And he would obviously be unable to find Maria and complete his assignment if he was locked up in a strong room somewhere on board.

So that only left one other course of action, as far as Tremayne could see. He needed to get inside that stateroom and, if Maria and the others were in there, just hope that he would be quick enough to shoot down the three men before one of them could turn his gun on her. He had to take the chance.

Again making sure that nobody was approaching down the corridor, he stepped up to the door which accessed the lounge of Lenz Kortig's stateroom and rapped smartly on it.

For a few seconds, he heard nothing, and wondered if he'd

guessed wrong, if Voss and the others had gone somewhere else on the ship.

Then he heard a distinct click as the lock was released from inside the suite, and the heavy wooden door started to open inwards.

Tremayne didn't hesitate. The instant he saw the door move, he kicked out with all his might, heedless of the noise. The door flew back violently, and a figure tumbled backwards as the edge of it caught the side of his head, and crouched on the floor clutching his temple and moaning in pain.

Tremayne glanced down at the man – it was Kortig, as he'd expected – and levelled his pistol, ready to take out Voss or the bodyguard if either of them suddenly appeared at the internal door, but he heard and saw nothing. It looked as if the others had gone somewhere else. He needed to find out where, as quickly as possible.

He backed up a couple of paces and reached behind him for the door handle. He swung it closed and clicked the lock to secure it, then stepped forward to the internal door to check that there was no one hiding in the bedroom. With the pistol levelled and his finger on the trigger, Tremayne checked every possible place of concealment, but the room was as empty as it had first appeared.

He strode over to the connecting door and walked back into the lounge. Kortig had moved, and was trying to pull some object out of the pocket of a suit jacket that was hanging over the back of a chair.

Tremayne guessed immediately that the man was going for a gun. He crossed the room in half a dozen strides, and then kicked out, just as Kortig pulled the weapon free and swung it towards him.

His shoe connected with the pistol the instant before the Prussian could squeeze the trigger, and drove it sideways out of his grasp, snapping one of the bones in his right forefinger as it did so. Kortig yelled with pain. The small, black semi-automatic weapon clattered across the floor to land in the far corner of the room, well out of reach.

Tremayne was in no mood to be trifled with. He tucked the Browning into his pocket, bent down and grasped Kortig's left arm, and thrust him into one of the chairs. The Prussian was still moaning with the pain from his injuries, his left hand cradling his right, the index finger bent back at an impossible angle. Blood trickled from the gash on his forehead and the left side of his face where the door had hit him.

Tremayne looked at him for a few seconds, then pulled out his pistol and sat down in the chair opposite him.

'I'll bet that stings a bit,' he said gesturing to the banker's ruined hand, 'and your face looks a mess as well.'

Kortig didn't reply, just rocked backwards and forwards with the pain.

'It's easy enough to hand it out, isn't it?' Tremayne went on in a conversational tone. 'But it's a bit different when you're on the receiving end. You were quite happy to shoot me in the corridor outside, and I promise you that the pain you're feeling from those two little scratches are nothing compared to what being shot feels like. And I know that from personal experience. Three men have fired bullets into me, and all three made the same basic mistake: they didn't hit anything vital, and because of that there are three bodies rotting in unmarked graves, one in England and two in Germany. But I'll tell you, getting shot hurts.'

'I need a doctor,' Kortig said hoarsely.

Tremayne shook his head. 'No you don't,' he replied. 'You're not going to live long enough to need a doctor.'

'What?' Kortig stopped rocking and stared at him. 'You wouldn't dare.'

'Try me.' Tremayne's eyes were hard and cold as he looked at the injured man.

Kortig couldn't hold his gaze, and hunched over again.

'I need you to tell me where Voss has gone, and where I can find Maria, the woman I was with.'

'Why should I tell you anything, if you're going to kill me anyway?'

'Because there are easy ways to die and there are hard ways. In your last few minutes on this planet, I can take you to places where you'll know pain more intense than you could ever have imagined. And I won't even need to lift a finger to do it.'

'What do you mean?'

'The black can on the end of this pistol is a suppressor. Some people call it a silencer. What it does is take away the bang, so that when I fire this weapon, the normal noise is reduced to just a dull thud. So I can gag you and then sit here, in this comfortable chair, and for the next half an hour or so I can just shoot bits off you, and nobody outside this cabin will hear anything to alarm them.

'I've never been shot in the stomach,' Tremayne went on, 'but I'm told that's the worst pain imaginable, so I'd probably save that until towards the end of our little question and answer session. But there are plenty of other places I can shoot you to persuade you to see things my way. I think the expression your friend Voss used was "concentrate the mind". By the time I've finished putting bullets through your ankles and knees and groin – that's always a favourite place – I can promise you that your mind will absolutely be concentrated.

'Or, as I said before, you can just make it easy on yourself and tell me what I want to know. Now, this is your last chance, Kortig. I've only got two questions, and I want two straight answers. First, where can I find Voss? Second, where's Maria?'

The Prussian stared at Tremayne, and obviously read something in his eyes that frightened him even more than the blunt threats the Englishman had made. Threats are easy to make. But Tremayne was clearly the kind of man who would always deliver what he promised. And that was the difference.

Kortig started talking.

'Gunther was going back to his stateroom when he left here,' he said. 'He told the bodyguard to take the woman to his own room and hold her there, but I don't know where that man's stateroom is, so I can't tell you. But Gunther will know the number, of course. He said he was going to question her, because he wanted to try to find out how much you really knew about our plan.'

Tremayne nodded his thanks. 'Now that wasn't so hard, was it?' he said, and stood up. 'And because of that, I'll even give you a chance.'

He walked across to the corner of the room, picked up the small automatic pistol which was lying there, took a couple of paces back towards Kortig, and tossed the weapon to him. It landed in his lap.

'You'll have to use your left hand to fire it,' Tremayne said. 'Now, you were ready enough to shoot me in the corridor and again when I came in here, so maybe it'll be third time lucky for you.'

Kortig moved with the speed of a striking snake, grabbing the pistol and raising it to point at Tremayne, his finger already starting to pull the trigger.

But fast though he was, Tremayne was quicker. The Colt coughed twice in his hand and Kortig slumped back in the chair, one bullet crashing into his chest and tearing his heart to shreds, the second ploughing through the centre of his forehead and blowing off the back of his skull.

'Or maybe it'll be third time unlucky,' Tremayne muttered, staring for a moment at the spew of blood, bone and brain matter sliding off the back of the chair.

He slid the Colt into his trouser pocket, and turned to leave the suite. Then his eyes fell on an envelope lying on an occasional table. It looked almost identical to the one he'd taken from Bauer's stateroom. He picked it up, broke the seal and took out the contents: it was another set of the same documents he'd seen before.

Tremayne slid the envelope into the inside pocket of his jacket. 'I'll see if I can hang on to these this time,' he muttered to himself.

He looked around again and found Kortig's door keys and a 'Do not disturb' sign. He let himself out of the suite, locked the door and hung the sign over the handle, then strode away down the corridor.

Chapter 58

14 April 1912
RMS *Titanic*

Gunther Voss was feeling reasonably satisfied with what had happened that morning though it was a shame that Jonas Bauer was dead. Both Voss and Kortig had tried to persuade him to let one of the bodyguards remain in his suite overnight, just in case Maitland tried to break in, but Bauer had been adamant. He was a light sleeper and believed he was big enough and strong enough to tackle the British agent single-handed.

Clearly, he hadn't been, Voss reflected, but there was nothing they could do about that now. Fortunately, Maitland had then fallen into their trap outside Kortig's stateroom, and now he was dead. Capturing the woman had been unexpected, because Voss had assumed Maitland would be working alone, but he hoped she could be useful. If she was another secret agent, albeit American, it would be worth interrogating her to find out exactly what both the governments knew before they killed her.

Voss stepped out onto the Promenade Deck and took a few deep breaths. One or two couples were already out on deck, walking briskly in the cold light of early morning, perhaps trying to give themselves an appetite for the breakfast which was already being served in the dining saloon. The day was really cold, the wind a keen-bladed knife which cut through all but the thickest clothing.

Voss didn't need the exercise, especially in those conditions. He had, quite literally, been up all night, and he was famished. He'd come to the Promenade Deck as soon as it was full daylight for one reason only: he wanted to make absolutely sure that there was no sign of blood on the deck planking or guard rails which might suggest foul play. Even if there was a patch of blood, of course, there would be little or nothing that the ship's officers could do to discover what had happened. But Voss would rather there was no evidence at all.

He walked twice around the Promenade Deck, his head bent forward as he searched for any stains, looking especially carefully on and near the guard rails, but he found absolutely nothing. It looked as if Vincent had done his usual competent job. He'd told the bodyguard to get some sleep afterwards – he, too, had also been up all night – and to meet him in the smoking room after lunch.

Voss strode back to the entrance and returned gratefully to the warmth of the ship. He began making his way down the staircase as he decided on his next move. He would, he thought, go down and question the girl after he'd eaten breakfast. That would be a pleasant, and hopefully informative, way to spend the morning. And then that night, once the public areas were again deserted, Vincent could dispose of the girl the same way he'd got rid of Maitland.

As he walked into the dining saloon, Voss licked his lips at the anticipation of what the day would bring.

Chapter 59

14 April 1912
RMS *Titanic*

Alex Tremayne held the Colt pistol inside his jacket, his left hand gripping the weapon awkwardly by its suppressor through the material. The corridors and passageways in the first-class accommodation section were now busy with people going to, or returning from, breakfast. He clearly couldn't allow anyone to see the pistol, and with the suppressor attached it was really too big to conceal in any of his pockets. And he couldn't remove the suppressor, in case he had to quickly use the weapon again.

He glanced in both directions along the passageway, picking his moment, and then rapped firmly on the door in front of him, the door to Voss's stateroom.

His plan, if so simple a concept really justified that title, was to force his way inside Voss's suite, make the man tell him where Maria was hidden, and then kill him. But it all depended on Voss being in his stateroom and, from his observations of the past few days, Tremayne knew that the Prussian appeared to spend most of the time in the public rooms, particularly in the smoking room. It was the second time he'd tried knocking on the door, and it now seemed clear enough to him that Voss wasn't inside. Tremayne knew he would just have to wait until later in the day, perhaps even that evening, when the man would return to dress for dinner, and then try again.

A couple of minutes later he was standing in his own stateroom, the first time he'd been in the room without Maria by his side, wondering where she was, hoping to God that she was still alive, and trying to decide what else he could do. He had no idea of the name of the bodyguard who'd taken her, and even if he had known, that wouldn't have helped.

He presumed that the bodyguards had also been travelling first class and he could hardly have knocked on every door on the off-chance of eventually finding the right one.

His fervent hope was that Kortig had been right, and that Voss would want to question Maria before he killed her. If he interrogated her during the day, they would probably keep her alive until that night, simply because it was much easier to force a person to walk out onto one of the open decks and then kill them or simply throw them over the side, than it was to lug a dead body down passageways and up staircases in order to dispose of it. So unless Voss had already killed Maria and dropped her body into the sea, she was almost certainly still alive, hidden somewhere on the ship.

With every fibre of his being, Tremayne wanted to find her, to wander the corridors hoping that he would hear her voice or glimpse her through an open stateroom door, but he was a professional, and he knew that course of action would be futile. Wherever Maria was hidden, the bodyguards would make sure she couldn't cry out, and certainly wouldn't have the door open.

Tremayne considered his logic another couple of times, and decided that it made sense. And that, in turn, meant that there was nothing he could do for the moment. Voss had already left his stateroom, and on past form he probably wouldn't return there until it was time to dress for dinner. And although at that moment Tremayne wanted to do nothing more than to go out and find Voss and stick the barrel of a pistol in his mouth and pull the trigger, he knew that in the public rooms, which were almost always crowded with people, Voss was essentially invulnerable.

He could do nothing but wait, and Tremayne also knew that perhaps his biggest asset at that precise moment was the fact that he was dead – or at least Voss thought he was. Sooner or later, the Prussian would start to wonder why he hadn't seen Vincent anywhere, or why Kortig wasn't in the dining saloon or the smoking room, but by that time Tremayne hoped he would be in a position to kill him. In the meantime, he needed to keep out of sight, and that meant staying in his stateroom. If Voss or one of his bodyguards saw him and realized he was still alive, he had no idea what they might then do to Maria.

Tremayne was tired and sore. The wound in his side was aching, and he realized he ought to inspect it, and probably change the dressing. Manoeuvring Vincent's dead body – a literal dead weight – over the side of the ship must have put a lot of strain on his injury.

He locked the stateroom door, placed Vincent's pistol on the occasional table, where it would be within easy reach, and then got undressed. He removed the bandages holding the dressing in place over his wound, and carefully peeled away the pad which covered it. The edges of the cut still looked ragged and raw, and there had obviously been some fresh bleeding, but not enough to concern him. More importantly, he couldn't see any sign of infection anywhere in the wound. He prepared a fresh pad, put it in position, and then tied the bandages around his torso again, getting them as tight as he could. It didn't look anything like as neat as when Maria had done it, but Tremayne hoped that it would hold.

Then he lay down on the bed, closed his eyes and waited for sleep to come, haunted by thoughts of Maria.

Chapter 60

14 April 1912
HMS *D4*

Just after twelve noon, Eastern Standard Time, Lieutenant Bernard Hutchinson bent over the plotting chart and compared the submarine's actual position with the location he had expected it to reach, based on the speed he had estimated the boat would be able to achieve in the prevailing weather conditions.

He checked again, and then nodded. They were a little behind schedule – only a couple of miles – but enough to be a worry. The sea conditions were still fairly calm, though it was bitingly cold, the water temperature obviously below freezing, and this was the indirect cause of the boat's slower than expected progress. What they were having to watch out for were the occasional icebergs, grubby dark lumps of floating ice that would do incalculable damage to his vessel if they hit one, but which were easy enough to avoid: with its twin propellers, the submarine was manoeuvrable, and the icebergs essentially stationary.

But the icebergs worried Hutchinson, and either he or William Evans were always on duty in the conning tower ready to give the appropriate helm orders as the submarine headed south-west. They were doing four-hour watches each and after dark, because of the extra concentration needed, two-hour watches. And although it was a tight fit, Hutchinson had also ordered two lookouts in the conning tower, day and night.

As well as avoiding the icebergs, they were also having to steam through occasional patches of broken floating ice, presumably the remains of bergs which had broken up further north. Most of these fragments were quite small, just a foot or two across, and wouldn't damage the submarine. Nevertheless, he and Evans invariably ordered a speed reduction every time they encountered one of these ice packs, just in case there were larger pieces lurking somewhere amongst it.

Hutchinson pulled on an extra sweater and his foul-weather clothing, and climbed up the first few rungs of the ladder into the conning tower. Then he called up and ordered the lookouts to come down while he took over from Evans. He stood back and waited as the two seamen clattered down the ladder into the control room.

'Cold?' he asked.

'Bloody cold, sir. Absolutely perishing.'

Hutchinson nodded. 'Get a hot drink and some food inside you,' he instructed, then pulled on his gloves and climbed up the ladder himself.

Evans was waiting for him in the conning tower, his nose red and raw from the cold, and most of his face invisible behind a woollen scarf.

For a couple of minutes, Evans briefed Hutchinson on the situation, pointing out the icebergs they'd avoided and the few which were visible ahead of the submarine; at least two of them would necessitate a slight change of course.

Finally, Hutchinson said he was satisfied, and took over the watch.

'Thanks, Bill. I have the boat,' he said formally.

But Evans didn't leave the conning tower immediately. He glanced at Hutchinson as the other officer swept the horizon with his binoculars.

'It's a bit of a rum do, this,' he said. 'I still don't really know what on earth we're doing out here in the middle of the Atlantic Ocean.'

Hutchinson lowered the binoculars and looked at his First Lieutenant. 'To be perfectly honest with you, Bill, I don't know either. But I suppose that's life in the Royal Navy. Some admiral comes up with what he thinks is a brilliant idea, a string of orders gets issued, and a shipload of poor unfortunate sailors spend a couple of weeks performing some completely pointless evolutions. A report gets written, filed and forgotten, the admiral gets promoted or retired, and life plods on in much the same way as it did before. I'd have thought you would be used to it by now.'

Evans smiled behind his scarf. 'I am, and I've certainly done my share of pointless exercises, but what we're doing now just seems to me to be ridiculous.'

'We'll just have to wait and see what the next signal says but hopefully, by tonight, we might be able to turn round and head for home.'

Chapter 61

14 April 1912
RMS *Titanic*

After he'd finished breakfast, Voss decided to enjoy a cigar, and had returned to the Promenade Deck. There, he'd spent a contented three quarters of an hour wreathed in blue smoke before he stood up to leave.

It was only as he was walking out of the smoking room that he wondered where Lenz Kortig was, and decided to visit his stateroom on his way downstairs. On B-Deck, he stopped outside the suite occupied by the banker, and smiled when he saw the sign attached to the door handle. Obviously Kortig had found the events of the night more than a little trying, and had decided to sleep in. No matter: he would catch up with him during the afternoon, or that evening at dinner.

Voss continued walking along the starboard passageway until he reached the forward first-class staircase lobby, and then began descending. He went down two decks, where the ornate and impressive staircase finished, and then took the more utilitarian stairs down to E-Deck, where each of his bodyguards occupied a first-class single stateroom. He checked a small notebook to find the correct number, then strode down the passageway before stopping and knocking at one of the doors to an inside stateroom.

'Who is it?

The voice was slightly muffled, but still audible.

'Voss,' he said. 'Open up.'

He heard the click as a lock was undone, and then a dark eye surveyed him through the crack where the door opened. As soon as the man recognized him, he opened the door fully and Voss strode inside.

The stateroom was substantially smaller than the suite Voss occupied, but the furniture and fittings were still elegant and of very high quality. The woman they'd snatched was sitting on a chair against one wall, her wrists handcuffed behind her back and a makeshift gag covering her mouth. She glared at Voss as he walked in.

'Any problems, Leonard?' he asked.

'No,' the man said, 'but I need to go to the lavatory and I'd like to get some breakfast, if there's time. I've had nothing to eat since dinner last night, and I've been awake for most of the last twelve hours.'

Voss glanced at his watch and nodded. 'Take your time,' he replied, and smiled at Maria. 'We've got all day,' he added, 'so we can do this nice and slowly.'

Once the bodyguard had left the stateroom, Voss took a seat in another easy chair facing Maria and looked across at her dispassionately.

'I think I need to explain the reality of your situation,' he began. 'Maitland – your friend, or employer, or fellow agent, or whatever he was – is dead. There will be no last-minute rescue or reprieve, so today is the last day of your life. At the end of it, I will tell Vincent to kill you, just as I did with Maitland, and you have a very similar choice to make. If you are prepared to answer my questions, to tell me whatever you know, then I will instruct him to make your death as painless as possible. A single bullet to the back of your head, and you'll be dead before your body even hits the deck. You'll feel nothing at all, that I can promise you.

'And,' he continued, 'if you cooperate with us, we can probably have quite a pleasant day, all things considered. I'll order a decent lunch and some wine, that kind of thing. On the other hand, if you decide that cooperation isn't in your nature, and you'd rather fight us, then I can promise you that the next twelve hours or so are going to be desperately unpleasant for you. I abhor physical violence, but fortunately I've always been able to employ men who not only are very good at inflicting pain but who enjoy it. Vincent, in particular, can do things with a knife and a rope that are unbelievably painful, and I would far rather spare you the agony. But, of course, the choice is entirely up to you.'

Voss smiled at her again, and nodded encouragingly. 'I suggest you think about that while Leonard enjoys his breakfast. Then, when he comes back, we can get started, one way or the other.'

Chapter 62

Maria stared across the small stateroom at Voss, impotent fury blazing in her eyes. She had no doubt that if she refused to co-operate, he would do exactly what he threatened, and she had already decided that she would go along with whatever Voss suggested. But she didn't have to like it.

The only possible way she could see of leaving the ship alive was if she could somehow kill Voss and escape from the clutches of his bodyguards, and that would only be possible if she was uninjured, and able to use some of her close-combat tactics. If she let Vincent or the other bodyguard go to work on her, she had no idea what damage they would do, but obviously her chances of turning the tables on them would be seriously reduced.

She still didn't believe Voss's promise to have her killed quickly and painlessly, and guessed that once he had obtained all the information that she had to give him, he would turn her over to the bodyguards for their entertainment until the time came to throw her over the side of the ship. And she knew precisely what kind of entertainment the bodyguards would have in mind. But that actually gave her some hope, because to enjoy her properly, they would need to unshackle her wrists; and her fists, elbows and knees could, in the right circumstances, become lethal weapons. But whatever happened at that stage, there was no way she would give in without a fight.

About half an hour later, there was a knock at the door, and when Voss opened it the bodyguard reappeared.

'Excellent,' Voss said, and gestured for the man to go and stand beside Maria. 'Now,' he went on, 'I'm going to ask Leonard to remove your gag. But before I do that, I want you to give me your word that you won't scream or yell when he takes it off. If you do Leonard will hit you very hard in the stomach and then will replace the gag. Do you understand?'

Maria nodded once.

'And do you promise that you won't scream or try and make a noise?'

Again she nodded.

'Good.'

Voss nodded to the bodyguard, who leaned over Maria and untied the gag from the back of her head. She licked her parched lips and looked over at Voss.

'Could I please have a drink of water?' she asked.

Voss nodded. 'Yes, of course,' he replied, and watched as Leonard poured water into a glass and held it to Maria's lips.

'So what have you decided?' he asked, when she finished the drink. 'Will you cooperate with us?'

'I'm not stupid, Voss,' she said. 'The choice you've given me is no choice at all. You think I've got information that you want and either I tell you of my own free will or you beat it out of me. Either way, the end result is the same, so of course I'll cooperate with you. I don't want to be hurt.'

Voss almost purred. 'Excellent,' he said. 'I thought you would end up being sensible about this. Now, I think the best thing to do is start at the beginning, with who you are – and who Maitland was – and who you were both working for.'

Maria nodded, and began speaking in a low voice. 'Very well. My name is Maria Weston, and I'm American, obviously. I work for the Bureau of Investigation, in Washington, so I'm a government employee. My boss assigned me to this operation, to follow you, and he knows exactly where I am and what I'm doing, and if you do kill me, you can expect more than a little trouble from him. The man your thug killed, the man you knew as Alex Maitland, was actually named Alex Tremayne. He was employed as an undercover agent – not an assassin, as you seemed to be suggesting earlier, Voss – by the British Secret Service Bureau, based at Whitehall Court in London.'

'He may not have been employed as an assassin, Miss Weston, but the equipment I took off your partner last night clearly shows that killing people was one of his jobs. A silenced pistol, a garrotte and some kind of poison are not the sort of things most gentlemen would carry about their persons.'

Maria shrugged. 'Extreme circumstances call for extreme measures,' she said. 'When our two organizations discovered what you and your co-conspirators had planned, we realized that the only way we could stop you was to kill you. And, yes, that's why Alex and I were sent on board this ship. In fact, Alex was ordered to carry out the executions, not me.'

She was choosing her words carefully, subtly trying to convince the two men that she had been little more than an assistant for Tremayne, just a bag carrier and a lookout, so that when the time finally came, they would not be anticipating that she could be physically dangerous. And as she started thinking ahead, towards the next things she would tell them, she suddenly realized that Voss had just said something very significant. Or, to be absolutely exact, it was something that he hadn't said, an omission, which was important.

But that was the least of her concerns right then. She knew that the mission she and Alex had embarked on had failed. Voss was clearly alive, and sitting right in front of her, and the deadline for the signal to be sent back to Mansfield Cumming was fast approaching, with nothing she could do about it. But at least, she reflected silently, she knew that the plan hatched by Voss, Bauer and Kortig was doomed to fail, not because of Alex Tremayne's ability as an assassin, but because Mansfield Cumming had prepared a contingency plan that was entirely independent of the ship itself. She smiled slightly at the thought that her captors would be joining her in the Atlantic Ocean within a matter of hours.

'Something funny?' Voss asked.

Maria shook her head. 'No, not really,' she replied. 'I was just thinking how quickly you managed to turn the tables on us, how easily an advantage can be lost.'

Voss stared at her narrowly, as if wondering if he was missing something, then shook his head and resumed his questioning.

'So this Secret Service Bureau that Tremayne worked for,' he said. 'How did that organization find out what we were planning to do?'

'It all started in Germany, in Berlin,' Maria began, 'with a man named Klaus Trommler.'

Chapter 63

14 April 1912
London

Mansfield Cumming stared at the clock on his desk, then came to a decision. He had heard nothing from Alex Tremayne, despite the urgency of his last message to the *Titanic*, and had no idea what progress the two agents had made. On the other hand, a progress report wasn't really what he wanted.

It had been made very clear to him by his masters in the British Government that the only acceptable solution, from their point of view, to the problem posed by Gunther Voss and his two co-conspirators was either confirmation of their deaths on board the ship or, if that failed, the destruction of the vessel itself. Whatever happened, the three men could not be permitted to reach America.

Cumming believed that he had given his two agents both adequate time to complete their assignments, and suitable tools to do the job. And they should now be in no doubt about the potential consequences for them personally, and for the rest of the innocent people sailing on board the ship, if they failed.

He shook his head. Alex Tremayne was undeniably the best agent that he had ever employed, and Maria Weston had arrived from Washington highly recommended. He hated the thought that they would not be coming back from this mission. But he also knew where his duty lay, and the lives of two people – of any two people – and even of the more than two thousand souls on board the *Titanic*, were expendable and irrelevant when you considered the bigger picture.

With a heavy heart, Cumming took a fresh sheet of paper and began composing the 'prepare' signal to be transmitted by the Admiralty to the captain of the submarine. That would ensure that the boat was ready in all respects to complete the assignment, if it came to that, and included the final rendezvous position and time, based upon the very latest information from the White Star Line.

Cumming still hoped, desperately, that Tremayne would somehow complete his mission and that he would never have to send the final signal, the message to 'execute', a military term that was, in the circumstances, horribly appropriate.

Chapter 64

14 April 1912
RMS *Titanic*

At that moment, in his stateroom on the *Titanic* some two thousand miles away, Alex Tremayne tossed and turned in fitful sleep, tormented by kaleidoscopic images that tumbled and coursed through his brain. Jonas Bauer taking his last breath; his fight with the two bodyguards on the Promenade Deck; Lenz Kortig's skull blowing apart as the pistol bullet ploughed through it and, above all, his last sight of Maria, standing in the cross passage in the grip of one of Voss's thugs with the barrel of a pistol pressed against the side of her head.

Tremayne woke up with a gasp, clammy and damp with sweat, and immediately reached for his watch to check the time. Just gone five. He stood up, took a towel and dried his body as best he could – the stab wound in his side meant that he couldn't take a bath, even if he'd had the time, and got dressed again, picking a clean white shirt and a black suit he'd not worn before on the ship.

He picked up the Colt automatic pistol, took out the magazine which he had fired two rounds from, and replaced it with one of the fully charged magazines he had taken off Vincent.

The problem, as before, was the suppressor, a black canister which effectively doubled the length of the pistol and prevented it from fitting inside any of his pockets. But he had to have the suppressor attached to the weapon before he dared fire it. The only solution was to unscrew it and tuck it away separately, and hope that he would have enough time to reattach the suppressor before he found himself in a situation where he had to pull the trigger.

Tremayne checked that the stiletto, which he'd cleaned properly to remove all traces of Vincent's blood, was secure in the sheath strapped to his left forearm, and that he had the two other magazines for the pistol in his pocket. When he'd finished, he looked at himself in the full-length mirror, and although a couple of his pockets bulged noticeably, nobody could possibly tell what he had in them.

Then all he could do was watch and wait until Voss returned to his stateroom.

Chapter 65

14 April 1912
RMS *Titanic*

It was late afternoon when Voss finally finished questioning Maria Weston. He was amazed at how much information that treacherous German clerk, Klaus Trommler, had managed to pass to the British, and how near they had come to wrecking his carefully planned operation.

But at least he now knew that the danger was past. Thanks to Vincent, he had discovered the plot to kill him and his friends on board the *Titanic*, and had then managed to outwit the two agents sent by the governments of Britain and the United States, and kill them. Or at least, his men had killed one of them, and the body of that interfering American woman would go over the side that very night.

All in all, it was a satisfactory result, and just a shame that Jonas hadn't lived long enough to see their plan come to fruition. As far as Voss was concerned, nothing could stop them now.

And that just left the woman to be disposed of. He looked at her across the small stateroom. She was still sitting in the same chair, her wrists manacled behind her back, returning his gaze.

He stared at her eyes for a few moments, unable to shake the irrational belief that somehow she had won. In those grey eyes he seemed to see a kind of knowledge, a calm serenity that spoke of enormous self-belief.

'Is there something else you should be telling me?' Voss asked.

'I don't think so,' she replied, shaking her head. 'Is there something you have to tell *me*?'

Voss nodded, then turned to the bodyguard. 'Leonard, replace the gag for me.'

When Maria was again rendered mute, Voss leant forward and spoke to her softly.

'You should never have believed me,' he said, a note of triumphant gloating in his voice. 'I don't know how Vincent will decide to kill you, but however he does it, however quickly or slowly, you might find that death comes as a welcome relief. I promised Leonard and Vincent that they could amuse themselves with you this evening, and I always like to keep my promises – at least to my friends and employees.'

Voss watched her face carefully as he said these words and pronounced her fate, but to his surprise her expression didn't seem to change, apart from a hardening of her eyes. It was almost as if that was exactly what she had been expecting him to say.

He turned back to the bodyguard. 'You and Vincent can do what you like with her,' he said. 'Just make sure that she's dead at the end of it. When you've finished, get rid of the body over the side, and make sure that you leave no evidence.'

Leonard nodded, and Voss stood up to go. Then he turned back.

'One more thing,' he added. 'She's probably going to make a

lot of noise, so don't start doing anything until seven o'clock, when most people in this section will be up in the dining saloon, having dinner.'

He looked across at Maria for the last time, and nodded his head. 'Enjoy yourself,' he said.

She stared back at him, her gaze unwavering, and for an instant he thought she nodded back to him. Then he opened the door and walked out.

Chapter 66

14 April 1912
RMS *Titanic*

Voss climbed back up to B-Deck, and stopped again outside Kortig's stateroom. But the 'Do not disturb' sign was still displayed, and when he tried the doors, he found that both of them were still locked. That was unusual, and for a moment he debated whether or not he should contact a ship's officer and ask that the door be opened, just to check that the banker was all right.

Then he shrugged and retraced his steps, descending to C-Deck and his own stateroom. If Kortig didn't appear for dinner, or in the smoking room afterwards, then he decided he would get the suite door opened, just as a precaution. And he knew he would soon need to raise the alarm about Jonas Bauer, lying dead in his stateroom, killed by the man he now knew had been called Tremayne. But the following morning would be soon enough for that. Vincent and Leonard still had the Weston woman's body to dispose of after they'd killed her, and so the less activity around the first-class accommodation areas that night, the better.

Voss turned down the passageway to his own suite, fished the key out of his pocket and opened the door. He glanced at his watch. It was a little before seven, so he just had time to dress for dinner, a meal he knew he would savour, even if this evening it looked as if he would probably be eating alone.

Chapter 67

14 April 1912
RMS *Titanic*

Alex Tremayne had spent the last hour standing just inside the open doorway of his stateroom, leaning against the wall and staring down the passageway towards Voss's suite, waiting for the Prussian to return.

And when he did, Tremayne almost missed him, because of all the activity that was going on in the passageways as couples and individuals moved around, entering or leaving their staterooms. When he saw the figure stop outside the stateroom door, for a moment he couldn't make out who it was. Then the crowd thinned slightly, and Voss's unmistakable features swam into clear focus.

That was all Tremayne needed to see. He stepped back into his stateroom, checked that he had everything with him that he would need, then locked the door of his room and walked straight down the passageway towards Voss's suite. As he got closer, he became more aware of the other people walking to and fro, and adjusted his own pace so that when he arrived outside Voss's door, there were very few passengers anywhere near him.

He checked again, looking in both directions along the passageway, then knocked three times on the door. For a moment, he heard nothing, and then a slightly muffled voice asked: 'Who is it?'

'Lenz,' Tremayne replied, imitating Kortig's voice as much as he could, though he guessed that from the other side of the door the sound would be so indistinct that Voss wouldn't be able to tell whose voice it was. At least, that was what he was hoping.

He heard a muttered comment that sounded like 'at last', then the distinct click of the lock being released, and the door swung open.

For a long moment, Voss stared at Tremayne, the blood draining from his face as he looked at the man who should have been dead, his own worst nightmare come to life. His mouth opened and closed as his brain struggled to comprehend what he was seeing, and form some kind of sentence.

Tremayne saved him the trouble.

'Hullo, Gunther,' he said, then smashed his right fist into the centre of his face.

Chapter 68

14 April 1912
RMS *Titanic*

Since Voss had left, the bodyguard – Leonard, a strangely incongruous name for a man in his line of work, she thought – had barely taken his eyes off Maria. And when he had looked away, it was usually just to check his watch. Maria guessed that he was waiting for seven o'clock so that he could start doing whatever he had planned for her.

Finally, he obviously decided he'd waited long enough. He went to the door and checked the corridor, and Maria could hear no sound of movement.

The bodyguard closed and locked the door. Then he walked over to where Maria was still sitting in the chair, and undid her gag.

'If you scream,' he said, 'I'll punch you in the mouth, break a few teeth. But you can talk to me, if you like. I might enjoy that.'

'Aren't you supposed to be waiting for Vincent?' Maria asked, sarcasm dripping from every word. 'Surely it's safer if there are two of you great big men to handle me? Or do you really think you're strong enough to do it all by yourself?'

He looked at her through narrowed eyes. 'You've got some spirit, girl, I'll say that for you, but you'll probably find it better if you just shut up and lie still. That way, I won't have to slap you around. And trust me, if I have to do that, I will. Now stand up.'

Maria obeyed. The bodyguard grabbed her by the arm and turned her round, and she heard the click as he released the handcuffs. The relief at being able to move her hands and arms was inexpressible, and she rubbed her wrists to try to get the blood circulating properly again.

'Now walk over to the bed,' Leonard instructed, 'and take off your clothes. All of them. And be quick about it.'

She bowed her head and walked slowly across the small room to the bed, where she turned to face him.

'Get on with it,' he snapped, 'or I'll come over there and make you do it.'

Maria started to undo the buttons on her blouse.

Chapter 69

14 April 1912
RMS *Titanic*

As Voss staggered backwards, Tremayne turned round, closed the door of the stateroom and snapped the lock to secure it.

But Voss was far from finished.

Tremayne felt a massive blow on his back as the Prussian charged at him, head down, like a bull, and slammed him against the door, driving the breath from his body. Then two powerful blows to his stomach completed the job. The second one caught the end of his stab wound, sending a searing throb of agony lancing up the right side of his chest. Through a red mist of pain, Tremayne hit out, punching with both fists, trying to gain some distance, create some breathing space.

Voss was fighting for his life, and it showed. He hadn't always had money. As a young man he'd worked in the mining industry, and that was a tough apprenticeship for anyone. He'd had his fair share of brawls along the way, and now he was drawing on his experience of every fight he'd ever had.

Tremayne's back was against the door, so there was nowhere he could retreat to. But retreat wasn't a part of his plan. As Voss lunged at him again, head down and fists flying, Tremayne kicked out, catching him in the stomach. And then he lifted his right arm above his head and brought his elbow crashing straight down. The point caught Voss on the back of the neck, and he dropped to the floor.

In seconds he was up again, back on his feet, but that brief respite was all Tremayne needed. He'd already spotted his cosh lying on a table near the door, along with the other devices Voss had taken from him. He took two quick steps over to the table, seized the weapon and, as the Prussian charged at him again, he swung it against the side of his head. There was a sickening thud as the lead-filled end of the cosh connected with Voss's skull, and he dropped to the floor, unconscious.

For a minute or two, Tremayne just stood where he was, catching his breath and clutching his injured side. Then he pulled Voss across the floor and propped him up against the wall. Voss was still out cold, and showed no signs of coming round, which was a problem, because Tremayne was worried sick about Maria, and the unconscious man lying in front of him was the only way he had of finding her.

He took a few moments to recover his weapons and tuck them away in his pockets, then went into Voss's attached bathroom and came back with a glass of water. He gulped a couple of mouthfuls and then threw the rest of the liquid into Voss's face. The man stirred slightly, but didn't open his eyes. Pain was a good way of waking somebody, Tremayne believed, so he walked across and trod firmly on Voss's right hand, grinding his fingers into the carpeted floor.

That produced a response. Voss groaned and his eyes flickered open. Tremayne stepped back, pulled the Colt automatic from one pocket, and the suppressor from another, and screwed it onto the end of the barrel, his eyes never leaving Voss.

'You fight well, I'll give you that,' Tremayne said, 'but this is the end of the line for you. This morning you offered me a choice of a hard or an easy way to die, so the least I can do is return the favour. Tell me where Maria is, and it'll be quick. If you don't, well, I've got plenty of ammunition for this pistol. It used to belong to a man named Vincent, but I suppose you'd already guessed that. So I can shoot you full of painful holes that won't kill you for hours, maybe days. Your choice.'

Voss stared at him, hatred smouldering in his eyes.

'You wouldn't dare,' he said.

'Try me,' Tremayne replied. 'I've already killed three of your bodyguards, as well as Bauer and Kortig, so I've got nothing left to lose. So that's what? Five or six? Who's keeping count? I promise you that one more killing won't make any difference to me. And with this suppressor on the pistol, nobody outside this room will hear a thing.'

'And what happens when they find the bodies?'

'Oh, I think I've already worked that out,' Tremayne replied. 'The bones of the bodyguards are probably all at the bottom of the Atlantic by now. Bauer unfortunately had a heart attack, and I think the authorities in New York will probably decide that you and Kortig had an argument, and you shot him with this pistol. Then, in a fit of remorse, you came back here and committed suicide with the same weapon. End of story.'

Tremayne levelled the Colt pistol at Voss's stomach. 'What they're probably going to find particularly sad is that you weren't such a good shot when you turned the gun on yourself, and the first few bullets unfortunately didn't kill you. Maybe you thought you should suffer for what you'd done. I don't know, and nor will they. But you will be dead, Voss, and that's a promise.'

He aimed the pistol carefully and prepared to squeeze the trigger. 'Now, for the last time, where is Maria?'

Chapter 70

14 April 1912
HMS *D4*

It took Bernard Hutchinson a long time to decipher the next signal sent to the submarine. Apart from the usual routing indicators, it consisted of four paragraphs. The first was the single word 'Prepare'; the second specified that the boat was to have two torpedoes, fitted with live warheads, loaded into the forward tubes and in all respects ready to fire, no later than eighteen hundred hours, six in the evening, Eastern Standard Time. That section he could ignore, because the tubes were already loaded and had been since just before noon that day.

The third paragraph simply amended the rendezvous position slightly and confirmed that the boat was to be at that location no later than twenty-one hundred hours that night.

The fourth and final paragraph was the longest. That instructed him to maintain a listening watch on his radio contact frequency, which he'd been doing, in any case, ever since he left Dover. It also told him to expect either the 'execute' or the 'return to base' signal shortly after twenty-two hundred hours EST. Whichever signal he received, he was to decipher it and then send an acknowledgement that he had fully understood his orders.

If the submarine was ordered to return to base, it was to remain on the surface and proceed at its normal cruising speed to a further rendezvous position with an oiler, and take on sufficient fuel to allow it to reach Dover. On passage, the torpedoes were to be removed from the tubes, the warheads taken off them and made safe, and all weapons returned to their normal peacetime status.

If the 'execute' signal was sent, his orders were entirely different. After sending the acknowledgement, the radio aerial was to be unshipped – an essential action before the boat submerged – and the submarine was then to dive and to remain submerged until after it had engaged the target which would be specified in that signal. Then, still submerged, the boat was to proceed for a minimum distance of twenty miles clear of the location of the engagement, then surface, re-rig the radio aerial and confirm that the operation had been carried out. After that, the vessel was to rendezvous with the oiler as before and return to base.

Hutchinson noted the slightly amended coordinates of the rendezvous position on a piece of paper, and walked out of his cabin into the control room. He plotted the new position on the chart, measured the distance the boat still had to cover in order to get there by the specified time, and ordered a slight change of heading and speed to ensure that it was easily achievable.

Then he returned to his cabin and locked away the code book and the signal in his safe, and for a few minutes simply sat on his narrow bunk, wondering yet again exactly what the Admiralty was playing at.

Chapter 71

14 April 1912
RMS *Titanic*

Gunther Voss looked at the man standing in front of him and weighed up his chances.

Voss knew he had at least one more card left to play and that Tremayne had made one mistake, because he hadn't searched or restrained him in any way. Voss was still wearing his jacket, and tucked into the right-hand pocket was something he never travelled without: a forty-one calibre Deringer pocket pistol. Possibly the ultimate close-range concealed weapon, it was so small it could be held in the palm of the hand, but contained two loaded chambers.

Although it was inaccurate at a range of more than a few feet, Voss had no doubt he could hit Tremayne with it. What he had to do was divert the Englishman's attention away from him, for the bare second or two it would take to draw and fire the pistol. Voss knew he would only get the one chance.

'She's still alive,' he blurted out, 'and she's being held by my bodyguard, in his stateroom down on E-Deck.'

'What number?' Tremayne demanded.

'I can never remember,' Voss said. 'It's written in a notebook in the pocket of the jacket I'm wearing.'

He lifted his right arm to reach for the breast pocket of his jacket, but Tremayne immediately stopped him.

'Not like that,' he snapped. 'Use your left hand, just the finger and thumb, and toss the book over to me.'

That was precisely what Voss had hoped he would say, because he needed to draw the pistol with his right hand, and Tremayne's attention would – with any luck – be held by the notebook he was going to lob across the floor of the stateroom.

Voss lowered his right hand to his side, where it was only an inch or two away from the pistol, and lifted up his left hand to slowly reach for his breast pocket. He slipped his finger and thumb inside and pulled out a small notebook.

'Throw it over here,' Tremayne instructed.

Voss tossed the book through the air, angling it so that it passed over to Tremayne's right.

But then something completely unexpected happened. He'd been hoping – and expecting – that the Englishman would switch his glance to the book as it fluttered towards him, and then Voss would be able to seize his chance.

The Englishman's gaze hadn't wavered, not even for a split second, and Voss was still looking straight down the barrel of the silenced Colt automatic.

'Now I have a bit of a problem,' Tremayne said. 'It could be you're telling me the whole, absolute, plain and unvarnished truth, and that in this little notebook I'll find a few room numbers and when I go and check them I might find Maria sitting in one of the cabins waiting for me. On the other hand, she might already be dead, floating in the ocean fifty miles behind us. Or maybe you've already killed her and your man is waiting until it's dark so that he can dispose of her body without anyone noticing.

'And because of what I know about you, I think the chances of you actually telling me the truth are really pretty slim. Now, for you, that's actually a good thing, because it means that I won't kill you, or not yet, anyway. First, I have to go and see if I can find Maria. If I can't find her, I'll be back to talk to you again. If I do find her, or discover that she's already dead, I'll be back to kill you. So now I need to make sure that you won't run away, because I'd hate you to miss our appointment.'

Tremayne gestured with the muzzle of the pistol for Voss to stand up.

'Put your hands behind your back,' he ordered, 'then turn around and face the wall.'

Voss did as he was told, because he knew that in order for Tremayne to be able to tie his hands, he would have to put down the pistol. Tying a rope or cord required the use of both hands, and that was a fact.

Voss stood up slowly and turned away, moving both hands behind his back as he did so, preternaturally alert for the slightest sound that would indicate that Tremayne had lowered his weapon, because that was the moment when he would make his move.

But Tremayne had no intention of trying to lash Voss's wrists together while the man was still conscious. That, he knew, would be a recipe for disaster. Instead, he shifted the pistol to his left hand, drew the cosh and cracked Voss sharply over the back of the head with it, enough to daze him, but not to knock him out.

Voss tumbled forward and fell on the carpet. Immediately, Tremayne pulled a length of cord from his pocket, grabbed the man's right hand, wrapped the cord around his wrist, and swiftly tied the ends around his left wrist as well. He pulled the knots tight, and made sure that Voss couldn't reach the cord with his fingers.

Then he stood up and looked round the suite. There was no obvious sign of the pouch that he guessed would contain further copies of the documents he'd already recovered from Kortig. But he remembered that the other man had kept them in his jacket, and that when he had previously searched Voss's stateroom he'd found no trace of them, which suggested they'd probably all kept the copies with them at all times.

He spotted Voss's dinner jacket hanging over the back of a chair, ready to wear for the evening. Tremayne walked across and felt around in the pockets. In one of them, he found two envelopes, one already opened, and the other one slightly larger, sealed and inside a heavy-duty pouch. He checked the contents of both. In the open envelope were the copied documents he'd already seen, and inside the sealed envelope he found the originals.

He tucked everything into one envelope, slipped that into the pouch and resealed it, and put it in his own jacket pocket.

He glanced back towards Voss, who had now recovered his senses and was staring at him with hate-filled eyes.

'I'll just hang on to these for safe keeping,' Tremayne smirked. 'I'd hate them to fall into the wrong hands.'

He ripped the page out of the notebook, took a final look round the sitting room to make sure he hadn't missed anything, stepped out of the stateroom, closed the door behind him and started walking quickly down the corridor, heading for the staircase that would take him down to E-Deck.

At the foot of the staircase, Tremayne eased the Browning

pistol out of his pocket and held it just inside his open jacket, then with his left hand he knocked firmly on the door of the first stateroom listed on the page. There was no response, so he waited a few seconds and then tried again, but with the same result.

He checked the number of the next one, and walked a few yards down the corridor until he reached it. He repeated the same sequence of knocks, and this time he also said: 'It's Voss. Open up,' in an American accent.

Now he heard a faint noise from inside the stateroom, then the unmistakable click as the lock was released, and the door opened just a crack.

Tremayne levelled his pistol and was about to kick the door wide open, when through the gap he saw a pair of grey eyes staring at him, and realized he was looking down the muzzle of another weapon.

Chapter 72

14 April 1912
RMS *Titanic*

The door swung wide open, and Maria stood in front of him, the pistol now held loosely in her right hand, and a slight smile playing over her lips.

'Well, buster, you certainly took your time,' she said. 'What have you been doing?'

Tremayne smiled back at her, a tidal wave of relief washing over him. 'Oh, this and that, you know.' Then he grabbed her in his arms and squeezed her tight. 'God,' he said, 'it's good to see you again.'

'That's quite enough of that,' Maria said. 'We've got company.'

Tremayne looked behind her, at the bed, where a bulky man lay on his side, his hands between his legs, breathing heavily and apparently in pain.

'What happened?' Tremayne asked.

'The usual. What you would probably expect to happen to a woman who finds herself in the clutches of a group of men who decide to kill her. They thought they'd have a little fun with me first.'

'Did they touch you?' Tremayne asked, the grip on his pistol tightening.

Maria shook her head. 'No. The moment a man – any man – starts thinking with the equipment he keeps below the belt instead of with his brain, they're usually quite easy to handle. I just undid a few buttons and waited for him to get close to me. Then it was just a matter of a knee in the groin, followed by a sharp punch in the throat. He was already over by the bed, where I was waiting for him, so I just pushed him onto it, snapped on the handcuffs he'd used on me, then walked back over here and picked up his gun to wait for either you or Voss to appear. He hasn't moved since, oddly enough.'

'How did you know that I wasn't dead?'

'I didn't, for sure anyway, but it was something Voss said that suggested you might not be. He was listing the weapons he'd taken off you – your pistol, a garrotte, and so on – but he never mentioned your stiletto, and I remember that when he searched you he made you put your arms in the air. I knew the stiletto was strapped to your left forearm, and so when Vincent took you off for your early morning swim, I somehow doubted if it was you who had gone over the side of the ship.'

Tremayne smiled. 'No,' he said. 'I'm sorry I didn't get to you sooner, but until I could get Voss by himself, I had no way of finding out where you were.'

'I presume Voss is dead?'

'Not quite. I wanted to make absolutely sure that I'd found you – that he'd told me the truth about where you were – before I finished the job. He's tied up securely in his stateroom. I'll go back there in a few minutes and sort him out. And I've recovered all three sets of copies, and the original documents, so we now know that Voss is a spent force, even if he somehow managed to get away. Once he's dead, it doesn't matter about the crates in the hold, because Cumming can arrange to have them collected in New York and the contents destroyed.'

'Excellent,' Maria said. 'So now let's stop wasting time and get that signal sent off to Mansfield.'

'What about him?' Tremayne pointed at the moaning figure lying on the bed.

'I think we can leave him there. I've taken his weapon, and he's not going anywhere in the near future. There was a certain amount of pent-up emotion in me when I kneed him in the groin. It's quite possible he'll never walk again.'

Chapter 73

14 April 1912
RMS *Titanic*

Lying on the carpeted floor of his suite, Gunther Voss was down, but not yet out. He thanked his lucky stars that Tremayne had been in such a hurry to go and find the woman, that he hadn't bothered to search him. The Deringer was still in his jacket pocket, though at that moment he couldn't reach it, but in his trouser pocket Voss carried a small knife with a very sharp blade. He normally used it to clip off the ends of his cigars, but it would cut through cord almost as easily as it sliced through tobacco. All he had to do was get it out.

With his wrists lashed together, it wasn't going to be easy, but he knew he had to succeed simply because the alternative didn't bear thinking about. He rolled onto his front and forced his bound wrists as far as he could over to the right-hand side of his body, but even arching his back and stretching his arms until he thought they would break, his fingers barely even touched the material at the top of his pocket, far less allowed him to feel inside it. He tried three times, but with the same result.

Then he had another thought: maybe gravity could help. He turned over onto his back, drew up his legs and then arched his back again so that his knees were in the air, but the knife stubbornly refused to fall out of his pocket. He rolled over, this time across to the side wall of his suite, lay on his back and walked his legs up the wall, until all the weight of his body was resting on his shoulders and bound arms. Then he wriggled his right leg up and down, trying to dislodge the knife.

And moments later, he heard a slight thud on the carpet beside him, and twisted round to look. There, lying right beside him, was the knife. He heaved a sigh of relief and brought his legs down from the wall as his fingers scrabbled to find the tiny instrument. His right hand closed around it, and then he knew that, as long as Tremayne didn't come back within the next two minutes, he could cut himself free.

Holding the knife firmly, he rolled onto his side and used the finger and thumb of his left hand to pull the blade open. It clicked into place, and then he moved it cautiously up towards the cord which held his wrists tight together. The first couple of times he tried it, the blade met nothing, but the third time it landed on something solid, and he immediately began a gentle sawing action, up and down.

Something parted, but his wrists were still lashed together, so he repeated the process, the sharp blade cutting through another part of the bonds that held him. This time, he must have hit one of the longer pieces of cord, because within moments he was free, the cord dangling from one wrist. He cut away the remaining pieces in a few seconds, then snapped the knife closed and slid it into his pocket.

He checked his jacket pocket. The Deringer was still there, with a handful of rounds, but he needed something with a lot more range. He ran through into the bed chamber, pulled out the presentation case from under the bed, and swiftly unlocked it. He took out both of the Lugers, pressed the button to release the magazine on each weapon, and opened one of the drawers in the wardrobe. Tucked away at the very back was a box of ammunition, given to him along with the two pistols. He loaded both magazines to capacity, slid them back into the butts of the Lugers, and put the rest of the ammunition in his jacket pocket. He had no holsters, but that didn't bother him. He tucked both weapons into the rear waistband of his trousers, where they would both be invisible and, more importantly, readily accessible.

Now all he had to do was find Tremayne, kill him, and make sure that he recovered the vital documents. Because, even with Bauer and Kortig gone, his plan could still work, and Voss had every intention of making sure that it did.

For a moment, Voss wondered if his best option might be to lie in wait in his suite. After all, Tremayne had told him that he would be returning, and Voss guessed that he would simply be able to shoot him down as he walked in through the door. But then he shook his head. Leonard, he now knew, was the only one of his four bodyguards who had survived their encounters with Tremayne, and he had a pretty good idea what his man had intended to do to the woman. There was a good chance, he thought, that if he got down to E-Deck as quickly as he could, he might well find that Tremayne was still in the stateroom there, exacting a messy revenge on Leonard for what he'd done to the American woman.

If he could burst in and surprise him, Voss knew that he could shoot down Tremayne, recover the original documents, and walk back up to his suite before any ship's officers or crew could turn up there to investigate the sound of gunfire. And that would also mean that all the blood would be down there as well, not spread all over the carpeted floor of his own stateroom.

He opened the door of his suite, checked up and down the corridor, then closed the door behind him and followed the same route Tremayne had taken, down to E-Deck.

Chapter 74

14 April 1912
RMS *Titanic*

Tremayne unlocked the door of their stateroom and then stood aside to let Maria enter first.

'We did it,' Maria said, with a hint of a surprise in her voice. 'For a while there, I wasn't sure that we'd be able to complete the operation.'

'There's still Voss,' Tremayne reminded her.

'I know, but you've got the documents and all the copies. Without them, there's nothing Voss can do, even if you don't kill him. The job's as good as finished. Let's get that signal sent off to Mansfield Cumming. There's less than three hours left before the deadline.'

Tremayne nodded, pulled out the notebook in which he'd written the decoded versions of the signals Mansfield Cumming had sent them, and opened it to start looking for the appropriate page.

'Do we need a special signal form or anything?' he asked, as he drew up a chair and sat down at the occasional table.

'Yes,' Maria replied. 'Just hang on there and I'll go along to the Purser's Office and get one. It's on this deck by the grand staircase.'

She was back in under five minutes, a printed form clutched in her hand.

'You have to use this,' she said, passing him the piece of paper. 'That's a form for a Marconigram, and according to the man I asked, it's the fastest way of getting a message back to London.'

Tremayne completed the administrative sections and in the large section at the bottom of the form, where the word 'To' was printed, he carefully wrote the address he'd been given, the address which he knew would ensure the message was sent straight to Mansfield Cumming as soon as it arrived in London. Then, below that, in the grid for the communication itself, he printed the prearranged message in block capitals, and added one piece of additional information:

PHASES ONE TWO AND THREE COMPLETE STOP LEVER
IDENTIFIED AND RECOVERED STOP TREMAYNE

There was no section on the form for a precedence indicator, so against 'Service Instructions', he simply wrote 'MOST URGENT' and underlined it twice, and then added 'RELAYING PERMITTED'.

Tremayne showed Maria what he'd written, but she frowned at him. 'He will get it in time, won't he?' she asked.

He looked at his watch. 'It's not even eight o'clock yet,' he said, 'and the deadline Cumming gave us was twenty-two hundred hours tonight, which is still over two hours away. I've marked the message "most urgent", so with any luck he'll get it within a few minutes. I certainly don't think there'll be any problem with it arriving within the next two hours. And this is the only way we can contact Mansfield. He told me on no account were we to let any of the ship's officers know what was happening, or what we were doing.'

Tremayne left the stateroom and walked quickly to the Purser's Office, where he handed in the form. The attendant behind the desk glanced at it, then carried it into the adjacent Enquiry Office, Tremayne following, where he inserted it in a canister which he put in a pneumatic tube system.

'That message is very urgent,' he said. 'I mean really, genuinely life or death important.'

'Don't worry, sir, it's a very efficient system,' he said. 'From here, it goes straight to the Marconi Office to be sent. They'll see the "Most Urgent" markings and get it sent as soon as possible.'

Tremayne thanked the man, paid for the message and then walked across the lobby but turned right instead of left. Once he'd finished off Voss, he could finally relax.

He glanced both ways down the corridor before he drew out his weapon, opened the door and stepped inside.

Then he stopped short. Voss was no longer lying tied up on the floor. Tremayne closed the door behind him, his eyes darting around the room, looking for hiding places, but there was nowhere a man could be concealed, at least not in that sitting room. He stepped forward to the door leading into the bedroom and took a swift, cautious glance in there as well, but again the only possible hiding place was under the bed, and one look was enough to tell him that Voss wasn't there either.

He walked back into the sitting room and picked up one end of the cord that was lying on the floor. It had clearly been cut, and Tremayne cursed himself for not having searched Voss before he left the room. But he'd been so concerned for Maria's safety that he'd got out as quickly as he could. That had obviously been a bad mistake, understandable though it was.

So where had Voss gone? Not to the officers on the ship, Tremayne was almost sure about that. Voss wouldn't want any official involvement any more than Tremayne would: it would hamper his movements far too much.

He tried to put himself in Voss's position. And then the answer seemed obvious. Voss would want to recover the original documents as quickly as possible.

From Tremayne being the hunter, it looked as if the tables might have been turned, and that now Voss would be pursuing him.

And hunting Maria. Tremayne turned on his heel and ran down the corridor back to his stateroom.

Chapter 75

14 April 1912
RMS *Titanic*

The Marconi Office was actually a number of interconnecting rooms located on the Boat Deck, staffed by Marconi employees. The transmitting equipment was rated at five kilowatts, making it one of the most powerful transmitters afloat, and had a normal range of only 250 nautical miles, but that was during daylight. At night, transmission ranges of up to 2,000 nautical miles were possible, and especially to receiving stations located either directly ahead or directly astern of the ship, because of the radiation characteristics of the T-shaped aerial.

At that time, the ship was just within range of a receiving station in southern Ireland, and from there the message could be swiftly relayed through the normal landline system to London. The range, in this case, was not the problem. Tremayne's message was delayed simply because of the workload.

The passengers on board the *Titanic* had been delighted to find that, for a comparatively modest cost, they could send telegrams to people they knew on other ships, to friends back in England, or people over in the United States of America, and they took full advantage of this facility. The Marconi operators were literally working day and night to handle the backlog of messages, and were not helped in this endeavour by the fact that the radio transmitter had broken down for several hours the previous day, and had also stopped working a couple of times on the fourteenth.

The messages from passengers had, of course, continued to arrive, and all were treated in the same way: no matter what the message contents, they were handled strictly in the order in which they arrived at the office.

As Tremayne's Marconigram arrived, the operator picked it up, glanced at the text and smiled at the 'Most Urgent' note at the bottom. Then he tossed it onto a pile with all the others, picked up the next message and began transmitting the contents.

Chapter 76

14 April 1912
RMS *Titanic*

Voss walked slowly along the starboard side passageway through the first-class accommodation on E-Deck, his right hand inside his jacket and resting on the butt of one of his Lugers, which he'd moved to the front waistband of his trousers. He passed a couple of people as he made his way down towards the small stateroom occupied by his surviving body-guard, but the area was still largely deserted.

Outside the room, he checked that nobody was in sight, then pressed his ear to the door and for several seconds just listened. He heard nothing to alarm him, certainly no sound of a beating. In fact, all he could hear was a faint moaning sound, and that could almost have been caused by some part of the ship's machinery. He checked around him again, took out the Luger and turned the door handle.

It was locked, and there was no response to his knocking. But Voss held the duplicate keys to the staterooms his men occu-pied – he was the one paying for their passage, after all – and he inserted the key and turned it in the lock. With the pistol held out in front of him, his finger on the trigger ready to fire the moment he saw Tremayne or any danger, he opened the door and stepped inside.

The stateroom was obviously empty apart from the man lying on the bed, who Voss immediately realized had been the source of the sound he had detected. Leonard was still curled up, his hands and handcuffed wrists clutched between his legs, and clearly in great pain.

Voss locked the door behind him, then stepped across to the bed on the other side of the stateroom. He grabbed Leonard by the shoulder and shook him.

'What happened?' he snapped. 'Was it Tremayne? What did he do to you?'

Leonard shook his head. 'No,' he groaned. 'It was the woman. She kicked me.'

Voss stared down at his incapacitated bodyguard for several seconds, digesting that information. He'd known that Tremayne and the woman formed a team, that she wasn't just along to act as his assistant or in a purely supporting role. Leonard was over six feet tall, heavily built, and extremely fit, but he'd been rendered helpless by a single kick from a woman about half his size. Now Voss knew he was facing not one but two trained assassins. He would definitely need Leonard's help to take them out.

'Can you stand up?' he asked, as he unlocked the handcuffs.

'Just about. God, that hurts.'

Leonard rolled over slowly and painfully to the edge of the bed, and lowered his feet gingerly to the floor. He stood up, resting one hand against the wall of the stateroom for support, his legs spread unusually wide.

'Try walking,' Voss instructed.

The bodyguard staggered a few steps across the room, then

turned and walked back, his face white with strain and perspiration springing from his brow. He was mobile, just about, but Voss knew that as a fighting force he was useless.

'Where's your pistol?' Voss asked.

'The woman took it.'

'Did you see Tremayne?'

Leonard nodded. 'Yes. He came along after she'd attacked me, and then they left together.'

'Here,' Voss said, taking the second Luger from the waistband of his trousers and handing it to Leonard. 'You'll have to stay here for a while, until you can walk again. If Tremayne or the woman come back, don't mess about: just shoot them.'

The bodyguard took it and laid it on the bed beside him. 'Is there a spare magazine?' he asked.

Voss shook his head and smiled slightly as he headed for the door of the stateroom. 'With those two,' he said, 'if you don't take them out with what's in the magazine now, you'd be dead long before you could reload the pistol.'

Chapter 77

14 April 1912
London

Mansfield Cumming had been at his desk the entire day, waiting for the message from Alex Tremayne on board the *Titanic* which would signal the successful termination of the operation. But he had heard absolutely nothing. He had reset the clock on his desk to American Eastern Standard Time, so that he would know the current time on board both the ship and the submarine which was now, he hoped, lurking in the path of the great liner.

The deadline he had given Tremayne was twenty-two hundred hours, ten o'clock in the evening, after which – assuming that no message had been received – he would have no option but to authorize the immediate transmission of the 'execute' signal which he had already prepared and which was lying on the desk in front of him.

By twenty hundred hours EST, Mansfield Cumming had given up any pretence of work and was sitting hunched over his desk, his eyes focused for most of the time on the hands of his desk clock, his thoughts racing as he pondered the reason for the delay. An hour later, at twenty-one hundred, there had still been no message, and he was fearing the worst, that Alex Tremayne, far and away his best agent, had failed in his mission. At twenty-one forty-five, fifteen minutes before the deadline expired, he instructed Mrs McTavish to contact the Admiralty by telephone, where several senior Naval officers were awaiting results.

'I thought you said, Cumming,' one of them remarked, 'that your man was competent, that he would do the job.'

'He's very competent,' Cumming replied, 'so I can only assume that something went badly wrong on board the ship. We did know that Voss was travelling with four bodyguards so perhaps we should have sent more men to deal with him.'

'With hindsight, anything is possible,' the officer said. 'But that still leaves us facing this current problem. I really do not wish to issue this order. Your man does know the deadline, and what will happen if he does not complete his assignment?'

'Yes. I made that absolutely clear in my last message to him. He's fully aware of what's at stake here.'

'Then for all our sakes, Cumming, I hope the message arrives within the next five minutes.'

'Can I recommend a delay of thirty minutes?'

'No, Cumming, you cannot. The window of opportunity for the submarine is extremely narrow. We have to give the order in a timely fashion, otherwise it will be impossible for the engagement to take place at all.'

When he ended the call, Cumming stared at the second hand of the clock on the table in front of him as it inexorably swept around the dial, counting off yet another minute.

Mrs McTavish knocked on the office door and walked in. 'You asked me to remind you, sir, when the time was up,' she said.

Cumming looked old and grey. He nodded. 'Yes. Thank you, Mrs McTavish.'

It was twenty-two hundred hours Eastern Standard Time.

As she turned away, Cumming stopped her with a final instruction. 'I expect the Admiralty will be telephoning quite soon, Mrs McTavish. When they do, do not connect the call to me. Just tell them that I am unavailable.'

Chapter 78

14 April 1912
RMS *Titanic*

In the Marconi Office, one of the harassed operators seized the next message from the pile and looked at it. The transmitting equipment now seemed to be working properly, but because of the earlier problems there was still a huge backlog of messages waiting to be processed.

'"Most urgent",' he muttered to himself, as he prepared to transmit the text. 'Every blasted message from a passenger on this ship is "most urgent". You'd think they'd have something better to do with their time than send this sort of rubbish.'

He was unfamiliar with military messages of any sort, and as far as he was concerned no one passenger's communication deserved any higher precedence than anybody else's.

The message was short, just a few groups, and within a couple of minutes the operator had marked it as 'Sent', and moved on to the next Marconigram.

Chapter 79

14 April 1912
London

Mansfield Cumming watched the minute hand of his desk clock move round, with what seemed like frightening rapidity, to the number five on the dial. When it reached ten past the hour, Mrs McTavish opened the door.

'I've had one of those admirals on twice, sir, and he sounded really annoyed. Do you still not wish to speak to them?'

Cumming shook his head. 'No, not yet. Just a few more minutes.'

At twenty-two fifteen Eastern Standard Time, as he heard the telephone ring in the outer office once more, he knew that he could delay no longer. He stepped outside his office and waited until Mrs McTavish had ended the call to the admiral whose voice was so loud that Cumming could make out most of what he was saying from where he was standing. Then he confirmed with her what he already knew, that no messages had been received, and handed her the 'execute' message for immediate transmission via the Admiralty's radio communication system.

Then he walked back into his office, shut the door and for some seconds sat at his desk with his head in his hands. Then he pulled open the bottom drawer, removed a bottle of single malt whisky that he'd bought on the Isle of Skye, and poured himself a large drink.

He held the glass of amber liquid up to the light and studied the way that it seemed almost to glow.

'Goodbye, Alex,' he said, 'and you too, Maria. God rest your souls.'

There were tears in his eyes as he took the first sip.

Chapter 80

14 April 1912
Crookhaven, County Cork, Ireland

The telegraphic station at Crookhaven was working at maximum capacity, despite the late hour, with a full complement of six operators on duty. Since the station had been established ten years earlier in 1902, the amount of wireless traffic from ships crossing the Atlantic had increased enormously. The job of the Crookhaven operators was to convert the radio traffic to normal telegraph and transmit the messages along landlines to their ultimate destination. In the early days, the station might only be in contact with one ship, but by 1912 traffic from over six ships at a time was the norm.

That night, one of the operators was working full-time just on signal traffic from the RMS *Titanic*, such was the volume of messages being transmitted from the liner, and he was finding it difficult to keep up. His head bent over his desk, he snatched another signal form and immediately began transferring the message to the telegraph, oblivious of the chattering of his companions and the constant tapping of the other Morse keys beside him. As soon as he'd finished that message, he reached for the next. And then the next, creating a production line of communications as he struggled to clear the backlog.

He took a brief break for a drink and a visit to the lavatory, then resumed his task. Tremayne's Marconigram was in the pile in front of him, marked for onward transmission to the London telegraphic address. But because of the volume of traffic being handled, it was almost fifteen minutes after its arrival before the operator finally picked it up and relayed it to its addressee and final destination.

Chapter 81

14 April 1912

HMS *D4*

The signal Lieutenant Hutchinson had been expecting arrived later than he had anticipated, at around twenty-two twenty-five EST. He already had the code book out on the table, and the moment the signalman passed him the sealed envelope and he'd signed for its receipt, he began deciphering the message.

As soon as he saw the size of the encrypted text, he knew what the contents would be. What he'd been hoping to receive would have been a simple three digit message – RTB, return to base – but he was looking at nearly a page of encrypted groups.

It took him ten minutes to complete the decryption, not least because the final section, which followed the series of precise orders he was to follow, was another personal instruction from the head of the Submarine Service, reiterating the crucial national, and international, importance of what he was being ordered to do, and the vital necessity of never breathing a word about the operation to anyone.

Despite this high-level reassurance, for several minutes Hutchinson sat on the edge of his bunk and simply stared at the decrypted signal, struggling to make sense of the implications. Firing a torpedo at an enemy vessel during a time of war was entirely justified. That was what he and his crew had been trained to do. Firing a torpedo at a completely unarmed civilian ship in peace time was utterly abhorrent to him. What he was being told to do seemed sheer madness. He could think of no possible reason why the British government would want him to sink the White Star Line's newest and most expensive passenger ship, the *Titanic*. But that was what the signal was instructing him to do, in absolutely clear and unequivocal language.

For a few fleeting seconds, Hutchinson considered not acknowledging the signal and simply ignoring it. But he knew that the signal logs on board the boat would clearly show that he had received the message, and then disobeyed it. So perhaps there was something else he could do. In fact, he realized, there was one thing he should certainly do.

He walked back out into the control room and summoned a signalman.

'Acknowledge that message you just received,' he instructed, 'and then add the following two words: "Confirm target". And do that right now.'

The signalman hurried away, and Hutchinson climbed up the metal ladder to the conning tower, where Bill Evans was on watch.

'All quiet?' Hutchinson asked. 'No ships?'

'It's clear all the way to the horizon,' Evans replied, 'but we're seeing a few more icebergs now, so we may have to do a bit more manoeuvring than we've done so far if we're going to stay in this area. Have you had the signal yet?'

Hutchinson nodded. 'It came a few minutes ago and it does instruct us to carry out a live firing. I've asked for confirmation, just as a precaution, but my guess is we'll be firing the two weapons in an hour or so.'

'At what?' Evans asked reasonably, looking around at the empty sea.

'A target ship will apparently be provided,' Hutchinson replied, stretching the truth more than a little.

'Sir?' The voice came from below, and Hutchinson looked down to see the signalman standing at the foot of the conning-tower ladder.

'Yes?'

'They've replied, sir,' he said, 'and in clear. The message reads: "Target confirmed. Course and speed as briefed. Execute." That's all it says, sir.'

Hutchinson nodded slowly. Now it was all up to him.

'Right,' he said. 'Get some men up here to drop the mast and stow the radio aerial, and rig for diving.'

'We're submerging?' Evans asked. 'With all these icebergs around?'

'Believe me, Bill,' Hutchinson said. 'You don't know the half of it.'

Chapter 82

14 April 1912
London

Mrs McTavish didn't even bother to knock. She simply swept the office door open, a piece of paper clutched in her right hand, which she waved at Mansfield Cumming as she strode across to his desk.

'The signal, sir, the message. It's from the *Titanic*. They've done it. Mr Tremayne and that Maria. They've done it!'

Cumming grabbed the paper from her and read the two brief sentences that it contained. Then he looked at the time it had been sent from the ship and realized that Tremayne had made the deadline. But the message had taken the better part of three hours to get to him.

'Quickly, Mrs McTavish. Get me the Admiralty, as fast as you possibly can.'

He was connected to his opposite number there in less than two minutes.

'Stop the attack,' Cumming said, almost shouting. 'My man has done it, but his message was badly delayed.'

There was a pause from the other end of the line, and when the captain replied, his voice was almost apologetic.

'I don't think that's possible,' he said. 'The boat's already acknowledged the "execute" signal. The captain queried it, but we've already sent confirmation.'

'You've got to try!' Now Cumming really was shouting, a vein in his forehead pulsing angrily. 'For God's sake man, do something.'

He heard nothing for about a minute, and then the officer came back on the line.

'We've sent an order cancelling the operation and instructing the submarine to return to base,' he said. 'The trouble is that we ordered the captain to dive his boat as soon as he'd acknowledged the signal, in preparation for the attack, and before he can submerge, he has to unship the radio aerial. That means he can't receive any transmissions from us until he resurfaces and puts the aerial up again. Stand by.'

There was another short pause before the captain spoke again.

'We've sent the signal six times now, and there's been no response of any sort. We'll keep transmitting, but I think we have to face the facts here, Mansfield. That submarine has submerged and it's going to prosecute the attack, so we'll need to be ready to react when the news breaks. This is going to be a complete disaster.'

As he ended the call, Mansfield Cumming thought that, if anything, the captain at the Admiralty was severely understating the magnitude of what was about to unfold.

Chapter 83

14 April 1912
RMS *Titanic*

The *Titanic*'s Marconi radio room was busy, messages being sent and received both from other ships operating in the north Atlantic and from shore stations such as Cape Race in Newfoundland.

An ice-warning message, the first of several, had been received by the ship at about noon that day, but nobody on the bridge seemed to be particularly interested. The *Titanic* was a huge ship, filled with watertight compartments and doors that could be closed electrically from the bridge to isolate certain sections of the hull in the event of any damage being sustained. Floating ice was not perceived to be a serious problem.

A second message had been received just after seventeen thirty EST, reporting three icebergs close to the liner's planned route, and at twenty-two forty, a third message had been received, this one from a ship named the *Californian*. That vessel reported so much ice in its vicinity that the captain had ordered the engines to be stopped until daylight the following morning, leaving the ship dead in the water and surrounded by ice.

That message was brushed aside by the operator on the *Titanic* because it wasn't prefixed by the standard urgency code 'MSG' – standing for 'Master Service Gram' – which would have ensured it was sent directly to the captain, the master of the ship.

So when, sometime later, the radio operators received yet another message warning of icebergs ahead, even though the source of this particular message was somewhat unusual, they didn't feel that it was worth reporting the matter to the bridge.

And in fact, by that time it was already too late.

Chapter 84

14 April 1912
HMS *D4*

Bernard Hutchinson was the last to leave the conning tower. Just before he did so, he glanced at his watch. Ten forty-six. He took a last look around the horizon with his binoculars, and there, slowly beginning to appear down to the south-east, he saw a faint glow of light. The *Titanic*, the ship he'd been ordered to sink, was just about to come into view.

He knew the vessel would be travelling at about twenty knots, perhaps even slightly faster, and would reach his location within the hour. He scanned in a complete circle once again, mentally noting the position of a handful of icebergs in his area. In those conditions, he would have much preferred to stay on the surface, and steer the boat from the conning tower, but that was now an option which he didn't have. But the boat wasn't going deep. It would remain at periscope depth throughout the operation.

He climbed down the ladder, securing the hatch above his head as he did so, then stepped onto the steel floor of the control room, shedding his foul-weather clothing as he did so.

'Dive the boat, Mr Evans,' he instructed. 'Maintain periscope depth.'

Evans issued the appropriate orders, and the metal hull of the small submarine suddenly came alive as water rushed into tanks to reduce its buoyancy and allow it to dive. The throb of the diesel engines, which had been an inescapable background accompaniment for the last few days, suddenly ceased as the boat switched over to electric power.

Within five minutes, the submarine was below the surface of the water, the screws turning just enough to provide steerage way, and Hutchinson was standing in the control room with his head clamped to the eyepieces of the periscope. Through the optics, the distant shape of the ocean liner was now just visible, though the ship was still too far away to be positively identified. But Hutchinson would absolutely ensure that he was targeting the correct vessel before he gave the order to fire his weapons.

He stepped away from the periscope for a few moments and glanced round the control room. Whenever the submarine was below the surface, these men all knew that technically it had already sunk, and all that was stopping it from continuing to plunge to the bottom of the ocean was the delicate balancing act conducted by the crew as water replaced air to subtly alter the boat's buoyancy. If anything went wrong, they all knew that the submarine could begin an unstoppable and fatal descent without warning in a matter of seconds, and their faces reflected this inevitable uncertainty.

'We're about to embark on an unusual manoeuvre,' Hutchinson said. 'I know we're out here in the middle of the Atlantic, but their Lordships at the Admiralty have decreed that while we're here we will engage a target ship. That vessel is now being towed into position, and I expect that we will begin our attack within the hour. Once we have fired our weapons, we will retreat for a distance of about twenty miles, remaining submerged throughout, and then surface and report the results of the attack.'

Hutchinson paused and glanced around again. Many of the crew looked puzzled, which was entirely unsurprising because none of them had been involved in anything of this sort before. And, he thought, they would probably look a lot more puzzled before he'd finished.

'The other unusual feature of this attack,' he continued, 'is that it is really a test of my abilities. I have been instructed to conduct the entire evolution by myself, with no help from any other members of the crew, except for the usual duties. That means that nobody else is to use the periscope for the duration of the attack. I will locate the target, plot a firing solution and issue all the appropriate instructions to release the weapons entirely independently. Is all that clearly understood?'

He'd been right. Now everybody looked confused. William Evans opened his mouth to say something, but Hutchinson got there first.

'Those are my orders, Bill. They don't make too much sense to me either, but that's what I've been told to do, so we'd better get on with it.'

Hutchinson went back to the periscope, carried out a complete sweep to ensure that they hadn't moved too close to any of the icebergs in their vicinity, then focused on the approaching liner. He could now see what kind of ship it was, because lights blazed from most of the decks, and even at a distance, he could tell that it was simply enormous. He looked at it for a few seconds more, then did another sweep.

It wouldn't be long now.

Chapter 85

Alex Tremayne was taking no chances. As far as he was aware, Voss didn't know which stateroom he and Maria were occupying, but he also knew that the Prussian could find out easily enough, simply by checking the list of first-class passengers who had boarded the ship at Southampton and looking for the name 'Maitland'. Staying in their stateroom could become a trap. They needed to get out of there, and merge into the crowds in the public rooms.

'He's still alive,' Maria objected, 'but he knows we've discovered his plans and taken the documents, so surely he'll just stay out of our way now.'

But Tremayne shook his head. 'No,' he replied, 'precisely because I've got those original documents. If he can get those back, he can still make his plan work, even though Bauer and Kortig are dead. Without those papers, Voss is powerless to proceed. The one thing I'm absolutely sure about is that he'll now be doing his best to hunt down and kill both of us to get them back.'

Maria didn't look particularly concerned. 'There are two of us, and only one of him,' she pointed out, 'or one and a half, I suppose, if you include his bodyguard. And we're armed and he isn't, because I took the bodyguard's pistol, and you took the one Voss was carrying.'

'You're quite right,' Tremayne agreed, 'but when I went back to Voss's stateroom, the presentation case was open on his bed, and both the Luger pistols were missing. Just because I didn't find any ammunition when I searched his room doesn't mean that he didn't have a box tucked away somewhere. And usually when you give somebody a weapon, it's also normal to hand over some ammunition. I think we have to assume that he's carrying one of the pistols, and by now he's probably given the other one to the bodyguard.'

'I should have killed him when I had the chance,' Maria said bitterly, concern giving her voice an edge.

'And I should have shot Voss, but I was worried that he hadn't told me the truth about where you were. We're going to have to be even more careful from now on. We'll have to carry our pistols at all times, stay in the most crowded public rooms, and even, I think, take it in turns to sleep. I'm not the only person in the world who can pick a lock, and I don't want to be woken up in the middle of the night to find Voss beside the bed getting ready to cut my throat.'

Maria shivered. 'But it's still two against two,' she said. 'We can beat these people.'

'We will beat these people,' Tremayne confirmed. 'There's something else I think we should do. I still reckon that I'll be the main target for Voss. It'll be me he comes after first, so it'd be a good idea if we split the copies and the originals. You take the originals and one set of copies, and I'll take the other set. We'll carry them with us at all times, just as Voss and the other two men did.'

'Can't we just destroy them? Burn them or something?'

Tremayne shook his head. 'Frankly, I'd rather do that, but there'd be no way of convincing Voss about what we'd done, unless he actually watched us destroy them. And don't forget that Mansfield Cumming wanted us to recover whatever lever Voss was going to use. We can tell him what we found and what the documents contain, but I'd rather hand everything over to him once we get back to London.'

'So what do we do now?'

'We go out for the evening,' Tremayne said. 'We take our weapons with us, and we go up to the à la carte restaurant, where there'll be lots of other people, and we eat dinner. Afterwards, we'll stay in the public rooms until the crowds start to thin out, and then we'll come back down here. I'll barricade the door as best I can. Then you'll go to bed and I'll keep watch until, say, five in the morning, and then we'll change over. We'll do the same tomorrow and every other day until we get to New York, and make it as difficult as possible for Voss to target us. And, obviously, if I get a chance, I'll do my best to make sure that Voss does his bit for nature.'

Maria looked puzzled. 'What do you mean?'

'I mean I'll try and throw him off the ship so that he can feed the fish. At least that way he'll have done one useful thing in his life.'

Chapter 86

14 April 1912
London

'Look,' Mansfield Cumming said into the candlestick telephone mouthpiece, 'you have to do something. If you can't raise the submarine then there's only one other option. You have to contact the *Titanic* and warn the captain.'

He listened for a few moments to what the other man was saying to him, then tried again.

'At this stage, I don't think it matters what reason you give. Obviously, you can't tell him that the British Government has ordered a Royal Navy submarine to sink this ship, but there must be other things you can suggest which will force the liner to divert from its route. It's winter, in the north Atlantic. There must be dozens of icebergs in the vicinity. Signal the captain and tell him that you have received an iceberg warning or something, and suggest he alters course to avoid that area by a few miles.'

He listened again.

'No, it doesn't have to be far. The *Titanic* can do better than twenty knots. Dived, that submarine can't even achieve half that speed, so the liner can actually outrun the sub, and the torpedoes have only got a fairly short range as well.'

Two minutes later, he finished the call and sat back in his chair. He hoped that the Admiralty would try to do something, but at this stage in the game, he had a horrible feeling that it was going to be far too little, and much too late.

Chapter 87

14 April 1912
RMS *Titanic*

Tremayne and Maria had eaten a fairly hasty dinner in the à la carte restaurant – neither of them had much of an appetite – and then retired to the lounge on the Promenade Deck – one of the more crowded public rooms – for an after-dinner drink. The American poker players were in there, already well into their game, and one of them called out to ask Maria if she'd like to join them.

But she shook her head. 'Not tonight gentlemen, thank you,' she said. 'I think I've had quite enough excitement for one day,' she added, with a smile.

She and Tremayne found a vacant table beside one of the large bay windows, and sat down there. Tremayne ordered drinks, and when they arrived they silently toasted each other.

'What do you think the ship will do about the dead bodies? Bauer and Kortig, I mean?' she asked quietly, making sure that they couldn't be overheard.

'I don't think there's a lot they can do,' Tremayne replied, 'except put them in cold storage somewhere. Unless they look very hard, I think most doctors would probably conclude that

Bauer did die of a sudden heart attack. After all, the only sign he didn't is a minute puncture mark in the crook of his left arm. There's obviously no doubt that Kortig was shot, but I made sure that I left no clues in his suite that could implicate us.

'There are no witnesses, and even if Voss or the surviving bodyguard were to come forward and claim that we did it, we have no connection with either of the two dead men, and no obvious reason to wish them harm. It would be our word against theirs. And there's no evidence either. I've already chucked Mansfield Cumming's bottles of instant heart attack over the side, along with the cosh and Vincent's pistol, the one I used to shoot Kortig. I've kept the stiletto and our two Brownings. So we're a couple of innocent passengers who just happened to be travelling on the same ship as two men who are now dead. And hopefully that will be the end of it.'

Maria nodded. 'That makes sense to me,' she said. She looked out the window and shivered slightly. 'It's a real shame the weather has turned so cold. There's no moon, and it's a real dark night out there. Let's hope tomorrow is brighter.'

At that moment, Gunther Voss stepped into the lounge, his gaze swivelling around as he searched the faces of the occupants. Within seconds, he saw Tremayne and Maria, and for a moment he just stared at them. Then he gave a brief nod, turned on his heel and left the room.

Tremayne watched him go, then turned to Maria.

'It's not over yet,' he murmured.

Chapter 88

14 April 1912
HMS *D4*

Hutchinson checked the time. It was just after eleven thirty, and his target was now clearly visible, and readily identifiable. He was trying to remain coolly rational about what he had been asked to do, reducing the evolution to a matter of geometry, of headings and angles and relative velocities, because only by doing that could he be certain of achieving the result that he wanted.

The forward torpedo room was ready, the two tubes, mounted vertically one above the other, were both flooded in preparation for weapon release, and the figure-of-eight-shaped single outer door had already been rotated to expose the ends of the tubes and allow the weapons to be fired. The submarine was steady on what he anticipated would be the firing course, which would send two torpedoes, with their 200-pound warheads full of nitrocellulose or gun cotton, streaking towards their target over a distance of a little under half a mile.

He ordered a slight heading change and reduced speed by half a knot. He checked the target position again, told the torpedo room to stand by and then waited for the perfect moment.

Five minutes, he estimated. That was all.

Chapter 89

14 April 1912
RMS *Titanic*

Voss, in fact, had done more or less what Tremayne had expected him to do. He'd checked the first-class passenger list, found the name 'Maitland' and noted the stateroom number. But he had been unable to force the door, though he'd frantically tried. Defeated, he'd returned to his own stateroom, locked and barred his own door, then dressed for the evening – he knew he had to keep up the appearance of normality – and had walked into the à la carte restaurant about five minutes after Tremayne and Maria had left.

After dinner, he'd tried Tremayne's door again, but the stateroom was obviously still empty. He guessed that his quarry would be haunting the public rooms as much as possible, relying on the passive protection of other first-class passengers, and he'd confirmed that when he saw them together in the first-class lounge. But sooner or later, they would have to return to the room, and that would give him the opportunity he needed. If he waited until the middle of the night, he could force the door, perhaps even use a bullet from his Luger to destroy the lock if he couldn't open it any other way. Then he could get inside, kill them both and grab the documents and get away, hopefully before the alarm was properly raised. He'd have to wait and see what the night would bring.

Then he had another idea. Voss walked back down to E-Deck, knocked on the door of his bodyguard's stateroom, and waited. A few seconds later, Leonard opened the door. He looked a lot better, and even seemed to be walking more normally.

Voss stepped inside the room, then turned round.

'Can you pick locks?' he asked.

Leonard shrugged. 'A bit,' he admitted, 'as long as they're not too complicated.'

'What about a stateroom door lock? And have you got the right tools with you?'

'Yeah, I've got a couple of picks in my bag.'

'Right,' Voss said. 'Get some sleep now, and I'll see you outside my suite at three fifteen this morning. Make sure you bring the picks and the Luger. We're going to pay a visit to that bastard Tremayne, kill him and the woman, and retrieve some property he's stolen from me.'

Leonard grinned. 'I'll look forward to it,' he said.

Chapter 90

14 April 1912
HMS *D4*

Bernard Hutchinson hadn't taken his eyes off the approaching ship for the last three minutes.

The *Titanic* was off his port bow – at that moment, it was at about red zero-three-zero-thirty degrees to the left of the bow– and still steaming ahead at about twenty knots. Hitting it was not going to be easy, he knew that. It was a relatively high-speed crossing target, but the advantage he had was that he knew its course and speed would remain steady, so calculating the weapon release point was a comparatively easy mathematical exercise. He'd done it twice already and checked it three times, and he knew that his calculation was correct. Then it would all depend on how accurately the torpedoes conformed to their specifications – on how their actual speed matched what the weapons were supposed to travel at, and how straight their course was through the water.

He looked at his stopwatch, waiting for precisely the right moment to order weapon release. Then back to the eyepieces, watching the ship's approach through the periscope.

'Standby forward torpedo room,' he ordered. 'Ready tube one.'

'Tube one ready, sir.'

And then something completely unexpected happened. Like some enormous primordial sea creature, a huge dark mass seemed almost to rise from the deep, directly in front of the *Titanic*, so large that, from Hutchinson's viewpoint, it obscured the deck lights around the bow of the vessel.

It was a massive iceberg, and as far as Hutchinson could see, the ship was heading straight for it.

Chapter 91

14 April 1912
RMS *Titanic*

On the bridge of the speeding liner, all was quiet and peaceful. All the instruments, the dials and the gauges, were displaying normal readings. The ship was travelling through the water at over twenty knots, so fast that to come to a dead stop from that speed would take the vessel almost half a mile.

But stopping, quickly or otherwise, was not the intention. The *Titanic*, along with her sister ship the *Olympic*, had been intended by the White Star Line to provide the fastest possible crossings of the Atlantic Ocean, from Southampton to New York, and on this, the ship's maiden voyage, the captain was clearly determined to produce a time that other ships would find difficult to beat. Conditions were almost perfect. The sea was calm and the night was dark but clear, and the captain had retired to his cabin after instructing that he was to be called only if visibility dropped, when he would then decide if a reduction in speed was necessary.

Two lookouts, Fredrick Fleet and Reginald Lee, were posted in the crow's nest, with responsibility to advise the bridge of any obstacles that they saw. Due to the replacement of one of the ship's officers, they had no binoculars – the only pair the ship possessed were in a locker in the cabin previously occupied by that original officer, and nobody apparently knew they were there – and they were relying on their eyes to spot obstacles in the water ahead of the speeding liner. But in fact the night was so dark that binoculars might not have been much help to them.

During their watch, neither man had seen anything to warrant sounding the alarm, but that changed, with horrific suddenness at twenty-three thirty-nine Eastern Standard Time.

A huge dark-blue, almost black, mass suddenly loomed out of the darkness, directly in front of the ship, and frighteningly close.

'My God,' Fredrick Fleet muttered, as he strained his eyes to make out what the object was. At the same time, he reached over and grabbed the pull cord to ring the ship's bell mounted on the mast, ringing it three times to indicate that an object had been sighted.

Then he grabbed the telephone fitted in the crow's nest, and by then he knew exactly what the object was.

The phone was answered by the Sixth Officer on the bridge below.

'What do you see?' the officer asked anxiously.

'Iceberg right ahead,' Fleet replied.

'Thank you,' the officer said, then rang off.

At that moment, the iceberg was under 400 yards in front of the speeding *Titanic*, less than half the distance the ship would need to come to a complete stop. There was only one possible option. They would have to try to steer around it.

William Murdoch, the First Officer on the bridge had sighted the iceberg at almost the same moment, and reacted immediately.

'Hard a'starboard!' he ordered, although the iceberg was slightly to the right of the bow.

The order was a hangover from the days of vessels steered by tillers, when to turn a ship to port, to the left, the tiller had to be pushed all the way to the right, to starboard.

The helmsman immediately turned the wheel all the way anti-clockwise. At the stern of the ship, the huge single rudder swung to the left in response.

Even before the helmsman had completed this task, Murdoch had seized the engine-room telegraph and rung 'All stop' and then 'All reverse full'.

In the engine room far below, alarm bells rang and engineers raced to comply with the emergency order from the bridge. But to actually achieve this was quite a complex operation.

First, the three massive propellers driving the *Titanic* forward would have to be stopped completely. Then reverse gear would have to be engaged, and finally steam pressure would have to build up again before the propellers would be able to start turning in the opposite direction. All of that would take time, but more importantly the sudden cessation of thrust would also make the ship less manoeuvrable and harder to turn. Arguably, this order from the bridge made a collision with the iceberg more, not less, likely.

On the bridge, the First Officer activated the switches to close the watertight doors below deck, isolating the forward compartments, as a precaution in case the ship did hit the floating mass of ice and suffer any damage.

Almost immediately, the ship's forward speed started to reduce, both by the cessation of power to the three huge propellers, and by the turn away from the massive iceberg. But the *Titanic* was still travelling quickly, and the iceberg was looming ever closer, its bulk seeming to virtually fill the sea in front of the liner.

But now the bow of the ship was moving slowly but steadily to port, to the left, towards the open water beyond the iceberg. It looked as if they'd been lucky, as if the vessel would manage to avoid a collision. It all depended on the shape of the iceberg below the waterline, on the submerged mass of ice that they couldn't see.

And then, just over half a minute after the iceberg had been sighted, the *Titanic* reached it. The bridge crew watched in amazement as the huge, dark-blue bulk of the floating castle of ice passed down the starboard side of the ship, so close that they felt they could almost reach out and touch it. They'd been incredibly lucky, but it looked as if they'd done it. They'd actually managed to miss it.

Then the *Titanic* shuddered slightly, a sensation that was barely even noticeable to most people on board. On the bridge, the officers and men could see the bulk of the iceberg move very slightly in the water, and immediately they knew what had happened.

The ship had hit the incompressible mountain of ice but it was only a glancing blow. It was even possible that the hull had not been breached, the impact had been so gentle. Personnel were despatched to the bow section of the ship to inspect the damage, with orders to report back to the bridge immediately.

In the meantime, the *Titanic* would come to a complete stop, just in case. Disaster had been averted.

Chapter 92

14 April 1912
HMS _D4_

Through the periscope, Bernard Hutchinson had seen the _Titanic_ slow down dramatically, and watched its aspect ratio change as the ship had turned away from the submarine, or rather manoeuvred to avoid the iceberg.

'Tube one ready, sir,' the forward torpedo room reported again.

'Wait,' Hutchinson ordered, his entire attention fixed on the scene he was looking at through the periscope.

Far from travelling at high speed from left to right in front of the submarine and providing perhaps the most difficult target of all, the ship now appeared to have come to an almost complete stop. He had no idea whether or not the _Titanic_ had actually hit the iceberg and suffered damage, or if there was some other reason for the ship's manoeuvres. What he did know was that he would now have to throw away his firing solution and recalculate it.

But as long as the ship was stationary, and more or less directly in front of him, the new firing solution would be the simplest possible. All he would have to do was aim the boat straight at the target and release the weapons.

The only problem was the iceberg, which lay in the water between the submarine and the *Titanic*. He would either have to move his boat away to get a clear shot at the ship, or wait until the *Titanic* herself manoeuvred away from the floating lump of ice. But even as he watched the ship through the periscope, he saw foam appearing at the rear of the *Titanic* and realized that the vessel was still moving, albeit slowly.

'Ten degrees left rudder,' Hutchinson ordered. 'Revolutions for two knots.'

As he listened to his orders being acknowledged, Hutchinson guessed that that would be enough. That would swing the bow of the submarine slightly to port, which would bring the forward torpedo tubes to bear on the *Titanic* as soon as it moved out from behind the iceberg.

And then he could issue the orders which would complete his mission.

Chapter 93

14 April 1912
RMS *Titanic*

Once it was clear that the bow of the vessel had only grazed the side of the iceberg, the *Titanic* was steered over to starboard to move the ship's stern clear of the ice and to prevent any further possible contact, while the officers on the bridge awaited the damage report.

Below the waterline on the starboard bow of the *Titanic*, several of the steel plates of the hull had buckled with the force of the ship's impact with the iceberg, rivets popping and tearing free, but had only opened up a small wound on the side of the ship, very close to the bow. Ice-cold water started to pour in through the hole and slowly began to fill the single compartment which had been breached: the forward peak tank.

When the officer returned to the bridge, the captain ordered the pumps to be started, confident that they would easily be able to cope with the volume of water entering the ship. But with only a single compartment holed, even without running the pumps, the *Titanic* would be in no danger: the ship had been designed to stay afloat with four of the forward compartments flooded. The impact with the iceberg was an irritation, but not a danger. The ship would have to complete the voyage at reduced speed, obviously, and they'd have to keep an eye on the adjacent compartments, just in case the watertight bulkheads somehow became damaged, but that was all.

The vessel's arrival at New York would just be a little later than planned. No records would be broken this time, no headlines made.

Chapter 94

14 April 1912
HMS *D4*

'Check weapons state,' Hutchinson ordered, as he saw the dark bulk of the *Titanic* begin to emerge from behind the iceberg.

'Both tubes ready, sir.'

'Very good,' he said.

The target vessel was moving very slowly, possibly barely having steerage way at that moment, but a flurry of foam from the stern of the ship showed that the propellers were again turning, driving it forward. Hutchinson knew he would never have a better opportunity than this. With a silent prayer that their Lordships in the Admiralty actually knew what they were doing, and that – for whatever utterly incomprehensible reason – his actions could be justified, he made his decision.

Again he checked the direction of the submarine's bow, looked across at the *Titanic*, mentally assessed the speed the ship was now moving at – only about two or three knots – and then acted.

'Ready tube one.'

'Tube one ready, sir.'

'Fire one.'

The submarine lurched slightly as the weapon was released. Hutchinson clicked a button on his stopwatch. 'Ready tube two.'

'Tube two ready, sir.'

'Fire two.'

Again they felt the lurch as the second torpedo was blown out of the tube by compressed air.

'Close the outer door.'

Hutchinson focused his entire attention on the huge ship about half a mile ahead of him. For a moment, as he watched the twin wakes produced by the weapons, barely visible in the darkness, he thought he'd over-estimated the speed the *Titanic* was travelling at. It looked as if both torpedoes would pass a few yards in front of the ship.

But then the vessel seemed to speed up, and he saw two distant flashes, one after the other, right by the ship's bow, as the two eighteen-inch Whitehead torpedoes slammed into the side of the *Titanic* and exploded. Each warhead contained 200 pounds of explosive and, allied to the damage the ship had already suffered, either of them on its own would have been enough to sink the vessel. The two together just made the ship's fate inevitable.

Hutchinson watched for a few moments. He'd done what he had been ordered to do. Now he had no other option but to follow his other instructions and leave the scene. He carried out a complete sweep around the boat through the periscope, making sure there were no other dangerous lumps of floating ice around, then took a final glance back at the doomed ship, still floating apparently serenely on the dark water, and issued his orders.

'Right full rudder. Steer zero-nine-zero. Revolutions for five knots.'

Immediately, the submarine began turning to starboard and started picking up speed.

Chapter 95

14 April 1912
RMS *Titanic*

The impact with the iceberg had been so gentle, and so insignificant, that very few of the passengers on the ship were even aware that anything had happened. When the two torpedoes struck the bow, the situation was entirely different.

Tremayne had just jammed the back of a chair under the handle of the lock inside their stateroom when he heard two dull explosions, and the whole ship seemed to ring like a bell, a bell struck twice by a massive hammer. He looked at Maria and shook his head.

'What was that?' she demanded.

'Unless I'm very much mistaken,' Tremayne replied, his voice subdued, 'that was the sound of Mansfield Cumming deciding to use both belt and braces. I think he ordered the submarine to attack the ship anyway, because that was definitely the sound of two torpedoes smashing into the side of the *Titanic*.'

'Are you serious?' Maria asked.

'I've never been more serious,' Tremayne said, his voice urgent. 'What the hell happened to our message? We need to get out of here, right now. Unless we're incredibly lucky, this ship is going to sink. I know that the *Titanic*'s huge, and a lot of people seem to think that it's unsinkable, but its hull was never designed to withstand the impact of torpedoes. I'd give the ship maybe an hour before it's gone.'

For a few moments, Maria didn't reply. Then she nodded slowly.

'I really hope you're wrong, Alex,' she said, 'but I have a horrible feeling you're not. We need to get out onto the upper decks as quickly as we can. And, by the way, I can't swim.'

Tremayne smiled bleakly at her. 'With the water temperature out there, whether or not you can swim won't make any difference. If we end up in the water, it'll be the cold that kills us, not drowning.'

They took the minimum they thought they'd need. The clothes they were standing up in and heavy overcoats to go on top, because if they ended up in a lifeboat they knew it was going to be extremely cold.

They knew Voss was still on the loose somewhere in the ship, though ironically both Tremayne and Maria could now relegate him to the status of an irritant, rather than a problem, simply because of the much greater danger they now knew they were facing. But just in case they did meet him somewhere, they took their Brownings but didn't bother with the suppressors. The chaos of the sinking ship – and Tremayne was still certain that was going to be the outcome – would cover up any noise. Finally, Tremayne took the envelope containing the copies, while Maria made sure that she had the original documents in the waterproof pouch.

They saw no sign of Voss, though already other passengers were hurrying along the corridors. They took the aft first-class staircase and, a few minutes later, stepped out onto the Boat

Deck and into the darkness of the night. There was no moon, and little that they could see. Tremayne peered around, shielding his eyes from the glow of the deck lights as he studied the area around the ship.

'I can't see anything,' he said, then paused. 'No, wait a moment. There's something over there.' He pointed down the starboard side of the ship, towards some dark object that lay at the very limit of his visibility, beyond the stern of the vessel. 'It's definitely not another ship – the outline is wrong – I suppose it must be an iceberg. We've seen a few of them already on this voyage.'

'What about the submarine?' Maria asked.

'If the captain's following the usual tactics, he'll have retreated as soon as he fired his weapons. But even if the boat was still here, and on the surface, it's far too dark to see it.'

Maria looked around. 'It's strange. I know what we heard, but up here everything seems to be absolutely normal.'

There was no sign of any unusual activity on the deck, no officers or crewmen in sight, just a handful of other passengers. But there was something else, something that they both noticed at almost the same moment.

'The engines have stopped,' Tremayne said suddenly. 'And the ship's not moving.'

The ship seemed strangely quiet, almost peaceful, in the blackness of the night, and they immediately knew that this was because the engines were no longer working. The ship was dying slowly under their feet, the beat of its mighty heart already beginning to slow down.

Chapter 96

15 April 1912
RMS *Titanic*

By midnight, only twenty minutes after the iceberg had been sighted, everything had changed, and there was absolutely no doubt that the great liner was doomed. The bow of the ship was much lower in the water than it should have been, and the stern was slowly beginning to rise.

'The torpedoes must have hit somewhere near the bow,' Tremayne said. 'That section of the ship is flooding fast, which is why there's such a bow-down attitude.'

Maria was strangely silent. If anything, she simply felt more numb than afraid. In a matter of seconds, it seemed, their lives had been completely turned around. Their very chances of survival now looked slim indeed. But something else, something very specific, was also concerning her. This was not the first time Maria had been on board a passenger ship, and she was perfectly capable of doing the mathematics.

When she and Tremayne had been exploring the ship after they'd boarded, she'd noted the number and type of the lifeboats, and had immediately spotted a discrepancy. She knew that the *Titanic* was carrying over 2,200 passengers and crew, and had been built to accommodate a maximum of sixty-four lifeboats, well in excess of the current Board of Trade requirement, which was based upon the gross tonnage of the ship and not upon the number of people it could accommodate. Unfortunately, there were only twenty lifeboats on board, four of which were canvas-sided collapsible boats which were not mounted in davits and would have to be launched by hand. The reality was that there were only sixteen wooden lifeboats on board, the biggest of which had a maximum capacity of sixty-five people, but some only forty. So at best, if every lifeboat could be launched, and every lifeboat was full, only about 1,000 people – well under half of the total number on the ship – could possibly be saved.

No matter what happened, or what anyone did, if the ship sank, over half of the people then on board the great luxury liner were going to end up in the Atlantic Ocean, and that meant they were going to die.

Chapter 97

Gunther Voss had been asleep when the two torpedoes smashed into the bow of the *Titanic*, fatally wounding the mighty ship.

The noise of the explosions and the shudder that ran through the hull of the liner woke him immediately. He had no idea what had happened, but he'd been on enough ships to know that something was badly wrong. Either the *Titanic* had hit something – quite a difficult feat to pull off in the middle of the Atlantic Ocean – or there'd been some kind of explosion inside the ship itself. Possibly a boiler had blown up or something of that sort.

He wasn't concerned for the safety of the ship itself. Everything he'd read about the *Titanic*, about its double bottom and multiple watertight doors, had convinced him that in most circumstances the ship was effectively unsinkable. Rather, he saw the incident as playing to his advantage. No matter what had occurred, it would cause panic and alarm on board, and with any luck that might provide him with the opportunity to tackle either Tremayne or Maria Weston, or better still both of them, and dispose of them in the confusion.

He got out of bed, dressed quickly in warm clothing, and tucked the Luger into his waistband. Then he removed the chair which he'd been using to barricade the door, undid the lock and stepped cautiously out into the corridor.

Passengers were running about in all directions, clearly aware that something was wrong, and he heard one or two of them saying something about the ship sinking. Nonsense. It was panic, pure and simple.

He guessed that Tremayne and the woman would have already left their stateroom, but he reckoned it was worth checking anyway. He strode along the corridor, stopped outside their door and rapped sharply on it. There was no reply, so he tried the handle, and to his surprise it opened beneath his touch. Holding his pistol at the ready, he stepped into the room.

As far as he could tell, almost all their possessions were still there, and for a moment he felt a prickle of unease. Why would they abandon everything and leave the door of their stateroom unlocked? Only one explanation fitted the facts as he saw them, ridiculous though he thought it was. Perhaps the passenger he had overheard had been right, and the ship was going down.

Voss abandoned his hasty search of the stateroom, walked out and headed for the staircase.

Chapter 98

15 April 1912
RMS *Titanic*

At five minutes past midnight, there was a sudden flurry of activity on the Boat Deck as a group of officers and men appeared and immediately set to work to remove the covers from the lifeboats.

'That's it, then,' Tremayne said. 'The *Titanic* is definitely sinking, and they're preparing to abandon ship.'

Almost as soon as the covers had been removed, teams assembled by each of the lifeboats and swung them out on their davits before lowering them to the level of the Boat Deck. And then they heard orders being shouted from below, and a stream of passengers began to appear, being shepherded towards the lifeboats by members of the *Titanic*'s crew.

Most of them were women and children, who had probably been asleep because they'd obviously dressed hurriedly, and started walking onto the Boat Deck, looking around them in confusion. Although the ship was lower in the water at the bow and the engines had stopped, the lights were still working, the heating system was keeping the temperature at a comfortable level, and there was, at that stage, no apparent sense of urgency being shown, and certainly no panic. But Tremayne knew that that would change over the next hour or so.

He again shielded his eyes against the glow of the deck lighting, and stared out to sea, looking all around the ship. The night was still absolutely black, with no moon, and no sign of what he'd been hoping to see.

'As far as I can see,' he said to Maria, 'there are no other ships anywhere near us. I just hope the captain's sent out a distress signal. Unless there's another ship within a few miles, just over the horizon, the loss of life is going to be horrendous.'

In fact, nobody had ordered any messages to be sent, and it wasn't until fifteen minutes past midnight, almost exactly thirty-five minutes after the collision with the iceberg, that the captain finally issued instructions to the wireless operator to transmit a distress call. The message sent by the stricken ship was brief:

CQD DE MGY 41.44N / 50.14W

The prefix 'CQ' had been in use for some time to identify telegraph messages of general interest, and also been adopted as a maritime radio call prefix. In 1904, Marconi had added the suffix 'D' to create a recognisable distress call, and 'CQD' was understood to mean 'All stations: distress'. It was also popularly believed at the time that 'CQD' meant 'Come Quick Danger' or 'Come Quickly Distress', but actually this was never the case.

The 'DE' simply stood for 'from' and indicated the identity of the calling station, in this case 'MGY', the international radio trigraph allocated to the *Titanic*, followed by the position of the ship at the time.

Two minutes later, at seventeen minutes past midnight, the

radio operator sent a further distress message, this time including the other international distress signal 'SOS', which had been adopted in 1908 as the international Morse code distress signal. The new signal read:

CQD CQD SOS DE MGY 41.44N / 50.14W

The emergency messages quickly generated replies from two ships. The closest was the SS *Frankfurt*, about 170 miles away, and the second was the *Titanic*'s sister ship, the RMS *Olympic*, over 500 miles away.

Even steaming at its maximum speed, the SS *Frankfurt* would still take about ten hours to reach the *Titanic*'s position, far too late to render any assistance.

Chapter 99

15 April 1912
RMS *Carpathia*

About sixty miles to the south-east of the *Titanic*'s position, the RMS *Carpathia* was steaming steadily eastwards towards the Mediterranean out of New York. The radio operator, Harold Thomas Cottom, was in his cabin, a room which doubled as both his accommodation on board the ship and the radio room, getting undressed and preparing to go to bed. Periodically, as he removed his garments, he would pick up the earphones and listen in to the radio messages being pumped through the ether using Morse code.

Suddenly, his ears, highly attuned to the subtle nuances of Morse transmissions, detected a message which he had never heard before. The three letters that had been transmitted consisted of three dots, followed by three dashes, followed by three dots. 'SOS', the recently introduced international distress signal.

Immediately, Cottom forgot about everything but his equipment. He sat down and waited for the message to be repeated, which came within seconds. The full message read:

CQD CQD SOS DE MGY 41.44N / 50.14W

With practised haste, he wrote down the entire message. Immediately, the *Carpathia*'s radio operator replied, to confirm that the message was accurate, and received an almost immediate acknowledgement.

The moment he knew that the transmission was genuine, Cottom ran out of his cabin, found the ship's First Officer, and showed him the signal. Together they briefed the captain, Arthur Rostron, who immediately realized that he was in a position to help. He ordered the ship to turn round and head north-west towards the *Titanic*'s stated position at its maximum speed of seventeen knots. The steam heating for the passenger cabins was switched off to provide more steam pressure for the engines, so that the vessel could travel as quickly as possible. Captain Rostron also told the radio operator to contact the *Titanic* again, advise the ship that the *Carpathia* was on its way and to obtain as much information about the situation on board the liner as possible.

When the *Carpathia* steadied on its new course, the time was thirty-three minutes past midnight EST, and at that moment the two ships were almost sixty miles apart. Even at full speed, the *Carpathia* would take nearly four hours to reach the *Titanic*.

Chapter 100

15 April 1912
RMS *Titanic*

Tremayne and Maria stood in the centre of the first-class promenade on the Boat Deck and watched the first lifeboat being lowered to the sea below.

'I don't understand this,' Tremayne remarked. 'That lifeboat's still less than half full. I've counted twenty-eight people in it, and it could hold over sixty. Why are they launching it already?'

Maria looked at the boat and shook her head.

'I'm worried,' she admitted. 'You notice that at the moment there's still no real sense of haste? Nobody's running about or shouting. I don't think that most of the passengers have actually realized what's going on. They probably still think that the *Titanic*'s unsinkable, and they'd rather stay on board, where it's warm and dry than take their chances in one of these little wooden boats. And there's the weight problem. These lifeboats probably weigh two or three tons each. Add a full load of passengers and you could almost double that. I think the ship's officers are worried about the weight of a fully laden lifeboat breaking the falls that lower it from the davits.'

Tremayne nodded. That made sense. But now he knew it was

time to say goodbye. He had to get Maria to safety. She'd stood beside him watching the lifeboat being lowered, and made not the slightest attempt to join the women and children who had crowded into it. She seemed determined to remain by his side. But Tremayne wasn't going to let her go down with the ship.

'You've got those original documents somewhere safe?' he asked, and she reached into her coat and showed him the pouch. Then he looked around.

The ship's crew were now loading a second lifeboat, the one numbered five, again on the starboard side. Tremayne took her arm, and began leading her in that direction.

'What are you doing?' she asked, tucking the pouch away again inside her warm coat.

'I'm putting you on that lifeboat,' Tremayne said firmly.

'And you're coming with me.'

'No I'm not,' Tremayne replied. 'The captain has ordered women and children first, so you can get into that boat and I'm going to stay here, on the ship, until he changes that order.'

'But you'll die,' Maria snapped. 'Don't you understand that? I've already told you. There aren't enough lifeboats to take even half the people who are on board this ship. Please, you must come with me.'

Tremayne shook his head. 'I've done a lot of things in my life that I'm not particularly proud of, but I'm damned if I'll go to my grave and have people say that I took the place of a woman or a child on one of these lifeboats. I would rather kill myself right here and right now. Besides, there's still unfinished business on board the ship. Gunther Voss is still here somewhere, and I need to take care of him before the end.

'You've done your bit, Maria, done more than your fair share on this operation. You can go back to Mansfield Cumming and tell him exactly what happened, how we achieved what he told us to do, and you can give him the documents.'

Maria looked at him for a long moment, then stepped close and wrapped her arms around him, hugging him tight. Tremayne bent forward and kissed her gently on the forehead.

'Go now,' he said. 'It's been a privilege to know you.'

Maria nodded, hardly trusting herself to speak. 'Be lucky,' she murmured, then turned and walked away.

A couple of minutes later, the lifeboat began the long descent down the side of the ship to the water, over sixty feet below. Maria stared up at Tremayne until his face was lost to view high above her.

Chapter 101

15 April 1912
RMS *Titanic*

Alex Tremayne had been able to do the mathematics as easily as
Maria. When he saw her lifeboat being lowered down to the
sea, he knew at that moment that he would be staying on board
the ship to the bitter end.

Oddly enough, the thought of his impending death didn't
particularly scare him. He knew that he and Maria had in-
directly saved Britain and her Empire from becoming embroiled
in a European war. There were not many men, he reflected, who
could claim to have achieved even a tenth as much as that in
their lifetimes. And Maria was safe, assuming her lifeboat didn't
get swamped or suffer some other catastrophe. That, to him,
was infinitely more important than whether he himself lived or
died. His only regret was that he hadn't known her for longer,
become a real friend, or perhaps even more than that.

He wasn't even particularly concerned now about Voss.
Maria had the original documents, and she was safely on board
a lifeboat that was even then pulling away from the side of the
ship, well out of his reach. As far as Tremayne could see, he was
going to die when the ship finally sank beneath his feet, and he

expected that Voss would share exactly the same fate. Killing him before the ship went down would simply spare him the agony of drowning in the freezing waters of the North Atlantic. Maybe he should spare him.

So he stayed up on the Boat Deck, where he would be able to watch the last minutes of the mighty liner's short life.

The lifeboats then began being loaded much more quickly from the deck now, as more and more people finally realized the life-threatening situation they were in, as the *Titanic* sank even lower by the bow.

By now the crew had obviously ordered all the passengers out onto the decks in order to abandon ship, and the crowds were growing by the minute as more and more people streamed out onto the Boat Deck. It was also clear that the appalling reality of the situation had become apparent to almost everyone: there were simply not enough lifeboats, and at least half of the people on board the ship were going to perish. And there was nothing that anybody could do about that.

It was a race for life. Getting in a lifeboat meant a chance to live: no seat meant immersion in the Atlantic Ocean and almost certain death.

In the crowds around the lifeboats some people were starting to panic, men shoving women and children out of the way in a desperate attempt to secure a place on board, and being forced back by the efforts of the ship's officers and crew, and by other male passengers. Tremayne heard shots fired as one officer fought to maintain some semblance of control over the lifeboat he was attempting to lower.

The air was pierced by yells and shouts of pain as men fought each other for precedence, either for themselves or their families. Women screamed as the realization hit home that there were no spaces left on the boats – for them or for their children. The number of lifeboats diminished steadily, and now every boat was not simply loaded to capacity, but dangerously overloaded, crammed with people.

A cacophony of noise rose, growing ever louder as the seething mass of people seemed almost to merge into a single terrified organism, its shape changing and growing as more and more passengers joined the throng and started trying to fight their way towards the last few remaining lifeboats.

Eventually, the crowds on the Boat Deck became so large and violent that Tremayne had to walk away. He had done what he could for Maria. He had saved her life, he hoped, and now all that was left for him was to wait for the end, for the huge ship to finally slip beneath the waves. He wondered if it would be peaceful when it came.

He climbed up onto the roof over the first-class lounge, the room where he and Maria had spent their last evening together, and where even then he could clearly hear the sound of music as the ship's band, the Wallace Hartley Quintet, continued playing in the lounge. They probably hoped that the music would help keep the passengers calm as the end drew near, but from what Tremayne had seen, that was a vain hope. He strode across to the compass platform in its centre and looked around. That, he thought, was probably as good a place as any to wait. At least he would have a good view of the final act in the drama.

Chapter 102

15 April 1912
RMS *Titanic*

Voss had been searching for Tremayne ever since he'd arrived on the Boat Deck, but he'd been unable to find him, simply due to the press of people clamouring to be allowed into the lifeboats. He'd been blocked at every turn, and he'd also been trying to check the occupants of every lifeboat before it was launched, to ensure that his quarry hadn't somehow been able to climb on board. If Leonard had turned up to help him, it would have made the search more efficient, but he had no idea where his bodyguard was.

But Tremayne was simply nowhere to be seen, and eventually Voss reached the uncomfortable conclusion that the Englishman must already have got off the ship somehow. He was making his way towards one of the last lifeboats still being loaded, shoving people out of his way and counting on his loaded pistol to guarantee him a place in the boat. Then, out of the corner of his eye, he caught sight of a familiar figure standing on the roof of the first-class lounge.

At last. He'd found him. All he had to do was climb up onto the roof, get the documents from him, and then make sure he still had time to get down to the Boat Deck and force his way on board one of the last lifeboats.

Further distress rockets were being fired from the *Titanic* in an attempt to summon assistance. In the Marconi suite, the radio operator continued to send messages which marked the increasing desperation of the situation, pleading for help for the occupants of the sinking ship. Just before zero-one-forty EST, he transmitted:

Women and children in the boats. Cannot last much longer.

Displaying traditional British calm in the face of adversity, at about this time the ship's band moved out of the first-class lounge and established themselves on the forward section of the Boat Deck, where they continued to play classical music and ragtime tunes in a vain attempt to keep the passengers calm. They would remain there, still playing, until the ship sank beneath them.

Tremayne looked around him at the throngs of people who had clearly realized that there was no room, that they were not going to get a place in a lifeboat. Many were still struggling futilely, trying with increasing desperation to force their way forward through the crowds, even though there was not the slightest possibility of getting a place. Others had clearly become resigned to their fate, and were frantically pulling on lifebelts, which would at least keep them afloat in the water. But Tremayne knew very well that drowning was perhaps going to be the least likely cause of death when the ship finally sank: it would almost certainly be the cold that would kill them first.

And there was another danger facing them. When the ship

sank, it would cause a massive suction effect that would drag down anything on the surface. A lot of the passengers evidently knew this, and had decided to try to get well away from the *Titanic* before the end, because Tremayne watched dozens of them line the side rails of the ship and then jump into the freezing waters far below. Sometimes, they swam away, but a lot didn't, and he thought he knew why. Their life jackets had slid up their torsos when they plunged under the water, and the rigid flotation pads rammed them so hard under their chins that it broke their necks. As soon as he realized that, he decided that jumping in wasn't the way he was going to go. He'd just ride the ship down and hope for the best. For the first time in his life he slightly regretted not believing in any kind of god: to have prayed might have been a comfort right then.

The noise of the crowd had changed, too, as the screaming began to die away. That sound was being replaced by sobbing and wailing as the mood changed from violent anger at being denied access to the lifeboats to increasing horror and desperation about the fate which now awaited everyone left on board.

Tremayne knew he was looking at the faces of over 1,000 people, all of whom would all be dead within the hour.

But as he looked back towards the stern of the ship, his focus changed. Gunther Voss, a Luger pistol grasped in his right hand, was walking clumsily towards him over the roof of the lounge, a roof which was sloping to an increasingly large angle as the bow of the *Titanic* sank further beneath the waves.

Tremayne's own pistol was tucked in his pocket and out of reach, and he didn't even bother trying to get it.

'Hello, Gunther,' Tremayne said. 'Come up here to watch the show, have you?'

'You know what I'm here for, Tremayne. Hand over what

you took from me, then I'll shoot you and at least that will save you from drowning.'

Tremayne smiled. 'And you think that's a good deal, do you?'

'It's the best offer you're going to get now.'

Tremayne reached into his jacket pocket with his left hand and pulled out the envelope containing the copied documents.

'These are what you're after, I think,' he said, extending his hand.

The bow of the *Titanic* had now sunk so far that the stern of the vessel was rising high out of the water, the strain on the steel plates in the mid section of the hull simply enormous, and clearly unsupportable. As Voss leant forward to seize the envelope there was a rending crash from the sinking bow section, and the whole ship shuddered as if it had received a mortal blow. The immense strain had caused the forward smokestack to break free from the superstructure and crash over the side of the ship and into the water. The huge mass of steel killed dozens of people struggling in the sea and created a huge wave which overturned one of the canvas-sided lifeboats. Alex was relieved it wasn't Maria's.

For an instant Voss looked away, and in that same instant Tremayne kicked out, knocking the Luger from his grasp to send it spinning off the roof.

'You don't concentrate enough, Gunther,' Tremayne said, drawing his own pistol and aiming it at Voss.

Then he smiled, and tossed the weapon away.

'But I think shooting you would give you an easy way out,' Tremayne said, with a tired smile. 'I'd only be doing you a favour. If you want these copies – and that's all I've got, because the originals are in a safe place, right out of your reach – you come and take them off me.'

With a growl of rage that was almost feral in its intensity, Voss leapt at him, and the two men crashed down onto the roof of the lounge and tumbled down the sloping steel plates towards the edge, struggling together.

Then the lights of the *Titanic* flickered once and went out for the last time. With a shattering roar, the stern of the ship simply fell away, vanishing from sight. The steel of the hull had finally given way, the metal ripped apart by the enormous weight, and the mighty ship was instantly torn in two. And at the same moment, the bow section dropped away beneath the struggling men with sickening rapidity, and plunged smoothly beneath the waves, vanishing for ever.

Almost immediately, he and Voss were totally immersed, both men gasping for breath in the freezing water as debris swirled all around them.

Chapter 103

15 April 1912
RMS *Titanic*

The shock of hitting the sea was overwhelming, the plunge into the icy water heart-stopping and brutal. In an instant, it felt to Tremayne as if his body temperature had fallen off the scale. He'd never been so cold in his life, never thought he could be that cold and still live.

The water swirled around him as the massive bow section of the *Titanic*, virtually one half of the huge liner, sank rapidly into the depths. But there seemed to be little of the suction effect he'd been expecting, perhaps because it *was* the bow, designed to carve through the waves, and it disappeared from view with remarkably little disturbance.

The stern of the ship was another matter altogether. With a tremendous roar, the after end of the vessel reared up out of the water, and for a few horrifying moments it looked as if it would topple down on him. But then it, too, vanished for ever beneath the waves, creating a swirl of water that must have sucked dozens of people to their deaths.

In the aftermath of the sinking, a sudden silence fell over the scene. No longer could Tremayne hear the rending of metal as the ship broke up, or the roaring thunder of the waves, and even the sound of the hundreds of people who'd been on the deck when the ship sank was stilled, shocked into silence by the suddenness of the sinking. For a few seconds, there was absolute quiet, and then the people in the water began to scream, their howls of anguish interspersed by gasps for breath.

He knew for certain then that there was no hope. The water was so cold that unless the survivors could be pulled out within minutes, perhaps an hour at the most, hypothermia would kill every one of them. For the rescue to be as quick as that, the ship would have to be actually on the scene already. Tremayne had looked towards the horizon before the *Titanic* sank, and there were no lights anywhere in sight, no other vessels within twenty miles at least. As with the number of lifeboats, the mathematics were unarguable: there was no ship closer than an hour's steaming, and within that hour everybody would be dead.

Within minutes, Tremayne guessed, the screams and shouts would start to die away to nothing, and then the scattered groups of people would slowly and inevitably turn into a floating carpet of corpses, the bodies buoyed up by their life jackets in a parody of life. And then, he guessed, the first of the creatures of the sea would arrive at the scene to enjoy the unexpected bounty.

But despite their predicament, and the inevitable certainty of both their deaths in the freezing water, Voss was still trying desperately to kill Tremayne. He swam straight for his victim, locked both his hands around the other man's neck and steadily tried to choke him.

Tremayne lifted both his legs up, placed his feet against Voss's chest and kicked out, breaking the man's grip instantly.

Tremayne was still holding the envelope, and as Voss swam forward again, he lifted it out of the water and tossed it to him.

'You're going to die, Voss,' Tremayne said, forcing the words out through his chattering teeth – the cold was intense, gripping his body like a vice. 'So you might as well have these back.'

The other man grabbed the envelope, but then renewed his attack, his face red with fury, apparently heedless of the cold.

Twice Tremayne kicked him away, but he knew he was weakening fast. Then he remembered his stiletto, the sheath still strapped to his left arm, and drew the weapon just as Voss surged towards him for the third time.

Tremayne held the knife out directly in front of him, gripping it with both hands, and Voss simply impaled himself on the blade, the needle-sharp point driving between his ribs and into his chest cavity.

For a moment, Voss just stared at Tremayne, his mouth open in a gasp of pain and surprise. Then he stopped moving, the light fading from his eyes, and floated slowly away, the hilt of the knife just breaking the surface of the sea.

Tremayne looked at the body and shook his head. 'I did do you a favour, you bastard, and that was one of my favourite knives.'

Chapter 104

15 April 1912
Atlantic Ocean

Alex Tremayne was a powerful swimmer, but he knew immediately that swimming wouldn't save him, not in those conditions. His biggest enemy was going to be the cold, simply freezing to death in the icy water. He'd heard that dying in that fashion was not an unpleasant way to go, though he'd never been entirely sure how anybody could possibly know that for certain. Still, he reflected with a rueful smile, there was no doubt that he would soon find out for himself.

The cold was intense, and already Tremayne could feel a deep chill starting to spread through his body. The heavy coat which he'd put on before he and Maria left the stateroom would have been fine in a lifeboat, but now it was waterlogged and hampering his movements. He fumbled with the buttons down the front and after a few seconds managed to shrug it off. But that would provide, he knew, only a temporary respite. He could now move more freely, and was no longer in danger of being dragged under by the sheer weight of the garment, but the cold was going to get him. There was no doubt whatsoever about that.

Swimming seemed pointless. There were no lifeboats anywhere near him, no wreckage floating on the surface that he could climb onto, and still no sign of any ships approaching. There weren't any other people swimming in the water nearby. Even Voss's body had drifted some distance away and, as he watched, the corpse slipped beneath the waves and didn't re-appear. He was going to die alone. It was fitting, perhaps. He'd lived alone for most of his life, and had no family who would mourn his passing. Though he hoped Maria might shed the occasional tear to his memory.

Then he sensed a sudden commotion in the water below him, as if some huge animal was rising to the surface, and something struck him very hard on the back of his head. For an instant, stars blazed in front of his eyes, and then he felt no more.

Chapter 105

15 April 1912
HMS *D4*

'Right,' Bernard Hutchinson said, 'I think that's far enough.'

The submarine had been maintaining a steady speed for the last four hours, heading east at five knots, and was then about twenty miles clear of the location where they had launched their two torpedoes. Now it was time to send the confirmation signal to the Admiralty in London and for Hutchinson to confirm that he had successfully completed his mission.

He did yet another complete sweep of the horizon through the periscope, and then ordered the boat to surface. As soon as positive buoyancy had been established and the vessel was securely on the surface, he clambered up the ladder to the conning tower and used his binoculars to check for anything he might have missed through the periscope. The night air smelt fresh and clean after the fug of the control room.

Then he clambered back down the ladder. 'You take the watch, Bill,' he instructed Evans. 'Steer the same course but get the diesels started and increase the speed to ten knots. But first, get the mast up and that radio aerial rigged, as quickly as you can.'

That operation didn't take long: the men had done it on many occasions. Five minutes later, Hutchinson was back in his cabin, writing the plaintext for the signal he was about to send, prior to encrypting it, when a signalman appeared outside.

'Yes? What is it?'

'There's been a new signal for us, sir,' the man said. 'It's sent in the clear again, and it's really short.'

'What is it?' Hutchinson asked again.

'It's just two groups, sir. The first is "Abort" and the second is "RTB". And that's all, sir.'

For a few moments Hutchinson just sat there, staring at his half-written signal. Then he muttered a curse, screwed up the piece of paper and tossed it to one side, a slew of conflicting emotions coursing through his body.

Then the signalman appeared again, now clearly in a state of excitement.

'What?' Hutchinson demanded.

'Sir, the air's full of radio messages about the *Titanic*,' he said. 'She hit an iceberg about four hours ago and now they think she must have sunk, because there's been no contact with her for well over an hour. The ship reported launching lifeboats, but there were no ships close by to help rescue them.'

'Right,' he said, and strode back into the control room. 'Right full rudder,' he ordered. 'Reverse course. Steer two-seven-zero. When the boat's steady on west, increase speed to fourteen knots.'

Then he called the signalman over. 'Acknowledge that signal from the Admiralty,' he instructed, 'and tell them that the *Titanic* has reported hitting an iceberg and is believed to have sunk, and that we are proceeding to the location to render all the assistance that we can. Send it in clear, and mark it "most urgent". No matter what they reply, ignore it. Don't even tell me about it. I know where our duty lies.'

Chapter 106

15 April 1912
Atlantic Ocean

At approximately three thirty in the morning, having proceeded at a maximum speed through treacherous waters, littered with ice and icebergs, and in consequence putting both his crew and his passengers at grave risk, the captain of the RMS *Carpathia* finally ordered his ship to come to a stop at the exact geographical coordinates supplied by the radio operator on board the *Titanic*. But they found absolutely nothing there. There was no sign of a ship, or lifeboats, or wreckage of any sort.

He could only assume that the *Titanic* had now sunk – if the ship was afloat, it was so big that it would almost certainly still be visible – and he presumed that the ocean currents in the area must have moved the wreckage and the lifeboats. The night was very dark and still. There was no moon and the surface of the sea was uncharacteristically calm, no waves or white horses visible anywhere.

The captain ordered his ship to begin steaming slowly, searching for lifeboats or debris, and had distress rockets fired, in the hope that some of the survivors would be close enough to see them, and would be able to respond with torches or rockets or whatever they had in the boats.

Fortunately, after some time without attracting any response, the rockets were finally seen by some of the people in the lifeboats, and they did what they could, lighting scraps of paper and pieces of dry clothing, anything which would burn. Some of the lifeboat crews began trying to row their vessels towards the *Carpathia*, and one of the officers in a lifeboat ignited a green smoke flare.

Finally, the crew of the *Carpathia* saw the first lifeboat and, at about ten past four in the morning, it was pulled alongside the ship, quickly followed by others. The survivors were assisted on board, clambering onto the waiting vessel using rope ladders and slings. Once safely below decks, they were provided with clean, dry clothing, hot drinks and food, and then their names were taken so that the sad task of identifying both the survivors and those missing, presumed dead, could begin.

After Maria Weston had undergone this brief processing operation, she went back up on deck, and stayed outside for the rest of the night, standing by the ship's rail heedless of the cold, her eyes ceaselessly scanning the water around the slowly moving *Carpathia* as she endlessly searched the wreckage and bodies for any sign of Alex Tremayne.

Dead faces, their skin turned white by the intense cold, their eyes open and staring sightlessly, almost accusingly, back at her from the surface of the Atlantic Ocean, the bodies buoyed up by the life jackets most of them were wearing. The very word 'life jacket' suddenly seemed to her like a cruel joke: the only purpose they were serving was to keep the bodies on the surface. They had done nothing to save the lives of the poor souls wearing them.

And it wasn't just the odd corpse. The surface of the ocean was literally covered with bodies, their limbs moving limply in the swell, their faces clearly visible. Maria couldn't even count them, there were so many. Hundreds and hundreds of men, women and, to her mounting horror, even a few children, passed silently beside the hull of the slow-moving ship.

In the end, that was what she remembered the most. Not the bodies themselves, but the silence of that appalling scene. No cries for help, no whimpers. Nothing. Just the silence as the ship moved through the sea of corpses.

She would only leave her post after dawn broke, when the *Carpathia*'s captain would reluctantly terminate the search and head slowly away from the area towards New York, her cargo the pitifully few survivors of the sinking of the greatest liner of the age.

Chapter 107

15 April 1912
HMS *D4*

It took the submarine nearly two hours to reach the position where Bernard Hutchinson had seen the *Titanic* steaming towards him, lights blazing. But, like the crew of the *Carpathia*, at first he could see no sign of a shipwreck, or even of the iceberg which had – according to the radio messages still flooding the airwaves – apparently done so much damage to the transatlantic liner. There had been no mention, as far as he could tell, of torpedoes hitting the ship.

Hutchinson and Evans were both in the conning tower, staring in different directions through the darkness, alert for the first signs of any wreckage.

'I can see the lights of a ship over there,' Evans said, pointing to the south. 'You don't suppose that's the *Titanic*, and it's all been a big mistake, do you?'

Hutchinson swung round to stare in the direction that his First Lieutenant was indicating. Then he shook his head.

'No. That's a passenger ship of some sort, by the looks of it, but it's too small to be the *Titanic*.'

The submarine was moving very slowly across the still,

dark water, and Hutchinson then ordered a heading change, so that it would proceed in the general direction of the ship they could see. He presumed that vessel was also looking for survivors.

Two minutes later, Evans saw a dark shape bobbing in the water just off the port bow.

'There,' he said. 'What's that?'

In moments, it was abundantly clear what it was. The body of a man wearing a dark suit, his body supported by a life jacket, drifted slowly down the port side of the submarine. There was absolutely no doubt that he was dead, no point at all in attempting to recover his corpse. When Hutchinson had briefed his crew on their way to the site of the sinking, he had made one thing absolutely clear: the D-Class boat was a very small submarine, carrying a crew of only twenty-five officers and men, who lived in cramped and generally appalling conditions. No matter what their personal feelings, Hutchinson said, they would have to ignore any bodies they saw and only attempt to save anyone still alive. Even then, he doubted the submarine could handle more than about half a dozen extra people.

'There's another one,' Hutchinson said, pointing ahead.

Evans nodded, and gestured silently over to his left.

Hutchinson looked, and then shook his head. The submarine was entering a veritable ocean of corpses, white faces staring upwards, sightless eyes wide open, their bodies rising and falling limply as small waves washed past them.

'Dear God,' Evans whispered, 'there are hundreds of them.'

Hutchinson ordered a further reduction in the submarine's speed, so that it was barely crawling along, nosing its way past the floating corpses. The bodies of men, women, and children drifted past the sides of the boat in a seemingly endless and macabre procession of the dead.

'We're too late,' Evans said. 'They're all dead. Didn't they have any lifeboats?'

'Not enough, obviously,' Hutchinson replied quietly. 'I suppose the cold killed them, those that didn't drown. I think we're wasting our time here, but we'll keep going, just in case.'

The submarine moved on, now encountering scattered pieces of wreckage as well as literally hundreds of floating bodies. There seemed little point in trying to do any kind of a formal search, simply because they had seen not a single sign of life since they'd arrived at the location. All around them, in every direction they looked, were floating bodies, the stuff of enduring nightmares.

'What's that?' Evans asked, bringing his binoculars up to his face and resting his elbows on the steel side of the conning tower.

Hutchinson stared as well, but for several seconds he simply had no idea what he was looking at. The shape in the water almost directly in front of the boat looked like some strange sculpture, small right-angle shapes interspersed with long sweeping curves. Then it suddenly dawned on him.

'I think it's a section of a staircase,' he said, 'a massive wooden staircase. All stop,' he ordered down the voice pipe.

The submarine eased closer, until the bow was almost touching the huge wooden structure. And then there was no doubt what it was.

'It must have floated out of the ship when it sank,' Evans said, staring at it.

And then, at almost the same moment, they both saw something else. A darker shape lying close to the centre of the floating staircase, a shape that Hutchinson was certain he'd just seen move.

'There's somebody lying on it,' he said urgently. 'He might be alive, and at least he's not in the water.' He leant forward, over the edge of the conning tower and issued crisp orders to the half-dozen men waiting on the foredeck of the submarine.

'Get a line across to that wreckage,' he shouted. 'Make it fast to the boat, and then a couple of you climb onto it. There's somebody on it. Find out if he's dead or alive.'

The first grappling iron clattered off the wooden structure and fell back into the sea, but the second time the seaman threw it, the steel spikes lodged around a banister rail. Within a minute or so, one end of the staircase was resting firmly against the side of the submarine, partially supported by the port-side ballast tank.

'Be careful,' Hutchinson called, as two of the men clambered over the side of the boat onto the wreckage and made their way over to the dark shape he had seen.

They bent over the figure, and then one of them stood up, turned and shouted back towards the submarine: 'He's alive!'

Manoeuvring the body of the semi-conscious man across the staircase was difficult, but the two seamen were both strong, and within five minutes they had reached the side of the submarine, where other willing hands were waiting to help them with their burden.

'Get him below,' Hutchinson ordered. 'Strip him and wrap him in a blanket. Get him warm.'

A few minutes later, the grappling hook was freed, and the submarine again resumed its slow and pointless progress through the sea of the dead. The boat remained in the area until dawn broke, but found no other living survivors. Then, reluctantly, Hutchinson ordered the submarine to reverse course, and increased speed to the east. They had to make their final rendezvous with the oiler, and still had a long way to go.

Chapter 108

30 April 1912
London

Maria Weston was in a black mood when she opened the door of Mansfield Cumming's office in Whitehall Court and walked in.

The *Carpathia* had taken three days to reach New York after picking up the survivors from the *Titanic*, arriving on the evening of the eighteenth of April. The final tally of survivors was 705, meaning that over 1,500 people had lost their lives in that single, dreadful night.

Maria then had to wait before she could get a passage on another transatlantic liner and return to Britain. She had checked the lists of survivors time after time, haunting the offices of the White Star Line in a vain attempt to find the name 'Alex Maitland' recorded. But eventually she had been forced to face the reality that he had done exactly what she had expected he would do: he had remained on board the ship to the very end, so that he could give other people the chance to live.

The eastbound voyage across the Atlantic had seemed interminable. For most of the time, she had remained inside her cabin – the accommodation she had booked did not merit

the term 'stateroom' – only venturing outside for meals. And
the mood on board the ship was sombre. Everybody knew
about the loss of the *Titanic*, and everyone on the ship, it
seemed, wanted to talk about it, and Maria simply couldn't
face that.

Mansfield Cumming stood up as she entered, shook her
warmly by the hand and led her to one of the chairs in front of
his desk.

'I'm so pleased to see you again, Maria,' he said. 'I know you
must still be in shock, but do you feel up to telling me what happened on board the ship?'

What she wanted to do more than anything else was take out
a pistol and blow a series of holes in Mansfield Cumming's body
until he finally died. Thanks to him, 1,500 innocent people had
died, among them the only man for whom she'd harboured any
deep feelings for a very long time.

'Frankly, Mansfield, the temptation to do you serious bodily
harm is almost overwhelming. Why the hell didn't you tell us
what you had planned for the ship before we set off?'

Cumming shook his head. 'Because at that stage we didn't
know. It was only when my agents in Berlin confirmed that Voss
had really good printing plates and enough paper to produce
counterfeit currency with a face value of over ten million pounds
that the government decided we had to have a backup plan. If
Tremayne's message hadn't been delayed for over three hours,
or if I'd managed to get the Admiralty to extend the deadline,
none of this would have been necessary. Believe me, Maria,
nobody regrets what happened more than I do.'

For a few moments she just looked at him. Then she replied.
'I think I can make you feel a whole lot worse.'

'How?'

'By telling the newspapers on both sides of the Atlantic what really happened to the *Titanic*.'

Cumming smiled at her and shook his head. 'I don't think so, Maria. Who do you think would believe you? Who would credit the British government with an act of such appalling brutality? And in any case, all the evidence is at the bottom of the Atlantic. No, I do understand your feelings, but you're a professional, and if you think it through I hope you'll agree that what we did was the only proper course of action in the circumstances. Now, can you please just fill in the blanks for me, and tell me exactly what happened on board?'

Maria really didn't feel like explaining events, but knew she really had little option. Sooner or later she would have to go through the debriefing process, and she might as well get it over with.

She explained how they had identified Voss and the other two conspirators, and how Alex had tackled them and finally eliminated two of them. Obviously she didn't know what had happened to Voss, but she presumed he'd gone down with the ship. And when she spoke about her fellow agent, her voice was quiet and subdued, as she tried desperately to distance her emotions from what she was saying, her voice cracking with the strain.

'And you were both, you and Alex I mean, certain about the plan Voss had hatched?'

Maria nodded. 'Yes. In fact, after Alex had tackled the two bodyguards who had been sent out to kill him, Voss actually admitted his involvement in the plot, and basically told Alex it was too late for him to do anything about it. No, there was no doubt about what they were trying to do.'

'As you know,' Mansfield Cumming said, 'Alex sent me a

message to confirm that you'd completed the mission, and in it he said that you had managed to find the lever, the information, that Voss was going to use to persuade the American president to do what he wanted.'

Maria opened her handbag and pulled out an envelope which she slid across the table to Mansfield Cumming. 'That's what we found,' she said. 'Voss had the original documents, and the other two each had copies of them. I think it's clear that they intended to blackmail the president into agreeing with what they were doing.'

Cumming opened the envelope, took out the documents and stared at them, his expression confused.

'What are these?' he asked.

'I'm fairly certain they could prove beyond any doubt that the American president has been engaged in illegal financial dealings with companies back home. Reading between the lines, I think he's been taking massive kickbacks from awarding government contracts. Those documents certainly have his signature on them.'

'That makes sense,' Cumming said. 'I think if Voss had threatened to release this information' – he tapped the paper-work on his desk – 'the president would have done whatever he wanted. I don't know if you're aware of it, but that man has an awful lot to lose. His wife controls the family finances, and if this did come out, he'd not only face political ruin and a possi-ble prison sentence – though by pulling a few strings he might have been able to avoid that – but he would also face cata-strophic financial ruin as well if he had to pay back the money. These documents are an incredibly powerful weapon.'

'So I suppose you'll destroy them now, will you?'

Cumming smiled slyly. 'We'll certainly keep them securely

under lock and key,' he said, 'but I'm not sure if destroying them would be in our best interests. Or not just yet anyway. You never know when we might need a favour from our cousins across the Atlantic.'

Maria stared at him. 'You do know that makes you almost as bad as Voss?' she said.

'Not quite. Now,' Cumming said, rubbing his hands together briskly, 'I do have some good news for you. You did very well on that last assignment, and you certainly deserve some leave. After that, I've got another little job I thought you could help us with.'

'No thanks, Cumming. I've had about enough of you and the sort of work you do to last me a lifetime. I came here to report to you because I had to, but as soon as I can I'm heading back to the States where I can find some sanity. I still can't believe you were willing to sink a ship and kill fifteen hundred people just to stop Voss.'

Cumming looked somewhat sheepish, and shook his head. 'I'm sorry you feel that way,' he said, 'but of course it's your decision.'

'It is. In this game, you have to be able to trust your own side, because you can't have any confidence in anyone else. I thought I could trust you, and so did Alex, but what happened proved just how wrong we both were. There's no way I'll ever work for you again. In fact, I don't even want to see you again.'

Without another word, Maria turned and strode out of the office, slamming the door closed behind her. Outside she stopped beside Mrs McTavish's vacant desk, tears springing to her eyes as her pent-up emotions finally gave way. She took out a handkerchief and dabbed at her eyes, trying to compose herself before she left the building.

She'd taken a couple of steps down the corridor when a voice from behind stopped her dead.

'Hello, Maria.'

She stopped dead and turned round. Alex Tremayne stood framed in a doorway, supporting himself on a stick, his left arm in a sling, his face unshaven and scarred by patches of raw red skin.

'Dear God, you're alive,' Maria whispered. 'I'd given up, completely given up all hope.'

'You did it,' Tremayne said. 'The last thing you said to me was "be lucky", and I was. You remember the grand staircase on the *Titanic*, with that huge glass dome above it?' Maria nodded. 'I don't know exactly how it happened, but I suppose the wooden staircase was so buoyant that it ripped away from its fittings and exploded up through the dome as the ship sank. I was floating on the surface of the Atlantic, waiting to die, when something rushed up from the depths below and smashed into me. Apparently it lifted me out of the water and provided a little shelter from the elements. The next thing I remember was waking up on board a British submarine, heading for Dover. I've got a broken arm, a sprained ankle and slight concussion, and I suffered a bit from exposure because of the conditions, but basically I'm fine.'

Maria stepped across to where Tremayne was standing and wrapped her arms around him. Tremayne grunted in pain and she immediately relaxed her grip.

'Sorry,' he said, 'I forgot to mention I've got a couple of cracked ribs as well. What did you tell Mansfield in there?'

'I told him to get lost,' she said defiantly. 'I don't care what he reports back to my boss in the States. I cannot and will not work for somebody who shows such callous disregard for human life. Have you seen him?'

Tremayne nodded.

'And?'

'Oddly enough, I told him pretty much the same thing, but in more robust language. As of now, I'm no longer a member of the Secret Service Bureau, and I don't think I'm going to lose much sleep over it.'

Maria looked at him. 'So you're out of a job, then? What will you do?'

'Nothing for a while, unless I can find a decent opening for a battered cripple, but I'm sure something will turn up eventually. What about you?'

'Well, I've burned my bridges here, that's for sure, so I was going to head back to New York. But I'm not in any hurry to leave.'

Tremayne nodded. 'Fancy a short holiday somewhere?' he asked.

'Good idea. One condition, though. Wherever you have planned, it'd better be a hell of a long way from the sea.'

Alex Tremayne smiled. 'You can count on it,' he said.

Author's note

This is of course a work of fiction, and the events I've described as taking place on the ship and in Berlin and elsewhere never actually happened. The *Titanic* really did hit an iceberg, literally a glancing blow, but that was enough to send the world's biggest ship to the bottom of the Atlantic Ocean.

The facts of the sinking are beyond dispute, the timeline well established, but still there are numerous unanswered questions. It is still not clear why the captain of the *Titanic* saw fit to ignore the numerous ice warning messages – at least seven – which had been passed to the ship during her last day on the surface. With hindsight, it could be argued that to proceed at full speed through waters known to be scattered with icebergs, with only two men aloft in the crow's nest – men who had no binoculars, and who were simply relying on their eyesight – to provide warning of any obstruction ahead, was an act of madness or, at best, criminal negligence. Exactly why Captain Smith chose this course of action is still a matter of conjecture.

It was popularly believed at the time that the *Titanic* was unsinkable, but this was not a claim that was ever made by either the company which built the ship, Harland and Wolff of Belfast, or the White Star Line: 'virtually unsinkable' was as far as they were prepared to go. In fact, the ship was designed to remain afloat with up to four compartments flooded. Unfortunately, because the ship turned away from the iceberg when it was sighted, a projecting part of the floating mass of ice scraped down the side of the vessel, doing remarkably little damage to the hull, but opening up a narrow gash which exposed six compartments to the Atlantic Ocean. That was enough to doom the ship.

In point of fact, if the lookouts had *not* sighted the iceberg, or the officer of the watch on the bridge had not turned the ship away, it's at least possible that the *Titanic* might not have sunk. If the ship had hit the iceberg square on, with her bow, obviously substantial damage would have been caused to the vessel but, crucially, only to the bow. This might have caused severe flooding in the forward compartments, but the closing of the watertight doors in this area – which was controlled from the bridge and was actuated before the impact – might have saved the vessel. But we will never know for sure.

Once the ship came to a halt, and the damage had been assessed, there were delays in orders being issued which are extremely difficult to understand. Within minutes of the impact at 2340 on 12 April 1912, it must have been absolutely clear to everyone on the bridge that the ship was going to sink, but it still took twenty-five minutes before the captain ordered the lifeboats to be uncovered, and it was an hour and five minutes before the first boat was finally launched. The radio operators were only instructed to send the first distress message thirty-five minutes after the impact with the iceberg, and it was one hour and ten minutes before the first distress rocket was fired.

No doubt there was considerable confusion on board at this time, but these delays in ordering measures to be taken, measures which clearly would not have helped save the ship, but which might have reduced the catastrophic death toll, is simply incomprehensible. In any sinking, time is of the essence. If the first distress message had been sent immediately after the collision, it is at least possible that more ships would have heard it and been able to render assistance. As it was, the first ship to arrive at the scene, the RMS *Carpathia*, didn't arrive until 0410 on 13 April, almost two hours after the *Titanic* broke her back and sank in two sections, and by that time every passenger and crew member who was not in a lifeboat was dead.

Many who jumped from the sinking ship died the moment they hit the water, their necks broken, ironically, by the life jackets they wearing. The buoyancy inside these flotation devices snapped their heads backwards, frequently with fatal results. Others drowned, obviously, but the vast majority simply died of cold, of hypothermia, in the freezing waters of the Atlantic.

Much has been made of the wholly inadequate number of lifeboats on board the ship, and many people seem to believe that if the *Titanic* had carried more boats, most if not all of the passengers and crew could have been saved. But it's worth pointing out that at the time, the number of lifeboats was – bizarrely – governed by the vessel's tonnage, not by the number of people carried on board, and the *Titanic* was in compliance with the prevailing legislation.

One fact that is not generally known is that when the ship arrived at Southampton, several of the lifeboats were removed before the transatlantic voyage, apparently to increase the amount of space available for promenading on the upper decks, and these boats remained behind at the port after the ship sailed. When news of the tragedy broke, the White Star Line ordered that the name 'Titanic' be painted out on each boat, to disguise their origin. And I know that for a fact because I was acquainted with a person, now sadly deceased, who was a descendant of one of the men employed to do this.

The reality of the situation, though, is that launching the lifeboats took so long that even if there had been a further fifteen or twenty boats on board, almost certainly the ship would have sunk before these extra lifeboats could have been launched, and probably the loss of life would have been about the same. The only possible advantage that extra lifeboats might have conveyed would have been to provide additional boats that people struggling in the water could have climbed into, assuming that the boats would have floated free of the ship as it sank. But even this is somewhat doubtful. Many of the people who were known to have been picked up from the sea and placed in lifeboats still died of hypothermia because of their sodden clothing.

Finally, there are the conspiracy theories, the most popular of which suggests that it wasn't the *Titanic* which sank at all, but her sister ship, the *Olympic*. Whether there's any truth in this suggestion is open for debate, but there are a few facts which are suggestive.

The two ships were for some time being worked on side-by-side at the Belfast dockyard of Harland and Wolff, the *Titanic* because it was still being built, and the *Olympic* because it was being repaired following a serious collision with the Royal Navy cruiser HMS *Hawke* in the Solent in November 1911. This collision had possibly snapped the keel of the *Olympic*, and also knocked one or more of the main propeller shaft bearings out of alignment. Damage of this sort would be frighteningly expensive to repair, and it's been suggested that the White Star Line did not carry sufficient insurance to cover the costs.

The theory goes on to suggest that the identities of the two vessels were swapped at Belfast, the idea being that the badly damaged 'new' ship would be deliberately sunk on her maiden voyage to allow the company to collect the insurance money, while the 'repaired' *Olympic*, actually the brand-new *Titanic*, would continue to operate as the company's flagship.

This may sound far-fetched, but some information has been produced by the conspiracy theorists which suggest that, at the very least, not all was well with the *Titanic*:

- The new ship's sea trials were severely curtailed and did not include a full power run
- During those sea trials, a fire was burning out of control in one of the coal bunkers
- Almost all the boiler room stokers, the men responsible for keeping the furnaces fuelled, left the ship at Southampton, refusing to sail any further in her
- There were several reports that the furnaces and boilers on the ship showed unmistakable signs of extensive prior use
- The *Titanic* apparently vibrated badly at speed, precisely the effect that would be produced by a misaligned propeller shaft bearing, the exact damage which had been caused to the *Olympic*
- The White Star Line enormously increased the insurance cover on the *Titanic* immediately before the ship's maiden voyage.

So is there any truth in the conspiracy theory? The bottom line is that nobody really knows. In those days, few parts of a ship were stamped with identifying names or numbers, so it is certainly possible – at least in theory – that the identities of the two vessels could have been changed. Certainly some parts of the *Titanic* ended up on the *Olympic* because the ship being built was cannibalized to get the repairs to the *Olympic* done as quickly as possible. There are also some anomalies relating to the internal design of the ship which now lies on the floor of the Atlantic Ocean. And in some ways it could be argued that it's surprising the *Olympic* had such a long and generally trouble-free life on the oceans of the world in view of the severe damage which she certainly suffered in that collision.

So I suppose you could say that it's case not proven, and much of the evidence for the theory is circumstantial at best.

But, *Olympic* or *Titanic*, there's no mistaking the incredible hold that this, one of the greatest and most publicized maritime disasters of all time, continues to exert on us all.

Acknowledgements

My thanks to Luigi Bonomi, my friend and agent, who had the idea and cracked the whip, imaginatively aided and abetted by Thomas Stofer. And to my delightful editors at Simon & Schuster – Maxine Hitchcock and Emma Lowth – who saw the potential and took a gamble. My grateful thanks to you all.

Jeremy Duns

The Moscow Option

October, 1969. Moscow. Paul Dark is a broken man.
A terrible mistake twenty-four years ago led to him
being recruited by Soviet intelligence, but he has
paid a heavy price for it.

Locked up in a cell, distrusted even by those he once
served, and with nothing for company but the ghosts of
his past, Dark is woken in the early hours and taken to
a secret location. There, he discovers that a terrible
calamity is looming – and that it is linked with the
final mission he undertook as a loyal British agent
during the Second World War.

Now the fate of the entire world rests on the shoulders
of one man: a traitor long past his best, who is soon
the subject of a massive man-hunt in one of the most
repressive regimes in history. Dark needs to make
it to a small island in the Baltic before it's too late –
and the clock is ticking.

ISBN 978-1-84739-453-8

Dean Crawford

Covenant

Humanity has always believed it is the only intelligent species of life in the universe. But while excavating in Israel, an archaeologist unearths a tomb that has remained hidden for 7,000 years. Inside lies a secret of such magnitude that the story of mankind is instantly rewritten – and its future thrown into terrible danger.

Only one man can piece history back together again. Only one man will risk everything to prevent a catastrophe that could tear the world apart.

That man is Ethan Warner.

ISBN 978-0-85720-469-1

Howard Gordon

The Chamber

Time is running out for Gideon Davis . . .

Angered when the Joint Terrorism Task Force ignores
evidence of an impending terrorist attack on U.S. soil,
Gideon Davis is left to launch his own investigations.

Enlisting help from his brother, Tillman, to infiltrate
Colonel Jim Verhoven's white supremacist group,
Gideon is thrown into the thick of a revenge plot
designed not only to overthrow the government
but to bring an end to democracy itself.

But when things get messy and the brothers are
forced to play along with Verhoven's plan in
order to avoid detection, they'll need the
help of Nancy Clement, Gideon's old
FBI colleague if they are to prevent disaster.

With non-stop action and ticking time bomb suspense,
The Chamber will thrill anyone who loved
Jack Bauer and *24*.

ISBN 978-0-85720-095-2

This book and other titles are available from your local
bookshop or can be ordered direct from the publisher.

978-0-85720-095-2	The Chamber	12.99
978-0-85720-469-1	Covenant	6.99
978-1-84739-453-8	The Moscow Option	6.99

Free post and packing within the UK
Overseas customers please add £2 per paperback
Telephone Simon & Schuster Cash Sales at Bookpost
on 01624 677237 with your credit or debit card number
or send a cheque payable to Simon & Schuster Cash Sales to
PO Box 29, Douglas Isle of Man, IM99 1BQ
Fax: 01624 670923
Email: bookshop@enterprise.net
www.bookpost.co.uk
Please allow 14 days for delivery. Prices and availability
are subject to change without notice.